"I urge anyone who is a fan of urban fantasy and paranormal romance to put Sharon Ashwood at the top of their list!"—Night Owl Romance

Praise for the Novels of the Dark Forgotten

Unchained

"An action-packed roller-coaster ride with thrills on every page. Sharon Ashwood always pens a fun read."
—Fresh Fiction

"A terrific action-adventure thriller . . . this is an enthralling, magical, great work by Sharon Ashwood."
—The Best Reviews

"What a rush! Gifted author Sharon Ashwood sweeps her readers up and keeps us breathless. . . . Ms. Ashwood's writing sucks us into her gritty urban fantasy world in *Unchained* and never lets us go! . . . Multiply the Wow Factor—the Dark Forgotten saga must continue!"
—Single Titles

"A fast-paced urban fantasy that will keep you hooked from cover to cover. Ms. Ashwood's characters leap from the pages, the romance is hot and passionate, and the monsters make me want to check under my bed. Superb and highly recommended!"
—Romance Junkies

"Ms. Ashwood has again woven a remarkable tale. She seamlessly pulls all the various threads together for that aha moment. I highly recommend the Dark Forgotten books. This highly original series has earned a permanent place on my keeper shelf!"
—Night Owl Reviews

"I loved it. I loved this. What more is there to say?"
—Book Faery

"I recommend *Unchained* and the first two books of the series . . . if you're looking for an action-packed, exciting paranormal romance with an incredible arc that will keep you enthralled and captivated till the final pages."
—Smexy Books Romance Reviews

continued . . .

Scorched

"One of the most original, entertaining, action-adventure fantasy novels of the year. Author Sharon Ashwood is clearly established as a major talent for innovation and re-creating the fantasy horror genre into a new level of entertaining excellence." —*Midwest Book Review*

"Sharon Ashwood has a way of making inanimate objects into fully functioning characters. In *Ravenous*, it was a house with a taste for trapping humans. In *Scorched*, it was the Castle. The beasts and beings that make the Castle—both in name and deed—brought a fantastical element to the story. It was as if the scenes were being played out in front of you and all you had to do was reach forward and you could touch the mythological beasts trying to survive in their ever-diminishing world." —Bitten by Books

"A unique blend of paranormal beings with a strong sense of survival to live in the human world and loyalty among unlikely friends. I enjoyed the quick-paced plot and look forward to reading more in this series." —Fresh Fiction

"It scorched me and left me wanting more. Fans of urban fantasy will devour these books. I can't wait to read the next one." —Manic Readers

"Sharp and stylish writing, plenty of action, a well-conceived and intriguing mythology and a great sense of dark atmosphere make *Scorched* a must-read for die-hard paranormal romance fans. . . . *Scorched* is a great continuation of the Dark Forgotten story arc, and Sharon Ashwood is definitely an author to watch." —BookLoons

"Sharon Ashwood tantalizes readers with *Scorched*. . . . All in all, *Scorched* is a roller-coaster ride of action, mystery, evil, and romance. Ashwood deftly interweaves the two story lines, keeping readers eagerly turning pages in this novel that just might keep you up late to finish it." —*The Romance Reader*

Ravenous

"With its splendidly original heroine and dangerously sexy hero, surfeit of sizzling sexual chemistry, and sharp writing seasoned with a generous dash of wicked wit, *Ravenous* is simply superb."   —*Chicago Tribune*

"Absolutely terrific. With demons, hellhounds, weres, and vampires waiting in the wings, I can't wait to see what happens next!"   —Alexis Morgan

"Sexy, suspenseful fun."
      —*New York Times* bestselling author Kelley Armstrong

"A multilayered plot, a fascinating take on the paranormal creatures living among us, plus a sexy vampire, a sassy witch, and a mystery for them to solve . . . *Ravenous* leaves me hungry for more!"   —Jessica Andersen

"Strong world-building. . . . Readers will look forward to the sequel."   —*Publishers Weekly*

"The heroine is gutsy, smart, and funny. As an urban fantasy, *Ravenous* is perhaps the best I've read this year."
      —The Shape of Imagination

"The world is interesting (I look forward to seeing more of it!), the romance gorgeous, the sex sizzling. There's plenty of action as well."   —Errant Dreams Reviews

"This tongue-in-cheek, action-packed urban fantasy hooks the reader from the opening moment . . . and never slows down."   —*Midwest Book Review*

"A fast-paced urban fantasy . . . nonstop action that will keep the reader turning pages long into the night."
      —Romance Junkies

"I think I have found a new favorite series. . . . I guess I have to wait for the next story, hopefully not for too long!"
      —The Romance Studio

The Dark Forgotten Series

Unchained
Scorched
Ravenous

FROSTBOUND

The Dark Forgotten

SHARON ASHWOOD

A SIGNET ECLIPSE BOOK

SIGNET ECLIPSE
Published by New American Library, a division of
Penguin Group (USA) Inc., 375 Hudson Street,
New York, New York 10014, USA
Penguin Group (Canada), 90 Eglinton Avenue East, Suite 700, Toronto,
Ontario M4P 2Y3, Canada (a division of Pearson Penguin Canada Inc.)
Penguin Books Ltd., 80 Strand, London WC2R 0RL, England
Penguin Ireland, 25 St. Stephen's Green, Dublin 2,
Ireland (a division of Penguin Books Ltd.)
Penguin Group (Australia), 250 Camberwell Road, Camberwell, Victoria 3124,
Australia (a division of Pearson Australia Group Pty. Ltd.)
Penguin Books India Pvt. Ltd., 11 Community Centre, Panchsheel Park,
New Delhi - 110 017, India
Penguin Group (NZ), 67 Apollo Drive, Rosedale, Auckland 0632,
New Zealand (a division of Pearson New Zealand Ltd.)
Penguin Books (South Africa) (Pty.) Ltd., 24 Sturdee Avenue,
Rosebank, Johannesburg 2196, South Africa

Penguin Books Ltd., Registered Offices:
80 Strand, London WC2R 0RL, England

First published by Signet Eclipse, an imprint of New American Library,
a division of Penguin Group (USA) Inc.

First Printing, June 2011
10 9 8 7 6 5 4 3 2 1

Printed in the United States of America

PUBLISHER'S NOTE
This is a work of fiction. Names, characters, places, and incidents either are the
product of the author's imagination or are used fictitiously, and any resemblance
to actual persons, living or dead, business establishments, events, or locales is
entirely coincidental.
    The publisher does not have any control over and does not assume any re-
sponsibility for author or third-party Web sites or their content.

There are a lot of people to whom I owe thanks for the Dark Forgotten. First of all, my critique groups and all the members who've passed through on their own literary journeys. Your fresh perspectives have been invaluable. Thanks go to Diana, for the friendship and especially the silly phone conversation that started it all, and to Catherine, for the endless cheerleading and proofreading. You're both brilliant and creative people. To Jo, who helped me through the publishing door with a kiss on the brow and a no-nonsense push. To Sally, my infinitely wise agent, and my editor, Laura, who waved her wand and made books happen.

It's one thing to write about magic, another to experience it. Gratitude to you all.

Prologue

"Till death do us part.

"Quite the statement, isn't it? When we utter those words, are we describing love, the bond of hunter and prey, or both? That is the question of the night.

"Good evening, my darkling listeners, this is your night hostess, Errata Jones, on CSUP. I'm coming to you from the glorious U of Fairview campus, on the radio station that puts the 'super' in supernatural. Tonight's program is filled with the usual basket of goodies, but first let's take a sneak peek at the main event. We're talking about love—and not the easy kind.

"Ever since the nonhumans came out of the shadows in Y2K, we've had to navigate the world with our claws in and our fangs firmly out of sight. Whether you're a vampire, a hellhound, or a werecougar like me, we've been meek and mild, not just with our human neighbors, but with each other. We've learned to get along. To sit at the same table. To act like friends and family. It's all been very civilized.

"But anyone who knows a real family, who knows what it is to truly *love*, will tell you passion isn't about getting along. It's the crash of undiluted personalities.

It's the thrill of the chase. It's the scent of blood and the heat of skin against your lips as you struggle against an inevitable surrender. It is undoubtedly beautiful, but never pretty.

"So the question is, ghouls and girlies, what about interspecies romance? If we drop the masks and give our sad little monster hearts away, will anyone still respect us in the morning? If we show them our true selves, will anyone be left alive?

"The phone lines are open. Talk to me."

Chapter 1

Tuesday, December 28, 7:30 p.m.
Downtown Fairview

*S**ome nights it sucks to be Alpha.*
   Lore winced as his fist crashed into bone.
And other times it just rocks.

He'd made it a bruising face shot, knuckle action splitting skin. The vampire flew backward into the bar, scattering the few remaining patrons—the dedicated drunks—like bowling pins. Lore closed in with supernatural speed, getting in a pair of jabs and a cross before the piece of Undead garbage had a chance to rebound.

The vamp roared with rage, fangs bared. Lore slapped his face, hard, with an open palm. "Manners!" Lore snarled.

The roar quieted to a hiss that unfortunately sprayed blood, spit, and whiskey like a faulty lawn sprinkler. Lore hated drunken vampires. It wasn't like they'd just had one too many. It took time and effort to pickle Undead blood, and most knew better than to lower their inhibitions that far.

With vampires, out of control was bad news. The

guy'd already cut a swath through Fairview's Old Town and damn near drained two humans before he'd even reached this bar called the Pit Stop—emphasis on the pit. Lore's job was to settle his tab but good.

He didn't see the fist coming for his solar plexus. Lore's breath went out with a whoosh followed by a sickly wheeze. Lore was big, hard-bodied and, hell, *half-demon*, but even a drunken bloodsucker packed a wallop. He doubled over, falling back just enough for the vampire to regain his feet.

The vamp tugged at the front of his filthy leather jacket, as if shaking out the creases left by Lore's attack. He dressed like James Dean, but had a face like the tire treads on a farm tractor—ugly, pocked and furrowed. Lore's aching ribs said that flat nose might have come from the fight ring.

Mr. Drunk and Ugly sneered, looking around at the last few patrons too stubborn or stupid to chug their drinks and go. One or two had figured out the ancient bartender had fled and were helping themselves to the stock.

The vamp pounded the bar, making glasses rattle. "Who let this mangy hellhound in here? No dogs allowed, or can't you read?"

Pure, predatory rage flooded Lore, as if the slur had tripped a switch. He launched himself at Mr. Ugly, smashing him back against the bar rail. He heard ribs snap, and the sound thrilled along his nerves. *Kill. Bite. Prey.* The urge was primal, written in his genes, as was the constant need to be the fastest, strongest, smartest. Survival demanded it.

It made him Alpha.

Mr. Ugly kicked, connected with Lore's knee. Lore's leg buckled under him, but he had the vamp in a death grip. They both fell to the floor, sending the nearest table flying. Ugly tried to bite, venomous fangs snapping on air.

Irritated, Lore banged the vamp's head on the dirty tiles. When the bloodsucker's eyes rolled up, Lore flipped him over, clamping the vamp's hands in his own massive grip. Lore reached for a pair of vampire-proof silver cuffs clipped to his belt. The sound of the metal closing around Ugly's wrists sent a bolt of satisfaction through his gut.

He pulled the vamp to his feet, using the collar of the grungy jacket as a handle. "Where are you from? I thought I knew everyone in this neighborhood, and I haven't seen you before."

Ugly was already coming around. "Bite my ass."

"No, thanks. I've already eaten."

Which was one reason why he patrolled in human form. Hellhounds generally had iron stomachs, but some of the pond scum he was forced to capture—you just didn't want them in your mouth.

Lore tried again. "Who's your sire?"

"I staked him back in the fifties."

"If you say so." His work here was done. If there was no sire to contact, then the human cops could figure out what to do with Drunk and Ugly. The odds were he'd be beheaded. Human law was pretty cut-and-dried when it came to rogue vampires on a tear.

Lore might have felt sorry for the guy, but there was no element of accident or even slightly poor judgment here. After chowing down on humans in full view of witnesses, this vampire was too stupid to live.

Lore hauled him out of the dark bar and out onto the darker street. His breath steamed in the cold air. The human police were already there with the special van they used for transporting supernatural prisoners. It was lined with a silver and steel compound nicknamed stilver. Nothing, not even fey, could get out of it. Just looking at it gave Lore claustrophobia.

Wordlessly, a patrolman he didn't know opened the rear doors of the van. Lore tossed his catch into the back, not bothering to make use of the three steps that folded down to street level. The cop slammed the door and looked up at him, his face tight with apprehension.

It wasn't surprising. Lore was a head taller and had fifty more pounds of muscle on the man, plus he'd just taken out the vamp with his bare hands.

"Where's Caravelli?" the cop asked. Alessandro Caravelli was the vampire sheriff in Fairview. Normally it was him breaking heads in the name of law and order. The other nonhumans paid his wages, but the Fairview City Police were more than grateful for the help.

Lore wiped his hands on his jeans, trying to get the vampire's stink off his hands. "On vacation. He hired me to fill in."

"For how long?"

"A few more days." Lore scribbled his signature on the clipboard the cop handed him. "Careful. That vamp's drunk and a biter."

"Another out of towner here for the election? Place is crawling with activists and looky-loos."

For the first time, a vampire was standing for office in Fairview's municipal election, and it was the first time nonhumans would be allowed to vote. Giving the monsters the vote was either Judgment Day or the dawning of the Age of Aquarius, depending on whom you asked.

Lore shrugged. "The vamp and I didn't stop to chat."

"What's his name?"

Lore handed back the pen and clipboard. "I've no idea. You need anything else for your report?"

"Nope."

"Have a good night," Lore said.

The cop didn't respond, but got in the passenger side. The van was in motion before the door closed. The cop was afraid, and the smell of it made Lore's stomach cramp with hunger.

"Hey, there. Barking at the moon yet?"

Lore glanced in the direction of the voice. Perry

Baker was ambling toward him from the direction of the corner store. The werewolf had a take-out coffee cup in one hand, mounded with whipping cream and chocolate shavings. Most shape-shifters had a sweet tooth. Something to do with the energy burn of changing forms.

"Hey," Lore said as his friend came to a stop beside him. "What brings you here?"

The werewolf yawned, showing strong teeth. "I needed a break."

"Feeling the need to get down and dirty on the streets?"

"The only thing I'm feeling right now is a slight sugar buzz." Perry shrugged, slurping the elaborate coffee. Like Lore, he was in his late twenties, but where the hellhounds were tall and big-boned, built for brute strength, the wolves were lean and wiry. His young, intelligent face was drawn with fatigue. "And the onset of a migraine. I've been marking Comp Sci exams most of the day. Who knew a doctorate meant slow death by HB pencil?"

Lore took out his cell phone, checking messages. There were plenty from pack members, but no more reports of bar fights or break-ins. "Looks quiet."

"Dinner?" Perry asked.

Lore still had the taste of the cop's fear in his mouth. "Sure."

By unspoken consent, they headed north toward Lore's place. There was a good burger joint around the corner that served their meat extra-rare. They walked a few blocks in silence, Lore's senses on alert.

"So," Perry said. "How's sheriff duty going?"

"There's something evil in Fairview."

Perry gave him a long look. "Uh, care to narrow that down?"

The wolf had a point. Fairview was supernatural central. Lore's own people had escaped here through a portal from a prison dimension. A few short years ago, while Perry had been wondering what degree to take next, Lore had been fighting for survival in a demon-filled dungeon.

The memory of the Castle—the deaths, the deprivation and slavery of the hellhounds—pissed Lore off all over again. Wanting to bite something, he kicked the base of a lamppost instead. Tension sang in his muscles. "I felt something."

"As in, an Alpha hellhound psychic gift kind of feeling?"

Lore frowned. It had been a premonition—the Alpha had the gift of prophetic dreams—but he could feel it too, just hovering on the edge of awareness. It was like a hair-raising charge of static. "I am the protector of my pack. Caravelli left me to guard the safety of the city. A large cloud of evil intent is floating around. I need to kill it."

The werewolf raised an eyebrow. "You see, that's why I hang out with you. Every time it's like, wham, I'm in a *Doctor Who* episode."

Lore grunted a reply. Now that he wasn't working up a sweat fighting, his hands were starting to ache from the cold. He slid them into the pockets of his jacket. "It's hard to explain."

"Hey, you're the premonition guy. You say there's floaty badness, I believe you." Perry slurped his drink again, but now he was watching the night, too, the set of his head and shoulders alert. Steam rose off the cup in filmy clouds, clogging the air with a syrupy-sweet smell.

Lore cast a glance at his friend. "Does floaty badness worry you?"

"I'm not sure yet. For me, magic is just another science."

"What does that mean?"

"I don't have your sixth sense. I like data."

They were across the street from Lore's condo building when a white and blue taxi pulled up at the building entrance. Both males watched as a young woman got out. The cabbie hauled a suitcase out of the trunk and held the door as she made her way into the lobby. She wore a navy blue uniform under a dark pea jacket. The short skirt left slim legs bare. Lore caught a glimpse of her face: long dark hair with bangs, high cheekbones, a pointed chin. Elfin more than beautiful.

Close, but not quite the woman he'd hoped to see. Not the one who reminded his body that it was past time to choose a mate.

I don't have time to watch women. Something is out there. But he couldn't turn away, even from this pale ghost of the one he wanted.

Suddenly his pulse felt hot and thick.

"Who's that?" Perry asked with avid interest. "I mean, impending evil and all, but look at those legs."

Lore had. Repeatedly. "She lives in fifteen-twenty-four."

So did another woman who might have been her sister—someone less observant might have mistaken them for twins. Lore had never figured those two out. This one wasn't home much. The other—the beautiful one—was a vamp, with all the mysterious allure of the Undead female. They were never home at the same time, and never with anyone else.

Perry cut Lore a glance. "You know her suite number off the top of your head?"

"Guarding is in my genetics. I watch the building for intruders. I know who belongs where."

"I suppose you know her name and phone number, too."

He had spoken to this woman—the human—once. They'd exchanged the bland chitchat of strangers while they'd waited for the elevator. "I know the name on the mailbox."

Perry looked amused. "You could go borrow a cup of sugar. One look at her and I want to make cookies."

"And they call me a hound dog."

"Ooh, ouch." Perry tossed his empty coffee cup into the concrete garbage bin by the curb. It arced neatly and clattered inside.

The door closed, and the woman disappeared.

Perry let out a gust of breath. "So, what do you want to do about the situation?"

Which situation was that?

Hellhounds couldn't lie. Lore struggled a moment against a compulsion to tell his friend the truth. *I want to find the beautiful one and take her, even if she isn't one of my kind. Even if it's utterly against hellhound law.* But he would rather stick his head in a ghoul's nest than have that conversation.

Fortunately, there was another way to answer. "You know your way around a spell book as well as a mainframe. Help me find out what dark presence I'm sensing, and I'll pay for dinner."

The werewolf rolled his eyes, obviously catching Lore's evasion. "Okay, Romeo. Just don't get ketchup on my grimoire."

Chapter 2

*N*othing brings out the predators like a seventy-percent-off sale.

Talia Rostova wheeled her Prius into the North Central Shopping Center for their After-Christmas Clearance Madness. The lot was jammed, vehicles crawling over the icy pavement in a slow-motion game of musical parking spaces. Exhaust clouded the cold air like the breath of dragons.

Talia thought of all those lovely bargains in the sales flyer, and felt a pang of unease. She'd been delayed at the nail salon, and now the door-crasher specials were in full swing. The mall was giving out half-price coupons for designer leather wear at eight o'clock sharp.

Unfortunately, it was now seven forty-five, and she still had to park.

Crum.

Aggression hung in the air, vibrating like a sour note above the rumble of engines and the crunch of tires on the frosty ground. Talia shivered, the mood rousing her own adrenaline. A vampire knew bloodlust when she sensed it. Bargain-hunters could be serious fiends, with or without pointy teeth.

Talia zipped into the last empty parking spot almost before she saw it. *I may be dead, but I'm fast.* Someone honked. Talia bared her fangs at the honker's blinding headlights, and the noise stopped.

Talia locked the car door and trotted toward the entrance of Howard's Department Store, the heels of her suede ankle boots slipping on the slick pavement. The temperature had been dropping all day, and the rain had frozen into treacherous patches of black ice. Vampire or not, she'd be flat on her designer-denim backside if she wasn't careful.

Howard's was still decked in Christmas splendor, all tinsel garlands and fairy lights. The glitter delighted her, pulling her through the doors like a fish on a line. Talia's family hadn't been into celebrating—that was Dad all over, every minute all about work even when she and her brother were little. Too bad she had to die to experience a little ho-ho-ho.

A kid of about fourteen shoulder-checked her as he pushed past. Jerked out of her thoughts, Talia grabbed him by the collar, hauling him up until his high-tops barely touched the floor. Bad for the manicure—after all, the polish was barely dry—but oh so squirmy-delicious. Her jaws began to ache, itching to bite. The kid's blood would be hot and tasty.

"Mind your manners," she said, showing a bit of teeth.

"Says who?"

"Says your nightmares. Y'know, I used to dream of doing this when I taught school. So how are you doing in English Lit?" She grinned wider.

The boy turned the color of Cream of Wheat, kicking against the iron strength in Talia's thin wrist. After a moment, the disbelief in his eyes melted to terror. She let him go, giving just enough shove to make him skitter.

"Skinny vampire bitch! The law's gonna stake your ass. Just you wait." He dove into the crowd before she could catch him again.

Stupid brat. Talia drew a breath, squashing the urge to pursue the running prey. Inhaling only brought a wave of warm, blood-scented air. She sucked in her lower lip. *Too many humans around. Shouldn't have done that.*

Calm, calm, calm. Close your eyes and think of coupons. Talia blinked, straightening her coat and scarf, swallowing down the saliva that suddenly filled her mouth. She'd been Turned for only three years. Her body still got ahead of her mind half the time. It made it hard to fit in.

Nope, shouldn't have done that. It had been pure instinct. It had felt so good. *You're supposed to be under the radar, not making the headlines because you chomped on a mall rat. You're as good as finally, totally dead if somebody back home sees your picture.*

Her phone jingled "Material Girl." Who had her number? She fished it out of her purse, her throat closing with panic. *If anyone finds you . . .*

It was suddenly too hot in the store. She turned around and headed back toward the entrance, the primitive part of her brain screaming that she had to flee. Her eyes skated over the caller ID the first time without reading it. The second time, she realized it was her own home phone number.

What the hell? Who was at her place? For a second, she froze, but curiosity won out.

She answered. "Hello?"

"Hey, girl, guess what."

Oh, thank God, it was Michelle. Relief made Talia suddenly giddy. "What are you doing home? You're not supposed to be there! I thought you were gone for weeks yet."

"You make it sound like I'm back from outer space." Her chuckle was dry.

"You might as well be."

Michelle was a hostess on the Queen Anne cruises, gone for months at a time. Since she was rarely in Fairview, she'd given Talia use of her condo.

"Yeah, well, some of the vacationers certainly behave like they're in orbit. So what are you doing?"

"Shopping. I came for a door-crasher special, but I think I missed out on the coupons." *I was busy sowing terror and dismay.*

"Poor baby. I'd have thought you were bored with shopping. I mean, it was never your thing before, well, before."

"Hey, if I'm going to live forever, I may as well look good." *Besides, it's an excellent disguise. No one would look at me and see the old, plain Talia.*

"I like your attitude."

Talia listened to her cousin's voice, a different kind of hunger flooding her. Michelle was the one person from Talia's old life who'd risked helping a newbie vamp. She drank in the warm, laughing voice on the phone, an ache in her lifeless heart. She wanted so badly to hug Michelle, to show her all the gratitude she felt.

"Listen." Michelle cleared her throat, a small, tight sound. "My schedule changed. I'm between cruises. I just got home."

Talia jammed her hand through her hair, her rings catching in the long, dark strands. "I'll get a hotel."

"Why? We've got two bedrooms. We live at the same address, and I haven't seen you in forever. It's reunion time, sweetie."

Talia realized she had wandered blindly into the dress department. Women milled around her with armfuls of clothes. They smelled warm and savory. "Are you sure that's a good idea? We agreed I'd always leave when you came back. Just to play it safe."

"I'm okay with you sleeping here if you're comfortable with it. I mean, you've had time to adjust, right?"

The words shocked Talia, and then her throat began to ache with emotion. Michelle's level of trust was incredibly rare. One bite and a vampire's venom enslaved a human with its erotic, fatally addictive high. Michelle knew she was taking a huge chance. Talia could hear the tension in her cousin's voice.

And yet Michelle was willing to give her a chance to prove she wasn't a killer.

"Let me think about it." Talia disconnected, suddenly losing her nerve. *I can't do this. Too much risk.*

Outside in the stark, black night beyond the tinseled doors, Talia saw a swirl of snowflakes. It never snowed in Fairview. The universe was going crazy.

No one ever invited a vampire to sleep over.

As kids, they'd had pajama parties at Michelle's house. Junk food, movies, secrets, the works. They'd steal Michelle's mom's cosmetics to play dress-up because Talia's mom never wore makeup—Dad's rules.

Michelle had always been her window into the normal world. Talia felt like a puppy shivering to death in a filthy alley, aching to get into that golden world of loving hands and warm fires.

On the other hand, a bad vampire joke went that family members were like potato chips. *Can't stop snacking once you start.* And she knew from gruesome experience that it was absolutely true.

Never trust a bloodsucker. Her dad had been right.

Michelle didn't have all the facts.

Talia clutched her phone, thinking of the warm voice still echoing in her mind.

Chapter 3

"And why is it, dear listeners, that we compare love to a flame? Because it warms us or destroys us? A poet would say both, and write another sonnet. That's a human response. A beast knows to be afraid of the flame. There's a reason the rabble carry pitchforks and torches, because when we love one of theirs, the building is sure to burn around us."

There's a bad moon rising.

No—that was just one of those strange, human turns of phrase. The moon was as it should be, past full and mostly hidden by thick, moisture-laden clouds. But there *was* a psychic foulness in the air, as if a poisonous veil drifted down from the mottled sky and coated the city in a slick of curses.

It's back.

Lore was on patrol, walking the streets of the downtown. He could sense the vibe, smell it, almost hear it in the hiss of tires on wet pavement. Since arriving in Fairview, he'd adapted to the urban landscape and come to know its moods. Now he could feel darkness creeping into its energy.

It was what he had attempted to describe to his friend earlier that night. Perry would try to find it in a book, bring his vast knowledge of the arcane to bear. But the evil was here, and Lore had to act *now*. That was his nature, both man and beast.

Must find it. The urge to track was building like a pressure in his chest.

Must kill it.

Long ago, that's what hellhounds like him had been bred for: to search out and destroy a threat before it struck. Half demons themselves, they'd taken out the supernatural trash long before Armani suits and smart phones ruled the courts of law. There had been no appeals, just the munching of bones.

And for now he was sheriff. That gave the blessing of law to the urges nature had already provided.

Find. Stop.

Despite the fact that his belly was full from dinner with Perry, the urge to hunt crawled over Lore's skin like an electric current. As hellhound Alpha, he was both psychically gifted and a superior tracker. The other hounds hadn't sensed the evil. Not yet. He would call the pack once he knew what they faced. A good leader always took the first risk himself.

Kept the taste of first blood for himself.

Even as that thought formed, the dark miasma that screamed along his nerves was getting thicker, gathering to the north.

He began to run, still in human form, but beast-quick. Long legs carried him through the empty streets, where old false-front buildings huddled between newer stores, diamonds of ice on their wrought-iron railings. It was bitterly cold. Few people were out. The sidewalks were slick under his boots, glittering with frost.

Lore dodged around a lamppost and raced past the Victorian facade of the Empire Hotel. Christmas lights still rimmed the paned windows. Down a block, music grumbled from a dance club where neon signs winked in the night, the cold turning their colors sharp.

The chill air bit as he sucked it down, but he barely noticed. A sense of danger beat in his ears like a rushing pulse. *Go faster!*

In some ways it was a blessing the danger was here, in the supernatural ghetto called Spookytown. Its people knew how to fight. Some of the foes Lore had faced could pick off humans as if they were cheese puffs on an hors d'oeuvres tray.

Not that he knew a thing about fancy food, but the image fit.

Close, very close. He could nearly reach up and touch the edge of evil.

But between one pulse and the next, the night changed. The presence had been a veil, a mist. Now dread filled the air like a liquid, filling his lungs and mouth, pressing against his skin as if to force fear into his very pores. Lore skidded to a stop, his feet sliding on the slick ground. His puffing breath smoked the air, his heart hammering in an instant of mindless terror.

The street went dead quiet.

A hellhound's deep bell sounded in the distance, howling a warning that something awful had brushed past. The dread was so palpable now, the rest of the pack had felt it. The cry was picked up by another baying *awooooo*, and another. Somewhere, a wolf joined. Then the common dogs, barking in backyards and alleys.

In every house and apartment window, lights flicked on.

Danger! Danger! Lore snapped back to himself, shoving the fear aside. Then a distant alarm began to whoop, coming from somewhere deep in Spookytown. Fire? Burglar? Had whatever it was gathered its strength and struck?

He couldn't wait any longer. Their town was in danger. Tonight, he was the sheriff, in charge of keeping it safe. It was time to gather the pack.

Come! With his mind and will, Lore sent the call to his people.

The response was instant. The hounds poured from alleys and empty lots, running in twos and threes. They flickered just on the edge of sight, rarely seen but for the instant of the kill—but Lore knew them all. They were *his* creatures of nightmare, with eyes like the inside of a red-hot coal. Bulky and deep-chested, they stood nearly as tall as man, the long snout and upright ears like the Egyptian carvings of Anubis. Each fang was as long as Lore's hand, each claw a killing scythe.

The few other pedestrians out on the streets vanished as if by sorcery.

Still in man-form, Lore ran at the head of the pack, his half-demon nature giving him speed. Following the sound of the alarm, they raced almost to the harbor, the cold, damp wind telling tales of kelp and the merciless deep. The rain needling through the glow of the streetlights was turning to sleet. Before long, it would be snow.

Ahead and to the left was the quay. Here and there, sailboats decked with Christmas lights shimmered above the black sea, reflections glittering like scattered jewels. Lore didn't stop, but turned right into one of the alleys that cut deep into Spookytown.

Abruptly, the alarm shut off. Now there were sirens: fire, police, and ambulance sending up an eerie wail. Lore cursed under his breath, noticing an odd glow overhead. When Lore left the alley and stepped onto lower Fort Street, his eyes confirmed what his nose had been telling him for blocks.

Fire. Scrolls of smoke—a black paler than the night—billowed against the sky in roiling curls. Scraps of brilliant orange and yellow waved in the cold black night, snapping like flags in a stiff breeze.

Lore swore again, the houndish language giving the words extra edge. The building on fire was the South Fairview Medical Clinic, the one place in town the supernaturals could find a doctor willing to help them.

As loss hammered into him, the sense of evil retreated a step. It was as if whatever vile intelligence was behind it had relaxed to admire its work. In that instant, it became an individual. It wasn't just a something but a someone.

Who are you? Lore demanded of the dark presence, but there was only silence. Did he detect smugness, or was he just imagining it? Anger ached in his jaw. *Why did you do this? What do you want?*

Lore scanned the scene. By sheer luck, the parking lot that wrapped around the clinic was empty. No cars, no garbage, nothing to burn between it and the buildings on either side. The fire hadn't spread yet.

It was a miracle. The building seemed to sag into itself, the walls folding inward amidst veils of white and orange. Lore could feel the blaze from where he stood. He'd seen fires before, but this was hotter than he remembered. Even the roar of it seemed wrong, not a crackle but the whisper of a thousand tongues.

He shuddered, fighting the urge to strike out in rage. He had to think, let human reason do the work. He needed a proper target before he let the killer inside slip his leash.

Down, boy. Lore took a long, shuddering breath. Police and fire crews were already there, ladder trucks clogging the street. The firefighters were hanging back, pointing and arguing. They sensed something was different about the fire, too.

Evacuees of the nearby apartments milled at the pe-

rimeter tape, joined by the patrons of several neighborhood bars. Fort Street was a noisy, crowded scene, but
beneath the chaos the taint of evil simmered like a bad
memory.

The pack had gathered behind Lore. He glanced over
his shoulder, feeling their presence like a weight on his
back. Their shaggy, black outlines seemed to merge, cre-
ating one massive beast with two dozen pairs of glowing
yellow eyes. They were waiting for their Alpha to give
orders.

Nothing worked in a vacuum, especially not magic.
Sorcery left stink and mess. Lore turned to the pack and
raised his voice. "Mix with the neighbors. Ask what they
saw, smelled, heard, anything. Find out everything you
can."

Although it was too dark to pick out details, Lore had
the impression of pricking ears, the wag of tails. Then
the many-eyed shadow dissolved into a mist. Moments
later, the dogs were replaced by a group of young men
and women, dark-haired and big-boned like Lore. Unlike werebeasts, half demons didn't have to get naked to
change form. They rematerialized dressed like humans,
but in ripped jeans and motorcycle boots, leather bracelets and knives that glinted like teeth.

The shaggy, wild aura around the hounds didn't vanish with their fur. It lurked in the strength of their hands
and the fluid glide of their walk. Silently, they melted
into the crowd.

He turned and began pacing the perimeter of the fire
scene, silently wishing his pack good hunting. Residue
from the evil presence hung in the air, drifting around
them with the ash. To someone with his gifts, it had a
smell and taste. *Bitter as poison.*

And then a shadow flickered in the darkness to the
left of the burning building.

Chapter 4

Prey!
Lore launched himself after it, his body responding before his mind had time to consider. The shadow was a figure, darting toward the mouth of a lane on the far side of the parking lot. Beyond was a jumble of by-ways and Dumpsters with myriad hiding places. Once in there, a fugitive would be difficult to find.

The figure was supernaturally fast, and only guilt made someone bolt like that. Lore poured on the speed, not daring to take the time to change to hound form. Other pack members were breaking from the crowd to help, but they were far behind.

His quarry was only a stone's throw ahead now, dark clothing a blur against the night. Lore lengthened his stride as far as he could, lungs straining against the chill air. The pavement was slick with frost, the sound of pounding feet magnified by the cold. He lunged forward, snagging the rough wool of the runner's sleeve.

The figure jerked away, springing forward with a desperate burst of energy. Lore bounded, using both hands this time to grab the coat. The runner crumpled to the ground with a frightened cry, Lore pinning him with his weight.

They both grunted as they hit the ground. Lore rolled the figure over, smelling the sharp tang of smoke on his clothes.

"*Madhyor!*" cried his captive. *Master.*

With a wrench, Lore saw the runner was one of his own people.

"Helver!" he snarled, putting an extra sting in the young hound's name. He dropped into the hounds' own language. "What are you doing?"

Lore fought the urge to howl with frustration. He was supposed to be chasing his invisible enemy! Instead, he'd caught a whelp pulling some kind of prank.

"Forgive me!" Helver blocked his face with his hands, as if expecting a blow. "The building was closed and empty. I went to see what I could take."

It was an easy enough thing to do. Locks were no problem for a half-demon hellhound—but that only made respecting property all the more important. It was a pup's first lesson.

"You stole from the clinic?" Furious, Lore ran his hands over Helver's coat, finding the pockets. *There are police everywhere.* Humans were quick to judge their supernatural neighbors, and harsh with their retribution. The whole pack would suffer for Helver's stupidity. Lore couldn't let that happen.

He expected pill bottles, but he found money instead. He froze, staring at the double fistful of fifties and hundreds. "Where did you get this?"

"The campaign office. They keep the donations in the safe."

For a heartbeat, Lore was stunned. Of course. The municipal election. The vampire candidate's headquarters occupied two rooms on the building's east side. Lore had been so focused on the loss of the medical facility, he'd momentarily forgotten.

He shouldn't have. The election added a whole new layer to everything that had happened that night—political angst galore—but he would have to think about that once he'd dealt with Helver.

The other hounds were catching up. He held up a hand, keeping them back. They gathered, standing at a distance with arms crossed and hips cocked.

Lore put on his Angry Alpha face. It wasn't hard. "How dare you touch what does not belong to you? Do you want to ruin the rest of your life? Bring dishonor on your elders?"

Helver lifted his face from his hands, eyes stricken with shame and fright. His cheeks were still rounded, not the hard angles and planes of the adult hellhound male. Lore's gut twisted with anger and fear for the youth. He wasn't a bad whelp, but not the smartest, and this new world they lived in was crammed with temptation. The hell they'd left had been brutal, but much, much simpler.

Lore was damned if he'd watch one of his pack lose his way.

He hauled the youth to his feet and gave him a savage shake, showing his strength. Helver took it meekly, not even lifting his head. Lore was his king. To fight back meant a fight to the death, and they both knew Lore would win.

The shaking didn't hurt. The real discipline would come later. So would a lot of questions, like who had put him up to the theft, but Lore had to focus on the crisis in front of him.

"Who set the fire?" he demanded.

Helver hung his head, breathing hard. If he had been in dog form, his tail would have been tucked in as far as it would go. "I didn't see anyone. I just felt—it was *bad*. And then it was hot. It was really weird—there was nothing, just heat, and then there were flames everywhere. I grabbed a fire extinguisher, but then things started to explode in the clinic—oxygen and I don't know what else—and it stank. I couldn't breathe past the chemicals, and it was just too hot. I had to go."

The hounds muttered among themselves, the sound both angry and concerned.

"There was no other person inside?"

"No, no one I could hear or smell. I hid behind the building until . . ." He trailed off.

"Until what?"

"I thought I could get away. With all the trucks and stuff around."

"Count yourself lucky that it was me who caught you." Lore could hear the sound of pounding feet. The humans were catching up to them. Lore pushed Helver away. The youth staggered several steps before finding his balance. "Go home. Stay there. Burn those clothes. They stink. I'll deal with you later."

Helver bowed, his hands over his face again in a gesture of submission.

"Run!" Lore growled. He waved at the hounds standing there. "Take him home."

They obeyed, crowding Helver into their midst before they ran in long, fluid strides. Lore stuffed the campaign money in his pocket, wondering how the hell he was going to return it to the vampires without starting World War III. They weren't the types to laugh off a youthful prank.

He turned to face the humans running toward them.

The one in front was one of those cops that looked like a cop: tall, chiseled, dark-haired, somewhere between thirty and fifty. Lore knew him. He was one of the few human detectives assigned to cover the supernatural beat.

"Detective Baines!" Lore stepped in his path. At the same time, he pulled his jacket closed and zipped it to hide the weapons strapped to his body. All hellhound warriors went armed to the teeth. Human police often took that the wrong way.

"Who was that boy?" Baines demanded, slowing to a stop. His men stayed a distance away, as if they were afraid Lore would bite.

"Why did you let him go?" Baines's voice vibrated with anger.

Lore's blood felt acidic with disappointment in Helver, but pack was pack. "He's not your arsonist."

Baines gave him a hard look, as if taking a mental snapshot. "I want a name."

"No." Lore kept his expression blank.

"What's your name?"

"Lore."

"Lore what?"

"Just Lore. I don't need two names."

"Well, Lore-with-one-name, your boy might be a material witness."

"He saw nothing."

The evil was gone now. Just the memory of it hovered in the air, mixing with occasional spits of sleet. The jack-o'-lantern orange of the fire mocked them, turning the sky to a sickly bronze. Nothing in nature had made that blaze.

"How do you know what he did or didn't see?" asked Baines between clenched teeth.

"I asked him, and hounds cannot lie."

Baines narrowed his eyes. "Won't, you mean."

"Can't. It's impossible for us."

He raised a skeptical eyebrow. "No shit?"

"No shit," said Lore. "We're your dream witnesses."

Baines held his gaze another moment, then grudgingly backed off. He lifted his chin, the gesture subtly aggressive, as if he were still burning to face off with more than words. It would have been a bad idea. Baines wasn't small, but Lore could snap his neck in an instant.

The detective flexed his fists. "Thanks to you, I don't have any witnesses. Yet."

"Sure you do," said Lore.

"Who?"

He nodded toward the fire. "The building itself. A few years ago, that clinic used to be a machine shop. It's all concrete and steel."

The detective's expression tightened, understanding dawning in his eyes. "Concrete doesn't burn."

"Concrete walls can be subjected to gas flames at one thousand degrees centigrade for four hours without structural damage. That's why they make fire walls out of concrete."

Baines stared.

"I was renovating a warehouse," Lore added. "I had to look it up."

"No kid set that fire," Baines conceded in a low voice. "The walls are melting."

Baines gave him a look. "What the hell does that?"

"A spell."

Baines's frown deepened.

Lore stared at the fire, feeling the echo of sorcery deep in the heart of the flames. The hellhounds had not faced this enemy before, but it was old and powerful. Now that he wasn't chasing his foe, he could test the flavor of the leftover magic, rolling it over and over in his mind.

Necromancy.

Chapter 5

Talia might be dead, but she still had a bad case of the creeps.

The scent of blood swamped her brain, swallowing sight and sound. She hesitated where she stood, her vampire senses screaming that something was wrong. That much blood was far too much of a good thing. The elevator doors whooshed shut behind her, stirring a gust of recycled air. Stirring up that maddening, tantalizing, revolting smell.

And there was something oddly familiar about it, a specific top note stirring the memory like a complex perfume.

Talia blinked the hallway back into focus. This was her floor of the condo building, and home and Michelle were at the end of the hall. She fished her door keys out of her purse and started walking, the glossy pink bag from Howard's banging against her leg as she walked.

Now her stomach hurt, her jaws ached to bite, but more from panic than hunger. That much blood meant someone was hurt. There were a lot of elderly people in the building. Many lived alone. One of them might have slipped and fallen, or maybe cut themselves in the kitchen. Or maybe someone had broken in?

Talia quickened her stride, following the scent. She pulled her phone out of her shoulder bag, the rhinestones on its bright blue case winking in the dim overhead light. She flipped it open, ready to dial Emergency as soon as she figured out who was in trouble. She was no superhero, but she could force open a door and control her hunger long enough for basic first aid. If there were bad guys, oh well. She'd had a light dinner.

She passed units fifteen-oh-eight, fifteen-ten, and fifteen-twelve, her high-heeled ankle boots silent on the soft green carpet. Fifteen-fourteen, fifteen-sixteen. She paused at each door, listening for clues. A television muttered here and there. No sounds of a predator attacking its prey.

Fifteen-twenty, fifteen-twenty-two. The smell was coming from fifteen-twenty-four at the end of the hall. *Oh. Oh!*

Fifteen-twenty-four was her place. *Michelle!*

She grasped the cool metal of the door handle and turned it. It was unlocked. The door swung open, and the smell of death rushed into the hall like the surf, drowning Talia all over again. That familiar note in the scent pounded at her, but she pushed it out of her mind, refusing to acknowledge that it reminded her of her cousin.

Instinct froze her where she stood, listening. There was no heartbeat, but that didn't mean much. Lots of things, herself included, didn't have a pulse. Reaching out her left hand, she pushed the door all the way open. The entry looked straight through to the living room, where a big picture window let in the glow of city lights. It was plenty of light for a vampire to see by.

"Michelle?" she said softly. *There's no one here. She must have left.*

Talia couldn't, wouldn't, believe anything else. She slid her phone back into her purse and set it down along with her shopping bag. *Get a grip.* But her hands shook so hard, she had to make fists to stop them.

She left the door open behind her as she tiptoed inside. She'd lived there for two months, but suddenly the place felt alien. Lamps, tables, the so-ugly-it-was-cute pink china poodle with the bobblehead. They might as well have been rock formations on another planet. Nothing felt right.

Her boot bumped against something. Talia sprang backward, her dead heart giving a thump of fright. She stared, organizing the shape into meaning. A suitcase. One of those with the pull-out handle and wheels. Big and bright red.

It was Michelle's.

"Michelle?" Talia meant to shout this time, but it came out as a whisper. "What the hell, girl?"

She groped on the wall for the light switch, suddenly needing the comfort of brightness. The twin lamps that framed the couch bloomed with warm light.

Oh, God.

Her stomach heaved. Now she could see all that red, red blood. Scarlet sprayed in arcs across the wall, splattering the furniture like a painter gone all Jackson Pollock on the decor. Talia shuddered as the carpet squished with wetness.

The smell could have gagged a werewolf.

She dimly realized one of the bookshelves was knocked over. There had been a fight.

"Michelle?" Her voice sounded tiny, childlike. Talia took one more step, and that gave her a full view of the living room. *Oh, God!*

Suddenly standing was hard. She grabbed the wall before she could fall down.

Her cousin, tall and trim in her navy blue cruise hostess uniform, lay on her side between the couch and the coffee table. Drops of drying blood made her skin look luminously pale. Beneath the tangle of dark hair, Talia's gaze sought the features she knew as well as her own: high forehead, freckled nose, the mouth that turned up at one corner, always ready to smile. Born a year apart, they'd always looked more like twins than plain old cousins.

They still looked almost identical, except Michelle's head was a yard away from the rest of her body.

Talia's eyes drifted shut as the room closed in, darkness spiraling down to a pinpoint.

Beheaded.

Talia's grip on the wall failed, and she started to sink to the floor. The wet, red floor. Sudden nausea wrenched her. She scrambled for the kitchen, retching into the sink. She'd fed earlier, but not much. Nothing came up but a thin trickle of fluid.

Beheaded.

She heaved again, the strength of her vampire body making it painful. Talia leaned over the stainless-steel sink, shaking. The image of her cousin's body burned in her mind's eye. Whoever had done it had meant to kill *her*. Taking the head was the usual way to execute vampires— a lot more certain than a wooden stake.

She died because of me. They thought she was me.

Talia's breath caught, and caught again, dragging into her lungs in tiny gasps that finally dissolved into sobs. She pushed away from the sink, grabbing a paper towel to mop her eyes. There was no time to fall apart.

But she did. She pressed the wadded towel to her mouth, stifling her sobs. The tears were turning to a burning ache that ran all down her throat, through her body, and out the soles of her feet.

This was no good. She had to get out of there.

Before whoever murdered Michelle came back.

Before someone called the cops and they blamed her, because she was the monster found next to the body.

Talia braced herself against the counter and stared into the sink until her eyes blurred and she squeezed them shut. This was the moment when the movie hero swore revenge, made a plan, and went after the bad guy.

All she felt was gut-wrenching grief.

A rustling sound came from the hallway, as if something had brushed against the shopping bag she'd abandoned by the door.

Talia spun around, terror rippling over her skin. So much for her earlier quip of *bad guys, oh well*. Macabre images flashed one after the other through her mind. Sheer willpower pinned her to the floor, making her think before she bolted straight into danger.

Normally, she would worry about hiding her scent from another predator, but the place stank so badly that wasn't an issue. Plus, whoever had killed Michelle had to be human. Nothing else would have confused one of their own with a vampire.

Slowly, she peered around the edge of the kitchen doorway. A figure hulked in the entrance to the condo, backlit by the lights from the hall.

Oh, God! It's—he's—coming this way.

Talia shrank back into the galley kitchen, squeezing into the corner between the refrigerator and the wall. She shrank down, making herself small, bending her head forward to hide her pale skin with the dark fall of her hair. There was no need for her to breathe, nothing to disturb the absolute stillness of the dead.

Except terror. She wanted to run so badly her muscles cramped.

The fridge hummed, the hard surface vibrating against her arm. *Trapped!* Through the curtain of her hair, she could see the stranger's wide shoulders blocking the hallway between her and the door. Her heart gave a single, painful beat, jolted back to life by the adrenaline rushing into her blood.

Tears of outrage stung Talia's eyes. She was frightened, absolutely, but she was also furious. Someone had killed Michelle, and now they'd come back. *Realized you screwed up?* she thought bitterly. *Figured out that was human blood all over your hands?*

It galled her to be so helpless. Talia had weapons, but they were stuffed in the top of the hallway closet, gathering dust. She'd thought she'd never have to use them again. Prayed for it.

Apparently no one listened to a vampire's prayers.

You're hiding in a kitchen filled with knives. Maybe she wasn't so helpless after all.

She could see the figure's shadow slide over the wall, stark against the bright patch of hallway light. His silhouette showed he was tall and big-boned, moving with surprising grace for such a large man. She caught a sharp tang of smoke and chemicals, as if he'd been near an industrial fire. The smell drowned her vampire senses, choking out anything else his scent might have told her. He was coming closer, pausing after each step, his feet all but silent on the carpeting.

Just a few yards more and he would be past the kitchen door. Then she could make a break for it. Even a fledgling like her could move faster than a mortal.

Closer, closer. The hiding place where she crouched was just inside the kitchen entrance. If she reached out, she could brush the toes of his heavy work boots with her fingers. Her fingertips itched, as if they had already grazed the dirty leather. He was so close she dared not lift her head to look at him. All she got was a good view of jeans-clad shins.

And then he was past. She rose in a single, smooth gesture, balancing on her toes. One careful step forward, and she reached the counter opposite the fridge. Silently, she slid a kitchen knife out of the block. *Just in case.* It was smarter to run than to fight, but he might corner her yet.

She heard his intake of breath as he reached the living room. She froze, the cool handle of the knife heavy and hard against her palm.

The urge to vomit washed over her again, but she didn't dare make a noise. Not even to swallow. She could hear him, just a few yards to the right, the brush of cloth on cloth as he moved around the gory, glistening carnage in the next room.

Three, two, one.

Talia darted toward the hall, inhumanly fast.

He was faster.

Huge hands grabbed her upper arms, hauling her into the air. She kicked, hearing a snarl of pain as the sharp heel of her ankle boot dug into his thigh. She tried to turn and slash, but the angle was wrong. Wriggling like a ferret, Talia twisted, using Undead strength to turn within that big-knuckled grasp.

She flipped over, dropping through the air as her attacker lost his hold. With an upward slash, she scored the knife along the flesh of his hand.

Ha!

His other hand came down like a hammer, aiming for the weapon. Talia spun and kicked, wobbling in the heels but still forcing him back. She used the motion of the kick to fall into a crouch, sweeping the blade in a whispering arc, claiming the space around her body.

Force the enemy to keep his distance. One useful thing her father had taught her. One of the few.

But as she came out of the turn, he grabbed her by the scruff of the neck—how long was his reach, anyway?— and heaved her to the ground like a bag of laundry. Before Talia could move, she felt a heavy knee in the small of her back. She tried to arch up, but he was at least twice her weight. Rage shot through her, riding on a cold slick of terror. She hissed, baring fang.

His hand was pinning her wrist to the carpet, immobilizing the knife. Gripping it hard, she twisted her hand, snaking the point toward his flesh. His other hand clamped down, peeling her fingers off the hilt one by one.

She did her best to scratch. A female vampire's nails were sharp as talons.

"Give it up," he growled.

She made a sound like a cat poked with a fork, half hiss, half yowl. The knife came loose. He sent it spinning across the floor, out of reach. Then she felt something cold and metal click shut around her wrist. The chill sensation made her flail, the motion jerking her elbow up to connect with solid flesh. His jaw? For a glorious moment, she felt him flinch.

Only to shove her back down and snap the handcuffs around her other wrist.

"There's silver in the alloy." His voice was hard and low. "You can't break them."

Talia rolled over, baring her fangs. The slide of metal against leather told her a gun had left its holster. The next thing she saw was a freaking .44 Magnum Ruger Blackhawk aimed between her eyes—loaded, no doubt, with silver-coated hollow-point bullets.

Their fight had brought them closer to the living room. The glow of the table lamps cast a wash of light over the attacker's face, at last giving her a good look at the man. Or, what she could see of him around the muzzle of the mini-cannon in his hand.

Shaggy dark hair, thick and straight and a bit too long. Dark eyes. Swarthy skin. Killer cheekbones. Young, maybe late twenties. Not classically handsome, but there was something heart-stopping in that face. Something wild. And he was *big*.

She'd seen him before. What was his name? Lorne? No, Lore. He lived somewhere on the sixth floor.

"Great," Talia ground out through clenched teeth. Everything was catching up to her, emotions fighting their way through shock. She was starting to cry, tears sliding from beneath her lashes and trickling down her temples. *Oh, Michelle, what happened?* "Just great. I'm about to be blown to smithereens by the boy next door."

He leaned forward, pressing the muzzle of the gun into her flesh. "Be silent."

Talia hissed.

The corner of his mouth pulled down. "Did the smell of her get to be too much? You needed a taste?"

"Oh, God, no." Talia caught her breath, feeling beads of cold, clammy sweat trickle between her breasts. Fear. Guilt. She'd been so afraid of hurting Michelle, been so careful. Accusing her now wasn't fair. "How can you say that? She's right there. Right over there."

"Then tell the truth."

Talia gulped, tasting death on her tongue. "I didn't do this."

"All the vampires say that."

"Wasn't this *your* doing?"

"I don't hunt humans. I go for bigger game."

The statement made her shiver. His hand was bloody where she'd cut him, but he didn't smell like food. Not human, but nothing she recognized. The realization came like an extra jolt of electricity. *What the hell is he?*

"Then why are you here? Who are you?" She struggled to sit up, awkward because her arms were pinned behind her back. He pressed the Ruger hard against her skin, but she barely noticed.

"Who is your sire?" he demanded.

Talia clamped her mouth shut. His dark, angry gaze locked with hers. It wasn't the cold stare of so many killers she'd known. His eyes were hot with emotion, a righteous, remorseless fury.

"Who made you?" His voice grated with anger.

Talia blinked hard, her heart giving another jerking thump of fright. "No, please, if you send me back to my sire, I'll be lucky if he only kills me."

"That's what happens when a vampire goes rogue."

Now she was starting to sob, ugly little gasps that

caught in her throat. "You can't send me back. I didn't kill her. I loved Michelle." She was begging, and put every ounce of her soul into it, holding his dark, burning stare.

A crease formed between his eyebrows. "Damn you."

The wail of a police siren ripped the night. Were they coming for Michelle's murder, or was there another tragedy tonight?

Lore pressed the muzzle of the gun like a cold kiss against her forehead. "I don't trust you. I can't tell if you're the killer or not. But I believe you're afraid of your sire."

Her mouth had gone paper dry. "What are you going to do?"

His mouth thinned as if he didn't like the question. He looked her up and down, all that anger turning to a smoldering frustration. Talia could almost feel it heating her skin.

"The human police will assume you're guilty and look no further. I'll give you a choice. Take your chances with them, or . . ." He trailed off, clearly mulling over his next words.

"Or?" The single syllable came out in a croak.

"Or you're my prisoner. Take your pick."

Chapter 6

"Hello, and welcome back to CSUP in the nighttime hours, with your host Errata Jones. Tonight we're talking love amongst the monsters—especially between the monsters and everyone else.

"One of the best-known stories of unrequited love was found in that good old classic, *Dracula*. I have it on good authority what happened was nothing like the book, but then where's the surprise in that? History is usually written by the winner. If Mina and Drac found true love—well, that's not the story her wimpy human husband wanted to spread far and wide.

"But the truth isn't hard to find. Think about it: Who was the crazy one in the story? The wealthy vampire making real estate investments, or the wacky Dutch doctor with his black bag of fetish objects and torture devices?

"In other words, context is everything. Before you judge a villain or a hero and especially your lover, it's a good idea to understand his or her motives."

* * *

Tuesday, December 28, 11:00 p.m.
Talia's condo

I can always get away.

Talia's mind was still reeling with shock, with grief, but her father's lessons came back to her with the cold, hard pragmatism of long training. Drill long enough, and anything could become reflex. Even the art of escape.

It was a desperate gamble, but she'd take her chances with a lone gunman—even this bruiser—over the human police. Humans weren't strong, but there were too damned many of them. Besides, so far she'd kept out of their data banks. Once you were in their computers, Unlife got infinitely more complicated.

On the other hand, a single attacker couldn't watch her every second. Until Lore got her to his den of thieves, or spy central, or resistance cell, or wherever the heck he operated from, she had a window of opportunity to break free.

Or so she hoped. He wasn't letting her stray an inch, keeping a hard grip on her arm. Talia made the trip down the stairs with the Ruger pressed into her ribs and her hands wrenched behind her back, wrists cuffed. The position made her shoulders ache.

It was awkward going, step-by-step, Lore never letting her get more than half a pace ahead. Their feet shuffled and echoed as they passed from landing to landing, neither speaking a word—Talia because she refused to let her voice show her fear. That just turned some bastards on.

Lore was letting the Ruger do his talking for him. Man, she hated the strong, silent, carry-the-big-gun type. Worse, she was fairly sure he wasn't short on brains. Silent didn't mean stupid. In his case, she was willing to bet the opposite.

The fluorescent lights in the stairwell hummed and flickered, the harsh glare showing every gum wrapper, every bit of chipped paint. She was starting to get dizzy from staring down so many identical flights of stairs. By her count they were halfway to the parking garage, where she would no doubt be stuffed into the trunk of a car and driven off to whatever new outrage the universe had planned.

But isn't that what you deserve? If Michelle hadn't taken you in, she'd still be alive. Just by being there, didn't you murder her as surely as if you'd swung that sword yourself? And she wasn't the first casualty, the first loved one you destroyed.

A stab of despair suddenly robbed her knees of strength. She sagged a moment, stumbling. Lore grabbed her arm and heaved her toward the sixth-floor fire-exit door.

"Where are we going?" She should demand answers, proudly rage against him, but instead her voice sounded breathy and weak. She had to fight, but she was drowning in grief.

He paused a moment to make sure the hallway was empty before marching her from the stairwell into the hall. "I'm locking you up, remember?" he muttered.

For a second, incredulity trumped everything else. "In your condo?"

"What do you want? A crypt? Sorry, not available."

A sick fear jolted through her. Keeping a prisoner took soundproofing, locks, privacy. It wasn't a spur-of-the-moment project.

She swallowed hard. "Keeping girls locked up is your special hobby?"

"Shut up." He shoved her against the wall, the gun between her shoulder blades while he unlocked his door. "Don't even think about making a noise. Vampires are hard to kill, but they still break."

Her cheek pressed against the wallpaper, Talia gazed longingly down the hallway, willing with all her might for a neighbor to wander into view.

But no one ever rescued her. She just wasn't that kind of girl. *You're a monster.* She could feel a tear leaking down her cheek, but she didn't dare move. *Save me, save me, save me.* She could hear Lore breathing, rattling keys in his left hand.

She could hear that his heartbeat was slightly fast, as if taking a captive was the exercise equivalent of a brisk walk. Her window of escape opportunity was closing fast, but there wasn't a damned thing she could do while the Ruger was still planted firmly against her spine.

She tried to care, but all she could see in her mind's eye was Michelle's dead body. *Why did I let her try to help me? Why couldn't I just leave her alone?*

"Consider this your formal invite." He grabbed her above the elbow and pushed her through the door. Talia stumbled. His fingers tightened, keeping her from spilling forward. "Sorry."

He let her go as she leaned on the corner of the wall, steadying herself. Lore's apology had been automatic. At some time in the past, manners had been drilled into him. That made her feel just a little bit better. Too bad that innate sense of etiquette didn't extend to, say, not handcuffing a girl on first acquaintance.

Is it anything more than you deserve?

Now she could hear the police sirens again. Rack lights splashed on the thin drapes, showing the first squad cars had arrived. But who had called? Lore hadn't had time. Perhaps another neighbor had found Michelle while investigating the sound of their scuffle? Or maybe the killer himself had called, anxious for his fifteen minutes of fame?

Lore had gotten her away from the crime scene just in time. She was safe from the law. But really, how safe was that? Talia looked around, sick with anxiety.

She saw at a glance the layout of Lore's place was the exact image of Michelle's. Corner suite, even the same color of paint—except these walls weren't splattered with gore. Remembering what lay upstairs sent a hot, queasy wave through her. Lore took her arm again, pulling her to the left.

"Hey! Take it easy. You're leaving a bruise," she snapped, summoning some attitude, but her words were faint.

"Vampires heal." But he let go, instead poking the gun in her ribs. "That way."

Lore propelled Talia into a dark room and flipped on the overhead light. *Oh, Lord, it's his bedroom.*

He wasn't Mr. Tidy. The queen-sized bed was made, its navy comforter dark against a brass bed frame, but clothes, magazines, and other junk littered the floor in the basic single male decorating scheme. Her heel caught on a wadded-up sock.

"Onto the bed," he ordered.

Onto the bed? Not bloody likely!

Forgetting the gun, Talia twisted away to face him. A furious tingling crept up her limbs, the shock of just too much emotion. She was either going to throw up or slug him the moment her hands were free. "What kind of male fantasy bullshit is this?"

"Fantasy?" His heavy-browed scowl fragmented, drifting into embarrassment.

Something inside her snapped. All of a sudden, Talia's nerve was back. So what if she was in handcuffs? She'd give him the fight of his life. "You sick bastard."

"Don't flatter yourself." He gave her a shove that made her sit with a bounce on the soft mattress. "I don't do dead people."

Her arms pinned behind her, Talia struggled to stay upright. The mattress was one of those poofy pillow-top things. "Then what are we doing here?"

"This is my private territory. No one comes here unless they're invited."

Anger stabbed through her. "Your personal den of iniquity, huh?"

"More like the one place I can get some peace and quiet. Or used to be. Now there's a vampire in my bed."

"I'm not in it yet, bud."

His expression dripped irony. "I always forget the chocolates and flowers." Lore holstered the gun and pulled a handcuff key from his jeans pocket.

"That's more like it." Talia turned so he could reach her wrists.

She felt his fingers working with deft efficiency. Her right wrist came free. She flexed her arm, making sure it still bent in all the right places. Then she felt him moving her left arm and heard a metallic *snick*.

"Hey!" she yelled, squirming around to see what he'd done. He'd fastened the empty half of the cuffs to the heavy brass post framing the headboard. Now she was chained to his bed. *Oh, gag me!*

He stepped back, his expression hard. "You may as well get comfortable."

Her stomach plunged. "This is my prison cell?"

"As I said, the crypt was already booked."

Oh, shit! She gave the cuffs a jerk because, well, it was mandatory in the shackled prisoner handbook. Metal grated on metal, the silver of the cuffs biting into the skin of her left wrist. She took in a breath that rattled with fear, but she forced her voice to steadiness. "You don't have the fur-lined model, huh? Those would be a bit more comfy."

His eyes narrowed. "Not my thing. Bondage is a bit too much like my day job."

The words felt oddly like a joke she wasn't getting. Maybe it was something cultural. He had an odd, halting way of speaking—no accent, but she was willing to bet that English wasn't his first language.

Talia clenched her fist to hide the fact her fingers were shaking. "What exactly is your day job? Village executioner?"

"I am the Alpha of the hellhounds."

Lore folded his arms. Even through the storm of emotion, Talia couldn't avoid noticing how the gesture showed off his arms and chest. All he needed were buckskin and a rifle and he could have been a brawny version of Daniel Day-Lewis in *The Last of the Mohicans*.

Then what he said soaked in. "Hellhound?"

"We are half demons."

"Isn't that like being a little bit pregnant?"

Lore gave a sudden, evil grin. He leaned against the brass rail of the footboard, looming over Talia. No one got to be Alpha just because he was a nice guy. If Lore really was the top dog, there was a savage streak to match the wild-man looks. "It means that if you do break out of here, there is nowhere you can hide. I can track the ghost of a ghost, and the whole pack will be hunting you right along with me."

Talia set her jaw, refusing to give in to a sudden wave of terror. "Why?"

Lore's grin faded as he took a step away from the bed. "I told you. I'm not certain whether you're innocent or guilty. I'm the acting sheriff in Fairview. Right now you're my responsibility."

"So you're the self-appointed detective on my case, is that it?"

"Be happy that I care whether or not you're guilty."

The handcuffs interfered with her sense of gratitude. "I didn't kill Michelle." Her voice cracked, and she gulped down a rising tide of grief. She was in danger. She had to keep her head straight. *Don't you deserve to die?*

"Were they trying to kill you?"

"Maybe."

"Who?"

"I honestly don't know." She looked away, hiding the tears that spilled out from under her eyelashes. *Oh, God, Michelle.*

"No possibilities?"

There were, but none that she'd admit to. Talia

shrugged as much as the handcuffs would allow. "No names come to mind."

"That's the difference between you and me."

"What?" She tried to glare, but her eyes were too wet to make it convincing.

"Hellhounds can't lie."

"Huh?"

"We're incapable of telling an untruth. *You* are not."

"Are you saying I'm a liar?"

Lore looked unimpressed. "You're on the run. I found you with a bloody corpse. You use a knife with considerable skill. You're *something* more than you're saying."

He turned and opened a drawer in a tall dresser. From where she was chained, Talia couldn't see what was in the drawer, but heard the scrape of metal on wood. When Lore turned back, he had another set of silver handcuffs in his hand.

Talia scrambled backward, squeezing herself into the corner where the bed met the wall. "What do you think you're doing?"

"Extra insurance."

She jerked at the chain with frustration. "Damn you, leave me alone!"

"It was your choice, me or the police."

Lore reached over her, his big body stretching easily over the wide mattress. Talia shrank against the pillows as his face came too close to hers. She could smell that burnt chemical scent on his clothes again. Beneath it was the musky scent of man—except it wasn't. It was richer. Darker. *Hellhound.* The hair on her neck ruffled. *Must be the demon blood, because Mrs. McCready's cockapoo never smelled that good.*

But there was no way she was letting him chain her other hand. His face drew close to hers, a mixture of caution and determination in his dark eyes. She flexed her fingers, calculating the angle between Lore's nose and the heel of her hand. With enough force, the right blow could knock him out. The squishy mattress would cost her momentum, but she was willing to give it—him—a shot.

Damn! He anticipated her move, his hand rising to block her, so at the last second she changed angles and went for his holster. Lore solved the problem by dropping on top of her, pinning her under his weight. Suddenly her nose was buried in his hair, her breasts crushed under his broad, strong chest.

"Get off me!" she hissed into his ear. His neck was right *there*, pulse pounding like forbidden candy. She'd heard some vamps liked demon blood.

Talia felt the strength in his body, the stretch and pull of muscle under cloth. She tensed, wanting the freedom to fight but only meeting a solid wall of hellhound wherever she moved. Lore grabbed her right wrist. *Nuts!* She cried out, the sound plaintive.

He stopped moving and simply held her there, their faces a breath apart. His eyes were so dark, there was almost no distinction between the iris and pupil.

"Are you going to be good?" he growled.

Talia squeezed her eyes shut. "Please don't cuff my other hand. You don't need to. I can't break free."

Her voice cracked, finally giving way to the terror of the situation. She was too young a vampire to break the silver cuffs, and not nearly as strong as a hellhound. She might as well have still been human.

Helplessness brought back bad, bad memories.

"Do you promise to be good?" This time the question was gentler.

She nodded, hating herself for her eagerness. "Yes. Yes, of course."

She was lying. He had to know that. It was the first duty of a prisoner to escape—even if she had no idea in the world how she was going to do it.

He rose up on hands and knees. Talia was trapped beneath him, caged by his limbs. The feel of his warm hands still clung to her skin. His touch had been businesslike. Appropriate, if chaining up a woman ever could be described that way—yet now there was something in his expression as he stared down at her, the second set of cuffs still dangling from his hand. Something *other*.

The look pinned her like a stake.

She resisted the urge to curl into a ball, an instinctive urge to cover her vulnerable parts. He was looking at her as if he'd just decided she might be good to eat—in more ways than one. Worse, she wanted to respond.

Talia swallowed hard, putting all her defiance into her eyes. Refusing to cave.

"Bad dog!"

Chapter 7

*B*ad dog?
    She had no idea.
    Prophets spare me.
    Lore banged into the stairwell and began running back to the fifteenth floor, taking the steps two and three at a bound. It had been a long night, but acute frustration made up for the bite of fatigue. His nerves were sparking like a faulty wire.

There was a human saying about heat and kitchens, and Lore was beating a retreat before he did something incredibly stupid. That vampiress—possibly murderess— was hot enough to set his fur on fire. When he'd had her pinned to the bed, every cell in his being had sat up and begged.

Definitely not something any hellhound should be thinking about, much less an Alpha. Hounds lived by a set of rules millennia old, and those rules said that no hound looked outside the pack for pleasure. They just didn't. For one thing, if they did stray, they couldn't lie about it afterward.

That was awkward, to say the least.

Lore stopped on a landing, breathing hard and glowering at the scuff marks on the wall. His skin felt prickly, as if he'd been standing next to a glowing furnace. Thinking about the vampire's slender body made it worse. He'd had to walk away without even taking the time to put on the second set of cuffs. Feeling her struggle brought out the urge to pin her down. Taste her. Take her.

The memory turned the tingling in his skin to an outright itch.

Maybe he was allergic. After all, she was as different from him as another creature could be: a vampire, a rogue alienated from her sire, and on the run from a crime. The very thing orderly, family-driven pack structure despised.

Moreover, Lore was the serious, down-to-business leader, the one voted least likely to cut loose and have fun. Now, here he had gone and handcuffed a babe to his bedpost. Whatever seed of chaos had infected the vamp-on-the-run was apparently contagious, and now it was crawling through his system.

Bad dog. Who talked to a hellhound like that? In a very, very unwise corner of his soul, he found it hilarious. He started up the stairs again, more slowly this time. His footfalls echoed like a giant's.

He should turn her over to the law. She wasn't hellhound business. And how was he going to decide whether or not she had killed her cousin? He was an enforcer, not a detective. He had other priorities, such as Helver and whatever other whelps were digging their way into trouble. Furthermore, there was that *something* haunting the night and burning down buildings.

Something he thought might be the result of necromancy. That kind of sorcery required a death, and usually a violent one.

Maybe the murdered girl was part of it all. Maybe his pretty prisoner was guilty as sin.

Lore reached the fifteenth floor and cautiously pushed open the stairway door. He'd heard the sirens earlier and, for the second time that night, he found himself on the fringes of a crime scene. The hair on the back of his neck ruffled, his territorial instincts roused by so many strange males in his building.

Uniformed police officers stood outside suite fifteen-twenty-four. A knot of official-looking men crowded the doorway, backlit by the flash of a camera taking multiple shots inside the condo. Someone was asking for security tapes of the front door. Lore knew the man was out of luck. The building was old, and with few thefts there had been no need to add cameras—until now.

"Stop right there," said one of the uniforms, holding up a hand. He was young and beefy, his features unfinished-looking.

Lore stopped, giving the cop the blank face hounds used with outsiders—except, for some reason, his vampire. She was like a sudden brain fever, making him behave in unusual ways. Perhaps keeping her in his bedroom was a really bad idea. He could almost hear Perry saying, "Ya think?"

"Crime scene," said the uniform. "Move on, please."

"What happened?" Lore asked, wondering how much the cops would be willing to say.

"Never mind. Move along."

"Wait." One of the other cops turned around. With a sinking feeling in his stomach, Lore recognized Baines.

"Detective," Lore said, erasing all emotion from his voice.

Baines hooked a thumb in his belt, narrowing his eyes as he walked toward Lore. His face was set, like someone had chipped it out of petrified wood. "Okay. I'll bite. Why am I seeing you at two different crime scenes in one night?"

"I live in the building."

Baines missed a beat when he heard that. A split second of surprise. "A hellhound? Here? This condominium is about as white-bread human as it gets."

"I lease from a friend." Who was a demon, but that was another story.

"Interesting."

"I pay my utilities. I keep my TV volume at a reasonable level. I help the little old ladies put up their Christmas lights. There've been no complaints." Lore let the slightest edge of annoyance creep into his words.

Baines recovered his cop face. "Uh-huh. Don't play the poor-little-monster card with me. If a guy wants to spend part of his time running around on four legs, why the hell should the cops care? If that guy is dragging a dismembered leg in his jaws, then I'll get excited."

Lore felt his eyebrows lifting in surprise. This was an attitude he hadn't encountered before. He liked it.

The detective remained expressionless. "What brings you to this floor?"

"I heard the sirens. I was curious to see what was going on."

Baines flipped open his notebook and turned to a fresh page. "There were two women living here. Do you know either of them?"

"I know one was named Michelle." So far he was telling the truth. That didn't mean he had to say everything.

"Michelle Faulkner was murdered tonight. There was someone else living here, a Talia Rostova. A near look-alike to Faulkner, to go by the driver's license. Who is she, besides a vampire?"

Talia Rostova. So that was her name. It swirled in his mind like an exotic cocktail. "A cousin, I think. I don't know for sure."

"They have any visitors?"

"None that I saw, but I live on six."

"Any idea where this Talia is now?"

Lore hesitated, trying to think his way around the direct question. Baines gave him a suspicious look.

"Hey, Baines," one of the other officers called. "There's a drawing on the wall. Looks like gang shit."

"Take pictures," said Baines to the other cop. "See what the boys back at the office can make of it. Not that they know squat about supernatural crimes." He turned to Lore. "Anything going on with the Spooky-town gangs?"

"The Dark Hand tried to infiltrate Fairview. They didn't succeed." Under Caravelli's direction, the hounds had made short work of those vampires.

Baines grunted. "I remember that."

Lore saw his chance to get into the condo again before every trace of scent was trampled away. He hadn't had much of a chance to check it out before Talia had burst from the kitchen. "I may recognize your drawing. I know the neighborhood and its people."

"This is a crime scene. You're not a cop."

Lore could feel the man's suspicion like a physical touch. He shrugged, keeping his face neutral. "You're in charge here, but I might see something you won't."

And I've got the suspect you really want chained to my bed.

Interestingly enough, though, Baines was considering a range of suspects and not just the vampire roommate. It improved Lore's opinion of the man.

The detective studied him for a moment. Beneath the wariness, Lore sensed a lot of curiosity. "Like what?"

"If you're dealing with graffiti, I can help. Vampires are big on signs and symbols. Do you know which vampires belong to which clan, and which monarchs claim ownership of them?"

Baines shrugged. "I know Queen Omara demands the loyalty of any vampire living here."

"There are things she doesn't know."

"And you do?"

Again, an image of Talia flashed through his mind. "I have my nose to the ground."

"You a snitch?"

"I keep order."

"I thought that was Alessandro Caravelli's job. He's the peacekeeper in Spookytown."

"He hires my pack from time to time. Right now, I'm his vacation relief." Lore gave a slight smile at the phrase. It was just so wonderfully, mundanely *human*.

After a long moment, Baines gave a small nod. "Okay. Maybe you should take a look at what we've got in there." He glanced toward the open door to the condo. "Put some of those booties over your shoes."

Lore obeyed, barely fitting the protective covers over his long feet. Playing along with the humans' rules irked him, but at this point he'd take answers wherever he could get them. He'd hoped for more information from the hounds who questioned the crowd at the fire, but they'd come up empty. Helver had given the most detailed account.

After leaving the scene of the fire, Lore had found the pup and made him explain himself again. And again. Lore was taking his time to invent an appropriate punishment for stealing the campaign money. He was still too angry to think straight, and it wouldn't hurt Helver to stew a little.

Unfortunately, the young idiot hadn't had anything useful to add to the story. No sight, sound, or scent of an intruder. Lore guessed the fire had been ignited from a distance. Definitely sorcery, probably necromancy. Maybe a warlock, demon or vampire. Big, thick spell books required the patience of an immortal.

He walked behind Baines, taking in the scene. It was crowded with officers and hot with all the lights in the place turned on. The brightness showed everything in lurid colors. Lore had watched enough crime dramas to know they could tell a lot from the way blood splattered during a murder.

The walls and ceiling had a lot to say.

Hellhounds knew death intimately. They were predators, and they'd been preyed upon in the prison where

Lore had grown up. He'd seen enslavement, torture, and cruelty for the sake of pleasure, and yet the sight of Michelle's body made his chest burn with sadness. She'd been a slight woman, her shattered body reminding him of a fallen bird. Slashes seamed her skin where she'd tried to fend off her attacker. The neck was a gory mess, clumsily hacked apart. Lore prayed she'd been unconscious by the time that happened.

The vampires executed their own with swords. Those wounds were, by comparison, precise. Lore guessed the killer had used something that required a lot of cuts—a dagger or a knife.

The camera kept flashing, the bursts of light setting Lore's nerves on edge.

The police had left the head where they had found it, apart from the body. The eyes were half-open, the lips slack. Lore turned away from the waxy face. It was far too much like Talia's.

An officer stood in the living room, making a sketch of the placement of the toppled furniture, the body, and the severed head. With no camera or sketch pad, Lore had to remember what was there: a floor lamp toppled, a small bookcase capsized, paperbacks everywhere, pictures askew. Michelle Faulkner had fought back.

Lore tensed as someone bumped into him. There were too many people, and no one was dusting for fingerprints yet, tweezing up bits of thread or vacuuming the carpet for evidence. He supposed even more personnel would arrive to tramp through the place.

To a hellhound, it was a stupid way to investigate. The first and most obvious tool was a good nose, and now there were too many scents crowding out any trace of the killer. The only thing Lore could tell for sure was that hellhounds and vampires were the only nonhumans who had been there in recent history.

His other sense—the one that gave him premonitions—was jangling with a sense of *wrongness*. The place stank of violence and terror.

"Where's the drawing?" Baines asked a young officer standing by the window.

"There." The man pointed to the living room wall.

With a ping of annoyance, Lore wondered how the hell he'd missed it earlier. Then again, it didn't exactly stand out—just more blood on a bloody wall.

"Well?" asked Baines.

Lore stepped closer. The symbol was crudely done, and at an awkward height. The blood was turning a rusty brown, soaking into the bland off-white paint. He estimated the distance to the floor. "It looked like whoever drew it knelt, scooping up the blood from the carpet with his fingers."

Baines nodded. "So, what does it mean?"

Lore's first impression was of a meaningless splodge. If he squinted, it reminded him of a pup's drawing of the summer sun. Or a squashed spider. Or a head with crudely drawn hair. What had the cop been thinking? Gang symbols had more style. "Honestly, I can't tell."

Baines shrugged. "It was worth a try."

Lore straightened, fixing the childlike scrawl into his memory. As he took one last look, he noticed there was a tiny squiggle disturbing the bottom smears. "There's something written beneath the blood. It's almost covered up."

Baines quickly bent down, bringing his nose nearly to the wall. "It's in pencil."

He pulled a penlight from his pocket and shone it directly on the small printed letters. The writing was ragged, the letters uneven. It reminded Lore of his own awkward penmanship.

"*Vincire*," Baines said. "Latin. Something about binding, I think. It's been years since I studied it."

"Latin?" Lore thought about the fire, dark sorcery,

Talia, and the dead body mere feet away. "What kind of a binding?"

Baines didn't answer. He straightened and looked out the window. "Huh. The snow's started coming down in earnest."

Lore followed his gaze. Fat flakes were twirling through the beams of the streetlights, the wind gusting them into spirals. A brief moment of wonder seized him. *So that's what snow looks like.* He'd seen pictures, but never the real thing.

"I dreamed that it would snow." In the dream, something was chasing him. The snow was so deep, he couldn't run. There had been no choice but to turn and face his enemy.

Prophecies came in dreams. They were the gift and burden the Prophets sent to the Alpha of the pack. The problem was deciding what was a prophecy and what were the aftereffects of the three-day-old pizza he'd left in the fridge. It seemed this time the dream was a warning.

"The snow's a nightmare all right," Baines grumbled. "Roads'll be hell by morning. No one here knows how to drive in this shit."

The detective turned away from the window, then stiffened. He was looking at a desk with a laptop pushed into the corner of the living room. Lore recognized the detritus of a thinker's profession: highlighters, sticky notes, bits of torn paper used as page markers, and more books than any one person could reasonably read. A teacher, perhaps? A stack of papers sat on one corner of the desk. The title page of the top one said *Paradise Lost*.

Lore wondered how anyone could sit still long enough to read that many books.

"What did the missing cousin do for a living?" Baines addressed no one in particular, raising his voice to be heard by all.

The answer came from the young cop who'd pointed out the blood on the wall. "Rostova's a sessional tutor at the university. She's got a master's in education and a bachelor's in Western literature."

Baines gave a low whistle. "So she knows Latin?"

"I guess, maybe," the young cop replied.

Lore understood why Baines had asked. There was a Latin dictionary sitting on the desk. The detective shifted some of the other books stacked on the desk. "Beginning Latin Translation. Virgil's *Aeneid*. *Pride and Prejudice. Anna Karenina*. A DVD of Hugh Grant's greatest hits. Good to have balance."

A ripple of puzzlement passed over Lore. He could usually sniff people out. But with her endless shopping bags, glittery cell phone, and ridiculous heels, Lore would never have guessed Talia was a teacher. She didn't put out the smart girl vibe. But then she didn't put out the knife-fighter vibe, either.

She was deep in hiding, and better at it than anyone had guessed.

Maybe someone had found her out, and gone after her. If so, why?

Or maybe Lore was entirely wrong, and he had a murdering fiend chained to his bed.

He looked out at the snow, watched it gusting down the cold, dry street like handfuls of sugar. It was starting to stick to the grass.

Baines came to stand beside him. "If this keeps up, the city's going to be shut down by morning."

"That will make it hard for our killer to run."

Baines snorted. "You'd be surprised how well they usually hide in plain view."

Chapter 8

Darak tasted the evil that hung in the air and ached to smash it.

Pluto's balls, some idiot went and got himself a spell book.

Wasn't that just dandy?

Who the hell in this backwater has that kind of power? For a pinprick on the map, Fairview was just full of surprises. Vampires standing for public office. Entire prison dimensions. And his personal favorite—invisible evil that set stuff on fire.

Come for the election, stay for the magic of mass destruction.

Darak heaved himself to his feet, stiff from crouching on the peak of the cathedral roof like an oversized gargoyle. He dusted away the snow that had collected on his sleeves and scanned the horizon while he took a slug from his flask.

The dark leathers he wore kept out the wind, but the cold seeped through seams and zippers. One of the old Undead, he could ignore it. What bothered him more was the smoke—not the comfortable scent of a hearth fire, but the reek of a burning building. The acrid stink had drawn him to the highest point he could find, and now he could see the source—a glowing maw of flame to the southwest, unnaturally fierce and bright.

Who or what had caused it? Only one way to find out. Go to the source.

Darak balanced on the roof's ridgeline, walking toe to heel along its length. Pride made him careful. Vampires could fly, but at close to seven feet and three-fifty, Darak was not exactly aerodynamic. Control was important, unless he wanted to drop like an anvil.

When he reached the roofline, he jumped, a streak of shadow against the black sky. The air rushed to meet him, snow stinging his cheeks. He landed lightly enough, boots skating on the frosty sidewalk. Pulling himself upright, he began walking toward the fire.

Darak and his blood-sworn kin were Undead, but they bowed to no queen or king. It had taken them two millennia to gain enough strength for true freedom, and they'd done it by force of arms. The honest way.

Darak didn't like magic or the people who used it. Weapons were far more reliable. Nevertheless, it took a cartload of power to start a blaze like that.

Power was interesting.

He stopped walking when he came to one of the telephone poles that dotted the street. An election poster jostled for space with ads for lost cats and ska-goth fusion bands. Darak read the poster with a sense of bitter amusement.

Elect Michael de Winter
Equality and fairness for all citizens of Fairview!
Choose a candidate with centuries of experience!
It's time for an interspecies perspective.

The vampire candidate. Like many, Darak's crew had come to watch the election.

Michael de Winter was backed by the vampire queen, Omara. Her goal was equal rights for the nonhumans—but a lot of vampires were nostalgic for the good old days of crowns and scepters. After all, vampires survived by feeding on the weak. A desire for dominance was natural.

Bottom line: Did the queen want to reign over more than vampires? Half the humans were ready to riot, so apparently they believed the worst. Meanwhile, Omara's vampire enemies waited and watched for an excuse to topple her throne.

Who said politics wasn't a blood sport? Among vampires, politics often ended in war—and that meant innocents would die.

Not okay.

That's when Darak and his brethren voted with cold steel.

He turned away from the poster and began walking toward the fire once more. Yes, it had taken true power to set that blaze.

Maybe Darak could use the fool with the spell book. If election fever turned bad, they might need an extra weapon in reserve.

Or maybe he'd just tear off the fool's head.

That sort of thing was his specialty.

Tuesday, December 28, 11:40 p.m.
101.5 FM

"Good evening and welcome back to CSUP. For those just joining us, tonight's program is all about the special bond between lover and beloved, hunter and prey. Where do the two intersect, and what does the battle of the sexes have to do with the battle between species?

"It brings us, my dark faithful, to the topic of slayers.

These days, it seems as if any cheerleader with a stake can get into the game, but I'm not talking about the wannabes or even those oh-so-scary mercenaries who accept a bounty on our lives. I'm talking about the crazies, the ones who kill from a sense of devotion.

"There are human tribes from Eastern Europe called the Hunters. They don't kill for sport or for money. It's a family tradition handed down from parent to child since the dawn of written history. To them, killing us is the purest act of love for their own kind.

"They're the ones I worry about when I turn out the light."

Tuesday, December 28, 11:45 p.m.
Lore's condo

When she heard Lore leave the condo, Talia curled up on her side, cradling her cuffed wrist in her free hand. Relief drained the last strength from her limbs. He hadn't hurt her, but she wasn't convinced he wouldn't. No one handcuffed a woman—a stranger—without the possibility of harm. That last look he'd given her was the pure, remorseless gaze of a predator.

But at least he was gone for the moment. She'd needed an interval of privacy to gather her wits. Too much had happened since she'd . . . had she really been shopping a few hours ago?

Now that she was alone, her emotions began to unfold from the clenched ball of pain lodged in her gut. Fear. Guilt. Loss. Loneliness.

Talia pressed her face into the coverlet, her feelings too crowded to cry just yet. She'd lost her mother, then her fiancé, and then the rest of her family. It was like a recurring nightmare where pieces of her flesh were torn away, leaving nothing recognizable. After Talia had lost her humanity, she'd thought there was nothing left to take—but the horror had come back again. She'd still had something to lose. Still more pain to endure. *One more time.*

Perhaps the last time. Michelle was all she had left. Now there was no one. Pink tears began to stain the pillowcase. Grief was finally finding release.

Michelle had been the one to anchor Talia, to patiently remind her that not everything was obliterated because she'd been Turned. She'd helped Talia pick the threads of her true self from the tangled, damaged mess she'd become. If it hadn't been for her cousin, Talia would never have gone back to teaching.

And she was only one of the many, many people who had loved Michelle. Tonight, a light had gone out of the world. *And it was my fault.* Talia sobbed in earnest. There was no way to bring her cousin back. Not even an ancient vampire could save someone after their body had been so badly broken.

Talia's tears slowed, the last thought pushing her from sadness to fear. *It should have been me who died.* A vampire would have known the difference between a human and one of their own. That meant the murder was either a huge mistake or a warning.

Who wants me dead?

Talia's stomach cramped as cold terror washed through her. There was her sire, who had reason to hate her. She'd escaped from his clutches and also swiped a small fortune on her way out the door. But would he really risk Queen Omara's wrath by coming to Fairview and beheading the locals? She had counted on the fact that he would not.

And then there was Talia's family. *Dad.*

In his eyes, she was no better than a rabid dog. The Talia he'd raised from a baby had died the moment the vampires took her for their own. If he caught her now, he'd butcher her without mercy.

Strike the monsters before they kill or corrupt an innocent human. That was what her whole neighborhood—

the tribe—had believed. When you saw the crossed-blade symbol of the Hunters, you knew you were dealing with monster-killing machines, bred for the job and trained from birth.

Talia pulled up the right sleeve of her sweater. Twin Hunter sabers, crossed at the hilt, were inked on the inside of her forearm. Against pale vampire skin, the fine detailing would never fade or blur. Nor could she ever get the damned thing off. Everything she wore, however fashionable, would be long-sleeved. Forever.

She made a fist, the design shifting along her skin. She'd never been big, but she'd always been good with firearms. She'd also been a risk-taker to the point of stupidity. She'd wanted her father's approval and at sixteen, she'd made her first kill. A ghoul. He'd given Talia the tattoo as a reward.

It was hardly a reward now. Everyone knew the Hunters' symbol. If the nonhumans ever saw the tattoo, she would be torn to shreds. Of course, now that she was one of the monsters, the Hunters only saw her as something fit to kill. Undeath was filled with interesting ironies.

Talia pulled the sleeve down again. What was she? Hunter? Monster? Teacher?

Prisoner.

Talia blinked, tears of frustration and sadness misting the lights into a blurry wash. The pillow felt cool against her cheek. She'd been in that room, on that bed, almost long enough that it was starting to smell more like her than the hellhound.

It smelled like grief.

Then grow a spine, will ya? She took a long, shaky breath, fumbling for enough anger to push her into action. Half her instincts screamed to hop the first night bus heading out of town. The other half was crying out for vengeance.

Either way, she had to get out of Lore's bedroom.

What would happen if he found out I was a Hunter?
Ground vampire patties with extra ketchup, probably.

No one was going to save her but herself. Heroes on
white horses were a myth. *I am not a victim.* She rolled
onto her back, scanning the room for escape possibilities.

First, she needed a tool to get out of the cuffs. She
wiggled toward the bedside table, stretching as far as the
handcuffs would allow. There was just enough play to
let her slide the drawer open and feel inside. Not much
there—just a library book on how to fix kitchen appli-
ances and a pack of spearmint gum. She pushed the
drawer shut.

On top of the nightstand were a bedside light, an
alarm clock, and some tattered paperback books. She
turned the spines of the books toward her. Lore's reading tastes leaned toward Westerns of the lone-gunman-
saves-the-town variety. It suited him.

Despite her fear, she'd noticed a few choice details
about her captor. The broad spread of his chest, the slim
hips, the skin shades darker than her own, as if he'd labored outdoors in the hot sun. A working man.

But not just a muscled body. Those dark eyes held an
entire universe of sorrow. Lore was the sort of puzzle a
woman could get lost in solving. She knew the type of
guy. Just one more piece, and the picture—or his soul—
would reveal itself.

Yeah, right. The guy had chained her up. She was so
out of there. She would not waste time dissecting his
psyche.

Instead, she was going to dismantle his alarm clock.
Talia's hand closed over it, feeling the vibration of its
ticks. It was one of the old wind-up ones, the kind with a
round face and twin bells on top. There should be something inside she could use to pick the lock of the handcuffs. She'd learned the whole Houdini skill set as a kid,
along with every kind of combat drill going. Who needed
summer camp when you had Dad and Uncle Yuri?

She dragged the clock onto the bed and turned it over. It seemed a shame to break it, but oh well. She popped the brass case off its back and watched the gears tick for a moment. There was a pin at the top that connected the hammer that rang the alarm to a spring. It looked almost like a hairpin. It would do, as long as the metal was neither too soft nor too brittle.

Holding the clock down as best she could with her cuffed hand, she dismantled the gears with the other. Once she had the pin out, she spent some time bending it so that it had a slight curve at the end, almost a hook. Holding it parallel to the cuff, she slid it just inside the lock, where there was a tiny notch in the keyhole. Applying even pressure to the pin, she levered it away from her. The lock gave a satisfying snick. She twisted her cuffed wrist at the same time, grinning with satisfaction as the mechanism gave way. She rubbed her wrists, glad to finally be free of the silver. The cuffs had scraped her skin raw.

Talia rolled off the bed, crossing to the window and looking out. Cold air seeped through the glass, a rim of ice forming at the bottom of the pane. With no breath to fog the window, Talia was able to lean in, her vision unobstructed.

Snow was falling at a brisk pace. That was going to add an interesting wrinkle to her escape. Before long, the roads would be clogged. She had to get moving.

She didn't want to ever see the place where she'd found her cousin's body again, but there was no way around it. She would just have to figure out how to get past the cops. She wasn't going anywhere without her weapons, cash, and decent boots. The dainty ankle boots she had on would be useless in this much snow.

And if the dog got in her way, she'd send him to obedience school. No one caught Talia Rostova twice.

Chapter 9

Darak had followed the evil to the fire, but there wasn't a lot to see once he got there. Bystanders, police, a city pound's worth of hellhounds were all doing what needed to be done—but none of that interested him.

The fire itself was okay, but he'd seen better sorcery. This one was a little heavy on the whole melting-walls thing. Showy and dramatic, but a lot of energy wasted to get a simple job done.

What got his attention was what the spell slinger had targeted. Campaign office—well, why not hit the most controversial location in town? But a medical clinic—that made Darak mad. It was always the ordinary folk who got it in the neck when the powerful began throwing their weight around.

He paced the sidewalk beyond the perimeter set by the fire brigade. Smuts fell from the sky with the snow, looking as if the flakes themselves were burning. One fell on his cuff and he flicked it away, feeling a hot kiss of embers.

There was no trace of the spell caster here. The sense of evil was dying from the scene along with the flames, burning down into a gray ash of wilted magic. By morning, it would be no more than a shiver up the spine.

That didn't do him a bit of good. Frustrated, Darak turned and stalked back along the sidewalk again. There should have been more. He wasn't a magic user, but he knew something about it. A sorcerer didn't just pull this kind of energy out of his ass. It had to come from somewhere: a sacred object, a ley line, or maybe a sacrifice.

There was nothing here. Whoever had cast the spell had raised the energy someplace else and redirected it. Darak glared back at the fire and its halo of snow and ash.

It was then he saw the woman. She was standing a few feet away, wearing nothing but a blouse and navy blue skirt. Her brown hair was neatly cut at shoulder length. She was shivering, clutching her arms because she had no coat.

Oh, no. He had a bad feeling, but he walked over anyway.

"Are you okay?" he asked.

She looked up at him, frowning the way some people did because they had to look up, and then up some more to find his face. "I'm not sure how I got here," she said, her voice holding both fear and annoyance. "It's snowing. It never snows here."

Darak took off his jacket and draped it over her shoulders. "Here."

Its size drowned her, but she looked grateful. Pausing to look around again, she seemed to notice the fire. "Is that the clinic?"

"Yeah. Too bad about that." He was wearing a pullover, but the wind bit through the loose weave. The whole chivalry thing obviously came from warmer climates.

"I hope the nurses don't lose their jobs." She looked confused. "You know, I think I need to go home."

He'd been expecting it. "Want me to walk you?"

"Please. I'd like that."

He offered her his arm. He was the last thing from a gentleman and most of the time was barely polite, but there was a time and a place to show respect. "Where do you live?"

She hesitated, searching the streets around them, then seemed to get her bearings. "Over this way."

Dread settled into his bones. He wondered how far it was, and how much time he had to talk to her. This sort of thing never got easier, no matter how many centuries rolled past.

They set off in silence, taking shortcuts through an alley and a schoolyard. The chain-link fence around the playground sparkled with frost. Darak stayed close to her side, careful not to let her out of his sight for even a second.

"I just got home tonight," the woman said.

He noticed she was pretty in a fresh, simple way. In other circumstances, she would have been pleasant to look at for hours on end.

"I was going to spend the night with my cousin," she added.

"Yeah?"

"She's like you."

"Like me?"

"You know. A vampire." She gave him a shy glance. "Sorry. I seem to be saying whatever pops into my head. I'm usually a better conversationalist than this."

"Don't worry about it." He wasn't much good at small talk at the best of times. "So your cousin's a vampire?"

"I was kind of afraid, but if no one ever gave Talia a break...." She trailed off, then stopped, turning to Darak. With a pleading gesture, she put one hand on his chest. "You've got to make sure she's okay."

They always made a request. It usually came near the end, so they had to be close to where it had happened.

He looked around. There were a lot of nice buildings, a few houses. Where would a woman like this live? Of course. Cop cars, over there. It looked like the kind of street that should have been quiet, but tonight it was jammed with ominous flashing lights and men with uniforms.

She was still looking at him, her eyes dark with worry. She barely came up to his collar bone. *It's surprising how many ask to keep their loved ones safe.*

"Of course," he said. "I'll check on her. Talia, right?" One vampire shouldn't be hard to find.

"I'd really appreciate it." She gave him a quick, uncertain smile. "My feet are so cold."

That would be because she was barefoot, but he didn't point it out. "Is that your building over there?"

"Y-yes. Wow, look at all the police. I wonder what's going on. Think somebody had a break-in?"

"Why don't we go in the back way?"

"Good idea."

Gently, he guided her to the corner, and they crossed with the lights. Nice and easy.

As they went around to the parking lot, she started to become agitated, looking nervously around her. They were passing through the rows of cars, stepping over the concrete ribs that kept them in tidy lines. "Thank you for walking with me."

"No problem. What's your name?"

"Michelle."

The back door was still a fair distance away, its light making a pool on the gathering snow. A single cop stood outside, looking bored.

She started violently, colliding with Darak in terror of something only she could see. His coat slid off her shoulders and fell into the snow. He caught her, wrapping his arm around her so that she was caged against his chest. He crouched down between a truck and an SUV, letting her sink safely to the ground. "Hey, take it easy. You're not alone. I'm here."

"What's happening?" Trembling like a fever victim, her slight weight began to fade.

They weren't going to make it through the door before her spirit fled the earth.

"Tell me what happened, Michelle."

Clamping her hands around her head, she shrieked, a piercing wail that reverberated through his bones. He hushed her, cradling her against his body. "Sh. You're safe."

Necromancy.

The word burned hot in his gut. He knew this for what it was now. The spell caster had gotten his power from this woman's murder. Now that the spell was winding down, she got to live through the horror all over again.

She was panting, a sheen of sweat coating her fine features despite the cold. "He came for me. He said it was a warning to Talia that she was next. Watch out for her. Please. Please."

"I will. I promise."

Her eyes grew wide, seeing something or someone looming closer. She raised her hands, warding off an invisible blow.

"Michelle—"

Stripes of blood blossomed on her hands.

"No!" He shielded her with both his arms, using his size and bulk to ward off the horror that only she could see.

She screamed again, so loudly that Darak squeezed his eyes shut.

In that split second, she was gone. He crouched in the parking lot, his skull still splitting from the noise.

The cop didn't come running. He hadn't heard a thing. It was Darak's special curse to see and hear the dead. One he loathed violently each and every day.

He picked up his jacket and stuffed his arms through the sleeves, sending the buckles and zippers jangling. Darak turned toward the back door with its single guard. It would be easy enough to hypnotize the human into letting him have a quiet look through the building. Odds were there would be no clues to the necromancer's identity, but he had to look.

Slowly, he got to his feet, swallowing hard as if he were choking something down. He rested his hand for a moment on the hood of the truck, taking a long breath of the icy air.

Pluto's balls, he hated these encounters. A hard ache lurked where his heart should have beaten. This jackass with a spell book had ruined Darak's evening. He had completely messed with Michelle's.

The jackass had to die.

Wednesday, December 29, 12:05 p.m.
Lore's condo

Once he was through scoping out the crime scene, Lore left the building, walking into the steadily falling snow. He'd learned a few things, including how the police intended to proceed. They were looking for evidence of who came and went from the building and when. They were looking for witnesses. They wanted to know about Michelle's and Talia's lives, whom they associated with, and why anyone would wish them harm. Mostly, they were looking for Talia.

Lore already had a head start on the last item. He needed to catch up on the rest, now that he had a road map to follow. It would have been more efficient to share information with Baines—the man was obviously no fool—but the hellhounds hadn't survived by trusting anyone else. He wanted solid proof of Talia's guilt before he left her to the mercy of the human cops.

He crossed the street, fascinated by the dizzying, swirling snow. It left cold kisses on his skin, chill and ephemeral as a ghost. Or a vampire.

Not that their flesh was that cold. It was cool and

smooth as silk, enticing as half-forgotten wishes. No, it wasn't the temperature, but the odd, hushed melancholy of the snow that made him think of the Undead.

Or perhaps it was the silence. Talia was too new to have that eerie calm. Instead, the chill, pure air reminded him of another Undead beauty.

Constance Moore and her son had lived in the Castle, the prison where Lore had grown up. Because Lore was a friend to her boy, almost a big brother, she'd included him in their daily lessons. She had taught Lore to read and write—rare skills for a lowly hellhound. His people had been little better than slaves, but Constance had never been anything but kind. Now her gift of knowledge gave him an edge for survival in the human world.

Perhaps it was the memory of Constance that made him protective of Talia. *Foolish.* They were entirely different people. More than that, he was a different person now, a grown Alpha with no time for sentimentality. Which was why he was standing in the snow with his cell phone, running interference for a pretty vampire he had no business helping.

Nah, he'd been suckered since the moment she'd tried to kick him in the head. He had a weakness for girls with some spirit. *Idiot.*

Lore began punching in a number. He'd gone outside because he was too wary to risk being overheard by the cops. Now he began pacing, impatient to get answers.

Fortunately, Perry was still up.

"Miss me?" the werewolf said dryly. "Or do you think I'm such a crack researcher I've found your answer to the floaty evil already?"

"Have you?"

"No."

"Too bad. Something else has happened."

"I heard about the clinic building burning. The vamps have gone bat-shit crazy about the campaign office."

Lore ignored the not-so-subtle bat joke. His mind

was on a straight road that he hoped led to confirming Talia's innocence. "There was a murder in my condo building."

After a stunned silence, Perry made a noise that wasn't quite a laugh. "What?"

"I'm not making this up."

The wolf swore. "What the hell is going on tonight?"

Lore looked up and down the street, his eyes searching the front of each neighboring building. The dusting of snow made everything look deceptively charming, like one of the humans' greeting cards. "My building doesn't have security cameras covering the entrances. Are there any around here that you can hack into?"

"I dunno. Depends on their setup. Are you trying to get me arrested?"

"You're too good for that."

"Says you. What's nearby?"

Lore named the businesses.

"Hm. The bank and the corner market are good bets. There's probably a traffic cam around there, too. Are we looking for anyone in particular?"

"The killer."

"We need more words than that, dog-boy."

"I don't have a description," Lore said, irritated. "Possibly two people—one to control and one to strike. Or else someone strong enough to hack off a head on his or her own."

There was silence at the other end of the line. "They took the head? That's an execution. Who died?"

"The woman we saw walk into the building tonight. The one who made you want to bake cookies."

He heard Perry's breathing quicken with anger. "I'll get back to you when I have something."

"Good luck." A puff of steamy breath followed the last words like a prayer.

Lore snapped the phone shut and considered his next move. First, he wanted to ask Talia about the Latin word on the wall. Maybe it meant something to her. Would she admit it if it did?

A car rushed by, skidding because the driver didn't know how to handle the slippery road. Lore stepped back, avoiding the clumps of snow kicked up by the tires.

Once he'd talked to Talia, then he'd visit some of the vamp clubs and bars. This wasn't the work of a local troublemaker. He was looking for a new face, and someone there would have gossip.

Normally, a newcomer asked permission of the ruling monarch to hunt in their territory. It was a means of keeping track of who was where. Sires owned the members of their clan; deserters were punished. Rogues on the run—like Talia—tried to stay off everybody's radar.

Come to think of it, the ugly vampire he'd arrested earlier was an unknown, too. *Interesting.* Was Mr. Ugly just another bloodsucker dropping in to cheer on the first-ever fanged candidate? With election fever in high gear, plenty of Undead had come to see history in the making. It would be easy for a murderer to get lost in the crowd.

Great. Just great.

Lore headed back toward his building and Talia, his protective instincts on alert. He went around to the back door, planning to use the stairs. As soon as he rounded the corner into the parking lot, he stopped dead. An unfamiliar scent hung in the air, plain as a billboard to a hellhound's sense of smell.

Lore's shoulders hunched, instinctively protecting his neck from attack. The presence was vampire. Male. Dominant. *Enemy.*

Lore searched the shadows of the parking lot, scanning for a darker shadow, a flutter of movement. Nothing. Even as he stood there, the scent trail began to dull in the cool, wet wind.

The stranger had passed through recently, but hadn't stayed. That was something to be thankful for. Still focused on Talia, Lore approached the cop standing outside the stairwell door.

"Did anyone come past here in the last few minutes?" Lore asked as he pulled out his driver's license to prove he lived there.

The cop shook his head. "No."

Lore pulled open the door and began the climb to his floor. With a low growl, he found the male had gone all the way up to his floor and beyond. Here the scent was fresh.

The cop was out to lunch. Or hypnotized. Vampires could wipe memories from a human's mind.

It didn't matter. He would find the source of the stink and remove it from his territory. There was no way a strange vampire was going to roam Lore's building. *Even the big ones taste like chicken.* Rotten, disgusting chicken, but whatever.

Shoulders aching with tension, Lore forced himself to stay on task. Talia first. Vampire after. He pushed out of the sixth-floor stairwell door and crossed to his suite.

When he turned the door handle, it was unlocked. A jolt of anxiety raised the hair on his arms. *Intruder!*

Lore burst into his condo. Empty. He slammed open the bedroom door, chest heaving.

The room was empty.

Talia was gone.

With a snarl, Lore wheeled and ran back into the hall.

Chapter 10

Wednesday, December 29, 1:25 a.m.
101.5 FM

Are you a nonhuman new to Fairview? Call the Good Hearth Cauldron Company for your complimentary welcome pack! No matter your species, we'll call on you with one of our lovely mini-cauldrons brimful of goodies! Coupons to local businesses! Treats from the Wily Wolf Delicatessen and Baba Yaga's Restaurant! Even an appetizer platter absolutely free with your first visit to Cthulu's Sushi House!

If you're a member of the vampire community, we have representatives standing by to arrange an appointment with Fairview's Undead registry. With many election visitors in town, appointment times are filling up fast. See us, and secure legal feeding privileges now. Bite safe; don't bite sorry!

* * *

Wednesday, December 29, 1:30 a.m.
Lore's condo building

Talia's anger and determination had careened into a brick wall.

She hid in the stairwell, the fire door open just enough to give her a crack to peer through. Carefully, she'd opened the noisy push bar without anyone hearing it. She'd assumed that late at night, the cops would have gone home. She had been wrong. There had to be a dozen still scouring the condo for clues. A few stood just feet away, almost close enough to touch.

If she let go of the door, the mechanism would close with a clatter and reveal her presence. A vampire could run faster than human cops, but she wasn't exactly sure where she was going to run to. All her ID, her money, her car keys, and her warm clothes were in her condo. Leaving Lore's bedroom hadn't improved her circumstances very much at all.

She couldn't go forward. She couldn't go back. She was stuck. Talia's skin shivered with the tension screaming through her muscles.

A uniformed cop walked out of the condo, interrupting someone who looked like a plainclothes detective. The latter was talking to a guy whose jacket was dusted with melting snow.

"Freaking vampires." The uniform was stowing a camera in his shoulder bag. "That was something else, eh?"

"Just wait till you see a werewolf kill," said the man with the snow on his coat. "I needed a wet vac to collect the remains."

The detective snorted. "Nice mental image, Bob. I'm going to remember that next time I have chili."

"Up yours, too, Baines."

"It's not funny," snapped the cop with the camera. "What's in there is not freaking funny. Sir." He added the last with a baleful glance at Baines.

The detective looked sympathetic. "Murder is never funny."

Bob lifted his voice, yelling into the condo, "You guys done yet? Can I bring in the gurney?"

With a jolt, Talia realized Bob was a paramedic. Or maybe a morgue attendant. He'd come to take Michelle's body.

"Just about!" came the reply.

No! Talia hadn't said goodbye. *I'm not done. I haven't had any time with her!*

The uniform was still rambling on. "Things are getting worse. It didn't used to be like this. Not before the monsters came out and started pretending to be all nice and normal. Their ordinary clothes and jobs and homes are just like the feathers on a decoy. Camouflage."

Bob murmured agreement.

"The nonhumans are not going away," Baines pointed out. "We know they exist now."

Bob folded his arms. "Then we should kill them. Plain and simple."

Talia shuddered, the hand gripping the door handle giving a slight twitch. It rattled faintly, making her still heart give a single thump of alarm.

"Whoa, Bob." Baines held up his hands, palms out. "Don't hold back. Seriously, though, is this any worse than a human kill?"

"That's a fair fight, sir," said camera cop. "The monsters are too strong for one of us."

That was true. Even without Undead strength, how could a human best the pure animal hunger in a vampire? *Our thirst is a ravenous, selfish monster.* Destroying others to slake it? Natural as breathing. From the first moment she woke to the night, Talia had learned how flimsy inhibitions were. Beneath that tissue-paper layer of reason was pure, bestial id.

"Okay, Bob," someone yelled from inside the condo. "Come and get it!"

"Just wait till they get themselves elected." The paramedic's voice was dour with warning. "They'll turn our own laws against us, and even monster lovers like you will start to see just how helpless we are."

Baines frowned. "Part of me wants to agree with you, but the evidence doesn't support that way of thinking."

The paramedic gave a short laugh. "Then I'll bring her out so you can take a good look." With that, he collected his gurney from farther down the hallway and pushed it into the condo.

Talia's eyes blurred with tears. *She's not evidence. She's not a* thing—*she was a warm, living woman!* A wave of hatred for the men rose in Talia's belly, followed by a flood of shame.

She was the monster. It was *her* presence in Michelle's life that had caused an ugly, violent death. Talia deserved whatever low opinion they had of her kind.

Baines turned to the uniformed cop. "All right, you want to arrest a vampire, here's a reason I'll buy into. I checked the registry for rogue vampires."

Registry? What registry?

"And?"

"The dead woman's cousin, Talia Rostova, is on there. A big-shot vampire from down east was her sire, and he's looking for her. Apparently, she's trouble. A thief, among other things."

Crap! Why did I keep my own name? What an idiot! Of course the sires had a registry. It was a simple way of finding rogues so that they could be returned to their clans for punishment. And why wouldn't they enlist the human police to help out?

Suddenly, switching identities seemed like a basic precaution. Naturally, there would be forgers, people who made new identities—but she didn't know who any of them were. That was way too James Bond. She'd counted on sheer distance to hide her, and the fact no vampire king would dare to enter Queen Omara's domain—especially not Belenos. He'd learned that the hard way.

She'd counted wrong.

I'm such an incompetent fool. The Hunters had trained her to fight, but not to hide. Now she would pay the price for that oversight.

No, Michelle's memory would pay the price, because they'd be looking for Talia instead of the real killer. Suddenly, making sure justice was served seemed more important than anything else.

It was the only thing she could do for Michelle.

The gurney came rattling out of the condo. All that was left of her cousin was a misshapen lump in a zippered bag. Talia felt a scream building in her throat. She began to shake so violently, she had to brace the door with her foot. Her shuddering rattled the safety bar.

Oh, God, Michelle. There were no tears. She was beyond that. It was more as if her body couldn't contain what she was feeling anymore. Any strength she possessed leaked from her body.

All that existed was the sight of her dead cousin.

She didn't hear Lore approach. Suddenly, she felt him like a hot wall behind her, and was drowning in the scent of him. He reached around her and put his hand on the door. She stared at it, barely comprehending what his presence meant. Dully, she noticed his knuckles were scuffed as if he'd been fighting.

"Let go," he whispered in her ear. "Hellhounds have power over doorways and the places between places. I can close it without anyone noticing."

Talia hesitated, unable to tear her eyes from the last glimpse of the gurney as it rattled toward the elevator. At last, though, she stepped back, colliding with the solid wall of his body. She stiffened as if she'd encountered an electrical field.

He closed the door silently, and then closed his hands around her upper arms. "You escaped."

"No, I didn't," she returned dully. "Here I am, back in your power."

He turned her around, never releasing her completely. Not for an instant. Almost funny, since what she'd just seen and heard had drained the fight out of her. Right at that moment, he could do what he wanted.

"We'd better get out of here," he said quietly.

Talia didn't have the will to move. She felt like a black hole, a pit of negative space. Lore, on the other hand, radiated urgency—not just impatience, but the hot fire of vibrant life. At first, she wanted to shrink away—not just because he was taking her captive all over again, but because he was simply *too much*. Too alive. Too male. She wanted to be alone with her grief, because that was all that seemed real.

Worse, with both of them on the landing, it was crowded. He had her trapped against the wall. She turned her face away, wishing she could sink into the hard concrete behind her.

"Come on," he urged, giving her arm a light tug. "The last thing we need is for Baines to walk through this door."

Talia finally looked up at him, meeting his eyes. She'd expected anger, but instead saw sadness. Not pity, but a tightening around the mouth and eyes that mirrored the ache in her throat. He saw her grief, and that dulled the hostility between them.

A part of her wanted the anger. It was easier to navigate. It would be simpler to strike out, push him down the stairs, leap over his body on the way out into the snowy night. Yet she couldn't—not when he was looking at her like he could read her soul. "Are you going to lock me up again?"

"Probably."

"Why?"

"I still don't know if you're telling the truth. And now

there's another vampire prowling this building. Can't you smell him?"

The moment he said it, the trace of another's presence penetrated her fog of distress. Talia shivered, suddenly freezing cold. "I heard the cops talking. There's a registry for rogue vampires. Maybe my sire figured out where I am and sent a bounty hunter."

His eyebrows twitched together. "Then what are you doing standing here?"

"I . . ." She couldn't answer. She'd been completely derailed by the scene playing out in her old home, which was now anything but a haven. All she could see in her mind's eye were scattered images of the cops, the gurney, the body. She gripped the wall, light-headed. *Vampires can't faint, can they? Do we go into shock?*

Lore gave her a grim look. "Trust me, you're safer downstairs. I'll make sure you're protected."

"I don't trust anybody." It had been her mantra for a long time. Michelle had been the exception.

"Suck it up. They have all the exits covered. Unless you've got that vampire hypnosis thing down pat, you're not getting out of here for a few hours."

He wrapped an arm around her waist, both supporting her and effectively capturing her against his tall body. She wasn't ready for that. She pushed him away, putting distance between them. He let her, but kept an iron grip around one wrist.

They went cautiously for the first few flights, but then picked up speed once the sound of their footsteps wouldn't carry to the crime scene.

"So what was so vital you had to risk your life to go get it?" Lore demanded once he closed his condo door behind them and steered her back into the bedroom.

"My personal laptop. My money. My driver's license. My everything." Talia pulled away and turned to face him. She was feeling steadier, but not by much. "Maybe I needed to say goodbye."

Oh, God, I'm back in his bedroom. Ugh! The thought suddenly gave her back her anger. "Don't you get it? My life just crashed and burned. Again."

He leaned against the door, blocking her exit with his body. The posture showed off the worn softness of his jeans. "Again?"

"What do you think?" She folded her arms and walked toward window. "There's a lot of starting over involved when you wake up a monster. A lot of losses. And they just keep coming."

Her mother. Her humanity. Her family. Her vampire clan. And now this. Her head was starting to clear, and a low, dull throb of anger was building. Someone had stolen her last ray of light, and she was going to make him pay. Michelle needed justice. That was something Talia the Hunter and Talia the vampire could agree on. No, not justice. That was too soft. *Vengeance.*

I am not a victim. I am the avenger.

Outside, the snow was still falling, but she barely saw it. She was still too shaken to take in much new information. She turned around to face him again. "You have to let me go. I'm going to find out who did this to Michelle. Then I'm going to chase him down and shred him with my teeth."

Lore gave her a startled look. "That's usually my line."

"Was that a joke? Because I'm completely serious."

Lore looked her up and down, from her dainty boots, up the length of her tight jeans and the curves of her sweater. His eyes warmed at what he saw, suddenly becoming intimate. Despite everything, she felt a rush of heat under her skin.

His gaze finally made it to her face. "I'm trying to find the killer, remember? Telling me you're going to bite your enemies probably isn't smart."

Talia's cheeks burned, but his words focused her. She had to be careful. She had to think. "We want the same thing. We want to find out who did this."

Not that she had any intention of working together. They'd just met, and she could tell by his expression that she wasn't quite crossed off the suspect list.

"What do you know about that vampire who was in the building? Do you really think your sire sent him to drag you home?"

"I don't know anything. It's just a strong possibility." Especially since Talia had not left empty-handed. Older vampires didn't like banks. She bet Belenos used one now that he was missing a few million in neatly bundled stacks of hundred-dollar bills.

She really hoped the cops didn't tear up the floor-boards upstairs.

Chapter 11

Wednesday, December 29, 1:45 a.m.
Lore's condo

She was so damned beautiful, Lore felt himself struggling to keep his upper brain in charge. The hound part of him didn't sweat things like murder and interspecies differences. It liked the little brain much better. *Female. Pretty. Soft.*

The part of him that could still string thoughts together realized that this was the first time Talia seemed open to conversation. Now was the opportunity to question her.

"Baines invited me into the crime scene," he said, doing a reasonable imitation of a rational being.

Her expression had gone from angry to thoughtful. "What did you find out?"

"I found out that you're a teacher." He gave a slight smile. "That's a very honored profession among my people."

She looked down, as if shy all of a sudden. This was obviously important to her. "I used to teach in a private high school. Now I tutor first- and second-year literature. My classes are online distance education." She grimaced. "That way I can't eat my students."

The sudden regret in her voice made him flinch. She raised her gaze to him, her guarded expression slipping a little. Her eyes were a striking bronze color. The shade reminded him of a hawk's—neither brown nor gold, with a hint of green rimming the iris. They'd probably been hazel when she was alive, but once a vampire tasted living blood, their eyes took on a metallic cast. It was an easy way to pick them out of a crowd.

Lore held that gaze. Hellhounds were safe from the Undead's hypnotic powers, and he felt compelled to prove it. Maybe to her, maybe to himself. He wasn't sure. He was too aware of her, and needed to control the situation. "You know Latin, don't you?"

"Yes. Why?"

"There was a Latin word written on the wall. A symbol was painted over it in blood."

She looked startled. "Huh?"

"Someone wrote on the wall in Latin."

"What for?" Bewilderment filled her features.

"Could it have had anything to do with Michelle?"

"No. Latin wasn't her thing. I'm the geek." Pinkish tears filled her eyes. She swallowed convulsively. "I can't talk about her right now. Not if you want me to make sense."

She swallowed again. "What did the words say?"

Lore's hands twitched at his sides. He wanted to comfort her, but holding her against him would shut down his thought processes once and for all. The questioning would end, and the reign of the little brain would begin. That would be giving in—to her? To himself? All he knew was that if he started something, it would be hell to stop.

"There was just one word. *Vincire.*"

She shook her head. "Why that?"

"What do you think it means?"

"It's in the imperative tense. It means 'be bound.'"

"Why would someone write that?"

"I have no idea. It sounds creepy." She seemed to be telling the truth.

It might fit with his necromancy theory, but he wanted to talk to Perry before he said anything. Lore moved on. "What were you doing before you came home tonight?"

"Shopping. What does it matter? Do you need an alibi? I have receipts."

A tear escaped, leaving a faintly pink track down her cheek. Before he could stop himself, he reached over and erased it with his thumb. Her skin was satin-soft, almost white against the deep tan of his skin. She looked up at him, eyes wide. She looked as vulnerable as one of those wild daisies that grew in the sidewalk cracks. There only by chance, and by chance as easily destroyed.

He withdrew his hand, heart stumbling. *No, don't do this.* Vampires seduced as easily as they breathed. His half-demon blood was good armor, but it wasn't bullet-proof. Pretty women didn't necessarily need magic.

He took a step back from her, hating that he did. "Why is your sire after you?"

"Because I ran away. Isn't that obvious?" He saw her gaze flicker away. *A half-truth.*

"Where did you come from?"

"A long way away." She sat down on the edge of the bed, as if she were suddenly tired.

"If you're in the registry of rogues, it's easy enough for me to find out who your sire is."

"If you ask the cops, they'll want to know why. You'll have to give me up." She shot him a glance. "Are you really ready to do that?"

Lore clenched his teeth. "Why did you come to Fairview? Why not go someplace else?"

"Michelle was here. Plus, you have a big supernatural population."

"That makes it easier to hide."

"Yeah."

That much made sense. "Where did you learn to fight like that?"

Her mouth tightened. "Why do you care?"

The need to touch her again itched through him. It made him impatient. "Think about it. If somebody wants to kill you, it would help to know why."

She held up her hands in a gesture of surrender. "I don't know! I'm just a schoolteacher. And you're about as subtle an interrogator as a troll!"

"Why did you run away from your sire?"

The repeated question got a reaction this time. She jumped to her feet, her eyes flashing with a sudden bolt of fury that made Lore want to fall back—but this time he stood his ground.

"My sire was pushy." Talia's words were quiet, almost inaudible. "Take a hint. It brings out the worst in people."

Lore gripped the bedpost, longing to press his lips against that flower-stem throat. Or maybe strangle her. He wasn't supposed to want her, but she was driving him crazy. "Who turns a schoolteacher into a vampire?"

Her mouth quivered. "Another vampire. There was nothing special about it."

That was a lie. He could smell it. "We're not getting anywhere unless you're honest."

She gave him an impassive stare with her golden hawk's eyes. He had to hand it to her, she was as cool as the snow blanketing the world outside. She had lied to him and defied him and escaped from his custody. He was Alpha. No one had ever flouted his authority this way.

The woman is pure chaos. A growl ripped out of Lore's throat, filling the room. He felt her tense, and his hunting instinct went on alert. *Fear. Prey.* Her eyes flared wide, obviously aware of the danger he represented.

He stalked closer to her, stopping when they were

only inches apart. She didn't back away as he expected she would. As she should have, a female yielding to a dominant male.

This was bad. Nearness made him far too aware of her. He couldn't risk getting any closer. The slightest movement, and their faces would have touched.

One of them had to retreat.

Instead, he touched his hands to her hips ever so lightly, barely brushing the fabric of her jeans. His palms tingled with the contact. She smelled so delicious. Her skin was inches away, petal-soft and pale as a lily. This close, he could see the faint spatter of freckles across her cheekbones, the texture of her lips. She was utterly still, too focused on his next move to take a breath. It was like looking at a statue. A beautiful statue.

I'm on a slippery slope.

They were at an impasse, both too stubborn to give way. *I can force her.* He meant that in a hundred ways: to yield, to answer his questions, to lie beneath him as he had his way. He was stronger. In the end, brute power would win, but it would never be a victory he would relish.

He needed her to tell the whole truth.

He had to surprise Talia into giving something away.

Slippery slope!

But how? She wasn't responding to him like a normal female. Maybe vampires weren't attracted to hellhounds. He knew *he* wasn't supposed to want *her.* Never mind that every two seconds he had to remind himself of the fact.

He had to grab control of the situation.

Or not.

Or maybe just grab her. Lore kissed Talia.

A slight gasp of surprise escaped her, but otherwise she didn't move a muscle. Only a slight trembling in her limbs told him she was even aware of his presence.

Her hair slid along his cheek, sleek and soft. Her lips

were cool, tasting of the cosmetics she wore. Beneath, he felt the press of teeth and the sharpness of fangs. *Beware of those.* Venom couldn't addict a half demon, but a bite would send him into a narcotic haze.

This was about as hazardous as kissing could get. That was a turn-on, too.

He nipped one lip, then the other, the plump softness of her mouth everything he'd fantasized. Her hesitant response said how completely he'd taken her by surprise.

Then he felt her hands sliding up his arms, so lightly they felt like the brush of a bird's wing. Oh, she was sweet. The kiss was filled with discovery and recognition, as if somehow he'd known how good it would be.

He didn't press further, but stood his ground, releasing her only when he was finished with his moment of possession.

As their lips parted, she took in a sharp breath, color flaring in her cheeks. "I thought you didn't do dead people."

He backed away. Every nerve in his body was prickling with the shock of her taste. He wasn't sure he *hadn't* ingested her orgasm-inducing venom.

Prophets spare me. She was delicious.

He grinned. "That wasn't *doing.* That was a peace offering."

"Huh?" Her fist clenched, as if she wanted to slug him.

"A kiss instead of more argument."

Her eyes sized him up in a new way that brought heat to his skin. For an instant, he felt the pull of attraction between them like a physical tug, guessing that she felt it as much as he did.

The moment didn't last long. The corners of her mouth pulled down. "Do you think a kiss will make me confess everything?"

Lore frowned, her accusation stinging all the more because it was true. "The cops want you for murder.

Your sire wants you punished. I'm trying to help you. Throw me a bone here."

She gave him a look of contempt that seared him to the quick. "You handcuffed me. Now you want to be my friend?"

"You felt that kiss as much as I did," he growled.

"As a human, I also felt food poisoning and root canals. We can't always pick and choose physical sensation."

Lore growled.

"Dog spit. Great." Wiping her lips, Talia took a deep breath and sat down on the edge of the bed again. Lore remained standing. She swayed a little, looking exhausted, but then pulled herself tall, as if mustering her dignity. "Tonight, I've been through an After-Christmas Blowout sale, the murder of the only person who cared for me, imprisonment, escape, and imprisonment again. Please leave me alone."

She really did look like she might fall over. Sadly, he didn't think kissing her again would get them any closer to a confession.

"If you answer one question."

"What?" She blinked at him. Fatigue pulled at every line of her body. Vampires were physically resilient, but they were subject to the same emotional storms as everyone else.

"Why won't you let me help you?"

She gave a shallow sigh. "Because you're like every man I've ever met. You're not happy unless I'm under lock and key."

"Nice guilt trip. I can't let you go."

"Because you don't trust me." She lay down on the bed, her arm shielding her eyes from the overhead light. "I can't trust my jailer. It's a matter of principle."

"Then we're at a standoff."

"Lock me in on your way out. I'll look forward to an exciting evening of counting carpet lint. You should try hanging some pictures. Do you know how boring your bedroom is?"

Lore raised an eyebrow. "I'll let *that* sleeping dog lie."

A beat passed. "Oh, great. Now I have to wash my brain out with soap."

Chapter 12

Lore set wards on the bedroom window and door, using the power over entryways that came effortlessly to the hellhounds. The wards would keep Talia in and everyone else out. He feared a door-to-door search by the police, so he set more at the front entrance, but these were designed primarily to make someone pass by. It wouldn't do to blow up the local cops.

The downside of using magic was that other magic users could detect it. Handcuffs, while primitive, were a better choice for that reason. However, he couldn't bring himself to put them back on Talia's wrists. His doubts had shifted. Now he was less convinced that she was a murderer, but he was dead certain that she was in deep trouble—and had been for a long time. He'd seen that kind of grief in people's eyes before. It didn't come from a single tragedy. It came from circling the drain for years.

There were people who had done extraordinary things to make his life better, and for no other reason than that they could: Constance Moore, Perry Baker, Alessandro Caravelli, and Mac, the fire demon who had helped to rescue the hounds from hell. Talia needed someone to be her champion, whether she trusted him or not. How could he let her go until he knew that she would be safe? Besides, wasn't clearing the name of an innocent woman the sort of thing a deputy sheriff was supposed to do?

The fact that he'd noticed Talia time and again in a very unsheriffly way had nothing to do with his protective instincts. Not at all. And nothing to do with the fact that the bow of her mouth drove him crazy.

Twenty minutes later, Lore stamped his feet as he pushed open the heavy oak door of the Empire Hotel restaurant lounge. A blast of heat and babbling voices swirled against the wall of frozen air outside. He took a moment, blinking the snow from his eyelashes. Christmas lights ringed the room, and pine swags adorned the walls. Frost veiled the windows, reflecting the lights in sparkles of red and green. Lore brushed the last of the melting flakes from his coat and headed into the gloom.

"Winter sucks. Can half demons get frostbite?" he asked the man behind the bar.

"You tell me," Joe replied. "It's coming down like crazy. You got your truck on the road?"

"Just. If this keeps up, the parking lot at the condo is going to be snowed in by morning."

Joe put a mug of black coffee on the bar and splashed some brandy into it. Lore hitched himself onto one of the barstools, resting his feet on the gleaming brass rail of the bar. He gratefully wrapped his hands around the steaming drink, inhaling the brandy-soaked fumes.

"Snow sucks," Lore said. "I thought it was supposed to be fun."

"This storm is nothing," Joe replied. "You should see the Caucasus in January."

"Where's that?"

"Mountains by the Black Sea. The most beautiful place in the world."

Lore shot Joe a glance. The bartender was slicing lemons, each cut quick and exact. They looked about the same age, but Joe—Josef—was a cursed immortal, part vampire, part werebeast, although he looked like a healthy human male in his early thirties and had no problem at all with sunlight. He'd been an inmate of the Castle, escaping a few years before Lore had.

"Why did you not go back to your homeland?" Lore asked.

Joe gave him a wry smile, the same one that advertised his doomed-but-definitely-available status to the human women who came into the Empire. They lapped up his charm like starving cats would a bucket of cream. Lore always wondered what Joe lapped up in return.

The barkeeper swept the lemon slices into a metal bowl. "They have not forgotten my old mistress in Trencsén. If they figured out I'd been part of her household, I'd either become a tourist attraction or a throw rug."

Lore had heard the stories of the Hungarian princess Joe called *ecsedi Báthory Erzsébet*. Elizabeth Bathory, the Blood Countess. She'd been rumored to bathe in the blood of virgins. That was likely more hysteria than fact. She'd probably just snacked on them.

"Besides." Joe shrugged. "I have friends here. Opportunities. I'm an entrepreneur now."

Lore followed Joe's gaze around the lounge. The place was filled with dark paneling and upholstery. The heavily carved bar ran the length of one wall, the elaborate mirrored cabinetry behind it a masterpiece of craftsmanship. Lore knew every inch of that antique oak shelving. He'd restored it himself.

"Business must be good," Lore said. "Only a few tables are empty."

"I'm open. The snowstorm's closed a lot of places." Joe refilled Lore's coffee. "What brings you here?"

"I'm meeting someone." He'd made some phone calls

on the way over. By human standards, it was an odd hour for an appointment, but some people were only available in the middle of the night.

"Better grab a table, then."

Joe turned away to serve a couple of werebears that had lumbered in for a beer. Lore slipped off the stool and walked toward an empty table in the back corner. The clientele was mixed, some humans, some supernaturals. Since Joe had taken over the place, he'd tried to appeal to a more upscale crowd. It seemed to be working.

Lore wondered where he'd gotten the money. He'd started as a penniless waiter only a few years ago. Another thing about Joe that inspired question marks.

Halfway across the lounge, Lore picked up a familiar scent. He stopped so suddenly, the hot coffee sloshed in his cup, burning his hand. He ignored the pain as he swung around, searching for the male vampire that had been prowling the stairway of Lore's condo.

He spotted him at once. Three figures were sprawled around a wooden table, two men and a female whose skin was so dark it was almost truly black. All were warriors—even more than their impressive muscles, Lore could see it in the alert carriage of their bodies. Weapons were out of sight, but their hands lingered close to belts, boots, and arm braces, all places Lore typically stashed his knives. These three were potential trouble.

They were also vampires.

His nose identified the larger male as the one who had been to the condo. He was big, hard-faced, and threw off a vibe that warned away other males. His hair was very short, elaborate designs shaved into the thick, dark stubble. His most striking feature was his eyes, an ice blue that contrasted sharply with an olive complexion. A scar ran along his jaw Lore would have sworn had been made by a cat's claw. A very, very big cat.

At his feet lay the ugliest dog Lore had ever seen. The

scarred bitch looked like a cross between a pit bull and a dozen other bad-ass breeds. Bandages wound around one leg and an ear was missing, the stump still pink. *Dog fights.*

Lore's hackles rose. Sensing his anger, the bitch got to her feet, putting herself between the hellhound and her master.

"Easy, Daisy." The big vampire patted the dog's flank gently; then those ice-blue eyes searched Lore's face. "You have a problem?"

Mostly Lore itched to rid the place of this vampire and his friends. The Alpha in him wanted to thin the testosterone haze hanging over the table. "Your dog is injured."

"I found her in an alley behind a dive in Northern Cal. She'd lost her last match and whoever owned her didn't waste a bullet to put her down." His massive hand engulfed her head, rubbing her remaining ear. His voice was rough, as if someone had crushed his voice box. "Old fighters have to stick together, eh?"

The dog tried to lean in to his hand and lick it at the same time. Lore relaxed, sensing the bitch's trust in the huge vampire. It was the best character witness possible.

Encouraged, Lore pulled up a wooden chair and sat down. The vampires gave him a hard look, lips lifting to reveal the tips of fangs. His blood rose, urging him to snarl back, but he didn't answer the challenge. His goal was to get information, not fight.

"Who are you?" the big vampire demanded.

"Lore, Alpha of the hellhounds and acting sheriff of the nonhumans."

The ice-blue gaze flicked over him. "We are visiting. Election fever has us curious."

Lore got straight to the point. The noise level in the place was loud enough to cover their conversation. "You were in the building where I live. Why?"

"Does it matter?"

"There was a murder."

"I didn't do it."

"Then—"

"He said he didn't do it." The second male picked up the pitcher of beer and refilled his glass.

He was of a different ethnic type, golden skinned and dark eyed. Black, curly hair framed features still soft with youth. He could have been no more than twenty when he was Turned, but he felt enormously old to Lore. All three of them did.

"I didn't say he did," Lore returned, pitching his tone between friendly and no-nonsense. "I've been told that I'm a bad interrogator, but I'm not that blunt."

"Your technique needs work," the young-looking one shot back, his eyes hostile.

Lore calculated the odds of taking all three vampires in a fight. They weren't good. Still, he had no plans of backing down.

"Peace, Iskander." The first one returned his attention to Lore. "I had an errand near your home. You can rest assured that I won't be back. Is that good enough?"

"What kind of errand?"

His expression defied Lore to press further. "It was personal."

And I'm a Chihuahua. "Do you know anything that would cast light on who beheaded the human woman?"

The dark-skinned female made a sudden gesture that rattled the golden bracelets at her wrists. Lore spared her a glance. She was slender and sleekly exotic, but obviously just as lethal as the men.

"Nia?" asked the first vampire.

"Darak," she said in a voice that reminded Lore of dark fur sliding through the night. "You said nothing of a murder. You said you were chasing power."

Nia, Iskander, and Darak. Lore at least had names.

"Because it is like saying the sun rose today. Inno-

cents die. And I did not find the source of power. Yet."
Darak stood suddenly, pushing back his chair. "It is time
for us to go."

The other two exchanged startled looks, but rose. The
dog stood, pressing close to Darak's leg. The vampire
turned to Lore. "You can tell your queen that we are
neutral observers."

The statement confused Lore. He got to his feet, dis-
liking the sensation of the vampires looming over him.
"Omara is not my queen. I'm not one of the Undead."

Darak gave an odd smile. "She has not demanded
your allegiance?"

"No."

That seemed to surprise him. "Will you vote for de
Winter?"

Lore shrugged. He cared little for politics. "I don't
know."

"Then whose side are you on? Are you for integra-
tion with humans?"

The questions irritated Lore. He was the one doing
the investigating. "What is it to you?"

"Nothing, but I grow tired of providing all the answers.
It is only fair that I get equal time to play interviewer."

Lore grudgingly played the game. "I am neither for
nor against de Winter. I hope for peace but I have one
hand on my weapon. The pack comes first."

The vampire gave a low laugh. "We have a few things
in common, Alpha of the hounds."

He turned to go. Lore grabbed his hard-muscled arm.
"Not so fast."

Darak wheeled, eyes wide. "You think you can hold
me here?"

"I need answers."

"I don't have any."

"You know something." Lore held the vampire's cold
blue gaze, the skin down his back prickling with tension.

Darak was one scary mother, clearly expecting Lore to turn tail and run. He held his ground. Slowly, those ice-blue eyes narrowed, changing from angry to speculative.

Darak leaned forward, so that only Lore could hear what he had to say. "The dead woman has a cousin. A vampire."

He could feel Darak's age and power like an electrical field. Lore felt the hair along his neck rise. *Talia*. "Yes."

"Keep her safe."

The words made his guarding instinct go on high alert. "What do you know?"

"A necromancer set a fire earlier tonight. A spell that raises that much power needs a death. That's why your neighbor was killed. Or part of it. Her cousin is in his sights. She will be next."

Lore went cold. "How do you know this?"

A strange look came over the vampire's face. Lore would almost say it was horror. "The dead sometimes speak to me. Leave the spell caster alone, deputy dog. Guard the girl and keep the town from going crazy over the election."

"I can't let the spell caster go," Lore said flatly. "Murder is murder."

Darak gave a shrug. "As you wish."

Talia is in danger. He knew that, but hearing it from this stranger made the threat all the more concrete. "Did the dead mention the name of the killer?"

"No." Darak stepped back, his enormous frame filling their corner of the lounge. "I don't think she knew it."

Darak turned and made his way toward the door, the dog and the other two vampires at his heels. This time, Lore let them leave.

What the hell am I supposed to make of that? Lore picked up his cup, then set it aside in disgust. The encounter with the vampires had made him edgy, itching to feel the crack of the necromancer's bones against his knuckles. The only plus was that Talia was safely behind magical wards—and what Darak had said proved that she was innocent. Unfortunately, a secondhand account from a ghost would never stand up in court. Lore would have to do better to clear her name.

And to do that, he needed more information.

Checking his watch, Lore noted it was past his appointed meeting time. He looked around, but didn't see the face he was looking for.

He also needed something stronger than coffee. By the time he got himself a beer from the bar, all the normal tables and chairs were taken, so Lore sat down in one of the soft leather seats clustered around a coffee table. Lore shifted uncomfortably, his jeans sliding on the leather seat. It was a bit like sitting on a giant black marshmallow. He just wasn't trendy urbanite material.

Irritated, he checked his phone and found a voice message from Baines, demanding to talk to him again. Lore deleted it. He'd make himself available when he had time.

A woman left a nearby table and sat down across from him. "You called me, and here I am. What can I do for you?"

Lore did a double take. "I'm sorry. I didn't see you."

The truth was, he hadn't recognized Errata Jones. The celebrity werecougar talk show host of CSUP radio, she normally wore a Goth getup of black leather. Only the chin-length jet-black hair was familiar. Today she wore a heavy cream sweater and jeans beneath a tweed coat, and her face was bare. For the first time, Lore thought she was actually pretty.

"I need your help," he said, deciding to be blunt.

"Do you? I wonder how I can help one of the mighty hellhounds?"

She tilted her head to one side a moment, considering him. Her eyes were green-flecked hazel, her skin more golden than he had expected. He'd bet good money the black hair was a dye job.

He waited patiently as she squirmed out of the coat, knowing better than to rush a cat toward a decision. She picked up her peppermint hot chocolate and crossed her legs. He could see her jeans were wet from the knees down, evidence of her trek through the snow. "Tell me," she said.

"Are you up for doing some investigative work?"

"I always wanted to be Brenda Starr. I'm more than just a sultry voice, you know."

She was indeed one of the smartest people Lore knew, though that intelligence was very different from Perry's. Where Perry found facts, Errata made connections. "I need answers from someone who isn't with the police. Strictly off the record for now, but you can have anything I know for an exclusive later."

Errata raised one eyebrow slightly. "Really?"

"There was an incident."

"Incident?"

"Beheading. Vampire. I don't think it's public knowledge yet. I didn't see any reporters."

"Hairballs!" She set down her mug again, leaning forward. "When? Are we talking slayers?"

"Not anything sanctioned by human or vampire law." He sketched out the bare bones of Michelle Faulkner's murder, finishing with what Darak had said. "My problem is that there are far too many strangers in town. Finding one spell caster won't be easy. I'm counting on Perry's help, too."

Errata made a face. "And the spell guy isn't the only new problem in town. There are rumors of pro-human fanatics arriving with plans to blow Spookytown to kingdom come. With so many visitors, mass carnage would be the height of efficiency."

"Who are we talking about?"

"Some say the Hunters."

"I didn't think there were any outside of Europe."

"There is one bunch who lives down east. They could be out here for the election along with everyone else."

Lore swore, and then dropped his voice. "This has to stay just between you and me. I have the prime suspect in the murder locked in my bedroom."

Errata stared. "What the hell?"

"It's a long story."

"You are *such* a dog. Who is it?"

"A female vampire."

Her whole body tightened, like a compressing spring. "You know bondage is only cool if it's consensual, right?"

He felt unwelcome heat creeping to his ears. "This is not for games. I can't turn her in to the police. She's not guilty. There's a good chance they'll execute her just to say they closed the case."

"So she's hiding with you?"

"Yes."

"Was that her idea?"

"Not exactly."

Errata sat back, looking away. "I get that you grew up in the Castle, where locking someone up was considered normal, but you can't do that here. This is, y'know, the real world."

He wanted to snap at her. "It's not like that. Help me prove her innocence."

Errata turned back to him, her hazel eyes grim. "What do you need?"

"Tell me if you can find out anything about Talia Rostova's history with her sire, starting with who that is. Something happened between them. This is more than just a rogue-on-the-run story." It had left a sadness in Talia he itched to fix.

"Is that part idle curiosity, or do you really think knowing her history will help you catch her cousin's killer?"

"Maybe." He sounded defensive even to himself.

Her eyes narrowed to slits. "Just be sure you know what you're doing."

I wish. "We don't have much time. She's a target."

Errata stood, a graceful movement worthy of a feline. "Then I'll let you know what I find out ASAP."

"Be careful."

Her lips quirked. "You and Perry. So good at stating the obvious."

"He should be there next time we meet."

Errata gave him a sly look as she picked up her coat and purse. "Tomorrow night. Your place. I want to see this vampire of yours. She must be something if you're going to so much trouble."

Lore experienced a wave of possessiveness for his territory and for Talia. "Yeah, okay," he said reluctantly.

"One condition."

"What?"

She was serious again. "You have to let her go. You can't keep a bloodsucker in custody without reporting it to the vamp authorities."

Lore narrowed his eyes. "Don't go there."

Errata leaned over him, showing tiny, sharp canines. "Caravelli's only a phone call away. If anyone else finds out . . ."

Lore made an irritated noise. "I've had her for only a few hours. Once it's safe, you can watch me shoo her out the door."

"That's what I needed to hear. I like you, Lore. I don't want you in trouble with the Undead, and I don't want to find out you have a hobby dungeon filled with pretty young vampires."

Lore gave her a caustic look, trying not to remember Talia's lips. "I'm a hellhound, not a sociopath."

"I think you just want to keep her for yourself."

"Scat!"

"Aha, you're blushing. You like her." She gave him a finger wave as she headed for the door.

"Just be cautious," he said again to her retreating back. "Be careful who you talk to."

"Yeah, yeah. Ta-ta, my brave puppy." She was moving briskly, like a mouser on a mission. Cats never listened.

Lore felt a stab of worry, afraid he'd sent Errata into danger.

Chapter 13

Lore dreamed of demons. Not half demons, not hell-hounds or incubi, but the real thing, pitiless and hungry. He dreamed of them chasing the hounds through the Castle corridors, shredding the stragglers with claws as cruel and curved as the blades of warrior fey.

Run! Run quickly! He was dreaming a memory, his breath quick with the echo of panic.

But there were the demon's searing balls of energy, sailing low over their heads, singeing the fur from their backs. The heat cut like a razor. Lore flattened his ears against his head, making himself as long and low as he could. He heard a yelp of pain. One of the other hounds wasn't as quick or as lucky.

The tunnel narrowed, the side tunnels coming less and less frequently. They ran so fast, the stonework blurred into a gray wash. They were being stampeded. At the end of the tunnel was a dead end. *It was a trap!*

There was one last chance, barely a crack in the wall to wiggle through, that would get them to safety. One by one the hounds dove for it, the youngest first, then the mothers, but it was taking too long. Everything in the dream slowed to an excruciating slowness. They wouldn't all make it through ...

Stop!

Lore jerked awake but lay still a moment, letting the scene shred and fall away in the calm, rational daylight. He tried not to remember the old Alpha turning, hurrying the other hounds past, and putting himself between the demons and the pack.

The old Alpha. His father.

That was the end of the dream, but Lore hadn't witnessed his father's death yet again. He'd awakened in time. For once.

Lore had been the last through that crack in the wall. There had been others who'd died.

Lore had just turned eighteen. He'd become the new Alpha that day.

It was a long time ago. He could feel the pressure of the nightmare like something scrabbling at the doors of his mind. It wanted to finish, to show him the whole gruesome scene. *No. Don't think about it.*

Lore sucked in a deep breath, forcing himself into the waking world like a swimmer breaching the waves. *Wake up!* There was a new threat to the pack and the yoke of responsibility was on his shoulders now. *Get up, get moving.*

But he slipped into a different dream. He saw Mavritte, one of the female hellhounds, looking at him with accusation in her eyes. "Do I not please you?" she asked, and then held up a long, thin knife, ready to strike it into his heart.

Lore came fully awake with a jerk, heart pounding. He looked around, letting the shock of the dream fade and the objects in his apartment become familiar and welcoming again.

He'd slept through the morning, making up for the

long night. Because his bed was otherwise occupied, he'd curled up in dog form, taking advantage of the soft lambskin throw in front of the TV. Now he got to all fours, shook himself, and padded to middle of the room.

A glance out the balcony doors told him the world was buried in snow. It was still coming down, the stuff mounding into a white caterpillar along the balcony rail. Along the streets, cars were slowly disappearing into drifts. Lore couldn't believe so much had fallen, and it was still coming down. A hush had fallen over Fairview. There was no hum of traffic—a bad omen for the state of the roads.

He thought of the dream of snow, and the mysterious terror he had to face. He thought of the she-hound Mavritte and the knife. Prophecy? Or anxiety that, as Alpha, soon he had to choose a mate from the pack? The urge to bond rode him like a constant thirst, and yet there was no one he wanted. It was a diplomatic disaster, and he couldn't even lie about it.

If only one of the hounds fascinated him half as much as the vampire in his bed. *But we never want what's good for us.* With a mutter of disgust, Lore turned from the window and headed for the kitchen.

Calling his magic, his hound form fell away, dissolving to mist and reassembling in his two-legged body. The sensation was like falling, every cell surrendering the subtle tension that glued it to its neighbor—floating free a terrifying instant—then gathering himself back together with the whoosh of an inhaled breath.

As the coffee brewed, he shook cereal from a box, feeling pleasant anticipation as the nuggets of Cap'n Crunch pinged into his bowl. Changing forms made him hungry.

Females were only one of his problems. There was the fire, the murder, the election, and the mysterious vampires he had met last night.

Where do I start?

Lore finished the cereal and looked in the fridge for

something else to eat. He hadn't gone shopping in a while, so all the good snacking food was gone. *How do I expect to catch the perpetrators of dark sorcery, arson, and murder if I can't even remember to buy groceries?*

Annoyed, he pulled open the vegetable crisper and then quickly shut it. *Prophets save me!* He was a hell-hound, not a biologist.

When it came to keeping the peace in Fairview's nonhuman community, the hounds were basically hired muscle. They guarded VIPs, broke up bar fights and sat on troublemakers until the sheriff, Alessandro Cara-velli, showed up to dispense justice. The hound/vampire partnership worked, but now one half was on holiday. Lore would get the job done, but he missed Caravelli's knowledge of the supernatural community outside of Fairview.

Unfortunately, the vampire had booked his holiday before the election date was set. He was missing all the fun. *Lucky bloodsucker*. Not that Caravelli didn't de-serve a break.

The vampire was vacationing in Madrid, travel-ing with his wife, his wife's grandmother, his baby daughter—that was a long story—his wife's sister and her husband, and their eleven-year-old girl. The women were witches, the brother-in-law an ex-immortal still set-tling into life in the twenty-first century. That was one Christmas family vacation sure to be memorable by anyone's standards.

Lore pulled his head out of the fridge and tried the cupboards instead. There were dog bones and straw-berry Pop-Tarts. He went for the Pop-Tarts, stuffing them in his old toaster.

Caravelli had been excited about the trip. This would be the vampire's first vacation in—what had he said?—a hundred and fifty years. He was finally getting some per-sonal time, leaving with a good conscience because the hellhounds were there to keep an eye on things.

The Pop-Tarts popped just as the appliance started to smoke. *Time to fix it again.* Lore pulled the plug out of the socket and grabbed a tart, burning his fingers, and ate it over the sink.

I can't call Caravelli at the first sign of trouble. That would be the worst thing—a holiday ruined, Lore losing face in front of the pack, and what would happen to Talia? For now, it was better if the Fanged One stayed in Spain, safely out of the way. The airports were probably snowed in, anyway.

Lore chewed, feeling a nagging sense of guilt. Murder, arson, and dark sorcery weren't exactly minor problems. Lore had a responsibility to ask for help if he needed it. He had a right to pride, but not to arrogance.

Lore started on tart number two.

He'd be an idiot if he didn't ask for information. Lore looked at the clock. It would be night in Spain. Stuffing the last of the tart in his mouth, he picked up the phone and punched in Caravelli's cell number.

The vampire answered on the third ring. "Caravelli."

"It's Lore. How's the holiday?"

"Women like to shop," he replied in sepulchral tones. "The only thing keeping me from eating someone is that I am mercifully unconscious during the vast majority of store hours. And it's a good thing the queen pays me well. I apparently need to keep my wife in overpriced shoes."

"Better you than me." Lore didn't buy the long-suffering husband routine. There was a vibrancy in Caravelli's voice that said he was really having a good time.

"Is this a purely social call?"

"No. I met three vampires last night who made my nose twitch. Their names are Nia, Iskander, and Darak. Do you know them?"

He heard his friend catch his breath. Given that vamps didn't breathe unless they were talking, that was saying something. "What were they doing?"

"Drinking at the Empire. They say they came into town for the election."

"They weren't causing trouble?"

"Not when I saw them."

"You're lucky. They're rogues. More like *the* rogues. They've been around since the time of Nero."

Lore's grasp of human history was vague, but he knew that was a very long time. "What do they want?"

"It's hard to say."

"That's helpful."

"They have a particular hatred for authority, probably because they began life as Roman slaves. Darak was a gladiator, famous in his own time. There are crowned heads who tremble at the mention of his name."

Yeah, whatever. "What did he do?"

"Whatever he wanted to. Basically, the gladiator doesn't pick favorites when it comes to the vampire clans. That's why they hate him. He's more likely to show up, cut off the heads of both sides of an argument, and then shower their wealth on the gardener and the scullery maid. He thinks he's Robin Hood."

The reference was lost on Lore. "And he got away with killing both sides?"

"No one will stand up to him."

We'll see about that. Lore rubbed his eyes, still feeling his late, late night. "There's more. You're going to be home in three days, so you should know."

"Know what?"

Lore told him the rest, keeping back only the fact that Talia was asleep in the next room. For a long moment afterward, Caravelli was silent. "I'll try and get an earlier flight."

"Finish your vacation. Don't spoil it for your family. What I need you to do is to get the queen to delay her arrival. She'd just be another target we need to guard."

"She's on my speed dial." Caravelli didn't have an

easy relationship with Omara, but he looked after her interests. "Look, I want to be there to help."

"I'm just doing legwork right now. Recon. I'm not pulling the trigger on anything until I know exactly what I'm up against. And I'll warn you that it's snowing hard here. The airports may not be open."

Caravelli made an exasperated noise. "Can I do anything else?"

"No. That's it. I'll call if anything else comes up."

"Good. Keep me up to speed."

"I will. Bye."

"Later."

Lore put the phone down, mulling over what to do next. He would welcome Caravelli's return, but he couldn't count on it. Not with this weather.

He was on his own.

Chapter 14

There might be Latin-spewing evil burning down the city, but Lore still was Alpha of the pack. Since questioning vampires in daylight was pointless and it was too soon for Errata to have found any answers, he would spend the afternoon finding out who had put Helver up to breaking into the campaign office.

Lore stood on a street corner downtown, or where he thought the corner should be. Snow hid the curbsides and muted the shapes of fire hydrants and garbage cans. It was still coming down, too, the heavy clouds making a twilight out of midafternoon. The buses had wallowed down the main roads without getting stuck, but he didn't hold out hope for tomorrow. The city didn't have much snow-removal equipment, and this storm was freakish.

Fortunately, he'd been born with an optional fur coat. Letting his human shape drop, Lore fell to a dark mist. The cold shocked him for a moment, seeping through the infinitesimal spaces between demon and nothingness. He swirled, buffeted by the rising wind. It took all his considerable strength to pull the particles of himself and re-form into a hound—ears, paws, tail, nose—his deep-chested body the last to form out of the churning mist. Lore shook himself, scattering the falling snow from his back. With a bound, he dove into the drifts, heading toward the cluster of city blocks the hellhounds called home.

He saw the pups first, bouncing in and out of the snowdrifts, rolling and wiggling in the soft white mounds, and tossing clumps of snow with their noses. Lore slowed to a trot as they raced in circles around him, seeming to barely notice the cold. *Where do children get all that energy?* He mock-nipped at a stubby tail as it flashed past.

He was tempted to give chase, giving in to the game, but a nudge of his psychic senses made him look down Heron Street. The urge to play vanished in a lurch of foreboding. There was a cluster of hounds in human form, hands in their pockets, standing in the intersection a block away.

There were two groups of hounds in Spookytown: his own Lurcher pack, and these others, the Redbones. When Lore and his allies had rescued his pack from the Castle, they had freed the Redbones, too. There were many casualties, and survivors from the two packs had amalgamated under the Lurchers.

Sort of. The Redbones' idea of getting along seemed limited to sharing a zip code.

Lore barked the pups out of the way and shifted back to human form. He turned down Heron Street to see what fresh hell the Redbones were plotting. He was willing to bet they were at the bottom of Helver's sudden interest in crime.

Blowing on his hands, he walked toward the group. They fell silent as they spotted him, leaving nothing but the eerie quiet of the traffic-free streets and the soft crunch of his boots through the new-fallen snow. He

counted five hounds, including the Redbones' leader—
the she-hound from his nightmare.

As he drew near, the female put a hand to her chest
and bowed. At her signal, the four males followed suit.
Lore had no illusions about the greeting. Mavritte was
an Alpha in her own right, bowing to Lore only because
so few of the Redbones survived. As leader of a dimin-
ished pack, her position was awkward. She could only
truly join her group with another by mating with the
Alpha or by losing to him in a fight—and losing was
usually fatal. Her best option was to do what she was
doing—maintain a truce with the Lurchers and treat
Lore as her king. If their positions had been reversed,
she'd expect Lore to do the bowing.

Not bloody likely. She was a bitch in every sense of
the word. Beautiful, but in a spine-chilling way. Like all
the hounds, she was tall, strong-boned, and leanly muscled. Her black hair was thick and cut to a shaggy cloud
that framed her face and showed off huge, dark eyes.
Despite the cold, she was dressed in more weapons than
clothes, and a generous part of the clothing was rings,
chains, and zippers.

He'd heard a Castle warlord had used Mavritte as a
body slave, tending to his physical requirements. She'd
eventually slit his throat. After that, she'd ousted her pack
leader and taken his place. Now she was looking at Lore
with dark, serious eyes. He had a fleeting urge to duck.

"Greetings, *Madhyor*," she said, giving him his formal
title.

She never did that unless she wanted something.

"Greetings, Mavritte." He returned the bow, showing
respect.

Lore took a quick survey of the others. All Mavritte's
favorites, and probably bedmates. All heavily armed.
Each one shifting to block an exit from the intersection.
He unbuttoned his coat, just in case he needed the freedom to move.

"I am glad we meet. There are matters concerning the Redbone pack that require your attention."

Lore felt like saying that the Redbones took three-quarters of his time already, but thought better of it. "Is this a discussion that can be accomplished indoors?"

She tilted her head, the gesture showing off the striking bone structure of her face. "It is better that we talk where no others can listen."

Lore looked pointedly at her friends.

"They are no one," she said with a wave of one hand. She wore gloves with the fingers cut out, all the better for gripping a weapon. "My business is with you."

"How fortunate for me."

Mavritte gave him a caustic look.

If she was going to thrust a meeting on him, Lore would take advantage of the situation. "I am happy to listen to any member of my pack, but right now I have a whelp to discipline for breaking pack law. Perhaps you know something of that?"

"Helver?"

"Yes."

She shrugged. "I heard about that. We all need money. Can you blame him for using a hound's natural gifts to get ahead? Besides, the bloodsuckers have wealth to spare. To listen to them, you'd think they were all emperors in their youth."

"Theft is lazy. There are means to earn our keep."

Building and fixing came as second nature to the hounds. Hauling lumber up a scaffold was easy. Engines surrendered their secrets with barely a struggle. The Lurcher pack had opened a business recycling everything from furniture to auto parts. As long as humans were wasteful, there was good money to be made by clever hounds.

"Picking garbage?" Mavritte shifted her weight to one hip. "What sort of a future is that?"

"We came from hell. Now we live in a place that lets

us earn and pay our way. We have hope that we can send our young to good schools, so they will live even better lives."

She laughed, a throaty sound of sheer amusement. "You're an idealist. I didn't think that was possible after the way we grew up."

"I think it's essential. What I say is also truth. We are living a life better than anything we dreamed of."

They were silent a moment, the snow drifting down. It caught in Mavritte's dark hair, ephemeral stars.

She shook it off. "The humans won't let us get ahead unless we force them. We are like the insects that hide in their cupboards, stealing scraps of food. One day they will grow weary of us and call the exterminator."

Lore felt a niggle of doubt. "Not all of them are like that. Many welcome us. Remember when we first came to Fairview? Some sent food and blankets."

Her voice softened. "There are always a compassionate few. I would rather have the respectful many."

"I don't see how raising a pack of thieves will gain respect."

"I grant you that, but it's time we consolidate. Seek power."

"What are you hoping for?"

She straightened, as if they'd finally reached the part of the conversation that mattered. "Wealth. A louder voice on the Supernatural Council. Fear, if necessary. You know how the Castle warlords worked. You learned their lessons as well as I did."

"Enough to know I never want to live in such a place again," Lore shot back. "Why re-create the very thing we fled from?"

She raised her hands in an exasperated gesture. "Because if we can't defend ourselves, the pack will fail."

"We are the peacekeepers that patrol Fairview. We are the ones who break bones and smash heads. How are we not defended?"

Mavritte thrust a finger into his chest. "You need to pick a mate. Pick me. Bind our packs once and for all."

Lore's mouth dropped open for a heartbeat. *Prophets save me!*

She folded her arms. "Do I not please you?"

That's what she said in the dream.

"You are beautiful and fierce. Strong. Powerful. Smart." Hellhounds could not lie, and she was all of those things.

"But?"

He hesitated. *But I don't trust you enough to give you half my power.*

She grabbed his face. His first instinct was to throw her to the ground, but then she pressed her lips to his. They were surprisingly soft, full, and hot. Her tongue danced at the entrance of his mouth, teasing, coaxing. He let her inside as her body pressed against his. They shifted slightly, adjusting for the bulge of weapons, the exact placement of hip and shoulder. They were a good fit. She was nearly six feet of warm, female hellhound, everything his genetic code had bred him to want. Someone who would give him litter after litter, and guard them with her last breath.

Lore crushed her to him, savoring the musky, honeyed taste of bitch. He'd always noticed Mavritte. Now he slaked his male curiosity, letting his hands wander down the taut muscles of her back. He had slept with plenty of the pack's women. Some would even say he'd been downright democratic in his interviews for a mate. Mavritte was certainly the most exciting, in a vaguely suicidal way.

Someday, the mating urge—that drive to take a female in a permanent bond—would drive him mad. Mavritte was right. It was past time to pick somebody, but it wasn't just a choice made by lust. There was more than pure biology involved. A hellhound chose with his soul.

He released her. They panted slightly, gusts of breath

forming clouds in the air. He could see the disappointment in her eyes. She would feel the failure as much as
he did.

"You're not the right one."

Scent. Taste. Something was off. He'd found Talia
more appealing, and she wasn't even the right species.
And yet Talia felt right. Was there something wrong with
him?

"I don't care if we're not the match for each other's
souls," Mavritte returned, her voice soft. "There are too
few of us left to search endlessly for one eternal mate.
The ones we were supposed to bond with could be dead,
killed in the Castle. We have to choose and move on."

Lore didn't reply. There was a chance she was right,
but they were still a bad pairing. They didn't think the
same way.

"I'd never regret having you in my bed." She looked
him up and down, but her bravado wobbled. However
she chose to spin it, her Alpha had rejected her.

"I am honored that you considered me worthy of interest," he said, and meant it.

Nevertheless, anger flared in her eyes, flickering out
of sight so fast he wasn't sure he'd seen it. "Go, then,"
she said. "Go look after the misbehaving whelp."

Lore made a move to leave, but she stopped him with
a hand on his arm. "Wait. How are you going to punish
him?"

"I must think of a way for him to make amends to
the vampires. Then I will give him to a trainer for a
few months." A trainer acted as a strict but fair task-
master, usually appointed to younger hounds who had
transgressed. The sentence usually meant a span of hard
labor on difficult, unpleasant jobs.

"Let Grash be his trainer." She nodded to one of her
men. "He is good at working with wood. He could teach
Helver much. Let the Redbones prove to the Lurchers

that we are also invested in the pack's welfare. If we can't bond one way"—she gave a lopsided smile—"we'll have to come up with other ways of integrating the packs."

It made political sense, but Lore didn't like it. He didn't trust Mavritte, especially in a conciliatory mood. Still, this was a low-risk way of extending goodwill. He would keep an eye on the situation, and set others to do the same. "Very well."

Mavritte nodded and folded her arms. "Good."

Lore studied her a moment. The snowflakes had made a crown in her hair. "Be well."

"Be well."

Lore turned. Grash stepped aside to let him pass, bowing as he did so. Lore nodded an acknowledgment, resisting an urge to growl. There was something about the Redbones that set his teeth on edge.

He was still stewing when he reached Helver's home. It was one in a string of ancient row houses, two stories high with identical green doors and peaked roofs. The hellhounds had repaired what they could, but the walls were crooked and the foundations cracked. *The homes of refugees*, Lore thought. One day, when there was enough time and money, he would tear them down and build afresh.

The grandmother of the family opened the door.

"Greetings, Osan Mina," he said, giving her his best smile.

Grandmother Mina had been littermate to his own osan, and was the closest he had now to family. She was dressed in a long skirt and apron, a white blouse, and a flowered kerchief that tied over her hair. She wasn't a tiny woman, but years of hard work had rounded her spine. He bowed low, as befit one who was so much younger.

"*Madhyor,*" she replied in the hound's tongue. "Sit by the fire and let me serve you tea."

The fire in question was a steam radiator, but Lore

didn't argue. He pulled up a wooden chair to the tiny kitchen table. The family had painted the walls in a bright yellow, with trim in brilliant blues and reds. Geometric designs ran along the edges of the ceiling. It was the same pattern the women sewed on the hems of their skirts, symbolizing the endless return of souls to the pack, life after life.

Grandmother Mina gave him tea in a mug emblazoned with the CSUP logo. Like so many in Spookytown, Grandmother Mina spent the day listening to the station. Then she put a plate of meat and bread on the table. The smell of it reminded Lore that he hadn't eaten anything solid yet that day, and refusing refreshments was an insult.

"Bevan wants to know what to do about the taxes for the warehouse," Mina said. "He told me to ask you when you next came around."

"He has my phone number. He can call me anytime." He turned the mug around, liking the fact it was warm against his chilled hands.

"He knows if you stop by his house, that will make his mother happy. A family feels blessed when the Alpha steps through their doorway." Mina patted his hand. "Osan Riva will have no one else fix her sink. She says you are the only one who can make the drains run right."

"Water flows downward no matter who fixes the drain."

"And Livrok wants advice on the batball team."

"Baseball." He put a slab of chicken onto a thick slice of bread and bit into it.

"That makes no sense. They don't hit it with the base."

"I didn't make up the name, Grandmother," he said, taking another bite.

"Why not? It would have made sense if you had done it. And don't forget my sister wants to know what to do now that her grandson is old enough to work a full day. He needs an occupation."

Which was the main reason Lore lived a little distance away. With the pack turning to him for everything—especially since coming to the human world—a sanctuary was essential. *And perhaps it is also a rebellion, along with the vampire in it?*

"Is Helver at home?" he asked. "I want to continue our discussion from last night."

"I know you do. I sent him to spend the afternoon with Erich and Breckan." Those were younger cousins.

Lore set his mug down on the table, irritated at her interference, but keeping his expression respectful. "Why, Osan Mina? He stole money from the vampires. Money I have to take back to them with an apology. He has brought dishonor on the pack."

"I want to talk to you alone. You can punish my grandson later." She pursed her lips as she sat down across from him. Although her hair had gone white, she was still lean and clear-eyed. Unlike other half demons, hellhounds were mortal. They loved, labored, and bore children. Grandmother Mina bore the testimony of all that and more in the lines of her face.

They were also the only species who had reproduced, aged, and died inside the Castle. Its strange magic had not affected them the same way as any other species. They were the worker bees of the nonhuman world, always in demand, never allowed the luxuries of the others.

He meant to change their status in this land, where hard work and imagination could take the common man to the heights of power. Opportunity was all they had ever needed, and already he had made great strides. Lore had scored a victory when he won a seat at the table with the other leaders of the supernatural community, and now sat there as their equal—but he still felt like a young boy beneath Grandmother Mina's dark gaze.

His cell phone rang. It was Baines again. He switched the phone off.

"What is more important than Helver's welfare?" he asked.

"He runs riot with the Redbone pack. They are not like us. They question your strength as Alpha."

"They're wrong."

"Is that all you have to say?"

"What should I say? That I will bite Mavritte on the nose?"

"You have to show the Redbones your strength."

"If they challenge me, it will be to the death. Mavritte isn't the type to stop at first blood."

"A fight isn't what we need."

"Then what?"

"You know the pack waits for the Alpha to choose a mate."

Lore shifted uncomfortably in his chair. "Perhaps that is a tradition that must fall by the wayside. Just because I haven't . . ."

Mina's eyes snapped. "It's not *tradition*. It's fact. We're neither human nor animal. Magic sometimes dictates how we live."

Lore stared stubbornly into his tea. The legend had it that until there was an Alpha pair, the females would not bear young. It was true that very few pups had arrived since his father's death and none since his mother had passed away. But how much was fact and how much simply tradition? How much would he let an ancient legend rule his life in a world filled with refrigerators and wireless Internet?

"Kirsta is willing. So is Zofia, Sasha's daughter. What is wrong with them?"

"Nothing."

"Then get on with it!" She twisted her fingers through the bright strings of beads around her neck.

"There is no hound I want to take to my bed. At least not permanently."

"No bonding means no young. No young means no future."

Lore was silent.

Mina released the beads, and they fell with a clatter. "If you don't do your duty, the pack will find an Alpha who will."

"I'm still young."

"Your father was younger. Why won't you choose? Have the humans tempted you? Are we no longer good enough?"

Lore pushed his tea away. "Forgive me, Osan, but you know me better. I walked back into the Castle time and again to rescue the last of our people, one by one. I am loyal to the pack."

"What about Mavritte?"

Lore stood. "I have already told her no."

"The Elders favor her. It would unite the packs."

"But I am Alpha." *And I am ambushed.* It was too much a coincidence that he was having this conversation twice in one day.

Mina rose and took Lore's hands. "Promise me you will think on this, *Madhyor.*"

"I will ask for a prophecy." It was a ritual answer, but a true one. He was going to need divine intervention to find his way through this mess.

"The Elders seek prophecy on your mate, too. So far, all is darkness. The Eldest threw the bones of divination, but they turned up blank."

Thank all the gods. At least that bought him some time. Lore bowed over her hands. "I honor your concern."

"Don't honor, act. Choose someone before the Elders choose for you."

Like hell they will!

Lore changed the subject. "Tell Helver that Grash will be his trainer."

Grandmother Mina gave him a surprised look. "Grash?"

He crossed the tiny kitchen toward the door. "It will make Mavritte happy."

"Are you certain this is wise?"

Lore put his hand on the doorknob, then dropped it. He turned to face her, needing to make his point. "Either we trust the Redbones enough to mate with them, or we don't. Merging the packs has to go beyond a mere pair bond. We need other bridges between us."

She pressed her lips into a dubious scowl. "I don't like Grash."

"I don't like any of them, but I sleep better knowing I am their Alpha. If they step out of line, I have the authority to take action."

"Spoken like an Alpha."

"Maybe, but our packs are small. We are still better off together. I will keep trying to make peace."

"You are your father's son."

"Be well, Osan."

"Be well."

Lore left the house, feeling oddly alone when the door closed behind him. *Would the Elders really force a mate on me? Choose a different Alpha?* What would he do? Take a female he didn't want or walk away from the pack, losing everything he'd ever known?

The once familiar street looked strange, smothered, and frozen.

Trapped.

Welcome to my future.

Chapter 15

Later, Lore stood at the foot of his bed, arms folded, watching Talia sleep. He could feel the sun setting, his demon sense tracking the moment twilight passed into night. Hellhounds belonged to that place between one state and other: doorways, dawn, the soft state between sleep and waking. Some believed that, once upon a time, the hounds had padded beside the souls of the deceased, guarding them on their journey to the Land of the Dead.

That was why they could not lie—there was no room in that critical passage for anything but truth. And perhaps that's why vampires fascinated him. Like him, they were caught on the road between life and death, never quite finding rest.

He watched Talia and waited for the sinking sun to work its magic. It was like admiring a painting, her still form lovely but curiously vacant. Vampires didn't die during the daylight hours, but their sleep was so deep it resembled a coma. The old ones could wake in the day, but not fledglings like Talia.

Even Lore could tell she was newly Turned. Awake, she was in perpetual motion, energy sparking every moment. She didn't have the stillness of the long-dead. Now she was an empty container.

What is her story? How did she end up like this?

Lore felt the horizon snuff out the last of the sun's glow. Talia's eyes flickered open. They reflected the dim light of the room like a cat, a sudden flash of yellow.

Lore knew enough to wait before approaching the bed. There was a moment when a vampire woke when the body was active, but the mind still asleep. For those first few seconds, the newly made were unpredictable.

Sure enough, she launched herself across the bed toward him. *A trapped animal. Nothing but rage, fear, and hunger.*

Lore grabbed her shoulders. "Talia!"

She froze, and the silence was potent. He could almost hear her mind booting up like a balky computer. Then he saw personality flooding back, filling up her face.

"You." The word was filled with meaning—disgust, relief, regret, and a touch of desire. Then he saw pain. "Last night . . . it all really happened."

"Yes."

"Of course it did." She sank back on the bed, jamming her hands through her hair. "Oh, God."

Lore picked up a glass from the dresser top. "I brought you blood."

"Get serious." Hunger and revulsion collided in her face. "Whose is that?"

"I keep refreshments in the fridge. Beer, cola . . . and this. For friends. The hospital supplies it, if you know the right people."

"Bagged blood is—it doesn't work. We can't live on it. And it's disgusting."

She was right. Vampires needed the life essence of their victims as much as the protein from their blood, but the O Neg alone could keep them going for a few days. "I'm told it's best cut liberally with vodka. I can make it into a cocktail, if you prefer."

"I'd be hosed by six o'clock."

"You'd stop complaining."

"I'll stay sober, thanks." She eyed the glass, hunger obviously getting the upper hand. "Any chance of going out for a bite?"

"You're safer here, where I can protect you."

"Who elected you my bodyguard?"

"I'm a hellhound." He handed her the glass, careful not to let their skin touch. He would not visit that slippery slope again. "Guarding is what we do."

"Don't I get a say in the matter?" She glanced up at him. "Don't watch me."

New vampires were squeamish about drinking blood, but he couldn't afford to make a mistake. "I'm not turning my back on you. You'd figure out a way to hit me over the head."

"Mangy beast." She took a sip of the blood and made a face. "Omigod is that awful!"

"It's a bit old."

"Ugh!"

He moved to take it away, but she waved him off. Closing her eyes, she chugged the blood, draining it to the last drop. Then she held out the glass, eyes still screwed shut. When he took it, she clamped her hand over her mouth, her throat working. For a moment, Lore wondered if she was going to throw up. A thread of guilt wormed through him. "I'll try and find a volunteer next time."

She drew a long, shuddering breath. "Next time I'll just bite you."

The rest must have done her good, if she was up to slinging insults. "I've been told demon blood is low in nutrients."

The look she gave him would have made a lesser hound grovel. Lore grinned. "You have to keep up your strength."

"You're a monster!"

"So are you."

She hiccupped. He wondered again if she was going to be sick but, to his complete astonishment, she started to weep, little mewing sobs.

This was too much. He abandoned the dirty glass on the nightstand and sat down on the bed next to her. He laid a hand on her head, feeling the smooth silk of her dark hair. Stiffening, she folded her free arm across her stomach, clutching herself.

"I didn't ask for this!" she muttered under her breath.

"I'm sorry." Lore stroked her hair, rattled by her silent, angry sobbing. These were tears of rage as much as sorrow, her teeth clenched against her grief. "I'm working as fast as I can to find out who killed your cousin."

When she didn't pull away, he wrapped his arm around her shoulders. Talia was small by hellhound standards, but that made her fit neatly into the circle of his arm. She was so slender, he could feel her bones move as she wept. The utter, aching sadness of it stirred memories of his own. Species didn't matter when it came to the kinship of sorrow.

Slowly, very slowly, Talia quieted. "You're warm," she murmured.

He pulled her closer. Vampires were always cold, and he had heat to spare. The perfumes she had been wearing had faded, and now he could smell her clearly, her unique musk imprinting on his memory. It smelled familiar, like a sweet tune he'd forgotten only to hear it in the most unexpected setting. He closed his eyes, memorizing the feel of her body against his. It felt so right.

This was wrong. He was the Alpha of his pack, and he shouldn't be holding a strange female. He could feel his motivations turning murkier by the second, the desire to see justice done mixing with desire of another kind. *So this is forbidden fruit.*

"What happened to you?" Lore asked. "How did you end up in this mess?"

She closed her eyes. He studied her finely veined eyelids, delicate as a moth's wing. "The answer depends on where you want to start."

"The beginning."

"When my brother turned thirteen, my father hung a picture over Max's bed so that it was the last thing he saw at night. It was of a succubus devouring the flesh of her lover. It gave him nightmares. As long as I knew him, Max never bedded a woman more than once."

Lore's stomach rolled over. "Disturbing, but how did that get you here?"

"It says everything you need to know about where I came from. The rest was all me trying to make sense of everything my father did to us. I try to tell myself I'm not a victim, but it's hard to believe sometimes. Home was like a prison, only stranger."

She fell silent, as if talking had exhausted her. Lore kept his arm around her, feeling the tension in her muscles. She might be slumped against him, but she was wound to the breaking point. In the quiet, Lore could hear some optimist trying to start his frozen car.

"I know what it's like to grow up in a prison," he said.

"How did you get out?"

"One day, by pure chance, a doorway opened and a few of us escaped. It took a while before we could figure out the place we'd come to. Your world is so different. I'd never seen the sky or growing things."

Talia put her hand on his forearm. It was a commonplace gesture, but it was the first time she'd made the first move to touch him. It made him feel humble and yet twice his size.

"As soon as I could, I went back for the rest. Many were held as slaves by the Castle warlords. We are stronger than many species, so the others kept children and wives as a guarantee that we would not turn on them. Many hounds would not leave their captive families behind. So I smuggled in goods that were scarce in there but plentiful here and bargained for every hound I could. Cloth. Books. Tools. Three pairs of shoes would buy a houndish child out of slavery. One by one, I got them out. Finally, I convinced the other species to help me rescue the rest of the pack who were still hiding in the dungeon corridors. It was a fierce battle, with many casualties. But no one was left behind as a prisoner."

Talia blinked. "No one?"

"No."

"You had nothing, and you got your people to safety. So why did this happen to me?" she whispered.

"No one asks to be the target of a killer."

She seemed to choke for a moment. He saw tears leak from beneath her long, dark eyelashes. They trailed down her cheeks, glistening with a faint pink sheen. "That's not it. I didn't ask to be Turned."

Lore stiffened, and she looked up. The stricken look in her eyes made her meaning clear. Few vampires were made, especially in these times when human law held sway. None were Turned without begging for it.

Unless Talia had already been murdered once before.

A cold, cold horror began to fill his chest. Beneath that, rage.

Chapter 16

Wednesday, December 29, 8:00 p.m.
101.5 FM

"**G**ood evening, this is the CSUP news on 101.5 FM in Fairview. At the top of our headlines tonight is the fire that destroyed the South Fairview Medical Clinic and the campaign office of Michael de Winter, the first nonhuman to stand for election to city council. Although preliminary investigations do not reveal traces of an accelerant, according to Fairview Police Detective Derek Baines arson is indeed suspected. The news has rocked all of Fairview. Already, accusations of a hate crime are finding their way into the national media. Queen Omara, sponsor of de Winter's candidacy, is rearranging her plans and will arrive in Fairview as soon as the weather permits."

Wednesday, December 29, 8:00 p.m.
Lore's condo

Talia heard the front door click shut. She was alone, lying on her side, her face to the wall. She'd cried herself into exhaustion and Lore had finally left, believing her asleep.

The anger and tears had been for Michelle, but also for herself. She'd pushed her own wounds aside for years, but they'd reopened, needing to be cried out, too.

Lore had simply held her. He hadn't tried to tell her everything would be fine, and that made her enormously grateful. She didn't need his lies—but then he'd said hellhounds couldn't lie. That allowed a slim margin of trust to grow between them.

But what was she supposed to make of him? Man-dog. Dog-man. Demon guy. She'd never met anyone like him. Hunters hunted monsters, they didn't get to know them.

So what if she was one of the monsters now? It was something she'd been careful not to examine too closely. Existence was a day-by-day bargain between self-disgust and her instinct to survive. She'd never looked at her fellow Undead as anything but walking corpses. Maybe that had been shortsighted, but a person's world view didn't change just because they'd been bitten. Waking up dead wasn't a great advertisement for interspecies relations.

But Lore was something else. As jailers went, he could have been much worse. There was no mistaking the power that clung to him like a second skin, but he hadn't hurt her. That counted for a lot.

He did seem bent on finding the truth. That gave them something in common.

On top of that, he was easy on the eyes. She was a sucker for the hard, strong kind of guy who worked with his hands. The kind you knew could fix the sink or the car or the horrible day you'd had with his oh-so-capable touch. She bet Lore was just that type. A haircut and some wardrobe advice, and he'd be a definite hottie. Oh yeah, and he could use some advice on the whole handcuffing thing. Definite turnoff if it wasn't handled just right.

But what did you expect from a monster? A wry

smile twisted her lips. *What does the word "monster" mean, anyway?* Did it really describe a guy who walked into the hell he'd escaped and bargained for the lives of his people? That was the stuff of legends.

No one was left behind. The words had power over her, because she had been abandoned when it counted most. Over and over again.

What had Lore asked? How did she end up in this mess?

The kickoff really had been the incident with Max and the succubus painting. Talia was just old enough to see the incident as a wake-up call. Killing monsters was the hub of Hunter culture, but so was despising anything that made a man weak. That included women. Lust happened, but it was something to be sniggered at or hidden in dark corners. Her father was already shaping the way Max saw his future loves.

Most of the Hunter women accepted that they were second-class warriors and not much else, but Talia's mom had been from outside the tribe. The male grip on Max was hard to break, but she'd given her daughter ideas. It was her mom that had given Talia the courage to strike out on her own.

Against her father's wishes, Talia left for university. She'd done brilliantly, found a job she loved, built the start of a sane life—but such a lonely one. There'd been no one to fill the place of the tribe and all the close-knit family bonds she'd had from the cradle. She still loved and hated them at the same time, and with such passion. Too bad there was no Toxic Homes Anonymous.

Hi, my name is Talia and I can't stay away from my homicidally screwed-up roots.

Her mistake had been letting family bonds drag her home again. Going back had cost her life. *I tried to be a good daughter. I should have tried harder to become a good wife.*

No, that last one would have been a disaster.

She sat up, pushing her hair out of her eyes. She'd survived her family, sort of. Even death hadn't stopped her. She'd soldiered through that like she had everything else—but each battle took a little more out of her. Michelle's loss had hit her hard. Grief had made it easy for Lore to capture her.

I can't afford that. If I'm going to make it past this, I have to keep it together.

Talia closed her eyes, realizing the whole murder-suspect thing meant abandoning her teaching position. She felt a sudden, nostalgic wave for the hush of the university library, the scent of fresh paper, and that eager nervousness of September beginnings. *I don't want to lose that, too.* Her students were her only real contact with the human world. The world of books was the one place where being a vampire didn't matter.

The price for survival just kept getting higher. The only way to stop paying was to clear her name and go somewhere her past couldn't reach her.

If she was going to find the killer, she had to be at the top of her game.

The bedsheets felt cool under her fingertips. She sat for a moment, watching the snow fall outside the window. Lore had left the drapes open, giving her a view of the winter scene. The drifting flakes invoked a sense of inevitability that was almost like peace.

Talia was definitely feeling—not exactly better, but calmer.

Okay, then, think.

She had defined goals: to find and punish Michelle's killer, and to escape someplace where the rogue registry couldn't find her. To accomplish either one, she needed her money, ID, clothes, and weapons.

She'd run out of Lore's condo once already—straight into the cops. She was going to plan properly this time. *I am calm and rational. I am in control. I spit in the eye of fate.*

First, she wanted out of the bedroom. The memory of being chained to the bed was making her claustrophobic. Talia rose, walked to the door, and tried the handle.

It was locked. She rattled the handle a second time, just to be sure. A tingling spread over her hands, creeping up to her elbows like a glove of electricity. A spell.

Damn him! Lore had been so sympathetic, so kind, she thought he'd given her a refuge, not made her a prisoner again! *Stupid, stupid, stupid!* She'd granted him a glimmer of trust, and this is what happened. *Fool!*

A sense of betrayal flared through her. She clenched her teeth so hard the back of her skull ached. She'd been had. *Now what am I going to do?*

She could pick a lock. There wasn't a thing she could do about magic.

Damn! She slammed the heel of her hand against the door in frustration.

Talia slid down the door until her rump hit the carpet. She was so going to tear the dog a new one once she got free. No one chained her up, locked her up, and fed her stale blood and got away with it! Fleas were too good for him.

Calm and rational, remember? She ground the heels of her hands into her eyes.

You haven't tried the window yet. With a surge of hope, she got to her feet, crossed the room, and tried to push it open. A zap of electricity numbed her arm. She yanked it away.

Her whole body felt the low burn of frustration. *Just let me go, you mangy bastard!*

The sound of the door to the main hallway opening sent her skittering back from the window. Stupidly, she felt like a teenager caught ransacking the liquor cabinet.

There were voices. Several, and ones that she didn't know. That threw a new wrench in the works. *Who are they? Police? Or the killer? The mysterious vampire?*

She glared at the door. *I'm caged here. A sitting duck.*

And Lore was out, nowhere around to protect her—and he'd locked her in so that she couldn't protect herself. *Idiot.*

She needed a weapon, and she needed her freedom. A quick look around the room revealed only standard bedroom stuff. She opened the closet. A weapon could be anything, if it could stab or club.

Like a baseball bat. There it was, hiding in the corner behind a pile of junk. Talia picked it up almost lovingly. It was an old wooden one that bore the marks of many, many games. Perfect for smacking anything short of a full-blooded demon. If it broke, heck, it would make a great stake. *Talia steps up to bat, and the crowd goes wild.*

Finding a weapon had taken only seconds. *Check.*

Now for the door. Would Lore's magic work on it if it wasn't attached to the wall?

The construction in the building was better than most condos, but interior doors were for privacy, not security. They crumpled like paper if you knew what to do. Hunter 101.

The thought brought a spark of satisfaction.

Talia stripped off her dainty, high-heeled boots. The bedroom was crowded, but there was enough room for a good kick. A couple of steps and a twist, and she would lead with her heel and the full force of her anger. She tested the carpet—just enough nap to give great traction.

It was a perfect strike from the right hip. The door crashed open, pounding against the wall in an explosion of splinters and drywall. Talia landed on the balls of her feet, her fists raised to cover her face. In the next second, she swooped to pick up the bat, ready to swing.

A faint whiff of ozone filled the air.

On the other side of where the door had just been, Lore was turning around, eyes wide with surprise. Astonishment turned into a frown as he planted his feet and crossed his arms, looking like an irate Egyptian statue. "Getting impatient, I see."

Astonished, she fell back a step. The doorway crackled, thin blue veins of electricity making jagged spider webs across the empty space. The spell guarding the door was still going strong. *Crap!*

"What's going on?" a male voice shouted.

"Nothing," Lore said in a flat tone.

Nothing? Her anger wasn't nothing. She shifted her grip on the bat, wanting to smack the superior look off his face. "I'm so done with the bondage games. C'mon, by now you must know I'm not the killer."

He made a disgusted noise. "The wards were for your protection, in case someone came looking for you." Eyes narrowed, he poked at the spot where the door handle had punched into the drywall. "I guess that wasn't necessary."

"Damned straight," she shot back, lingering anger making her surly. *I trusted you. I cried on you, and you locked me up again.*

"Are you sure you're all right?" the voice yelled again, but this time there was amusement in the tone.

"Yes!" Lore snapped.

"Oookaaayy, I'll take your word for it." The voice dissolved into a chuckle. "Next time try a dating service. It's safer."

Talia's cheeks burned with outrage. *What the hell?*

With a grumpy expression, Lore made a gesture and said something under his breath. The crackle of electricity stopped. The spell or ward or whatever it was fell away.

Lore stood aside. "You can put the bat down. You're free to go, if that's what you want."

"Seriously?"

His dark eyes flicked away, as if he was embarrassed. "You're innocent."

Talia dropped the bat and hurriedly pulled her boots back on while he stood watching like a grim sentinel. Relief warred with awkwardness. She'd been psyched up for a good ass-kicking, and now nothing. She was mentally stumbling, all revved up with nowhere to go.

How does he know I'm innocent? Did it matter? She pushed past his solid bulk, suddenly feeling like the bedroom walls were closing in. He could change his mind. This whole thing might be a trick.

An urge to run warred with curiosity. What had Lore found out?

Talia nearly collided with a woman taking off a gorgeous black-and-white tweed coat. The woman looked up, and that made Talia slow for a microsecond. *Werecougar*, she thought instantly, looking at the bone structure of her face. The creatures were rarely seen south of the Yukon, but they were unforgettable. Her skin was the dusky tone of café au lait, her posture that of a runway model.

"Nice coat," Talia said, not sure what to do next. Instinct said to dive for the door, but she was curious. Who was this? Why was she here?

"It's a Burberry," the cougar returned, and Talia recognized the smooth voice.

"You're Errata Jones!" Talia looked from Errata to Lore.

"And you're Talia Rostova." Errata hooked the Burberry on a coat tree that was crammed with wet outerwear. Lore had several guests. Of course he did—whoever had been teasing him before was male.

These strangers know who I am! Talia realized with shock. *So much for keeping me safe!*

"Don't look so worried." Errata fixed Talia with intense hazel eyes. "Lore knows what he's doing."

I'll bet! Talia rounded on him, but something stopped her before she could vent her feelings. He looked exhausted and unhappy and more than a little apologetic. The urge to scream at him withered as it reached her throat.

Oh, God, it's the puppy-dog eyes. Or Stockholm syndrome.

Errata leaned close, murmuring into Talia's ear, "He likes you, you know. I can tell."

Talia stared at her, both curious and aghast. Lore was narrowing his eyes at them both.

A sly smile played on Errata's mouth. "Loyalty. Agility. You could do worse than a guy who can catch a Frisbee in his teeth. Just think what else he can do without using his hands." The werecougar shrugged, keeping her voice so quiet only Talia could hear her. "Not that he doesn't need work but, hey, he comes when he's called."

Talia stepped back, stunned by an irrational urge to defend Lore. She drew a breath to protest, but then the most gorgeous guy she'd ever seen emerged from the kitchen holding a plastic bag of blood.

The man held up the bag, pointing to the tiny writing stamped on the bag. He looked from Lore to Errata. "Did you look at the expiry date on this? You could kill somebody with this stuff."

Errata gave a delicate snort. "Oh, come on, Joe. You're three parts vampire and one part hellbeast. It's going to take more than funky blood to do you in."

Talia stiffened, her Hunter sense on alert. This guy was a *volkodlak*, Turned by a curse that made him immortal and very hard to kill.

"This is Joe," Lore said, sounding irritable. "Ignore him."

In response, Joe gave her a smile that did funny things to her stomach. He was too pretty for words—a dimpled chin, blade-straight nose, cheekbones sharp enough to cut diamonds. There were no fangs to spoil the sensual curve of his lips—she knew those only came out for feeding.

Talia gave herself a mental shake, woozy from too much hot guy. She had to say something to break through his charm, so she focused on the blood. "I wouldn't drink that, if I were you. It tastes like a garburator bled to death."

With a sigh, Joe vanished back into the kitchen. She heard a *thwack* as he dumped the bag in the sink. "Then let's get this show on the road. I have to take over the bar at nine thirty."

"You're a bartender?" she asked in surprise.

"Bar owner." He gave her another smile that should have carried a warning from the surgeon general. "I own the Empire Hotel."

Oh, God. This guy was in the hospitality industry? His species were ravening killers—weren't they?

Lore gave Joe a grumpy look. "Time to sit down."

Joe winked at Talia and headed for the living room, following Errata. Lore put a hand on the small of Talia's back, guiding her. Still annoyed at being locked up, she pulled away.

He dropped his hand, but leaned over to whisper, "I get it. You can look after yourself."

Talia was about to deliver a scathing retort—she'd think of one any second now—when she realized there was another person in the living room. He was watching the news on the TV without the sound, and clicked it off as they walked in. He was handsome in a boyish way, brown-haired and green-eyed.

Talia experienced a shock of recognition. "I know you. You work at the university."

He offered a hand. "Perry Baker. Comp Sci."

She took it. He had a nice handshake, firm but not a bone-crusher. Warm, but with a different energy than Lore's touch. *Werewolf.*

"Talia Rostova. English Lit. Distance Ed, mostly."

"Perhaps we met at a faculty party?"

"No. It was the day they had all the nonhuman faculty in for orientation."

He rolled his eyes. "Oh, right. The don't-eat-the-students speech."

Perry laughed, but it had a nervous edge. She was glad he was there. Werewolf or not, another professor represented something from the university, the one place she had a right to belong.

Talia took a quick scan of the room. The view was nearly the same as from her living room, though several floors down. The main difference was the big, comfortable furniture that marked it as a man's domain. No bobblehead poodle dogs here. Just a hellhound, a werewolf, and a vampire/werebeast cross. Oh, and a werecougar. *What is this? Wild Kingdom?*

By now everyone else was sitting: Joe and Errata on the couch, Lore in an armchair, and Perry on the rug in front of the fire. It was a subtle demonstration of the social position of the three males. Lore had a chair to himself, Perry had none—but he didn't seem worried about it. They'd tactfully left an armchair for her.

An instant of fright passed through her. She wasn't used to dealing with so many new people anymore. On the run, she'd learned to isolate herself. Instinct made an outcast cautious—the straggler from the herd was vulnerable—and here she was faced with a roomful of lions and wolves.

Taking a breath, she sat and got straight to the point. "So what's up? How come you think I'm innocent all of a sudden?"

Perry spoke up. "First, you didn't actually have time to kill your cousin, hide the murder weapon, and change into clothes that weren't covered in blood."

Talia gave him a startled look. "How do you know that?"

"I hacked into the traffic cameras. You drove home minutes before Lore found you." The werewolf gave a self-satisfied smile. "Yes, I'm that good."

Sudden relief flooded her. *Someone believes me.* It wasn't the answer to all her problems, but it mattered. It meant that she wasn't absolutely alone as she had been a moment ago.

Perry's eyes turned serious. "I also don't think you're a necromancer."

All heads were turned to the werewolf, intent in a manner that was decidedly not human.

"A what?" Talia knew that a necromancer was a sorcerer that summoned the dead. It just wasn't what she'd expected to hear.

"Lore told me about the crime scene. There was a Latin word and a symbol drawn in blood. It suggested a spell."

A vague dizziness came over Talia, and she leaned back in the overstuffed armchair, grateful for its big-boned, manly man support. "A spell? You mean someone killed Michelle to work magic? That makes no sense."

Perry nodded. "It actually does. Once I knew what I was looking for, references to such spells weren't hard to find. They bind the power of death to the spell they want to work. It's considered by those in the craft to be a forbidden practice, but since when have rules stopped anybody from doing evil?"

"But why?" Talia shook her head. "If the murder was for something like that, why Michelle of all people? She wasn't involved in the supernatural." *Except for me. I was her one link.*

Lore took a deep breath. "I met someone last night who had a theory that her death was connected to the arson at the clinic."

Talia listened to his deep voice, her mind scrambling to make sense as he described first the fire, and then his encounter with three rogue vampires in the Empire bar.

"I remember them," Joe said. "A pitcher of draft brown ale, three glasses. Paid cash. They didn't cause any trouble, but they sure looked like it."

"This Darak guy talked to Michelle's spirit?" Talia said incredulously.

"A few vampires have such power," Joe replied. "It's rare, but sometimes the old ones can see the dead."

The thought horrified her. "Then Michelle's spirit . . ."

"The spirits don't stay earthbound once the spell has consumed the energy released in their death," Perry said in a comforting voice. "She's gone. You don't have to worry about her."

Talia nodded gratefully, forcing down another wave of grief. She couldn't fold now. Not in public. Not when she was getting solid information. *Justice comes first, grief later*.

"Is it possible that you have a personal connection with the attacker?" Lore asked, looking at her closely.

Talia answered honestly. "I know of a few vampires who did some sorcery, including my sire, but I don't know of anyone who does necromancy."

"Few would admit to it," said Perry. "Forbidden spells, remember?"

Talia bit her thumbnail. "Do necromancers ever kill vampires? I keep thinking it was me who was meant to die. But wouldn't most people be able to tell the difference between a human and a vampire? Michelle looked like me, but a sorcerer should know she was alive, right?"

Perry looked at her curiously. "I doubt you were the target. By all accounts, humans work best for a death spell. What I want to know is why someone burned the clinic and constituency office—and why use such a labor-intensive method? What's the point? It's not going to stop the election."

"But think of the effect it has," said Joe. "It's showy and scary. It's going to bring the queen running to find out who the hell is on her turf."

"I asked Caravelli to tell Queen Omara to delay her trip." Lore shifted irritably in his chair. "It didn't work.

He called tonight. She's coming as soon as she can. The only saving grace is the snow. The airport is closed."

"But that means Caravelli can't come home, either," Joe added.

Lore rubbed his eyes, as if tired. "We're on our own, and we have until the weather breaks to solve this."

Errata had sat silently through most of the exchange, but now she stirred. "If what we've guessed is true, the necromancer is one of Queen Omara's enemies. Unfortunately, that's a rather long list."

Joe turned to Lore. "I'm coming in late to this party. Is that why you asked us here? To play were-detective?"

"Yes," Lore said simply. "I asked you because you've been around the longest. You've seen more than any of the rest of us."

Joe shrugged. "Glad to know I'm good for something besides mixing appletinis, but aren't there human police working the murder case?"

"And what good are they going to be against a necromancer?" Lore replied.

"Good point." Joe fell silent, musing for a moment. "I was a soldier. Cutting off a head isn't easy. Whoever did it had to be strong."

Perry got to his feet, pacing over to the window. Talia could see him in front of his classroom, pointer in hand. "With this kind of a spell, the necromancer him- or herself has to do the killing. Because of the enormous amount of time it takes to build the right skills for this kind of magic, I don't think we're looking for a human." He turned to face them. "Sorcerers are usually immortals, or at least long-lived."

"You're not immortal," Errata returned.

"Yeah, but I'm a genius. Not a fair comparison."

Lore shook his head. "A vampire would traditionally use a sword for a beheading. It didn't look like a sword wound. That's the one detail that doesn't make sense."

Talia clamped her hand over her mouth, desperately trying to keep the image of Michelle's corpse out of her mind. At the same time, the logical part of her brain scrambled to put the facts together. "What about an immortal who for some reason couldn't use a sword properly?"

Lore gave her a sharp glance. "What are you thinking?"

She got to her feet, her stomach roiling with tension. She'd figured it out, but she needed a few minutes to decide what telling the truth would mean. "I think I need some air."

"It's freezing cold outside," said Errata. "Take my coat."

Talia headed for the door.

Lore jumped up. "What if someone sees you? We know you're innocent. The police don't."

"I'll take the back stairs and stay out of sight."

She heard Errata's voice, low and urgent. "Let her go."

Talia hesitated before grabbing the Burberry. If she took it, she'd be obligated to bring it back, and every instinct screamed to run. She grabbed an old, ratty jacket instead. It hung to her knees and looked like Lore had worn it while rebuilding a diesel engine.

She banged out the door and into the airless twilight of the sixth-floor hallway.

I am in so much trouble.

Chapter 17

Outside the fire door at the building's back entrance, the parking lot was a glittering snowscape. Talia stood in the tiny clearing someone had shoveled so the door could swing open. Beyond was a knee-high drift that stretched across the lot to the street. Rows of snow-covered cars made the landscape look like an inverted egg carton.

She knew it had been snowing, but this was way more than she'd expected. Back in her hometown, winters had been worse than this, but they'd worked up to it. A body had time to brace itself. This had come on freakishly fast.

She flashed back to the big hill behind her childhood home. Kids knew how to play even when adults were mired in life-and-death problems. She and her brother, Max, had found a big refrigerator box and used it for a toboggan, sliding down the hill over and over until every last bit of their clothes was soaked. There had been a snowball fight after that, one bunch of neighborhood kids against another. They'd known everyone in the area. They were all pretty much related, anyway. Cousins of cousins.

Her mom had been the odd one out. Whatever had

made her marry Dad? Why had he, the ultimate Hunter, picked a wife outside the tribe?

Opposites attract?

But not forever. Her father had all but crushed the life out of her mom—not with his fists, but with the hard edge of his will. Why had he wanted to kill the radiance in her that moved his heart? *Because loving someone makes you vulnerable. Weakness is never the Hunter way.*

More to the point, why had it taken her mother so long to leave? She had to have stayed for Talia and Max, toughing it out as long as she had. She left just after Talia had gone away to school. Too bad cancer had killed her a year after she'd found freedom.

The men had blamed Talia. If she hadn't escaped to university, the family would have stayed together. That had been the weapon they'd used to drag her back home: guilt.

They made me feel like a monster even before I was Turned. Most of the time that made her angry, but sometimes she believed those old accusations. *You're selfish. You insist on having your own way. Then everything gets worse.*

The facts could be twisted to fit that theory. She'd left for school and lost her mother. Escaped to Fairview and lost Michelle. Tried to break up with her fiancé and lost everything—right down to her life.

Talia took a step forward. Her high-heeled boots skidded on the frosty ground. There'd been enough of a melt during the day to coat the sidewalk with ice, and then another fall of snow to hide it. She caught her balance, holding her arms out like airplane wings. Cold stabbed at her toes. Clearly, Jimmy Choo knockoffs weren't designed for Arctic exploration.

She heard the rattle of the door behind her, then Lore's voice. "You're going to break something before you make it to the street."

"Can't you give a girl a moment to think?" Her words

drifted up on sudden puffs of steam, surprising her. She needed to breathe only when she talked.

He was silent for a moment. "Wouldn't you think better where it's warm?"

Carefully, she turned around to face him. His mouth twitched, like he was fighting a laugh. "I think the tweed would have looked better on you."

His smile brought heat to her cheeks. Talia looked down at herself. She looked like she'd crawled out of a Dumpster. "I wasn't sure I was coming back."

"So you took my coat?"

"If you never saw it again, I'd be doing you a favor."

He chuckled. "Where would you go?"

"A hotel."

"With the police on your tail? And maybe a necromancer?"

"I'm the evil Undead. I have tricks up my sleeve, and about forty dollars in my pocket."

"Good luck with that."

Talia skittered on her heels. "I'm screwed, aren't I?"

Lore crossed the ice patch toward her, his heavy boots finding plenty of traction. "You seemed bothered by the conversation upstairs."

"Aren't you?"

"Errata found the name of your sire. King Belenos. You have some impressive enemies." He caught her arm before she could fall. "You said you didn't ask to be a vampire."

Her chest tightened. "I didn't."

His look went deep into her. "How did it happen?"

Talia pulled the coat closer around her throat. "I . . . it's a long story. All you need to know is that Belenos is a few boards short of a coffin. And he hates Queen Omara."

"I know." Lore shifted onto drier ground. The movement brought him closer. "He's been here before. Last time he tangled with one of our slayers and she handed him over to the queen for punishment."

Talia nodded. "Queen Omara maimed him in ways that a vampire can't fix. He can't swing a sword anymore."

Lore gave her a sharp look. "You think it's him, don't you?"

Talia swallowed. She'd lived in fear of revealing her sire's name for two reasons. One, it made it more likely that Belenos would find her. Two, it brought anyone curious about her past closer to the fact that she'd been a Hunter. A prickle of anxiety skittered down her back.

Now Lore and her friends knew about her sire. She was walking on a tightrope, Belenos on one side, all the rest of the nonhumans on the other. If there was a third side available, her family would be itching to kill her, too. It was hard to know which to worry about first.

Don't go there. If she did, she'd be paralyzed. She had to focus on the idea that Belenos had killed Michelle. *My God, this means he must be in Fairview!* She so had to get her weapons from Michelle's condo.

Talia took a shaking breath. "Belenos is a sorcerer. He hates the queen. Besides that, he likes a cat-and-mouse game. If he found out I'm here, he'd kill Michelle for the simple reason that I loved her. He'd do it just to make me afraid."

"I believe that. Darak said your cousin's spirit was worried that you were in danger, too. Is Belenos a necromancer?"

"If it's nasty magic, he's probably done it. Frankly, the idea that he's anywhere nearby is going to give me nightmares."

"There's a report that you stole a lot of money from him."

Damn Errata! "He owed me a new life. After all, he stole my last one. I took enough to get away." Okay, so maybe that was understating, but he owed her.

"Blood money?"

"I think of it as disability insurance." Talia nearly spit

the last words. "Stealing's not what you'd call honorable, but it was my ticket out of his house of horrors."

She dropped her head, not wanting to meet Lore's gaze. No one else would understand what she'd done. Not unless they'd been there. She could feel his interest like a gentle hand probing her, wondering who she was. *I'm toast if you ever figure that out.*

Talia shivered, feeling like a child in the huge coat. The sleeves dangled past her hands, the hem almost to her knees. Lore put his arm around her, drawing her close to his body. The coat he was wearing was cleaner, but just as plain. He'd left it undone, leaving access to his body heat. Talia curled close.

Wait a minute! It didn't dawn on her until a second later what had just happened. He'd taken possession of her so casually, she hadn't noticed. She twisted her neck to look up at him.

He had a half-serious, half-amused look.

"You're presuming a lot, dog-boy—you know that?"

"You looked cold."

She dropped her guard an inch. "How come you don't have a nice hellhound girlfriend?"

A pained expression crossed his face. "Who says I don't?"

"I'd lay good money that none of you three canines are taken."

"Are you?"

Talia looked down, her mind sliding over unwelcome memories. "No. I was engaged, but I broke it off." Talia pulled away from him, suddenly not wanting a male touch.

"Whatever he was like, I'm not that guy," Lore said softly, the tug of his fingers protesting her movement. "Just so you know."

What was he saying? Was this some sort of flirtation? Talia nearly stammered. "No, you're the guy who chained me up."

"I had my reasons."

"You kissed me." It was an accusation.

Without his body next to hers, the cold air wrapped around her.

He gave a low laugh. "Was it a bad kiss?"

He moved forward, as if he might kiss her again, but she planted a hand on his chest and used her vampire strength to hold him back.

Talia frowned up at him. He was backlit by the light over the door, his features blurred by shadow. Above, there was a break in the clouds where the stars glittered like chips of ice. She was balanced on the point of decision: go or stay, trust him or run like hell. She couldn't think past the memory of his lips on hers.

How can I be breathless when I don't breathe? Irritation and an unwanted desire chased each other in an annoying loop.

"What do you expect from me?" she said, her voice a mere whisper.

Lore gave a smile that was at once sad and amused. "I don't expect anything. I want you to come back inside and help me find Belenos."

He held out his hand.

She dropped her arm, no longer pushing him away. He didn't try to close the gap, but stood there, waiting.

Talia felt the night closing in on her. A few flakes fell out of the darkness, catching on her sleeve. Running from Belenos had worked for a while. She'd built a life that wasn't ideal, but she'd been able to teach and no one, especially no man, had interfered. Yet now her freedom was withering away again, bit by bit.

"The snow isn't going to let me get away, is it? I bet all the roads out of town are blocked."

Gently, Lore reached out and caught her hand. His was warm, engulfing hers in welcome heat. "Come inside. I'll put on a fire."

She followed him inside, wondering how much she dared trust the moment.

Chapter 18

"This is Errata Jones taking the early shift on CSUP for Oscar Ottwell, who will be returning to us next Monday. Happy holidays, Oscar. I hope Santa Claws filled your stocking to the brim.

"To resume our coverage of current affairs in Fairview: Rumors are everywhere about who's in town for the election. We've heard about everyone from the Headless Horseman to Elvis checking in to our Spookytown hotels, but what's fact and what's fiction? Well, I'll give you one clue, my nighttime faithful. Not everyone is friendly.

"We've not been able to confirm this report, but word has it Hunters are in town. Lock your doors, my furry friends. The bogeymen are out and about and just to freshen up your sense of dismay, I've put my pretty paws on a few of their how-to manuals. If I ever decide to skin myself, now I know the drill. Stay tuned for choice excerpts—and I warn you these may not be suitable for all listeners."

* * *

Thursday, December 30, 5:00 p.m.
Lore's condo

When Talia woke up, she was free.

She was still using Lore's wide bed, but this time she was between the sheets, curled up in the bliss of soft pillows and a thick comforter.

Lore had taken her out of the cold and back to the meeting. The gesture had felt oddly symbolic, especially after that first wave of fright she'd felt when meeting the others. Yes, she'd been isolated too long. Rejoining the group in the living room had been an emotional victory.

She'd take her triumphs where she could. Talia rolled over, feeling a slowness in her limbs that said she hadn't eaten enough yesterday. It was the same lassitude she'd felt after a bout of the flu. Not really sick anymore, but not really well, either. *How long am I going to remember details like that?* In ten years, was she going to remember the taste of apples? The glitter of sun on a swimming pool?

She stared at the window, tucking the comforter under her chin. There was still ice on the glass, and the snow was blowing in veils across the sky. Hard to tell if it was still falling, or just swirling around.

It had been a night like this when she'd tried to go home again. Christmastime, but her family didn't celebrate much of anything. She'd slipped out of her sire's house and walked for miles through the snow wearing nothing but bedroom slippers. Thinking clearly wasn't easy during that first year as a fledgling.

She'd come toward her father's house from the back, where there was a rising slope dotted with pine trees. Making her way down the dark, cold incline toward the familiar back gate, she'd slid from tree to tree, her hands scraping over the rough bark, her head reeling with the tingling scent of pine. The kitchen window had glowed softly, giving a certain grace to the tiny, hard-used house.

Through the window she could see the Arborite table with the silver legs, the padded chairs with tape over the rips in the vinyl. She'd eaten all her meals and done all her homework at that table. It was the one place her family came together twice a day, morning and night.

Until her mother went away, running back to her own people. Afterward, her father had taken away Mom's chair and put it in the garage. With that one gesture, he'd obliterated her place, erased her from the family home. Her father wasn't a learned man, but he understood symbolism.

The memory had penetrated Talia's addled brain enough to be cautious as she'd approached the house. With the instinct of a wounded dog, she'd come home to beg for help. If anyone knew how to reverse a vampire's curse, it would be her father and his cronies—but she remembered the chair. Her father worked in a world of absolutes.

When she'd gathered her courage and crept close enough to see in the kitchen window, her father and her uncle were eating dinner. Steam rose off the bowls of stew, reminding her that her feet were blocks of ice, and hunger—though not for stew—cramped her belly.

But now her seat was gone from the circle of chairs around the table. Gone the way of Mom's, vanishing from the family circle. She was no more to them now than a monster with a familiar face.

Talia had turned away, creeping back to the sire who had sucked the life from her body. Just as well. If she'd gone into the kitchen, someone would have died. They had always eaten with guns on the table, ready in case of attack. It was the Hunter way.

She'd been captured and Turned by the vampires out of vengeance. What a knee-slapper, to change the Hunter girl into the thing her family hated. Perhaps they thought her father would feel a pang, slicing off his daughter's head.

Now, *there* was a joke. He'd do his duty without a flicker of doubt. That was how they'd all been trained. Talia. Her brother. Ready to die or kill. The man who had been her fiancé, Tom, had died when she had, but oh so differently.

She couldn't think about Tom. They'd never really loved each other. Her father's choice for son-in-law, Tom had wanted the traditional Hunter home, and children to raise in the tribe. Talia wanted to please her dad, but not that much. She'd split up with Tom, but that didn't make what had happened any less horrific. And then there had been Max . . .

Talia rolled out of the bed, memories making her restless. If those nice monsters in the living room last night knew what she'd done over the years, the nonhuman lives she'd taken, they would have turned on her. Might still. She had to accept that truth.

But I can't run away. Michelle was murdered. I have to settle that score, no matter where that leads.

And she'd made progress. Now she knew it was Belenos she was hunting, and now she had her freedom. *As long as things suck less today than yesterday, I'm on a roll.*

She realized Lore had rehung the bedroom door while she'd been sunk in the deep sleep of the Undead— but he'd left it ajar. The dresser was piled with some of her personal belongings: clothes, toiletries, and her courier bag. Surprise stopped her in her tracks. Wouldn't a crime scene be locked up for a while? Had Lore used his talent with locks to get inside?

She grabbed the courier bag and laid it on the bed. When she unzipped it, the contents looked undisturbed: papers she was supposed to mark, library books, and the usual litter of pens and sticky notes. Beneath the papers, her netbook nestled in a side pocket. She grabbed it, caressing the smooth black surface. Police usually seized computers, didn't they? They would have taken her laptop for sure. Someone had made a mistake by leaving the netbook behind.

Flipping it open, she booted it up and went immediately to her e-mail account. There were three new messages in among the spam; all were from students. Just to be on the safe side, she left all of them unopened. She'd just been curious to see if anyone had noticed she was missing. Apparently not. If she'd still been part of the Hunter community, they'd have been over at her place the next day to see if she was sick. Even if the community was toxic, it had been a home.

She closed that browser window and opened another, tapping in the URL for a private site she'd discovered a few months ago. She keyed in a password—it had taken her some effort to figure it out, but not all that long, considering—and waited while the site let her in.

It was Hunter central, pulling in info from the European tribes as well as her own. The main component was message boards, a lot of them in languages other than English. She clicked open the one marked "North America" and scanned the new entries.

There he was. Max, her brother. She looked at the name with longing, wishing there was some way in hell she could let him know she was still here, still anxious to hear that he was all right. It was an itch as strong as any drug addiction, and just as hard to shake.

She read the message he had posted: "Following Big Red. Back later."

Big red was Hunter slang for vampires. Red for blood. Max was on a hunt. Or had been. The message was almost two weeks old. Worry clamped around her heart, squeezing painfully. *Why hasn't he posted since?*

A feeling of angst cramped her gut. Some of Belenos's clan had tried to be nice to her, even if she'd been nothing short of hostile. Slowly, reluctantly, she'd begun to see them as people. *Who were you going after, Max? Did they really deserve it?*

It wasn't the first time she'd had the thought, but it was the clearest. It made her stomach cramp with anxiety. *Don't kill anyone I know, okay?*

She logged out and closed the netbook, letting her hands linger on the cover. Afraid of detection, she never lingered on the site long. It was the only link she had to home, and she wasn't going to risk losing it—no matter how queasy news from her old life made her feel.

Sliding the netbook back into her bag, she went back to the pile of her belongings on the dresser. No ID, no guns, no money. The police had probably taken the first two, and Lore didn't know about the cash hidden under her bedroom floorboards. She might have to wait a while before she could safely retrieve it, but there was no question that she'd do it. She'd need money to make a fresh start someplace else.

Talia searched through the clothes, trying to find a complete outfit. It was a man's selection. Half were practical things—sturdy socks and plain T-shirts, her coat and sturdy boots—and the rest were filmy excerpts from the realm of male fantasy. *How embarrassing.* He'd obviously found her lingerie drawer. In the end, she settled on jeans and a sweater, and headed for the shower.

When she walked out of the bathroom, she heard a rustle and the low murmur of the television. She padded barefoot into the living room. A newspaper scattered the floor. Something that looked like a disemboweled toaster littered the coffee table, half-repaired.

Lore was leaning back on the couch, eyes closed. He looked utterly exhausted. His breath was coming on a slight snore.

Talia's approach hadn't wakened him. That wasn't a surprise. All vampires moved with near silence.

And she was lost in his good looks. He wasn't pretty, like Joe, but his features were cut cleanly, the bones broad and strong. It was the kind of face that would only improve with age. She wondered who he looked like, his mother or father. Which one had given him the slight cleft in the chin? Which one had passed on that sweep of dark eyelashes?

Where had he gotten that sense of fair play that made him protect a wanted vampire, just in case she was innocent? Yes, he'd held her prisoner, but he hadn't hurt her, and he'd let her go. Talia was well aware that it could have gone so very differently.

She took a silent step closer to the couch. Whatever sixth sense that made hellhounds good guardians kicked in. Lore started awake, bolting to his feet before he was fully conscious.

Talia held up her hands, palms out. "Easy. It's just me."

He relaxed, letting out a huge breath. "Sorry. I dozed off. I've been with the pack during the day and up most of the night."

"Pulling double shifts?"

"Yeah." He rubbed his eyes, sinking back onto the couch. "I dropped by to check on things here."

Check on me. Talia felt unaccountably warmed by the idea.

Lore scrubbed his face, as if to wake himself up. "I've got my best hounds looking for Belenos, but so far no joy. Last time he came, he hid right under our noses in the Castle. I don't think he'll try that one again, but he'll come up with something equally clever."

"We're only guessing that it's him."

"That's why I haven't raised a general alarm. I want proof before I start a panic." He looked up. "I got fresh blood. Will that hold you for an hour or two?"

"Uh, great. Thanks. I'll get some in a minute. And thank you for getting my stuff. You ran a risk to do that—I mean, it's bad enough you're hiding me, but you broke into a crime scene to get my toothbrush."

He looked up, clearly a little pleased with himself.

"The biggest risk was going through your closet. I could have been killed by an avalanche of shoes."

"Yeah, well, a girl needs her footwear." She sank onto the other end of the couch and looked at the TV. *Scooby-Doo* cartoons. "That your hero?"

"I thought it might inspire my detective skills."

She couldn't help a laugh. That earned her a grin. He had the best smile, all white teeth and mischief. Then she noticed how big he was, filling his end of the couch with long, muscled limbs.

Her mouth went dry, her palms prickling with unfocused nerves. She curled up, tucking her feet under her. As always, she was a little cold.

She could feel his body heat even with an arm's span between them. "What sort of things does an Alpha do for his pack?"

He made a dismissive gesture. "A lot of different things. I deal with the human world on the pack's behalf. I represent the hounds on the council of nonhumans, so I'm the liaison with other species. We have a business that recycles things, like furniture and mechanical parts, and I run that. I settle disputes and oversee building projects—we're renovating a lot of the houses we bought to bring them up to code. The pack does a lot of security work in Fairview, and I'm the deputy sheriff, except right now I'm the sheriff in charge."

No wonder he's tired. But she could see he was proud, too. The hounds had come from nothing. Their success owed a lot to his drive. "What's it like, being in a pack? Do your parents live here?"

Leaning forward, he picked up a piece of the toaster and fiddled with it. "My parents died in the Castle."

"I'm sorry."

He gave a slight shrug, universal guy-speak for something he couldn't or didn't want to talk about. "Being part of a pack is never being alone, even when you need to be. That's why I have this place. I get a bit of peace and quiet."

"You have a lot of responsibilities." *Understatement of the decade.*

"An Alpha is father to his people." He gave the words an ironic twist. "Seriously, they're my family. Why wouldn't I do what I could to help them?"

Talia envied him with a swift, sharp pain. Even with everything his position demanded, it had to be worth it. He wasn't alone. She looked down, staring at the tweedy pattern of the couch cover.

He passed her a section of the paper. "Fashion column?"

She took it automatically, not sure why he'd offered it. Then she realized it gave her something to hide behind, a safety screen. For a guy—for a *demon-dog*—Lore was surprisingly perceptive. Enough to make a girl self-conscious.

She folded the section back to see the editorial. It *was* her first go-to spot in the paper, though she wasn't sure how he'd known. Oh, wait. He'd seen her closet. She read the caption under a photo of a woman in a boxy dress. "Wow. The return of shoulder pads. Now, that's real horror."

From the corner of her eye, she caught him watching her, his dark eyes intent. She understood that look. He liked what he saw. *Oh, God.*

She lowered the paper, her face turning to him with infinite slowness. He was drawing her like a magnet. Like a flower following the sun she'd never see again.

This is insane. Yet she was doing exactly what her body demanded down to her last cell. Her mind, on the other hand, was numb with shock. Their lips met with a bump, and she realized she'd leaned into the kiss with more hunger than she'd thought.

I kissed him! Where the hell did that *come from?*

But she knew. The moment had been building for the past couple of days. Curiosity. Attraction. A lingering wisp of anger. *Oh, God, he tastes good.* Savory. Spicy.

What began as exploration deepened in seconds. She shifted her weight to her knees so she could get closer to that delicious heat, feel the hard wall of his chest against her body. She braced her arms on his shoulders, leaning in, teasing, tugging at his mouth. She took her time, as if the kiss held a lingering echo of some delectable treat.

His tongue flicked across the bottom of her canine teeth, a quick tease. Her jaws tingled with the urge to bite, egged on by the feel of his broad hand sliding down her ribs, his thumb brushing the edge of her breast. She inhaled sharply, feeling his hand slide beneath her sweater, caressing her back.

Two could play at that. She ran her lips down the angle of his jaw, her tongue flicking the pulse that beat there, hot and salty. At the same time, she worked her fingers underneath the bottom of his T-shirt and began to explore upward, letting her fingers find the hard ridges of muscle that flexed beneath her touch. All that hard work he did paid off. No gym membership required here.

His fingers were playing with the edge of her bra, tracing the lace along the cups, giving feather-light strokes to her nipples. A burning low in her belly made her want to squirm in delicious ways, to explore the hardness beneath the zipper of his jeans. The urge to bite was growing into an ache. Her mouth was watering, already feeling the slide of flesh against her teeth.

Talia pulled away before instinct took over. She whimpered in frustration, her lips still seeking his even as she moved to slide off his lap. Sex and biting were inextricably linked for vampires. Sex also meant undressing, and that meant uncovering her tattoo.

Danger.

Lore's eyes met hers, the knowledge of her arousal in his dark gaze. It was a very male look: sure of himself and filled with anticipation. He had only to tighten his grip, and she was his. She felt his muscles flex, the calluses on his wide palms rasping against the soft flesh of her waist. His strength closed around her, pointedly keeping her in place. She could read it in the set of his lips: She would surrender and like it—whenever and as often as he chose.

Talia's mouth went dry, even as other parts of her grew wet in response to his challenge. Fear and desire were a potent brew, and with him she might enjoy the taste.

Yet he released her, his fingers reluctant to let her go even as she drew away and straightened her sweater.

"I can't," she said, her teeth near chattering with the repressed tension in those two words.

The look in his eyes said she would and she could.

"Not yet?" he replied after a long moment. "I'll take a rain check." His smile promised everything she'd just shied from—everything dark and dangerous and private.

Rain check? Oh, God, let this drought end. But how could it? How could it ever?

"I'm not the right kind of girl. You don't know what you're getting into," Talia said, wishing that didn't sound so clichéd. But it was true. *My daddy will skin you alive. Right after he stakes me, that is.*

"I could have a nice hellhound girl if I wanted one." Lore's head tilted, and he gave her a mischievous look. "Maybe you're my walk on the wild side."

Talia dropped her jaw. Her love life could have been summed up on the side of a cereal box. "You've got to be kidding me."

"I am. A little."

The phone rang. Lore picked it up. "Hello?"

Talia grabbed a couch cushion, thinking she might smother him with it, but then she heard Perry's voice, sounding excited. Lore's expression grew intent.

"What?" he asked. "No, don't worry. I'll come to you."

He hung up the phone and stood up in one gesture.

"What's going on?" Talia demanded.

When Lore looked down at her, she nearly ducked. Anger and triumph flared in his eyes.

"Perry says he's got proof that Belenos is here. More surveillance video."

"That was fast!"

Lore gave a tight smile. "Perry was sure to point out that he knows all the best shortcuts. I'm going to go see what he's got. Maybe there will be enough of a clue to catch the king."

Thursday, December 30, 6:00 p.m.
University of Fairview

Lore had to go to Perry because the werewolf was stuck at the university. In the midmorning, a power outage had made the pipes freeze and burst, flooding the downstairs computer lab. Plumbers had made it in, but Perry was called to assess the damage and do what he could to rescue his digital babies.

Lore had been able to drive his truck as far as the university's main parking lot, but going was slow even with chains. Driving in real winter conditions, he'd quickly learned, was a question of concentration and planning. That didn't mean more than ten percent of Fairview's residents concentrated or planned. With so many cars spinning out of control, telephone poles and mailboxes were becoming endangered species.

He was almost pathetically grateful when he was able to park and make the rest of the way on four feet. Now he was making good time along the path to the Cambridge Building, taking the deep drifts in long bounds. Lore rounded the corner of the building, catching a blast of damp, bitter wind in the face.

He hoped Perry's evidence was good. Frankly, Lore was worried that the airports would be cleared and

Omara would show up. The queen was overwhelming at the best of times, and Lore's plate was more than full as it was. With Belenos, rogues, murder, the election and the Prophets knew what else running amok on his watch, a lesser hound would have been babbling by now. Lore was keeping it together, but he was starting to feel punch-drunk.

The strain was clearly affecting his judgment, if he was spending couch time with Talia. What was he doing? He was supposed to be choosing a mate from the pack, not flirting with vampires. Especially vampires—if Errata's sources were right—with possible slayer connections. He wasn't going to jump to conclusions, but that would explain why she could fight like a professional and why she was so closed-mouth about her past. But whatever she'd been, things had changed. What the hell had happened to her?

It would be easy, even smart, to distance himself from a woman who was not only the wrong species but most likely had been raised in the archenemy's camp. But she was in trouble, and he couldn't help himself. Her kiss was like nothing else. Once he'd tasted her, there was no going back.

Was his attraction the appeal of forbidden fruit? Was it rebellion because he didn't want Mavritte or one of the other she-hounds?

No.

Talia was beautiful and smart, and she was brave. He didn't know all her story, but she was clearly a survivor. No one mourned as deeply as she did without knowing how to love. No one sat down to swap information with a roomful of shape-shifters unless she was prepared to meet them halfway. And to run away from Belenos *and* steal from him? That showed the kind of spirit Lore wanted guarding his back.

The Alpha couple was a partnership. He'd led his people out of hell, and then gone back for the stragglers.

He needed a mate who could do the same in a pinch. He needed someone who wasn't afraid to kick down the bedroom door and come out swinging a baseball bat. To put it in terms his beast understood, she had to smell right.

Talia was all that and more.

He was spending that couch time for a very good reason. He intended to have her. Hellhound tradition be damned; he wasn't going to pass up a woman like that before he even got to know her. *It's the twenty-first century, and we're not in hell anymore. Get with the program.*

Lore ducked his head and forged on, finding his way by the occasional emergency lights over the building entrances. He'd just about zoned out, hypnotized by the rhythmic sound of his paws in the snow, when a doorway opened and Perry stuck his head out. "I've got hot coffee! Fido's balls, you look like an Arctic troll!"

Hot coffee! Hallelujah! Lore was about a hundred feet away. He shifted his gait to a higher gear.

He almost felt the shot flick through the air before he heard the crack. It smacked into the doorframe inches from Perry's head. He ducked back inside as Lore made a bound for the corner of the building.

Sniper rifle, Lore thought, morphing back into human form. He dug for his sidearm through layers of coat and sweater. A gunshot was a big jump from beheading with a sword, but then Perry wasn't a vampire. Lore would have bet his hind paw the rifle used silver bullets.

Lore sighted down his firearm and searched the roofline of the building opposite the doorway. It was the most likely spot for a marksman to hide, but with no moon, all was inky shadows. Hellhound sight was good in the dark, but not good enough.

He listened instead, trying to catch the sound of a boot scraping tile, a window sliding closed. He was far away, but sound carried oddly in the cold, dark silence.

All he heard was the hiss of blowing snow and the rustle of his own clothes as he breathed.

Then, out of the corner of his eye, he saw the door swing open again. *No, stay inside!*

Perry threw something just as the rifle cracked once more. The object flew upward in an arc worthy of a professional pitcher, heading straight for where the gunman hid. It started small, no bigger than a baseball, but it grew as it spun through the air, blooming into a ball of light that drowned the campus in an eerie blue-green light. Lore shielded his eyes with his arm, squinting through the glare. He saw a man on the roof leap to his feet, falling back into the shadows. Lore squeezed off a shot, but the angle was bad. He got a glimpse of dark clothes, but nothing more.

The ball exploded, fountaining sparks like a Roman candle. The campus fluttered with plumes of blue-green light, the falling stars hissing as they hit the snow. Sorcery or chemistry? Lore wasn't sure—Perry was adept at both—but it had bought him a glimpse of the suspect.

He blinked away the last afterimages from the exploding ball. Scanning the building again, he saw nothing—no shooter, no sign of movement. Crouching low, Lore crossed the distance to the other building. A bullet whined past his ear. He ducked and rolled, floundering a little in the heavy snow, but came up close to the building wall.

That shot had come from a different angle. The shooter was on the move. He got to the end of the building and, gun at the ready, rounded the corner. There was a door, open just a little because the heavy, wet snow had jammed it.

Lore slipped inside. With the power out, it was dark. The door led straight to a large spiral staircase that wound around a huge, hanging metal sculpture. A mental calculation said the last shot had probably come from the third floor. Lore started up the stairs, hoping the shooter wasn't simultaneously descending somewhere else in the building. It was the best he could do. There were too many exits to cover, so a fighting chance was all he had.

Just enough light came in the stairwell windows to find his way. Stopping at the second floor, he strained to catch any sound of movement. A cold breeze stirred the metal shards of the sculpture, making them turn on their long, thin chains. Nerves chattered at the edge of Lore's mind, but he tuned them out.

Instead, he started up the stairs again. He'd gone three steps when he heard a single *scuff*. He froze. Overhead, two of the metal shapes bumped together in the air currents with a sepulchral clang.

Lore backed down the stairs, gun aimed at the second-floor landing. An electricity-deprived soft drink machine dripped softly, ice giving up the ghost. Lore peered down the hallway leading from the stairwell to the classrooms. A shadow flickered across the far window so fast it seemed a trick of the eye. A ping of grim satisfaction ran through him.

Quarry spotted. Now the real work began.

He slipped out of the stairwell, picking up speed. When he reached the window where he'd seen the figure, a wet footprint glistened on the tile floor, just visible in the light from the window. Lore crouched, squinting at the mark. He could tell it was the right size for an adult human male, but not much else. He followed the direction of the print, heading for the south side of the building.

There were fewer windows there. There seemed to be no emergency lights in that part the building, or else something had malfunctioned. All Lore could see was the outline of an intersecting hallway ahead. He moved cautiously, aware he could easily run into an open door or bit of wall. He'd survive that, but perhaps not the noise he'd make.

But then he noticed light creeping along the floor. It was coming from the left, up ahead, where he guessed the shooter had gone. As he drew nearer, Lore raised his weapon, focused on the south corridor as it slowly came into view.

He stopped midstride. The shooter was walking casually down the hall, his rifle—a box-type semiautomatic—slung over one shoulder. He had a flashlight in the other hand. Lore got an impression of someone fit and tall with collar-length hair—but not Belenos. Lore remembered the vampire king as a bigger man. Who was this guy? Lore took aim.

"On your knees! Now!" he roared.

The light vanished. The figure didn't turn or even flinch, but bolted like a flushed rabbit. Lore fired, hoping to scare the guy into stopping, but no such luck. Lore ran after him, afraid to stop and change to his hound form. The seconds it would take would be enough to lose his prey.

He'd gone about fifty steps when he lost sight of his quarry. He stopped, listening, but there was nothing to hear. Instinct made him fall to the ground a second before another bullet zinged through the air. Lore saw the muzzle flash. The guy was using a classroom door for cover. Lore returned fire, the bullet striking sparks off the door handle.

The guy dove for the emergency exit a few feet away. They had traveled a nearly complete loop back to the main stairwell. Lore cut down a side hall and aimed for that instead, hoping to head the shooter off when they reached the main-floor landing. Firefights in a stairwell weren't pretty, and he'd as soon have the element of surprise on his side.

He galloped down the stairs and jumped the last

steps, dashing to the fire exit door across the building foyer and ripping it open. He was late. The shooter was already two flights below, heading for the basement. Thankfully, the emergency lights were working here. Lore charged after him, stripping off his suffocating coat along the way.

Closing the gap between them, Lore followed the shooter into the subterranean warren of language labs, lockers, and bare concrete. Lore got a few more details— the guy was wearing a watch cap and black clothes. Caucasian. Human? Graffiti snaked along the walls as they streaked past. The runner turned, crashing through the fire doors that passed into a tunnel that ran between this building and the computer lab.

This is what Lore had been hoping for: an easy shot in an area where there was nowhere to hide. The runner had gone straight into a perfect kill zone.

"Freeze!" he bellowed, the walls ringing with the word.

Without stopping, the shooter turned to his right and opened a door in the side of the tunnel.

What the fuck? Lore charged toward him. He'd been in this underground passageway before. There was no door.

But the shooter passed through it.

Lore slowed, fighting momentum, ready to grab this unexpected doorknob.

But there wasn't one. No knob. No door. No seam where the door might have been. There was only grubby concrete wall, and a tingling sensation when he touched his hand to the concrete blocks. *Magic.* Magic not even a hellhound's power over doorways could break.

Fury shocked him, leaving his skin tingling and raw. It took him beyond swearing. He simply backed away, turned, and walked quickly to the end of the tunnel to the Cambridge underground entrance. His jaw clenched, and eerie, cold anger gripped him like an invisible beast.

Sorcery. Hate. Prey. Escape. Tear. Bite.

As he stalked into the basement computer lab, he could smell damp concrete. A mop and bucket in one corner reminded him there'd been a burst pipe. He walked up the wheelchair ramp to the main floor, wondering where Perry was. Lore pulled out his cell and pushed the speed dial to Perry's number, but it went to voice mail.

The ramp ended near the door. Lore looked around, noticing a red smear on the wall. *Blood?* Automatically, he looked down. There was more spatter on the floor.

No! Perry had been hit. A trail led away from the door, the teardrop shape of the drips pointing down the hall.

Lore ran in that direction, pulling out his cell phone again. He hit redial, listening for Perry's phone. He heard the tinny strains of "Blue Moon" coming from a cluster of couches up ahead. Lore sprinted toward the sound, a sick feeling in his gut.

Perry was lying on one of the couches, shivering and drenched in blood.

Chapter 19

"Silver bullets?" Talia breathed into the phone.

She could hear the tension in Lore's voice. "The bullet was a safety slug filled with silver pellets. The penetration wasn't deep, but a lot of metal got into his bloodstream."

Talia knew very well what that meant, because she'd used those rounds herself. Organ damage, and then death. *Oh, God, Perry.* It was a bad way to go, but at least it would be relatively fast. "Meet me at the front door of the hospital in half an hour."

She hung up the phone before Lore could argue. Talia had been mostly okay with staying at the condo while Lore went to the university, but now she couldn't sit around any longer. No one used those slugs but professional monster-killers. They were hard to get, expensive, custom-made, and this was her area of expertise.

Among the Hunters, she had been one of the very best shots. She knew where to get specialized ammunition, who made it in which back room, and what their maker's marks looked like. Safety slugs mushroomed on impact, so conventional ballistics was tricky, but there might be other clues as to where it came from. With a stroke of luck, she might even figure out who pulled the trigger. Perry had found the images that proved she had come home too late to kill Michelle. She owed him whatever she could offer.

A sixth sense told her to hurry. Fortunately, she'd already solved the problem of weapons. A search earlier that evening had revealed the locker where Lore kept his toys. There was a lock box protected by one of those zappy spells, but she found a knife in a sheath she could strap to her calf. It had probably been meant for Lore's forearm, but whatever.

In a determined flurry, she bundled into her coat and ran out into the snow. A few of the main buses were running, and there was no way she could be identified under a hood, scarf, mitts, and layers of sweaters. Everyone out on the streets looked like a bundle of knitting projects. She doubted anyone could even tell she was Undead, much less pick her out of a lineup.

The bus took longer than she expected, but it successfully dropped her at the edge of the hospital grounds. The parking lot was largely empty, but plenty of people had slipped, skidded, and snow shoveled their way into Emergency. The desk at the entrance was mobbed, making it easy to simply walk past. The nurses were too busy to care about one young woman wandering by, craning her neck to find one tall hellhound.

The gray tiled floor was covered in wet footprints. Talia could see the occupants had filled every bench. She caught the stink of wet wool and coats that had gone too long without dry cleaning. Chatter filled the place, mostly folks swapping bad weather stories.

After the quiet of Lore's bedroom, Talia was overwhelmed by the noise. Plus, she was hungry. She'd refused the icky refrigerated blood and now she was regretting it. The ambient smell of the hospital wasn't helping. Beneath all that antiseptic was ... *Oh, don't go there.*

The sight of Lore leaning against the wall, one leg bent and arms crossed, banished all thoughts of hospital food. The memory of his taste brought saliva to her mouth. She walked up to him, untying the long striped scarf she'd swiped from his drawer.

"Hey," she said.

"Hey." Now that she was close, she could see the strain around his eyes.

"How is he?"

"The doctors put him on hemodialysis to clean as much of the toxin out of his blood as they can. They say it's the only thing that works on werewolves."

"What's the prognosis?"

"They don't know yet, but at least they've got plenty of blood donors. I think all of Pack Silvertail showed up."

They reached the elevators and Lore punched the button. "Perry was lucky to get a bed. Not all hospitals are equipped to treat shifters."

Talia understood. A lot of people still believed that werebeasts would automatically heal if they changed form. That worked with small injuries, but few could summon enough energy to change after trauma and massive blood loss.

The elevator arrived, disgorging an orderly pushing an empty gurney. They got in and the doors closed with a shudder. With glacial slowness, it started going up. They were alone, but she could smell the hundreds of warm bodies that had come and gone throughout the day, some cleaner than others.

Talia glanced at Lore. A deep frown line creased his brow. She reached out and took his hand, squeezing it. Startled, he glanced down, then squeezed back.

"I'm glad you came," he said.

"It's good not to be alone when things go bad."

He couldn't quite manage a smile, but the worry line relaxed.

The elevator doors opened and they exited on the third floor.

"I hate hospitals," Talia grumbled. Health care administrators seemed to search the world over to find the most stomach-turning shades of paint. This ward had walls the hue of squished caterpillar guts.

She trailed Lore down the corridor, unbuttoning her coat. They'd rounded the corner, heading to the area marked NONHUMAN PATIENTS when Lore slowed, putting a hand on her arm. Up ahead she could see a cluster of people hanging around the doorway. Many of them looked related—lean and compact, with brown, wavy hair. They moved like they were on springs, filled with restless energy. A few paced back and forth, the others doing their best to stare down the nurse. *Wolves.*

There were a few more who weren't shifters—including a tall, dark-haired human. Handsome in a square-jawed, no-nonsense way that belonged to action movies and cop shows. *Baines.*

"Oh!" She pulled aside, hugging a pillar.

Lore stopped dead, moving so that he blocked the hallway. "He doesn't know you're innocent."

And the guy with the evidence she needed lay in a hospital bed with poison in his blood. Slowly, Talia turned her back to the crowd. All her nerves were on alert, all the colors and sounds of the hospital suddenly too sharp. "Why don't you go check on Perry? I'll meet you in the cafeteria in an hour."

"Baines is looking for me, too."

"Should we go and come back later?"

Lore looked unhappy, but shrugged. "Baines doesn't have anything on me. He just wants to talk. I'll get rid of him."

"Then go check on Perry. I'll stay out of sight. And

look, I know a thing or two about specialty ammunition. I want to get a look at what's left of the slug."

"That's evidence. Baines is going to want it."

Talia bit her lip, wondering if she was saying too much. "Whatever he can do, I'm better. Trust me on this."

Worry furrowed his forehead again. "I'll see what I can do. Be careful."

"I will. I'll see you in a bit."

Kissing her lightly, he squeezed her hand and left her there. Talia stuck her hand in her pocket, wishing she could keep the warmth of him a moment longer.

Wow. Weren't they in couple mode?

There's no way it can last. There's too many reasons why it won't work, starting with the fact that you're a monster and *a monster-killer. How's that going to play with his pack?*

Talia hunched against her inner voice, wishing it would just shut up for ten seconds. She liked what was going on with Lore. The fact that he had protected her made her feel worth protecting and, dammit, she meant to enjoy that for as long as she could.

She went back to the elevator, taking it to the main level. It wasn't hard to find the cafeteria from there. The greasy smell might as well have been a flashing sign.

Talia suspected the place was designed with the hospital's future revenues in mind. It was the typical mix of cardiac-arresting doughnuts and fried food, dirty tables, and lighting so bad no one would notice that she was a vampire. About the only things she could ingest there were the cashier or herb tea. She was contemplating her options when she saw Errata at one of the tables by the wall, scribbling in a notebook.

She was about to walk over when she caught sight of someone else out of the corner of her eye. *What the hell?*

Talia turned, frowning in the direction she thought she'd seen her brother. *That's crazy. Max is thousands of miles away.* Shaking herself, she blinked the image away.

It was unsettling. She'd been thinking about him and had seen his name on the bulletin board that morning. Obviously, she was missing him a lot.

Talia headed over and sat down opposite Errata. The werecougar looked up. Her eyes were red from crying.

"Hi," Talia said softly. "Lore's gone upstairs. I'm waiting for him here."

Errata closed the notebook and took a swallow of coffee. She looked like a woman trying to compose herself. "Why Perry? Everybody loves him."

Talia felt a pang for her. There was never only one victim. "He had evidence that he was going to show Lore. Maybe somebody knew about it." By *somebody*, she meant Belenos.

Errata gave her a look that said she understood what Talia was getting at. "But how?"

"Or what? Do you know what he found?"

Errata shook her head. "I've been at CSUP all day. We're short-staffed because of holidays. I was going to meet him late tonight. Then Lore called me at the station."

Once again, Talia thought she saw Max walk by in the distance. This time she got a better look, and it made her sit bolt upright. "Excuse me." She stood up, feeling suddenly light-headed. "I just saw someone I know."

"Is everything okay? You don't look happy about it."

Without answering, Talia strode quickly between the tables, heading for the corridor where she thought she'd seen him pass. It had been a glimpse, his head and shoulders above the half wall that separated the eatery from the main hallway, but his profile had been clear. Talia knew Max's face as well as her own.

What the blazes was he doing in Fairview?

A chill ran over her body as she put puzzle pieces together. There weren't a lot of options. Max did only one thing: He hunted, and he used silver safety slugs. Perry had survived, and professionals came back to finish the job if they didn't succeed the first time. As long as her brother was here, Perry was in danger.

No, no, I must be having a brain cramp. This can't be real. She reached the hallway and looked around, dreading and wishing for a glimpse of Max's dark head.

She nearly missed him in the hospital crowd. He was turning into the service stairway that led down to the basement. The tension in Talia's shoulders cranked up a notch. *What's down there?* She ran to follow, wishing she had more than a knife to defend herself.

Max was her brother, but he would likely kill her on sight. Stupidly, that didn't stop her from longing to cry out after him. She wanted to see recognition in his eyes one more time.

Slipping through the door, she stood on the landing for a moment, listening to the sound of footfalls descending. Why was he going down there? There was no underground parking at the hospital. That was all outdoors.

Silently, she followed, scanning for some clue as to what drew Max. Weren't morgues usually in the basement? *Creepy.*

She reached the bottom of the stairs, putting her hand on the knob of the fire door that separated the landing from whatever lay beyond. Nerves urged her to hurry, to try to catch up, but experience told her to play it cool. She listened a moment, and was rewarded with the *shush-thump, shush-thump* of a heartbeat. He'd heard someone coming, and was waiting on the other side of the door. Talia debated, her hand hovering above the door handle. Abandon the chase, or find out what her brother might know? That meant confronting him.

The quiet was broken by the sound of a round being chambered. He knew he was being followed.

This was a dance she'd done before, but it usually ended in a death. She'd have to be good, very good, to make this end well.

She grabbed the door handle and pushed it open with

as much force as she could muster. In the same gesture, she tucked and rolled, making herself as tiny a target as possible. Max fired at where her head had been moments before.

Regaining her feet, she grabbed him from behind and slammed his face into the painted concrete of the wall. He grunted with surprise, dropping the semiautomatic. Talia yanked his head back, using his hair as a handle.

"Talia!" His voice held pure horror.

"Sh!"

Max was silent.

She waited, forcing away the chorus in her heart that was cheering, *It's Max! It's him!* Were they safe? After the gunshots, she expected a sudden rush of security guards, or morgue workers. Somebody.

Nobody came. For whatever reason—budget cuts? shift change? the weather?—the basement was deserted. A shielding spell? There were such things, to keep passersby from noticing a crime. If someone had used one, she wouldn't necessarily know.

"Talia." Her name came out in a croak.

That yearned-for look of recognition was in his eyes. She breathed in the familiar scent of him, childhood coming back in a rush of remembered laughter, fights, shared meals, and shared secrets. He was solid proof that she'd had a life and people who loved her.

But that life hadn't been kind to him. Once, dark-haired Maxim Rostov would have given Joe a run for his money in the hot-guy department. The few years since she'd seen Max had been hard. He was only thirty, but he looked haggard, his dark eyes eating up the rest of his face. In his own way, he'd suffered as much as she had. *Poor Max.*

"You!" he snarled. "What are you doing here?"

She flinched at the rage in his voice. "I ran away. I had to get away from Belenos. This was on the other side of the continent."

He was immobilized, her fingers laced through his hair, her other hand pressing him into the wall. She was stronger than him now, and she could smell the fear coming off him in waves. Tears welled in her eyes. *She* was doing this to him. His little sister. "If I let you go, are you going to try to kill me?"

She hoped he would say no, and wished even harder that she could believe him. "I still love you. You're still my brother."

"You bit me!"

It had been one of the king's embellishments of cruelty. He'd taken both brother and sister, but Turned only one. Then he served up the other for dessert. Barely days old, burning bright with hunger, she'd had no self-control.

Guilt seared her like acid. "I'm so sorry."

Max bucked, struggling to get away. "Bullshit."

"It's true. I am. At least Belenos let you live."

"He made me a venom junkie."

That shocked her. Then Talia understood what had happened. Her brother hadn't been for killing. The vampire king had other suffering planned for him. Dozens of bites. Dozens of doses of addictive venom. Degradation of the chief Hunter's son had been the objective.

She hadn't known. "Oh, Max."

"I kicked it." Slowly, he turned his head to fix her with furious eyes. The movement must have cost him a clump of hair. "I beat what he did to me, which is more than I can say for you."

His disgust hit her with the force of a blow. She felt her lips growing cold with emotional shock. "He made me dead. That's a little harder to cure."

Suddenly Max blinked hard, confusion crumpling his face. "I know. You're one of *them* now."

"I'm still Talia."

He began to silently sob, his anger finally giving way to grief.

"Oh, Max." She bent close, meaning to kiss his cheek, but he reared away, nearly breaking free.

"Don't bite me! For God's sake don't bite me!"

It was an addict's cry not to send him back to that corrosive hell.

"Don't bite me, Talia, please!"

She hadn't meant to, but he shouldn't have put the idea in her head. Talia felt her mouth going dry, parched as if it were stuffed with dust and ashes. His struggling didn't help. Fear, struggles, heat, and the scent of blood and sweat added up to only one thing: prey.

Suddenly, Talia was shaking with hunger. She was starving. It had been days since she'd had a proper meal—too long for someone as newly Turned as she was. All she could see was fragile skin, all she could smell was his panic. Older vampires would make a game of seduction. She was too raw for anything but selfish urgency.

She began to salivate.

When she struck, skin would break with a springy resistance that reminded her of grapes. As her fangs breached flesh, there would be the first gush of hot comfort, and the blessed release of the venom. Her teeth ached with it, a pressure that built the hungrier she became. Now it would discharge, flowing from her into his veins and sending him into bliss. Oh, yes, she would give him a rush of pleasure.

In just a moment.

Unless she could hang on. She *had* to hang on. It was her brother. That would be weird and wrong. The first time, it had been a cruel trick. This time, she was in the driver's seat. She could resist.

She hoped.

Max fought back, egging on the predator inside her. Talia couldn't see his face and didn't want to. The intimacy of the moment wasn't something she wanted to remember. Tears leaked from the corners of her eyes as she struggled against the urge to take him. She was panting, trying to find enough air to relieve the ache that racked her whole body.

Back away, back away, back away.

She could almost accept the blood-drinking thing. What she really hated was the loss of control.

A clattering of heels broke her hunger trance. The door burst open and Errata nearly smashed into them. Talia looked up, hoping she wasn't sticking out her fangs like some B-movie Draculette.

The werecougar was staring at her openmouthed. "What are you doing?"

Duh, isn't it obvious? Sucking on a victim just outside the local morgue. Saves on body fluid cleanup. How's your night been going?

"Hairballs, something told me I should check on you. Talia, talk to me." Errata took a slow step forward. "Who is this guy?"

Talia swallowed hard before finding her voice. It came out strained and hoarse. "My brother."

Errata grabbed Max's arm, pulling him out of Talia's clutches. "Then don't eat him. That would make Thanksgiving really awkward."

Talia felt an irrational urge to yank him back, but reason was starting to claw its way through the feeding frenzy. Max flattened himself against the wall, glaring at Talia. Errata had her phone out, calling somebody for help.

Talia bent and picked up the semiautomatic, her fingers shaking with need denied. She couldn't bring herself to look Max in the face.

So much for the movie-of-the-week family reunion.

Errata put away her phone. She looked from Talia to Max curiously, taking in his nondescript black clothes, the gun, and his glare. Her look said she had him pegged as very, very bad news. "What's going on? What's he doing here?"

"Is this your friend, Tal?" An unpleasant leer came

over Max's face. "I always wanted to meet a girl who was all pussy."

His head whipped to the side, smacking against the wall. Errata's hand had moved faster than Talia's eyes could follow.

"Next time, the claws are out," Errata hissed. "I don't care whose brother you are."

"Don't!" Talia automatically stepped forward to defend him.

The malevolence in his eyes froze her where she stood. *What's happened to him? He was never this cruel.*

But who was she kidding? Hunters killed monsters. Would they sweat a little rudeness? *But he's not like that. I know him.*

Errata gave her a look that was close to pity.

The door slammed open again; this time Baines burst through. He flashed a badge. "Derek Baines, Supernatural Crimes Division. Stay right where you are."

Lore arrived a moment later, his expression baleful. He looked at Errata. "The detective was standing right next to me when you called."

When he caught sight of Talia, his expression said his worst fears had been confirmed. Detective Baines didn't realize it, but he'd just found the elusive Talia Rostova. She slid the gun into her pocket and out of sight.

Baines took a step toward Max, but he looked at Errata. "There was an altercation?"

With her stomach turning hard and heavy, Talia began a slow fade down the hallway one step at a time. Until her name was cleared, she was in trouble if the police figured out who she was. If she was on that frickin' registry, they'd hand her straight back to Belenos.

But this was Max. Was she going to abandon him? Was she going to sell him out as the gunman who'd shot Perry?

But he's my brother.

The worst they had on him was nearly being eaten

by his vampire sister. Max would be okay. Talia had his gun—they wouldn't even pick him up on a weapons charge.

He shot Perry. He tried to murder someone.

But that was what Hunters did. That was the family business.

Perry had helped her.

But it's Max.

Talia quickened her pace, panting from the tug-of-war inside her. She'd put two doorways between herself and the cop. The harsh overhead lighting showed the lines between each floor tile, making the hallway into a game board of squares. Talia felt like a pawn sneaking out of the path of the rooks and knights.

Max shrugged. "Look around. Obviously you've got no reason to hold me."

"Give me a minute," Baines said dryly. "You're already starting to annoy me."

"Hey, I'm the victim. These chicks are psycho." He pointed at Errata. "This one hit me and *that* one bit me."

For the first time, Baines looked directly at Talia. She saw recognition light in his eyes.

Shit!

"Wait," said Lore, a considering tone in his voice. "I know this guy."

Max took that moment to shove past Errata and bolt in Talia's direction.

Lore stabbed his finger at the running figure. "He's the gunman from the university!"

"What?" Errata exclaimed, a world of trouble in the one word.

Max moved fast, pumping arms and legs in a desperate rush to freedom. He covered the distance to Talia in a few strides. Instinctively, she grabbed for his arm. She felt her sharp nails dig into the cloth of his jacket, tearing through to the skin beneath, but he kept running, shaking her off as if she were a pesky dog.

Talia stumbled, bouncing off the wall, but lunged after him. "Max! Come back!"

Her boots slid on the polished floor, struggling for a grip. She heard Lore calling her name, but her eyes fixed on the back of Max's jacket.

She couldn't leave everything unresolved. He couldn't get away.

With a thunder of echoing footfalls, the others were coming after them. Baines was human-slow and would be left at the back of the pack. Talia, on the other hand, was a vampire with a head start. There was no way Max could outrun her. She dodged after him as he took a right turn. Signs hung from the ceiling, announcing what lay down each corridor, but they flashed by before she could read them. Smells told her they were places with plenty of chemicals and equipment. These weren't the places where healing was done.

Max took a sudden left turn. Talia was only a few paces behind him now, and she was getting angry. "Stop!" she snarled.

He had to. At the end of the short hallway was a dead end, a blank wall with no door, no poster, nothing. But he didn't slow.

"Stop!" Talia cried again, now afraid he was simply going to brain himself like a bug on a windshield.

Max roared something she couldn't understand and jumped *through* the wall, his body melting into the painted concrete and disappearing. Talia's brain wrenched at the impossible, nonsensical sight. A blast of outrage singed her. Jumping through walls was cheating.

Just like Max to pull a fast one on his little sister.

So Talia did the only thing that made sense. She jumped after him.

Chapter 20

Talia expected she'd keep on running. That was the problem with leaping into the unknown. It was, really and truly, unknown.

Instead, she fell. It was probably only a dozen feet—nothing for a vampire—but she'd only just grasped what was happening when the ground leaped up to smack her. *Wham*. She lay for a moment, stunned and hurting. Her skin tingled like she'd stuck her whole body into an electrical current. Was that the aftermath of some sort of magic spell?

Cold, damp ground. Outdoors? No. Wherever she was lying was mercifully bare of snow.

She got to her hands and knees and looked around. Her first instinct was to call out for Max, but common sense stopped her. He was hostile, and she was horribly vulnerable. It was completely dark. Not nighttime dark, which had enough ambient light for a vampire, but pit of Hades dark. Only a glimmer showed in patches of what seemed to be a ceiling. *Where am I?*

Skin crawling with nerves, she sniffed the air, trying to get some information about her surroundings. She could feel a slight movement of air, but city smells mixed with something musty and older. Almost sweet. Definitely stale. Somewhere in that cocktail was the stench of rat. The furry bastards were one of her few real phobias. A vampire sunstruck into her daytime sleep wasn't safe in rat territory. They weren't picky about whether or not flesh was dead.

Talia shuddered, getting quickly to her feet before she began to dwell on the thought. Her boots crunched on sand and dirt, but that was over something uneven but harder. Brick maybe. The sound was oddly muffled, as if it wanted to echo but the surfaces nearby were too close. Stretching out her arms, Talia felt nothing. Not *that* close, then.

Carefully, she moved toward the lighter patch of darkness ahead, pulling on her gloves as she went. Where was Max? There was no sign of him, not a whiff. Part of her was grateful, part pissed, part afraid. When had he learned to walk through walls? It wasn't impossible—a simple teleportation spell was something a sorcerer could make for someone else—but it was entirely out of character. Hunters didn't use magic. They were utterly against it.

Something is very wrong. Unease burned in her stomach. It was one thing that she was caught in a moral dilemma between ratting out her brother and turning in an attempted murderer, but magic made everything more complex.

Perhaps Hunters had started out protecting human villages and maybe they'd had the moral high ground once upon a time, but this was a different reality. To hate and kill someone just because they weren't human—to hurt someone like Perry—was completely wrong.

Monsters were monsters until they were your friends. Talia's beliefs had been changing for a long time, but this sealed it. Shooting Perry had made it personal.

And if the Hunters were using nonhuman powers? That was going from wrong to perverse. That was becoming the thing you despised in order to destroy it more effectively.

That's just repulsive. What the hell is Max up to? And if he was around, her father and the rest of the tribe wouldn't be far away. That meant all of Spookytown was in danger: Lore, Errata, Joe, and eventually Queen Omara. *Omigod they're here to stop the election!*

Nonhumans getting the vote—that was exactly the sort of thing that would make the Hunters go crazy. Talia felt a surge of alarm, the rush of adrenaline making her still heart beat for a dizzying moment. But what did Perry have to do with it? Why shoot him? She might be glimpsing some of the picture, but she still didn't have the whole thing.

Whatever. She'd found out something important, and she had to warn the others. If that meant her Hunter past was revealed, she'd have to suck it up. Talia balked at the thought, a surge of apprehension tingling through her. *I have to do it. There are a lot of lives at stake.*

Crap.

Talia had to get out of there and find Lore. But where was out? Wherever the spell had taken Max, she'd merely gone for a ride on the tail end of the magic—and apparently fell off along the way.

She stopped a moment, hugging herself in the intense darkness. It was really, really hard to pretend she wasn't afraid when she had no cell phone, no idea where the heck she was, and no way to find out. *Not fear. Don't give in to fear.*

Sunrise was just a few hours away, and she didn't have forever to get someplace safe. She stood under the brighter patch of dark, craning her neck to see straight up. Her vampire's eyes made more sense of it than a human could, but even she needed more light than this to get a clear picture. All she could tell was that the patch was a square broken into smaller squares, like a paned window. A very, very feeble light shone through.

Talia tried to rearrange her perspective, testing theories about where she might be. The hospital was northeast of downtown. How far might the spell have carried her? Just through the wall? Or miles away?

She saw motion above, a blur of light sweeping from left to right. Then she understood. *Those were bus headlights. I'm under the street in Old Town.* She was standing in one of the old service tunnels that used to run to the basements of the shops and hotels. Back then, coal was delivered to underground storage areas—not to mention slaves, opium, whores, and smuggled liquor. Talia had read a little of the town's history on the Internet when she'd first arrived—Fairview had played its part in making sure the West was not so much won as partied into a stupor.

That little bit of research had paid off. She remembered that thick blocks of glass were built into the sidewalks of Old Town to provide light to the tunnels. Over the years, the glass had turned a deep purple color, but they still did their job, more or less. That's what was overhead. The old glass bricks were letting a tiny glow from the streetlights shine down to her. *Okay, score one for the history geek. Now, how the hell do I get out of here?*

In the old days, the tunnels had been accessed through iron grates that opened onto metal stairways that led below street level. According to the Web site, most of those had been paved over for safety reasons. The best she could hope for was to find a door to some old building and use her Undead strength to break through it.

It looked slightly lighter straight ahead, so she started trudging in that direction. Her body temperature was always below normal, and now she was starting to feel the cold in a serious way. She wouldn't die, but she could slow down like a lizard left in the fridge—and then there would be rats.

No mistakes. No delays. It was dark enough that she

could walk by a door and not notice it, so she roamed from one side of the tunnel to the other as she went. Occasionally she felt a ripple of *something* pass by. Ghosts? She was no witch, but she could tell these tunnels weren't empty. There was a presence besides the rats down there—and she really didn't want to know more.

Talia picked up her pace, pushing her frozen limbs. She was heartened by the fact that the blocks above her seemed to be growing brighter, as if moving into a busier part of the downtown. She hadn't gone far—perhaps eight city blocks—when she came to an intersection of sorts. The other tunnel was newer, lined with concrete. A sewer? A storm drain? Who knew? She liked history and old books. What she knew about modern city engineering could have fit on a credit card, but tunnel number two had a ladder about twenty feet away. *Yes!*

Water had frozen at the bottom of this passage. Talia picked her way across the slick, gripping the wall with tense fingers. When she reached the ladder, she realized with a burst of relief that it led up to a manhole cover. As she climbed, the chill of the metal ladder leached through her gloves. Her feet were numb, and she had to be conscious of where she set them, one rung at a time. Giving commands to her body was like operating a robot, distant and imprecise.

The heavy cover was more problematic, mostly because it had a thick layer of snow that fell into her face the moment she scooted it aside. Grunting, Talia clambered out and shoved the cover back into place. She heaved a breath, grateful for the fresh, free air. When she looked around, trying to get her bearings, the first thing she saw was a blue neon sign flashing on the snow. It announced Nanette's Naughty Kitty Basket. Her joy dimmed a notch. *Oh, great.* She'd rejoined the world above right outside a strip club that featured the werebeast equivalent of horny alley cats.

She struggled to her numb feet and walked in the

other direction. It was an alleyway, but sheltered from the elements by high brick walls. There was not as much snow and walking was easier.

Only when she was halfway down the alleyway did Talia realize where she was. Three tall, dark-haired males stood in front of an arched doorway set into the brick wall. The door was made of vertical oak planks strapped with black iron—the sort of thing one would expect in an old castle or cathedral—except the subtle throb of magic that seeped from it was like nothing she'd felt before. The three guards were too much like Lore—big-boned, shaggy, and tough-looking—not to be hellhounds.

Of all the places in Fairview, she'd avoided this spot deliberately. *The Castle.*

She'd been raised to fear and fight monsters. This was the entry to an entire prison dimension filled with them. Some called it Hell, though that wasn't literally true. It was a war zone where factions battled through the eternities, scrabbling for brute power. Lore's people had escaped, but only with massive losses. Ever since arriving in Fairview, Talia had paranoid fantasies of being thrown inside, losing access to even the remotest scraps of her human existence. *In other words, kind of like high school.*

She started to turn and retrace her steps when one of the hounds called out, "Miss, are you lost?"

Do I look that clueless? She straightened up, forcing herself to look confident. She yelled across the distance that separated them, "Where can a girl get a hot drink around here?"

The hellhound laughed. "The Empire is right around the corner, and I'm off duty in half an hour."

He had an accent that reminded her of pirates and hearty drinking songs. It made her realize how well Lore had mastered English. She gave the hound a salute and moved past the Castle door, hugging the opposite wall of the alleyway and feeling a shiver up her spine as she crossed the field of energy it gave off. In contrast, the hellhounds leaned against the door, smoking and huddling in their thick, warm coats. There was a big thermos at their feet, and she bet there was more than coffee inside.

Though they seemed relaxed, it was all she could do not to run like a child scampering by a haunted house. The alley's entrance had iron gates propped open. Only when she'd passed through those did she take a long, deep breath, feeling the shadow of the prison fall away.

Then, all at once, she was in the heart of Spookytown, the busiest part of the Old Town area. Lights dazzled in the snow. There were few vehicles, but handfuls of pedestrians walked by, laughing and chattering. The occasional snowball whizzed past. It was a nighttime place, and it was in full swing.

The lights of the Empire glowed like the proverbial beacon, turning the snowdrifts to a field of glitter. Talia felt a blast of welcome heat on her face as she pushed through the door. She'd been in only once before, and looked around to get her bearings. The noise was a deafening wall, half the room talking at the top of their voices, the other half singing along to a piano player banging out an old jazz standard. It was crowded, thick with the smells of food, wet clothes, and warm bodies. It was life.

The first face she saw was Joe's. He stood behind the bar, pulling a pint. When he looked up and saw her, his first reaction was surprise, quickly followed by concern. She pushed through the crowd toward him, earning some astonished looks from the patrons crowded around the tiny wooden tables.

Joe set the pint on the bar, sliding it toward a jolly-looking werebear, and gave Talia his full attention. "What happened to you?"

"Do I look that bad?"

Joe's eyes widened a notch, as if forcing himself not to react. "You're damn near blue. Look at your hands."

She wasn't sure how he could tell. She was still bundled against the cold. He reached across the bar, taking her wrist, and pulled one of her knitted red gloves off, and she saw what he meant. Her skin had lost what little color it had, turning a grayish white. The mauve polish on her nails only helped the gruesome corpse effect. "Oh, God. I've got to get a fresh manicure."

Joe called over one of the other bartenders, asking him to watch his customers.

"You don't need to worry about me. I'll be fine," Talia said, her teeth chattering a little as she warmed up. It was as if she'd stored up cold, and now it was getting the chance to sweep through her thawing flesh.

"Yeah, right. Here." He wet one of the bar towels in the sink and wiped her face like a mother would her sticky child. The towel came away coated in dirt and blood. Blood? She must have hit her head when she landed in the tunnel. "Sit down."

Too weary to object to his bossy tone, Talia perched on one of the tall bar stools. She should have been sweating in her coat, but she was still shivering. Slowly, she pulled off the other glove. Her fingers felt thick and clumsy. If vampires got chilblains, she was in for a no-fun time when the feeling came back.

Joe was mixing something, foaming it up like steamed milk. Concentration furrowed his brow, reminding Talia just how handsome he was, how perfect his bone structure. A bit too much like fine art for her taste, but she'd have to be blind not to notice.

He poured his creation into a mug and added a generous shot of brandy, and then set the concoction in front of her. "Drink this very slowly."

Talia looked at it with suspicion. "Not that I'm not grateful and all, but it's pink."

"Stop whining and drink it. It's good for cold vampires. I call it the Empire Bites Back."

She picked the thick mug up carefully, aware that her fingers weren't quite under control. She sipped, catching a swirl of spices and alcohol and, under that, the salty richness of blood. "My God, it actually tastes good."

"You won't find that in Lore's fridge."

She laughed, feeling suddenly better. "I don't think he has a cappuccino maker anyway."

"No, but he could probably build one out of a fax machine and baling wire. The boy's a genius with mechanics but sadly lacking in the domestic arts." Joe gave a prize-winning smile. "He needs a good woman."

Talia already felt the effects of the alcohol. She'd never been a drinker to begin with, and now the brandy glowed like a tiny sun in her belly, sending out happy rays. "Mmm."

"Is that moan of pleasure about Lore or the drink?"

She took another sip. "For the record, there have been no moans of pleasure between my former jailer and me."

"Give it time. I know doggy love when I see it."

Talia's head spun—either from the alcohol or his comment or both—but she was just about tipsy enough not to care. "He's a hellhound and I'm a vampire. Doesn't that make it weird?"

"I'm an immortal living vampire bartender who occasionally turns into a giant wolfhound. Weird is relative." He gave her an assessing look. "You're starting to look better. You're lucky."

"I wasn't outside all that long. An hour. Hour and a half max."

Joe gave a rueful smile. "In this age of instant heat, people have forgotten how deadly weather can be. Now, tell me what happened."

Talia set down her mug. "I was at the hospital with Lore."

"Why?"

"To see Perry." She could tell from his look that this was news. "Perry was shot."

"What?" Joe's face registered shock.

"Perry called Lore to say that he had found something out about, you know, what we were talking about the other night. Lore went up to the university to see what it was. When he was there, Perry got shot by a sniper. With a silver-pellet safety round."

Joe swore, long and in several languages.

"The sniper showed up at the hospital, and I chased him. He's a Hunter, and what's weird is that he used magic to pass through the wall." She didn't say Max was her brother. It was the cowardly way out, but she felt cold and sick. She was giving Joe the important facts. The rest could wait until she felt up to accusations and rotten tomatoes.

"A Hunter? Are you sure?"

She blinked, staring into her drink. "Yeah, I knew him from before . . . before I was killed."

Joe gave her a curious look. "Okay. Go on."

She ended her story with her walk through the underground. "It didn't strike me until just now, but it's odd that there weren't homeless down there. It's cold in the tunnels, but it's out of the wind and snow."

"Even the human homeless are better at sensing threat than those of us who live comfortable lives." Joe refilled her mug with more of the warm, delicious Empire Bites Dark. "Those tunnels haven't been safe for weeks."

"Why not?"

"I've heard stories about something living down there. People start talking three beers into their evening." He made a gesture that took in the whole bar. "We get a mixed clientele in here. More and more human yuppies going for a walk on the wild side, but the core clientele is still the longtime Spookytown residents. If there's something going on, they know about it."

"Do you think there's a link to the election?"

Joe shrugged. "Maybe. Nothing surprises me anymore."

He pulled out his cell phone. "I'm calling the others. They're going to want to know you're safe, and I want an update on Perry."

"Me, too." Talia wrapped her hand around her mug. She was just about ready to unbutton her coat. Her toes were a mass of pins and needles, bringing back childhood memories of long walks home from school. She and her brother used to stand over the forced air ducts in the floor to warm their bare feet while their mother brought dry socks. Somehow, the cold hadn't seemed so bad as a kid.

Nothing had. *What the hell, Max? You never asked me if I was all right.*

And she hadn't had a chance to tell him about Michelle. Had he already known that she was dead? It was an ugly thought. Talia bit her lip, wondering what the Hunters were doing and how deeply Max was involved.

She looked up as Joe closed the phone. "How's Perry?"

"I talked to Errata. He hasn't regained consciousness."

"Oh."

Joe grimaced. "Lore filled me in a bit more. Now that the police know you're still in the area, they'll be looking for you that much harder. It's better if you don't go back to Lore's place."

Talia glanced at the frost-painted windows, dreading the cold outside. "How late are you open?"

"As long as you need."

She gave him a startled glance.

"Hey," he said, picking up a knife and cutting the end off of a lemon. "Take it easy. That's what friends are for."

Talia took a breath to speak, but changed her mind at the last moment.

"Thank you," was all she said.

Chapter 21

Darak was walking downtown, minding his own business, when the guy a block ahead walked through the alley wall.

For a moment, he wondered if that last blood donor had been knocking back more than Jell-O shots. She'd been the cheap and cheerful type, but he hadn't expected chemically altered. It would be a sad day when vampires had to start demanding organic.

Or, something might be more sinister than a funky meal.

Lengthening his stride, he covered the distance to the piece of old brick wall. His boots scrunched on snow and sand, the buckles and metal bits on his jacket jingling in chorus. It was cold enough that the bricks wore a rime of frost that sparkled in the streetlights.

He pounded on the spot where he'd seen the figure disappear just to be sure there hadn't been a door. Back in the day, secret passages were denarii a dozen.

His breath came out in a puff of surprised steam

when his fist passed right through the bricks. *Gah!* He snatched his hand back. He'd seen too many ghosts to enjoy that.

Except that his hand felt like it was crawling with ants. *Magic.* Someone was using spells to take a shortcut.

An unexpected ripple of triumph curled his lips. After Michelle's ghost had fled, he had looked long and hard but had found no real clues to the spell caster's identity—but this was something. There might be two or three magic users in a city at one time, but not a whole phone book of them. In his experience, one always knew about the others. If he could find the man who walked through walls, he'd be on his way to the necromancer.

Portals closed fast, sometimes in seconds. Without wasting another moment, he pushed through, feeling as if an entire swarm of bees was pressed against his body.

And stepped into an old corridor. It felt clammy, like a basement. The floor was covered in worn green broadloom, the wallpaper flocked red vinyl. A hotel? Something skittered by on the floor. An abandoned hotel?

He was alone. Seconds after the figure used the teleportation spell, the magic would have begun to decay. Darak had followed, but he hadn't gone as far. His quarry was somewhere up ahead.

He sniffed the air. Yes, there were other vampires nearby. He began marching toward the smell, the heavy thump of his boots barely muffled by the thin carpet. A feeling of profound creepiness descended on him. Outside of his own movements, the place was utterly silent.

He pulled out his Smith & Wesson. It was a .357 Magnum loaded with vampire-ready ammunition. He was a "just in case" kinda guy.

A pair of fire doors blocked his path. He was tempted to kick through them, doing the bad-ass thing, but magic made him wary. He opened the door a crack, looking and listening. He could hear male voices now, and detected maybe a few dozen individual scents. The long hallway ended in a meeting room. One of the doors was propped open with a chair, the barely padded kind found at wedding banquets everywhere. The chair was kept company by a pair of vampires holding assault rifles.

Darak opened the door slowly and went through, sauntering as if he had every right to be there. One of the guards started talking to his shirt cuff.

How many voices did he hear? Three? Four? It would be better if he asked nicely and they told him what he wanted to know. Then they could all get on with their nights. But he was always up for a good Plan B.

Through the doorway, he caught a glimpse of a long, bare table and more of the banquet chairs. Vampires, mostly male, were sitting and standing around it, looking at a large map. His view was eclipsed by four more males hurrying to intercept him at the door, presumably called via shirt cuff intercom. Better than the shoe phone, he supposed—but then few humans that age would have remembered Maxwell Smart.

The four newcomers all had assault rifles, too. One of them looked like the figure who had gone through the wall. Well, magic portals were one way of ensuring a fast commute to work.

The first of the newcomers caught sight of the Magnum. In a blink, he lunged for it. He was fast for a vamp, but Darak was older, faster, and overall meaner. The vamp hit the wall and the next one was on his knees, the Magnum at the crown of his head, before the rest had their eyes focused on the problem.

The guy on the floor was panting, a thin sound trickling from his mouth. Darak hadn't even warmed up. He heard the click and rustle of the assault rifles getting ready and aimed. "It's going to take a lot of bullets to bring down this much Undead body mass. I can take you all out before it starts to itch." A lie, but if you said it with the right amount of bravado, it usually worked.

"What's your business?" said the lead flunky.

Good. Questions made things better. Darak slid the Magnum back into its holster, but didn't let his hostage up. "Darak of Clan Thanatos seeks audience."

He didn't have a clue with whom, but that's what he'd come to find out.

More shirt cuff dialogue. Up close, he could see curly wires leading to the vampires' ears. He wondered how many of this happy gang there were, and how far they were spread out. What the hell had he stumbled on? Darak felt the stirring of misgivings.

Finally, the one in charge nodded, motioning the others aside. Darak barely resisted the urge to step on his victim. He let him up instead. The guy scrambled away on all fours for a few feet before getting to his feet and running behind the others. Yeah, *he* had a future as muscle. Not.

Turning his shoulders to fit through the door, Darak pushed past. He took his surroundings in at a glance. The room was large enough to seat a hundred people. Chairs and folded tables were stacked along the wall, some sitting on a platform on casters, as if they would be rolled away at any minute. Cheap chandeliers hung from a damp-stained ceiling, the glass baubles fluffy with dust. Otherwise, there was no furniture to get in the way of a fight.

Then he looked back to the vampires gathered at the table. His heavy tread hitched when he saw who was in the center seat. He'd found his necromancer. *Mother-effing Sons of Dis!*

"Looking for someone, rogue? Or should I say Brute? That's what they called you in the arena, is it not?"

Belenos, King of the East, gave him a beatific smile, and what a horrible smile it was. Darak's eyes watered with the desire to look away. Belenos had been a warrior of the north, as tall and strong as a Viking ship's prow. Now he was a mass of scars, one eye completely gone. He was using his right arm, but something about his

movements looked wrong. There was no way he would
swing a sword freely until it healed—if it healed. Beheading his victim must have been hard.

"Yes, this is what the bitch queen did to me."

"Omara?" Darak was perversely impressed. It took
talent—and sorcery—to hurt a vampire that badly.

"She broke the law, maiming another monarch."

He was wrong. Technically, she hadn't broken any
rules. Killing was forbidden; punishing for trespass was
not. The story went that Belenos had been trying to kid-
nap one of the local witches at the time, so Darak didn't
have much sympathy for the poor-me routine.

"If she hates you that much, why are you in her
territories?"

"Frank, aren't you, gladiator?"

"Saves time."

"You don't bow to royalty?" He made a gesture to a
flunky, who began to roll up the map. Whatever was on
it wasn't for sharing.

"No."

"I thought as much. Are you in town to cheer on the
democratic election?"

"No."

"You're not buying this move by Omara to put her
puppets in public office? It would take a fool not see
she's moving in on the human power structure."

"I don't do politics, any flavor."

"Ah, yes." Belenos looked amused. "Your reputa-
tion for utter neutrality among the vampire kingdoms
is remarkable. I'd say you hate all us monarchs equally.
If you had a weakness, I'd say it was a taste for Robin
Hood dramatics in favor of the downtrodden."

"I don't do tights and lacy shirts, either. Clan Thanatos is a mercenary unit."

"Is that why you're here? For a job?"

Darak thought quickly. His misgivings were turning
into full-scale alarm bells. The map on the table, from

what he'd glimpsed, had looked like a diagram of the sewers. Whatever Belenos was up to was going to be on a big scale. "The opposite. I'm looking for whoever started the fire at the medical clinic. I could use a skill set like that on my team. Necromancy is a rare talent."

"I'm flattered," Belenos said dryly. "But I'm otherwise occupied."

Got you, bastard. Hearing the confession gave Darak a spark of satisfaction. "Too bad. We pay well."

"Maybe I have a job for you instead," the king said. His look was thoughtful. "You could be exactly the tool I need."

"Yeah? We don't come cheap."

"Then what does it take to buy your time? What do you want?" Belenos fixed him with his one topaz eye.

I want to go home. I want to kiss the soil of Rome and walk the streets a free man. As an outlaw, as the murderer of his noble sire, it was the one thing his size and strength couldn't win. The Undead never forgot a crime.

The spike of painful longing came unbidden, as if summoned by the sorcerer-king's gaze. Darak turned his head away, focusing instead on the table. Besides the rolled-up map, there were candles, an incense burner, and a small quartz ball no bigger than a plum sitting on an ornate gold stand. *Magic.*

The king was watching his face. "I see there's something you want. If it's within my power, it's yours. A small price to pay for a job well done."

Amnesty? As a king, Belenos could arrange it. Maybe. Possibly. It wasn't out of the question.

Yes it was. Belenos was scum. Instead, Darak named a ridiculous figure, just to see what would happen. "Half up front."

Belenos shrugged, as if that were coffee money. "Agreed, but once you're paid I get a hostage to hold until the job is done to my satisfaction."

"Standard terms."

"It won't be straight combat. I've got other allies—or perhaps I should say *interested parties*—who are prepared to cover the usual assault activities. I would need you for more targeted work."

"What are our orders?" Darak asked, tension roughening his already gravelly voice. For a fee like that, the stakes had to be high. *What the hell is going on?*

Belenos sat back, lacing his fingers behind his head. "That's something I can't tell you until the time comes. And when that will be depends on the weather."

That's interesting. "How many men will I need?"

"More is better. Many of the best fighters are out of Fairview at the moment, but I understand there is a pack of hellhounds doing guard duty. I've run into them before. Nasty brutes."

Darak grunted. He remembered the hound in the Empire. Young, serious. Carried himself like he'd seen more than a few battles. "When do I need to have the men readied?"

"When the airport is opened again."

"What's the signal?"

"I'll find you." Belenos's eye flicked to the quartz ball on the table. *So he's using it for remote surveillance.* "You'll have your instructions then. In the meantime, bring your hostage to the pier midnight tomorrow and collect the first half of your payment. And don't think you can take my gold and run. I'll be watching your every move. Go about your usual business. Muster your men, but do it quietly."

"I've done this before," Darak said dryly, a little offended.

Beneath that was a well of anger. He was looking at the necromancer who had hacked off the head of a human woman, and the atrocity was clearly the farthest thing from Belenos's mind. Men like him had sent the gladiators into the arena for an afternoon's sport. Men who thought lives came cheaper by the case lot.

Darak masked his disgust behind the blank obedience of a hired thug. "Is the mark coming in by plane?"

Belenos fixed him with a wary stare, perhaps realizing that he'd been far too obvious. Maybe torture had damaged his wits as well as his body.

Darak guessed he wanted someone killed. Someone high level. Who better than a band of known rogues to bear the blame? Using them gave Belenos deniability.

The king's fingers twitched, the one sign that he realized Darak had cornered him. "Yes. I provided an incentive so that individual would arrive ASAP."

Ah. "The fire."

They crossed glances. Darak kept his face brutish and stupid, exactly what Belenos would believe of a former slave. *He wants us to kill the queen.*

Darak's body went cold with the knowledge. *Jupiter's balls, he's going to have revenge for what she did to him.* Belenos would claim it was politics, but this was purely personal spite. Looking at the ruin of the king's body, it wasn't hard to understand.

"Dismissed." Belenos stood and snapped his fingers. A dozen of the other figures stood and gathered around him. It was a warning to Darak not to overstep the role of hireling.

It sure as hell wasn't a dance number.

With a nod, Darak backed away, calculating the odds of shooting Belenos without getting shot himself. The math was ugly.

He'd found out far more information than he'd hoped for. More than he'd bargained for. Now he just had to get the hell out of there and figure out what he was going to do about it. Belenos had to go, but he was a big fish with lots of protection.

Darak had Nia and Iskander, but the rest of Clan Thanatos wasn't even in town. If he took on Belenos tonight, he'd end up like Daisy, bleeding his last in a back alley.

"Good night, rogue," Belenos said absently. "I'm glad you came along. It's been a busy night." He turned to one of his men, the human Darak had seen walk through the wall. "So how is your sister, Talia? Did she mention me?"

Talia. Wasn't that the dead Michelle's vampire cousin? The one he'd promised to protect? *What does she have to do with any of this?*

"Good night, sire." Darak made it to the door.

The guards parted, letting him through.

Darak stormed down the hall, back the way he had come. He had no idea how to get out of there, but would rot in hell before he asked for directions from Belenos's drones.

He pulled out his cell phone and hit a speed dial. "Nia. How fast do you think the rest of the clan can get here?"

Chapter 22

"Good evening, this is CSUP coming to you from the U of Fairview campus. I'm your hostess, Errata Jones. There's a community alert going out tonight about a confirmed sighting of a Hunter believed to be the assailant who shot a popular Comp Sci teacher here at Fairview U, Professor Perry Baker. The details will be on the upcoming news, but for now let me shed a ray of light on exactly how dangerous these people are.

"I mentioned that I'd found some of their manuals. Well, one of them makes pretty interesting reading. It's a Hunter child-rearing manual, or basically how to raise a good little psychopath. Even their nursery rhymes are all about killing. Imagine your little ones singing this while they play in the backyard:

Vampires with the slice of steel
Fairies cannot iron heal
Silver kills the man-faced beast

And demon hound has soul released
The day mercuric metal drives
Into his veins; Then death arrives.

"Sweet, isn't it? They know from the time they can toddle just what kills each and every one of us."

Thursday, December 30, midnight
Empire Hotel

The bar was the only part of the Empire open to the public. The hotel side, currently closed for restoration, was a tribute to Old Town's bygone glory. High ceilings held the remnants of gold-leafed plasterwork and Italianate frescoes. Beneath the drop sheets covering the lobby floor was a marble mosaic. Joe had found the original chandeliers in the attic. What he hadn't found was an electrician willing to bring the place up to code at a price Joe could afford. Part of the problem was that he wanted to convert the old gas fixtures to electric so he could keep the look of the original decor.

"Why keep everything the same? Wouldn't it be cheaper to update?" Talia asked.

Joe gave her a guarded look as he led her up the winding grand staircase. "I have a sentimental attachment to the place."

His tone said no more information was coming, so she didn't press.

Derelict didn't begin to describe the condition of the upstairs. A few bare bulbs hung from the high ceiling, giving just enough light to wind their way through a litter of construction debris. Wallpaper hung in shreds. It looked like a pipe had burst at some point, because water stains marred the plaster ceiling. Talia caught a faint smell of mildew.

"I know, it looks like wolverines slept here," Joe commented, stepping over a pile of paint cans. "I've cleaned out a couple of the rooms for personal use."

He took a key ring out of his pocket and unlocked the double doors to a suite. He hit the light switch, which turned on a couple of tabletop lamps. "There's no room service, but the sheets are clean."

Talia stepped inside, her breath catching as she took in the room. "It's beautiful."

Joe's face lit up with the first real smile she'd seen from him. Not charm, but genuine pride. "I'm glad you like it. I'm going slowly so I get everything right."

There was a small sitting room separated from the bedroom by an ornate plasterwork archway. There wasn't much furniture in the sitting room, just a couch and chair, so she could see the deep green wallpaper and paler green wainscoting below. The floor was covered by an area rug that left a border of oak marquetry visible around the edge of the room. A small fireplace was set into one wall.

Talia walked under the arch into the sleeping area. The half-tester bed looked original, as did the mahogany dressing table and chest of drawers. The forest green color scheme carried on through here and into the beautifully appointed three-piece bath. Joe had managed to find the right balance between Victorian ornament and a simpler modern aesthetic.

Or had someone given him decorating advice? She turned to ask, but found she was alone. Whatever Joe's mysteries were, they would remain a secret for tonight.

Friday, December 31, 1:15 a.m.
Empire Hotel

A strange bed, however lovely, didn't make for happy dreams. At least not on top of magic, and hidden tunnels, and the nightmare prospect of freezing into a coma and being chewed by rats.

Sure, Joe's drinks and a hot bath had warmed Talia back to her normal self, but they'd also made her sleepy. She'd laid down for a midnight nap, safe in the luxurious emerald oasis hidden in the derelict hotel. Safe, or as safe as Fairview got.

Except from her memories.

Belenos, King of the East, had stood beside the stone table where she was stretched out, her arms folded across her chest like the effigy on a sarcophagus. Later, she'd find out she'd been like that for days, losing her humanity little by little as Belenos fed on her, then fed her, and finally stole her life. Those memories he'd ripped from her mind. Turning a victim was a trade secret held only by vampire royalty. It wouldn't do to let the minions make their own toys.

The last thing she'd remembered was falling on the muddy soccer pitch behind the high school. There had been five Hunters—Talia, her father and brother, Uncle Yuri, and Tom. She'd just told Tom she wouldn't marry him, so when she'd taken the bullet to the back, he'd barely cast a glance over his shoulder as he ran with the others. They'd left her there, fleeing before the mob of vampires that had risen out of the grass like a flock of nightmare crows. From where she'd lain in the grass, crippled and helpless, Talia had watched the Undead levitate into the clear, moonlit sky.

If they'd wanted all the Hunters dead, they could have had their wish, but this was vengeance. This was Belenos's piece of theater: a death for a death, but with a twist.

Her father had killed Belenos's second-in-command. Turning the great Hunter Mikhail Rostov's daughter into the very thing he hunted was the vampire king's idea of an artistic punishment. In short, the Hunter struck, the vampire struck back, and Talia paid the price.

When her eyes had opened on her Unlife, they hadn't

focused all at once. Belenos had been dressed in a white suit, his long red hair like a cape of flame. She'd had a sudden, crazy idea he was an angel before her vision had cleared and his Nordic features had emerged from the haze. She'd guessed what had happened in a microsecond. She was dead, not stupid.

He'd bent over her, grasping her chin to keep her face turned to his. "Congratulations, my duck. You survived."

His touch had jolted her fully awake. She'd tried to sit up, but he pressed a hand to her chest, keeping her pinned to the cold stone. "Not so fast."

Talia's body had raged at the confinement. She felt enormously strong. Belenos's blood was potent, and she was bursting with its power. She was terrified. Horrified. Revolted, and yet when she gazed on her maker's face, she vibrated with a reverent lust.

She was his slave, and they both knew it.

She folded her hands over his, stroking the long, strong fingers. At that moment, he was her universe, and she ached to obey in the same moment she longed to rip into his veins and drink what she needed: more of the powerful, amazing blood that had Turned her into a dark goddess.

"There is something you must do for me," he whispered.

"What?"

"Drink."

She clutched his hand, ready to raise his wrist to her mouth, but he pulled away and gave her a paternal smile. "No, it's time for you to take your first steps. To learn to *hunt* for yourself." He said the word with all the irony it deserved. Imagine teaching a Hunter to hunt for blood, ha-ha.

She rose to follow him, her limbs as unruly as a newborn colt's. Then she smelled the most delicious scent, sweet, fresh, and *human*. Hunger hit her like the blast of heat from a kiln.

"There you are, my child," said Belenos, taking her by the hand and leading her a little way. They seemed to be in an underground crypt. More of her sire's overblown sense of drama.

Tom was chained to a heavy iron ring in the wall, a metal dog collar around his neck. He was naked, his shaggy blond head matted with blood. Obviously cold, he huddled close to the floor.

A pitiful thing, said a new, dreadful voice in her mind. *You never loved him. You thought he was weak, your father's puppet. You knew he couldn't protect your happiness—and you were right. He ran away when he should have saved you. Go ahead, make a meal of him. At least it'll be fast. Faster than the slow death of spreading your legs for a man who is half the warrior you are.*

That voice terrified Talia, even though it had a point. It was vile, and it was *part* of her. It was the voice of a real hunter, not humans with visions of species purity and moral stick-up-the-assedness. Belenos had given her more than just fangs. He'd turned her into a *killer*. Part of her wanted to dance, paint herself with that rich life-blood, and shriek with the sheer ferocity of what she had become.

Tom must have seen it in her face. His eyes went round, the whites showing as terror and revulsion twisted his face. "Oh, God, Talia, you're one of them!"

You could have turned back to help me. Instead, you ran.

But what arrowed into her heart was his disgust. She had become the Vile Thing. Worse, he smelled good, like a chilled orange when her body raged with fever. Quenching. Succulent. The object of a desperate craving.

This isn't me.

But it was. Her body raged with the urgency. A new, unfamiliar aching in her jaw told her there was venom waiting to render her meal cooperative, to give him a lustful bliss more potent than any wedding night.

"I brought him just for you," said Belenos.

She looked up at her sire, and realized she loathed him: every pore, every cell, every hair of his fox-red mane. Her feelings had turned on a dime after that look on Tom's face. Shaking, her voice came out barely more than a whisper. "I don't want to play your games."

"Ah, but my games are all you have left," he said, his voice sinuous with anticipation. "You're just a pitiful dead thing."

With one hand, he hauled Tom to his feet, with the other tilted the man's head to the side. Chains swayed and scraped against the stone, a sound like the gates of Hell dragging open to swallow Talia whole.

Belenos bit down, sinking enormous fangs into Tom's neck. Tom screamed, a pitiful wail of despair. Talia's insides jerked, responding to the cry of prey. Her teeth suddenly felt enormous in her mouth.

Blood sprayed all over the king's white suit as he tore out Tom's throat. He looked up, his face a mask of gore. "Are you going to join me? I've got your brother for dessert."

She couldn't remember what happened next. The reel of memory stopped short, as if it had been sheared away with a pair of scissors.

Perhaps forgetting protected her from insanity.

Talia twisted as she lay on top of the bedclothes, caught in the web of remembered imagery. She cried out, half of her already trying to wake up. A sharp sound brought her fully conscious, followed by a cold swirl of air. Her mind groped, trying to understand what she'd heard, but the unfamiliar surroundings disoriented her.

She bolted upright, aware something was in the darkened room, but not able to see it. Steeling herself, she reached out her hand toward the shadowy form of the bedside lamp. She touched the cool brass, letting her fingers slide up the base until she found the switch. Hesitating a moment, she swallowed, afraid of what she might see. That cold breeze curled through the room again, reminding her that *something* had opened a window.

She clicked on the light. It cast a feeble puddle of light across the bedclothes. Talia blinked, a ripple of fear slithering up her arms.

A huge shape hulked at the end of the bed. It seemed made of rags of shadow, scraps of it feathering away as the shape moved, as if stirred by the breath of Hell. Utterly black, it seemed more an abyss than a solid body, except for the two sparks of demon fire that were its eyes. *Hellhound.* Once she named it, she could make out the upright ears and long, pointed snout. The hounds weren't made to be seen by human eyes, but she was a vampire.

"Lore?" she whispered.

The savage snarl told her otherwise. Talia's hand darted under the pillow, grasping the gun she'd taken from Max. It felt hard and real in her palm, far from the magic talisman she needed to dispel this nightmare.

The hound crouched, baring teeth as long as Talia's hand. Ropy saliva trailed from its jaws, glistening in the lamplight.

"Hold it there, bud," Talia snarled in her turn, showing the hound her weapon. "Good doggy."

The hound sprang, the movement too quick for real animal bones and muscles. With a gasp of alarm, Talia fired, the gun in a two-handed grip as she rolled off the bed. Plaster exploded from the ceiling, showering dust on the bed. The hound landed with a thump that sent pillows flying, swinging its massive head around with another ferocious growl. Its lolling tongue was scarlet against the black fur, the teeth starkly white.

Talia thought she had hit the beast straight in its chest. With a burst of horror, she guessed that the bullet had passed through the hound without a trace. *Demons!*

Before it could lunge again, she dropped to the floor, rolling beneath the high Victorian bedstead. Paws thumped to the floor. Moments later a black snout pushed aside the dust ruffle, snuffling greedily.

Talia shot out from the other side of the bed, using all her vampire speed to dive into the bathroom and slam the door shut behind her. Splinters of glass covered the floor tiles, cold air streaming through the smashed window pane. *So that's what woke me up.*

Claws tore at the bathroom door, sending Talia scrambling for the window. The toilet tank made a good step up, but she'd shred herself on the jagged teeth of glass sticking from the frame. *Suck it up. Vampires heal.*

Then the scrabble of nails abruptly stopped.

Chapter 23

A deep baying rattled the drinking glass at the edge of the sink, stealing a sob from Talia's throat. The hound's cry was like the last moan before the sun and moon winked out.

But it hadn't come from outside the door. This one was farther away.

Her attacker answered, an *awoo-woo* that echoed in the tiny bathroom, making Talia feel like she was inside the dog. She shook with it, momentarily frozen.

A crash of splintering wood followed. Fresh snarls shredded the air.

Dog fight. Talia jumped off the toilet, not sure what to do. The dynamics had changed. Someone new had come.

Had someone finally shown up to help her when she needed it?

She cracked the bathroom door open, peeking out. The bedroom was empty, but she could hear the thump and crash of battle in the living area. Her gun in hand, she crept out of her hiding place. Whether or not bullets worked on hellhounds, she wasn't going unarmed.

The room was a writhing mass of shadow, like a dark star wrestling its way to implosion. Flashes of crimson eye and white fang streaked through the blackness, but it was impossible to see where one hound ended and the next began.

Then suddenly it was Lore, his hand around a woman's throat, pinning her to the floor. His movements were fluid, too quick to be human.

The woman was dark and muscular and starkly beautiful, like the spirit of wild Arctic tundra—and about as friendly. She struggled under his grip, giving an unholy snarl of fury.

"What's going on?" Talia demanded from the shelter of the arch that joined the two rooms.

Lore's shoulders bunched with the effort of holding the woman still. His eyes flickered to Talia for a moment, but his opponent had his attention. "Mavritte?"

The female spat back in a language Talia didn't know.

"She tried to eat my face," Talia said acidly. "I think I deserve to listen in on the conversation."

Lore's expression was still more hellbeast than man. "This is Mavritte of the Redbone pack. Beware of her."

He let his prisoner twist out of his grip. She was on her feet in seconds. Talia scanned the woman, looking for vulnerable points, weaknesses in her stance. There weren't any. *Crap.*

"I protect the pack," the woman said to Lore in a low-pitched, husky voice made for whispering dirty secrets. "It is you who wastes time with other species."

"How did you find this place?"

"Because I am a skilled tracker."

"Tell me!"

She spit in derision. "You left the hospital in pursuit of a pretty young vampire, wringing your hands because she was lost in the snow like a newborn lamb. I thought to ask the Castle guards who had passed by them this night. They told me to look in the Empire."

He came looking for me. Talia's throat ached with

astonished emotion. *My God, he told the truth when he said he'd protect me.*

Hellhounds really didn't lie.

Lore glared at Mavritte. "How did you know I was at the hospital?"

She grinned, a baring of teeth. "Not all wolves are your friends. Your professor had other visitors. Some would like to be *my* ally."

Lore closed the distance between them, looming over her. "If I had been a little faster, you would have never made it here alive."

Mavritte folded muscular arms beneath her breasts, looking like Mr. Clean's badass girlfriend. "By rights, the Alpha is mine to mate." She thrust out an accusing finger at Talia. "What fantasies do you indulge with this blood-hungry corpse? *This* is what you would betray us with?"

"Hey!" Talia snapped, misty longing giving way to annoyance.

Mavritte glared. "She is a breach of everything we believe!"

Lore made a grab for the other hound, but she ducked and wheeled, putting herself out of reach. He sank into a half crouch, ready to spring. "Be careful what you force me to do."

"The hellhounds need a bonded pair. You are pack father, the fertile seed. You can't make the dead our pack mother."

"Whoa, who said—" Talia lost her words, too astonished to keep going.

Mavritte rounded on her. "You do not care for him?"

Talia dared not look at Lore. "Yeah, but grab some dignity, girlfriend. No catfights, and I don't do bikini mud wrestling."

Mavritte looked confused. Maybe hellhounds didn't get the specialty channels. She turned to Lore. "She will not fight for you."

Talia couldn't resist a glance at Lore. He looked like he was going to explode, but she couldn't tell if he was embarrassed or infuriated by the conversation. "It is not the human way."

"Then what good is she?" the hell bitch asked.

Talia folded her arms, mirroring Mavritte's stance. "Hey, I'm not stopping him from finding a hellhound girlfriend."

"Enough!" Lore interjected.

Mavritte ignored him. "Then whose fault would it be that he will not have me?"

"Gee, I dunno."

Mavritte dropped her arms, holding them at her sides, slightly away from her body. Ready to grapple. "Don't mock me, vampire."

"Enough!" He grabbed Mavritte by the arm. He looked angry, but stricken. "Leave. Leave us. And leave Talia alone."

Mavritte broke his grip with a sweep of her arm. "You have no right to throw me out."

Lore's face flushed. "I have every right to a minute of peace! I have a right to myself. To my privacy. I have the right to be with who I choose. *I have done enough.*" He spit the last words as if he were throwing a gauntlet at her feet.

"I have the right to be heard by my Alpha."

"Hearing you is all that I've done from the moment you left the Castle!"

"If you will not have me to mate, I challenge you for leadership. I have to protect the pack."

Talia's jaw dropped. *Holy crap!*

Lore's face went granite-hard. "Mavritte, don't. I don't want to fight you."

She slammed both hands against his chest. "I demand it of you. By pack law. And don't think I will be an easy victory."

Lore pushed her toward the door. "I refuse. Pack law

cannot be invoked simply because you are angry that I don't want to bed you. Try this again and I will shame you in front of both packs."

"You would not dare!"

"Go, lick your wounds. Lick Grash. I don't care."

Mavritte turned. "You can't do this."

"And yet I do." Lore shut the door in her livid face.

He held the door handle a long moment, as if expecting her to burst back into the room.

Talia remembered to close her gaping mouth. "What did she just say? She wants to fight you?"

Lore held up his hand, signaling her to wait. After a long minute, he dropped his hand from the door. "She's gone."

Talia grabbed his arm. "What the hell is going on?"

He put a hand over hers, squeezing it gently. "Mavritte is angry. No one refuses her, and now I have. Her pride is wounded. She will get over it."

Talia wasn't so sure. "I think she wants to kill me. Is she going to try to kill you?"

"She won't hurt either one of us."

"How can you be so sure?"

The look he gave her was matter-of-fact. "I am Alpha. She can't change that."

Talia let him take her hand, warming it between his own. He seemed so utterly certain of his powers.

He was sure of her, too. He took her hand, pulling her to the pool of lamplight. The movement drew them into the bedroom. Talia could see raw scratches snaking down his arm, following the swell of his muscles. Suddenly, she wanted him. She wanted her tongue on those wounds, tasting the spicy blood she always sensed just under his skin.

He was wearing another one of those tight T-shirts that showed off every one of his chest muscles. *Doesn't he own anything else?* she thought irritably. Her fangs began to ache, matching the slow burn deep in her belly.

She wanted to kiss the place just under his ear, where even on a work-hardened hellhound, the skin would be soft as apricots. Tasty. Yielding.

She wanted her mouth all kinds of places, and the very thought of them was making her squirm. *This can't happen. He has to know the truth of who I am. What I've done.*

"What's the matter?" Lore asked, cupping her face in his hands.

"No one's ever come looking for me before. In a good way, that is."

He took a step closer, sliding one hand behind her back. "Never?"

"How do you think I ended up a vampire?"

"Tell me."

She shrugged, wishing she had the strength of will to put distance between their bodies. It was as if she had to leave room between them for the story she didn't want to tell. Lore seemed to feel her movement, because he stopped her with a soft caress.

Talia bowed her head. "I . . . I was with some people who were having vampire issues. We were ambushed. It turns out the easy kill we thought we were going to make was a trap. I was covering our retreat. Back of the pack was a bad place to be."

With the lightest brush of his fingers, he tipped up her chin so that she looked at him. His dark eyes seemed to absorb all the light in the room, drowning her in their soft, deep brown. "That makes no sense. Was no one watching out for your safety? Hellhound guards go in pairs."

That was Tom's job. "My partner was able to get away. I wasn't."

"No one stopped to help you." It wasn't a question, but a conclusion.

"Mission is more important than people. That's what we were taught."

Lore pulled her to him, closing the embrace. "No, no. People are the mission. Survival is a battle won one child at a time. Any loss means the whole pack is weakened. We live and die together."

Talia closed her eyes. He had just risked himself for her sake, facing down one of his own people. No one had ever done anything like that for her. She couldn't stand hiding from him one second longer.

And yet she hesitated, swamped by the sensation of a free fall into the unknown. *He'll hate me. He might even kill me.*

But he deserved to know who he'd saved. And maybe, just maybe, she deserved the right to stop hiding.

The giddy feeling continued, reminding her of that leap of faith through the hospital wall.

"The man I was chasing, Max. He's my brother."

"So Errata said."

"We were raised Hunters."

He pushed her away enough to look down on her. "When Errata looked into your background, she thought that was a possibility. When your brother showed up at the hospital, she knew it wasn't for a family reunion." His voice was quiet, but tight with apprehension.

She felt as if her insides were falling away faster than the rest of her, leaving her hollow and empty, as desolate as the tunnels beneath the city streets. She pulled up the sleeve on her right arm, showing him the tattoo. "I was born a Hunter. Raised that way. My father taught me to kill anything that wasn't human."

She could see him putting the pieces together, his gaze moving back and forth over her face. "Which made you a tempting target for someone like Belenos."

"Revenge."

"And your father never tried to rescue you?"

"If he ever finds me, he will kill me. That was the whole point of Belenos's little joke. You should have seen the look on my brother's face. He was . . ."

He was a recovering addict, terrified that she'd return him to that hell. Talia choked on the memory of Max's anguished plea not to bite him. "The Hunters are here and they're using magic and I think it's something to do with the election."

Lore studied her face, his brows drawn together. His expression said that he'd taken in her last words, but he let them go. He kept his focus on her, as if she were the only thing that mattered.

"From the very start, I should have guessed what you used to be. Your past doesn't surprise me." His voice was careful, as if he wasn't sure yet what her confession meant. "The way you fight. The way you handle a gun. New vampires usually have little experience with werebeasts and half demons. You're wary around nonhumans, but you aren't afraid."

Talia waited for some sign of his rejection, bracing as if a surgeon were about to cut her flesh without benefit of freezing. "I guess I gave myself away," was all she could manage.

Lore's gaze was still fixed on her face. "Not to anyone else. Your cover is good. The clothes. The teaching job."

"That's not cover," Talia said, a touch of heat creeping into her words. "I'm a girl. I like pretty things."

His lips twitched. "You have a lot of clothes."

"Paws off the closet."

There was a small change in his posture as his muscles relaxed. "I wouldn't dare."

His easing off made it possible for her to unwind a little. "And I didn't lie when I said that all I want to do is teach. I don't mind kicking ass, but I'd rather do it in the classroom."

"I've heard of the human male's fascination with naughty schoolgirls, but I think they've overlooked the teachers."

"You don't hate me?"

"I don't think so."

Confusion crept up on her. "I have plenty of nonhuman blood on my hands."

He ran his thumb over her brow, smoothing out her frown. "For that, I'm sorry. But I don't think you would do the same things now, would you?"

"No. I'll fight, but it will be for good reasons."

He bent and kissed her. They'd kissed before, but this was different. A new seriousness charged the moment.

"You smell right to me," he said, his voice suddenly husky.

"Mm." His scent was perfect—the warm, spicy musk of him locking her attention to him and him alone. She drank him in, one long deep breath reminding her how wonderful the presence of a warm, solid male could be.

"I thought you didn't do dead people."

"I'm in an experimental mood."

"Rebel without a chew stick."

"Shut up."

His lips were surprisingly soft, his hands warm and rough as they cupped her cheeks, positioning her just so for another kiss. She folded her fingers around his, pulling his hands down to her waist. He didn't need more invitation than that. His hands slid under her sweater, gently kneading her flesh.

She watched the strong architecture of tendon and muscle in Lore's neck as he bent to kiss her again and again. Talia felt her hunger whisper through her blood, as subtle as the slide of silk on skin. As her desire rose, so did the urge to feed. One did not arrive without the other.

Lore's palm crept to her breast, cupping it, caressing her nipple through the lace of her bra.

"If you keep this up, I'm going to bite you," she said, the words barely above a hiss of inhaled breath.

"I know. It won't hurt me. I'm a demon, remember?"

"Half demon."

His words were quick, his breath hot and urgent on

her cheek. "Demon enough that you can't live off me. Demon enough that I won't become addicted to you. That doesn't mean I won't enjoy it."

Encouraged, she let her lips slide to his jaw, running her tongue down the swell of his throat, exploring the ridges and valleys, the texture of his tanned skin. He had smelled delicious. He tasted exotic. The sweet ache in her jaws was matched by an insistent burn low in her belly.

Hands spanning her waist, he hoisted her upward, depriving her of his taste. Instinctively, she wrapped her legs around him, her hands gripping the bulk of his shoulders. His dark eyes held her spellbound, the mix of emotions complex as a rare wine. But this time, they held something she hadn't seen before.

Pleasure.

Raw. Unchecked.

Talia was suddenly wet with anticipation. "Take me," she said.

In two strides, they were at the bed. She slid away from him, giving him room enough to pull his shirt off. Talia felt a sudden jolt of pleasure. Lore was big, but he was lean, nothing obscuring the fluid play of muscle under his skin. She stroked his chest with both hands, unable to resist that simple act of possession.

As her hands reached the waistband of his low-slung jeans, she popped the button, then fingered the tab of the zipper. It was how she imagined Christmas morning should be, poised to rip the paper off the best present ever.

He put his hand over hers. Feeling suddenly awkward, she started to draw back, but he tightened his grip, guiding her hand as she unzipped the jeans, the cloth springing away from the opening as it grew. He wasn't wearing anything underneath, and he was ready to come out and play.

He is the pack father. The fertile seed. Lore was more than well equipped for the job.

Her body suddenly felt hot and heavy. Talia sank to her knees, stripping off his jeans as she knelt on the soft bedroom carpet. His thighs were roped with muscle, the legs of a long-distance runner.

Talia's stomach gave a flutter of excitement. *No wonder Mavritte was pissed she couldn't have him.*

"Talia," he whispered, his hands weaving into her hair. "I want to make you remember my touch always."

The words had a vaguely ceremonial sound, as if they were a ritual declaration.

"And I'll give you something to remember."

She took him in her mouth, tasting the pungent salt of male. With fangs, it was a delicate operation, and one normally reserved for the most intimate of lovers. That she went straight to the most erotic gift she could give said much about how badly she wanted him.

And here he probably thought this would be ordinary foreplay. A demon might not become chemically addicted to venom, but they would still feel its extreme erotic high.

She cupped the warm heat of his sac, giving it a caress just on the right side of firmness. She heard the hiss of his breath, felt his fingers dig into her hair. Then she braced her other hand on the hard surface of his hip, bringing her mouth to the soft, silky inside of his thigh.

And delicately broke the surface, no more than a deep scratch. Lore's muscles jumped, but she held him still, using vampire strength. Her venom seeped into his flesh, straight to a male's most erogenous area. His skin grew suddenly cold beneath her lips, and then flushed with heat. Lore moaned words she didn't know, but completely understood. A vampire's bite was painful, but the rush turned you into a single, taut nerve singing with pleasure.

She released him, judging how much sensual overload would be just right. He was still saying something in his own language, his voice low and husky. When they'd

begun, he'd been almost ready, but now he was fully en-
gorged, hard and long. Talia felt her eyes growing wide
as he pulled her to her feet. His eyes had gone to black,
the whites disappeared somewhere in that stare that was
more demon than man. Perhaps she'd overdone it?

He grabbed her, crushing her lips under his, a low
growl rumbling in his chest like an earthquake. She felt
it in her breasts, pulsing where her nipples were pressed
against his chest. A thrill of pleasure streaked all the
way to her thighs. She fumbled for the fastenings on her
own clothes, her fingers clumsy with urgency.

Talia wasn't going to waste this moment. She was
an immortal, but she wasn't convinced another opportunity like this was going to come along again in her
Unlifetime.

She had barely shimmied her jeans and panties over
her hips before he jerked them down her legs. As she
pulled her sweater off over her head, he was unhooking
her bra, his mouth already on her breasts. He bore her
down, spreading her before him on the bed, covering
her with his big body.

"You're ready," he murmured. "I can smell it."

Talia was quivering, feeling like she'd given herself
a venom overdose. She ached from her breasts to her
thighs, her whole body begging for him. In her sire's
court, she'd been made to pleasure others, but no one had
given themselves to her. It had been so long. "Please."

He thrust inside, the first push deep and on the edge
of painful. She twisted under him, wanting him gone,
wanting more of him, and just wanting. He slid partway
out, pushed again. This time, her hips rose up to meet
him, a thin cry escaping from her lips.

He was breathing hard, sweat trickling down the
heavy swell of his arms. Orgasm began to stir in her
belly, the first clouds of a gathering storm. Suddenly,
the bloodlust swamped her, shredding through her as if
those clouds carried electricity. With each of his strokes,

she arched against the mattress, the sweetish taste of venom in her mouth as it leaked from her fangs.

And then the storm began to break. Her muscles clenched around Lore, pleasuring him as he stroked into her. He murmured encouragements in his own tongue, but he was too far gone for finesse. His rhythm began to break, growing ragged as he growled again.

The vibration in his body tipped her over the edge. Talia's mind blanked, a white supernova of sensation as he released. The wet, hot flood of him filled her as he cried out, the hard force of his final thrust pinning her to the bed.

In that moment, she struck, fangs sinking deep into his neck. Blood filled her mouth as his heart sped, the exotic flavor of demon teasing her. A second wave of pleasure rolled over her, hardening her nipples to hypersensitive points. Tiny contractions fluttered through her, milking him in time with his pulse.

As this second orgasm crested, her venom released fully. Lore moaned as it flooded his blood, hardening him once more. He started to rear up, but she held him tight. She sucked, taking her fill, the heat of him bringing a false flush to her skin.

Their hips began to rock together as she fed. Pressure began to build again, this time gentler, more gradual. The sound of flesh on flesh, lips on flesh, the mixing sigh of breath filled the lamp-lit room. Like all demons, Lore healed quickly, the flow of life stopping just shy of satisfaction.

Talia rolled him over, still impaled on his shaft, and began to rock. His eyes were pools that held nothing but sensation. He reached for her breasts, cupping them, rolling the nipples with his thumbs. She was wet with needing him, but he was big enough to still be tight as she stroked him. She felt full—bursting with his blood and seed, but greedy for more. A contraction lanced through her, making her shudder.

"Come for me," Lore whispered. "Come for me, and let me finish you."

She rocked again, so sensitive that the stroke seemed to reach all the way to her throat.

He thrust up, and that ended it. She cried out, her sharp nails scoring deep into the flesh of his shoulders. With a snarl, he pulled her under him, driving into her again and again, until in a final push he came one last time, filling Talia until she felt she could hold nothing more.

He rolled his weight off her, and she rolled with him. Draped over Lore's chest, Talia fell into an abyss of weightless afterglow. He was panting slightly, one arm curled protectively over her back. She could hear his heartbeat, strong and quick. She turned her head so she could see his face. He was watching her, his eyes hooded.

"So is hellhound tasty?" he asked, his tone dry but gentle at the same time.

"An acquired taste, I think."

"As the Alpha, I have prophetic gifts."

"And what do you prophesize?"

"That you will never be left behind again."

"You going to handcuff me in a safe place?"

His lips curled in a very male smile. "Would you like that?"

Talia felt her energy flicker, like a short in her personal power line. She raised her head, looking toward the window. *No, not yet!*

Lore rose up on one elbow, lifting her up along with him. "What's wrong?"

She sat up, feeling suddenly naked instead of seductively nude. "Dawn. You should go."

He touched her hair, running his thumb along her cheekbone. "Why?"

Anger and shame stabbed through her. She pulled

away from his touch. "Because I fall into a coma and make like a dead person."

Lore seemed to be digesting this, his eyebrows drawn together. "You were in my apartment for several days. I know what happens."

But they hadn't made love then. Now they had something to lose. "Turning into a corpse is a deal-ender for so many relationships. I don't want that."

Strength was draining from her like a bath with no plug in the drain. Talia was starting to shake, her muscles too starved for energy to sit up. She lowered herself onto the pillow, tears of frustration filling her eyes. *Why couldn't we have had a few more minutes before the night had to end?*

Wordlessly, Lore lay down beside her, cradling her against him. Gently, he kissed away the wetness that had leaked from beneath her lashes.

Talia's heart hurt, strained with too much emotion. Ecstasy. Attraction. Sadness. Anger. It wasn't fair. She'd been so strong, a sex goddess, an equal to Lore just minutes ago. Now she was an invalid, withering away in his arms. An object of pity.

Why doesn't he just go?

"Do you hurt?" he asked, his voice soft with concern. He was warm, a walking furnace. He felt so good.

"No. I go numb. It's like dying every morning." If only she could hide, keep him thinking she was the Talia of an hour ago . . . but she could barely move.

"Sh." He brushed a hair from her face. "Once, the hounds guarded souls on their journey to worlds beyond this one. When you are with one of us, when you are with *me*, you can sleep soundly."

Despite herself, Talia managed a smile. "You'll be my guard dog."

He touched her nose with the tip of his finger. "Absolutely. You'll not be alone. Not one step of the way."

She could feel the darkness rushing toward her. "I'm always afraid I'll never wake up."

Lore watched as her face went slack, her lips parting slightly. At the last second, he had seen her fear. An unexpected sadness ached in his throat as she faded from life to wherever the vampires slept.

He hadn't expected to feel so alone.

Chapter 24

Friday, December 31, 4:00 p.m.
Empire Hotel

Talia woke. When her mind finally organized itself, remembered where she was and what had happened, she found herself staring at Lore's naked back, her gaze following the roll of muscle as he shifted his weight. He was sitting at the end of the bed, typing into his cell phone.

He'd stayed through the day. *I'm not alone.* When was the last time she had awakened with someone? Years. Long before Belenos had taken her. *It was with Tom.*

She held that thought at arm's length, not wanting to acknowledge it. Guilt had kept her solitary for years, but last night something fundamental had changed.

She'd told him who the real Talia was, and he hadn't rejected her.

I'm not alone, she thought again, this time feeling the wonder of it. *After all that's happened to me. After all the things I've done, whether I meant to or not.* Cautious joy crept in, not sure how long it would be welcome. She wasn't used to being happy.

Lore thumbed off the phone and twisted around so that he could see her. The gesture was fluid, not at all human. For a moment, she wondered how much of him was pure camouflage. Really, what did it matter? Human? Hellhound? Lore was Lore. *Since when were you the poster child for interspecies tolerance?*

Since she had six and a half feet of über-gorgeous male giving her a wake-up smile. *I had sex. Oh, golly, I had sex*! She did her best to keep the jubilation off her face.

"Good morning," he said.

"Hey." She rolled onto her side to face him as he set the phone down and bent to kiss her. He tasted just as good as she remembered. "What's going on in the world outside?"

"The humans are going to start celebrating New Year's Eve in a few hours."

"I bet Joe's looking forward to a busy night. How's the snow?"

"I hear cars. They must have cleared more of the roads."

I bet I could get out of town now. Only now Talia didn't want to leave. But if she stayed, where could she go? She had to get the money from Michelle's condo and consider her options.

"I was just talking to Bevan, my Beta. The police are watching the condo building. Baines is looking for both of us now. He knows I'm hiding you."

Obviously, he'd guessed her thoughts. She rose up on her elbow. "I'm so sorry you got dragged into this."

"It's my job." He stroked her hair with his palm. "We'll figure this out. For now, we can stay with the pack."

"Doesn't that put them in danger?"

"From Detective Baines? I don't think so. The human police never venture into Spookytown after dark."

"Maybe they met Mavritte."

He gave a dry chuckle. "She has a way of making visitors uncomfortable."

Talia pulled the blanket closer around her. "That includes me."

He gave a small shake of his head. "I won't allow her to bother you. I've given her a long leash, but it ends there. You're my guest. Everyone will know you're to be protected."

She pulled her arm out from under the covers, looking at her tattoo. "I guess I shouldn't say anything about this."

He gave her a considering look. "Not yet. Let the hounds get to know you first. They're good people, but the Hunter legends go back long before our time in the Castle. Fireside tales to scare the pups."

Talia felt herself flushing. "I guess I am your walk on the wild side."

"And what a lovely view it is from here."

"Thank you," she said, because that was all she could think of to say. Her mind was spinning, curious and terrified at the notion of meeting an entire pack of hellhounds. Lore was an impressive enough presence that he filled a room just by being in it. It was hard to imagine him times dozens more. No wonder the police kept their distance.

Lucky for her. It was ironic that she'd spent so long hunting monsters, only to end up relying on them for protection.

"Don't look so worried." He traced his fingertips down her shoulder, leaving her skin tingling with anticipation.

Talia didn't reply. She was too mesmerized by the obvious strength in his chest and arms. She'd felt that strength last night, the memory of it sending fresh explosions of need through her core.

Lore took hold of the edge of the blanket and gave it a firm tug, pulling it loose from her fingers. "We don't have to leave right away."

"Good."

By the time they finally made it out of the Empire, Talia had lost count of the favors she owed Joe, including the use of his washer and dryer to get the tunnel mud out of her jeans. Lore led her down the mostly shoveled sidewalks. Icicles clung to the rooflines, showing the temperature had risen during the day, but it was bitterly cold now.

Thankfully, their walk was short. She hadn't been down these streets before, but the air of hard work and not enough money reminded her a bit of her old neighborhood. A group of young people, neither teens nor fully adults, stood in a tight cluster by the entrance of a convenience store. At least a few were vampires. A werebear—he had to be by the size—was lifting his truck out of a snowbank. A movie theater was having a midnight showing of *Rocky Horror*. Talia wondered what the monsters made of that.

Lore turned south, and Talia knew at once they were in his pack's territory. A pair of colossal black hounds sat at the entrance to the street. They stood as Lore passed, dipping their huge heads. Lore acknowledged them with a nod and slipped his arm around Talia.

The gesture was as much territorial as affectionate. Her independent streak objected, but Talia understood the necessity on werebeast lands. She was a guest, not an invader, as long as Lore gave her his protection. Without it, she was vulnerable.

He kept his arm circled around her until they reached his destination, a green door in a row of old, two-story houses. Before he could knock, the door was opened by a woman Talia guessed to be around seventy. She wore what looked like traditional dress, hand dyed and embroidered, along with sneakers and an acrylic cardigan. It was the kind of mix Talia had seen before in ethnic communities. In another generation, little trace of the traditional would remain.

The old woman said something in the hellhound language, giving Talia a sharp look. She tensed, feeling very much like she Did Not Belong.

"This is Talia," Lore replied in English. "She is a friend who needs to stay for a night or two."

"Come in. Our bread and meat are yours." The woman spoke slowly, with a thick accent. The words sounded ritualized but also routine, much like someone would offer a cup of coffee.

"Thank you, ma'am," Talia replied. The welcome relieved her. She didn't want to get Lore into trouble with his pack.

"This is Osan Mina," Lore said. "She is one of our Elders."

He put his mouth close to her ear. "'Osan' is like grandmother, 'Obar' like grandfather. Anyone who is an Elder is called 'Osan' or 'Obar.' They are terms of respect."

"Got it."

"Thank you." He sounded relieved in his turn. Apparently one did not slight the Elders and get away with it. Talia understood; her own grandmother had been the sweetest woman she'd ever met, until somebody ticked her off.

"I'm honored to meet you." Talia gave a slight bow to Osan Mina, as she'd seen Lore do. It must have struck the right chord, because the woman stepped back, gesturing them inside. As they took off their coats and boots, Talia looked around with interest. Everything was done in colors so bright and varied the air seemed to vibrate.

"Is Helver at home?" Lore asked, following Mina into the kitchen. Talia trailed after him.

Mina replied, still in English. "He helps Obar Ranik get snow off roof."

"I need to go see him. I've let him stew long enough."

As Talia and Lore sat at the table, Mina filled an enamel kettle and set it on the stove. "You have tea first. You go out, everyone want to talk. You not come back to Mina and Talia."

Lore gave one of his trademark grins. He might treasure his private apartment a few streets away, Talia thought, but on some level he must have enjoyed being at the middle of everything. He was the go-to guy.

There was a small stack of books at the end of the table. Talia saw a child's reader on top. "Do you have grandchildren, Osan Mina?"

"I have grandson, Helver."

"That's his," Lore said, nodding at the stack of books. "He's a young man, though, not a child. Most of the hell-hounds are just learning to read English."

The teacher in her perked up. "Do you have classes?"

He shook his head. "Nothing formal. Volunteers come when they can."

That made Talia's head spin. Reading was as natural to her as breathing. "I saw the stack of books by your bed. How did you learn to read?"

"When I lived in the Castle, I had a young friend who was an incubus. His mother taught me. Constance was kind to me because I looked out for her son."

Talia picked up the reader and opened the cover. The book looked well used, the pages scribbled over with crayon. "What about the hellhound children? Do they go to school?"

"We're still looking for someplace that will take them. Half-demons aren't welcome in very many places."

Talia put the book down, trying to distance herself as a blast of anger roared through her gut. Humans complained that the other species didn't integrate well into society—but how could they, when access was barred to something as basic as elementary education?

Mina put a tray with tea and cups on the table.

"Why not set up a private school?" Talia said. She wondered if anyone had published educational materials suitable to other species. *See Were-Spot Run. See Spot Eat Dick and Jane.* It had possibilities.

Lore put his hand over Talia's. "Can we do that?"

She noticed Mina looking at their hands, and slid hers away. "Sure. It's not simple to get through all the paperwork, but setting up a private school can be done. I can help."

Lore still watched her intently. Just being the focus of his attention made Talia's mouth go dry, and that loss of control made her cautious.

"Just like that?" He sounded incredulous.

She shrugged. "You could even make funding it an election issue."

Lore's eyes narrowed, as if he were imagining the possibilities.

Mina didn't look happy. The old woman's expression insisted that Lore belonged to the hellhounds, not to a vampire waif. Talia doubted her credentials would impress the likes of the old woman and Mavritte. Forming any kind of a permanent bond with their Alpha, even a business arrangement, would probably spell trouble.

The realization turned her insides to stone, but a large part of her didn't care. *I have a master's in education. This is about the kids.*

Lore's cell rang. He flipped it open. "Hey, Bevan."

Mina poured tea and silently slid a cup across to Talia. She took a tiny sip to be polite. It wasn't blood, but she could get a small amount of hot liquid down without feeling sick. Lore stood and took his call into the next room. Without him, Talia had a sudden pang of awkwardness, and she cast about for a topic.

"How many school-aged children are there?" she asked Mina.

The older female shook her head. "There was big

fight to leave Castle. Many have no parents. For every house where hounds live, there live two or three young."

Talia wasn't sure how many that was, but it was a lot. "Orphans?"

Mina looked confused. Maybe she didn't know the word.

"They have no mother or father," Talia prompted.

"They have pack. They have what they need."

They need a school.

She was spared by Lore's return. "I'm heading over to Bevan's place. I'll make it quick."

"What's up?" Talia asked.

"Just a fire I have to put out. The Elders have decided they need their own meeting house. He has some suggestions, but I have to figure out how the pack is going to pay for renting a room in the community hall. I don't know why Obar Ranik's basement isn't good enough anymore."

Mina sorted. "Osan Ziva is jealous. She thinks the Prophets belong to everyone, not just Ranik."

Lore sighed. "It's the season."

Talia was intrigued. Did every community have its petty disputes? "What season?"

"The first full moon after the solstice. Our winter holiday. Now that we are out of the Castle, we can keep the old traditions."

"It is when Prophets give blessings," Mina said. "We have feast."

"Sounds like fun."

Lore gave a rueful grimace. "Only if I find a room so the Prophets don't play favorites. I'll be back in half an hour. This isn't a priority, but it's the best way I can catch all the hound warriors at once. They've been looking for Belenos, but no luck. We've got to rethink the search."

"Hard to smell one vampire in a city full of strangers," Mina put in. "Not pack business."

Lore let that pass without comment. He touched Talia's shoulder. "You'll be okay?"

"Sure." Actually, she dreaded being left to make small talk, but she wasn't going to complain.

Mina slurped her tea, the noise disapproving, as Lore left the room.

Talia put on her best face and turned back to Mina. The old woman's stony look rekindled Talia's dread of being thrown out into the snow. Lore's back was turned. The incentive for Mina to make nice would drop like a stone. *What do I talk about?* Kids? Teaching? Her usual fallbacks were danger zones because of the school idea.

Talia gave what she hoped was a warm smile. "My grandmother always gave me her mending to do when I went to her house. She made me learn to darn socks."

"Smart woman." Another derisive slurp of tea.

The conversation died. Talia toyed with her mug. The bright, primary colors in the room felt like a heat lamp. She was going to start sweating any moment.

Osan Mina suddenly spoke. "Lore needs hellhound woman. There will be no pups until he takes mate. The females do not become fertile."

Talia set down her tea before she spilled it. *Too much information!*

"Really?" Her voice was too high. She wondered if that was what Mavritte had meant about Lore being the pack father. "How is that possible?"

Mina's eyes were unexpectedly compassionate. "That is our tradition. That is how it must be. He has one mate. We die, we are reborn, we find mate again. Paired always. Never outside pack."

Despite her shock, Talia felt a puzzle piece fall into place. Half demons were immortal, and yet hellhounds aged and died. *Reincarnation.* That was how they could be both eternal and mortal at the same time.

Talia rubbed at the design on the side of her mug. "Lore hasn't—uh—connected with his female yet?"

Mina shook her head. "Castle killed many who do not come back. Packs are smaller. Loved ones gone for good."

It was true that souls could be destroyed—or at least taken out of the reincarnation circuit—by powerful magic. "She's gone forever?"

Mina shrugged. "Who knows? It is one thing an Alpha can never prophecy."

Talia was getting confused. Did he have someone waiting or not? "You don't know who your once and forever mate is before you meet them?"

"Strong hounds find them. The weak die alone." She gave Talia a hard look. "Alphas must be strong. Finding mate is test."

Talia got the picture. If Lore didn't take a mate, not only was the pack supposedly infertile, but he would look like a weak leader. In beast packs, weak leaders were killed.

Irritation and alarm prickled through her. So why was Lore paying so much attention to a Hunter-turned-vampire? She was the worst possible girlfriend he could have. Was she a last-minute fling before he got down to the business of being a literal father to his people? Talia folded her arms, more upset than she had any right to be.

Girlfriend? Get real. They'd slept together. It wasn't like they had a committed relationship.

I'm prettier than Mavritte.

I'm also deader.

Thick, sour jealousy threatened to suck her down.

Lore had meant more to her than a onetime fling. She was pretty sure he felt the same way, but maybe he wasn't thinking like an Alpha. Talia had little to lose. He risked far more by being with her. *Why the hell is he doing it?*

Why the hell was she letting him? People close to her got hurt: Tom, Max, Michelle. Call it bad luck or a vampire curse; she didn't need to add Lore to the list.

A sharp rap came at the door. With that unnerving

swiftness Talia had seen in Lore, Mina was out of her chair. "Who is it?"

She asked the question in English. *How does she know it's not one of the hellhounds?*

The knock repeated and then the door opened. Apparently, Mina didn't keep it locked.

Whoever it was called from the front entry. "I'm looking for Lore."

Talia recognized the voice, but it took her a moment to place it. By the time she searched her memory, the speaker was in the kitchen. She jumped up, putting her chair between herself and the visitor.

Chapter 25

"Detective Baines," she said, her voice tight.

"Talia Rostova," he returned. The detective looked tired and cold, but there was triumph in his expression. "I was looking for Lore in hopes that he could tell me where you were. This is even better."

He's going to try to arrest me for murder. How do I play this?

Mina gave a low growl and blocked him from moving a step farther into the kitchen. Baines pulled his police ID out of his coat pocket, holding it in plain view. "This is police business. I suggest you stand aside."

"This is my home. No place for humans."

The old woman's vehemence warmed Talia's heart, even if it was for Lore's sake.

"Then perhaps Ms. Rostova would like to come with me onto neutral ground, like down to the station."

"Talia is our *Madhyor's* guest. I look after her. You not taking her."

It didn't take a genius to see that this wasn't going to end well. She wasn't going to accept Lore's protection if that meant getting the pack grannies arrested. "Osan Mina," Talia interrupted. "It's all right."

Mina gave the detective a look that should have flayed the skin from his flesh, but she stood to one side. "I get Lore."

Talia gripped the back of the kitchen chair. "That would be a good idea."

Pulling herself to her full height, Mina strode out in a swirl of skirts. When the front door slammed, Talia felt the tension in the room spike. She was alone with the cop, and he smelled warmly human. Hunger began to toy with her self-control, a cat flicking at its feathery dinner.

Baines pulled out one of the kitchen chairs and sat down. The gesture reminded Talia of her father carrying the chairs of his wife and then his daughter to the oblivion of the garage. The table was the battleground for who had the right to eat, much like a lion's pride crowding in for a share of the kill.

There was no issue of permission as far as Baines was concerned. He apparently took whatever chair he liked. In his own way, he was an Alpha, too.

"Sit down," he said, meeting Talia's eyes for a microsecond before they slid away. Despite his confident pose, he was wary of her vampire abilities. She was too new to be expert at hypnosis, but he couldn't know that.

Talia sat. She was stronger and faster, but she still had butterflies. Baines's confidence was a weapon all its own. The one thing that comforted her was the conversation she'd overheard when they'd taken away Michelle's body. Baines had been more open-minded than the others.

"It was brave of you to come into Spookytown alone," she said.

"How do you know that I don't have backup?" As if to even the score, he took out his firearm and placed it on the table, his hand resting on the silver-plated grips. Silver to indicate it had vamp-killer bullets.

"An educated guess. It's too cold to leave someone

standing outside, and I doubt too many humans would like to stand on the street in the dark in the middle of monster territory. Not unless they had a SWAT team handy."

He made a good imitation of a chuckle. "You're a smart woman."

"It's just logic. What do you want?"

"I thought if I could get you alone, you might talk to me."

"Isn't that a bit naive?"

"That depends on whether or not you answer my questions." He leaned back in the chair, completely casual except for the weapon. "That's all I want for now."

"Do I get a lawyer?"

"No. The law hasn't gone that far for nonhumans. At least, not yet. Did you kill your cousin?"

She'd seen the question coming, but hadn't expected it so soon. "No."

"Why should I believe you?"

"There's evidence that the timeline doesn't work. I got home too late."

"What evidence?"

"Perry Baker has it." Talia suddenly realized it was an illegal surveillance tape. She could be getting Perry into trouble. The worst part was that Perry might never wake up to care.

"Baker's in the hospital unconscious and flirting with organ failure. Where is this evidence? What is it?"

Talia shook her head. "If I tell you, you'll send your men to find it. I know what they think of nonhumans. They'd like to shoot us on sight. Do you think I'm going to turn my safety over to their goodwill and professionalism?"

Baines gave her a long look. His heart rate was quick, but steady. Alert, but not afraid.

Talia picked up the teapot. "Thirsty?"

"No, thank you."

She warmed up her own tea. Not that she wanted it, but she was determined to look as cool and collected as the detective.

Baines cleared his throat. "You're looking for guarantees."

"I'm looking for fair play." Talia's mind felt clear, almost detached. It was the zone she fell into when trying to make a difficult shot, or to teach a class a difficult concept. She could see everything, action and reaction, how each choice would change the pattern of what came next.

Baines watched her, not moving. "What does fair play look like to you?"

"If you agree to my terms, I'll do my best to give you the evidence so that your department can forget about me and move on to finding the real killer. If you don't want to play ball, leave here now, but you leave alone. If you try to take me with you, you won't make it out alive. I don't want to sound ruthless, but you've backed me into a corner."

"Who is the real killer?"

"Belenos, King of the East."

"Your old sire?"

"There's good circumstantial evidence." Perry had found surveillance tape with Belenos on it, and it had been at the university. If the tape with her arrival back at the condo was in the same place, everything she wanted was in his office at the U.

"What's Belenos doing here?" Baines asked. "Is he nuts? This is Omara's territory."

"He is frigging crazy," Talia agreed.

"What's between you two, anyway?"

Talia looked down at her hands, picking at her chipped nail polish. Memories felt like heartburn, hot and bitter.

"About a year after I was Turned, Belenos came out here on some harebrained scheme. Omara took Belenos captive for a few months. The high-level vamps are always fighting, but he must have really ticked her off because she played with him in a bad way. When he came back he was crazier than ever. She'd broken his body, but she'd done something to his mind, too."

Talia took a breath, trying to steady her stomach. "He slaughtered half his court the day after his return."

She closed her eyes, replaying the scene in her head. "His house has this white stone floor. The blood soaked in. Apparently it takes some kind of super-industrial cleaner to get it out, but he won't let anyone do it. He likes to walk on the stains where he tore their heads right off their bodies and the blood sprayed all over his feet. And over the rest of us who were still standing there, waiting to be next. Anyone who tried to run was next."

Her body remembered the moment just as well as her brain, and nausea rose in a sweaty tide.

"What set him off?"

"It hurts him that he's not beautiful anymore. He thought we were mocking him."

"Were you?"

She gave a single, low bark of laughter. "No way. We were terrified. The only good part is that there weren't enough guards left to cover all the exits from Belenos's house of horrors. That gave me an opening to beat feet. I bolted and never looked back." With a suitcase full of cash.

Baines was chewing his lip. Humans never understood that monsters were people, but also monsters. They were misunderstood, just not in the way the do-gooders thought.

Talia cleared her throat. "Now, do you want the evidence or not?"

He paled a degree. "I go with you. Otherwise it will be useless in court."

"Agreed."

"Am I safe?"

She looked pointedly at his gun. "As long as I am."

There was every chance Baines could turn on her. He might even have a whole detachment waiting just outside the Spookytown border. She couldn't know—but this was the best shot she had of getting justice for Michelle and freedom for herself. If she could help nail Belenos's ass to the wall, so much the better. Humans might be useless against necromancy, but they had the weight of law and bureaucracy on their side. That had its own kind of relentless horror.

Baines nodded. "When we're done, we'll talk about that guy who jumped through the wall."

Talia felt a pang, but if this was her night to set things straight, she couldn't falter. It would break her heart, but she knew she'd have to make Max accountable for what he'd done. He was human. Baines was the human police. "I'll tell you what I can. In a place of my choosing."

The moment she said it, she felt like she was going to throw up.

"Are you all right?" he asked, real concern in his voice.

"Let's just go before Lore gets back." She cast another glance at the gun.

If things went south, she didn't want him in the way.

This was her risk to take. He had a pack that needed him.

Chapter 26

Friday, December 31, 7:15 p.m.
101.5 FM

"**A**nd a Happy New Year's evening to all you listeners out there in Radioland. This is Signy White, your pinch-hitting hostess for tonight on CSUP, your super supernatural station. Errata Jones is off.

"To begin tonight's countdown to the New Year, it's only natural to look at where we've been and where we're going. There's an election in three weeks that might bring us the very first nonhuman to sit on city council.

"Speaking as one of the Undead, it's pretty exciting, but I want to hear from those of you who aren't vampires. Do you believe that a bloodsucking city councilor will make a difference to Spookytown? Will he represent your interests?

"Put it another way: Will Michael de Winter be better or worse than a human? The phone lines are open. Cast your vote and let's have some fun!"

* * *

Not surprisingly, even the die-hard students stayed home from the university on New Year's Eve. When Talia and Baines pulled up in his unmarked cruiser, the parking lot was nearly empty. A plow had been through, making just enough space for a few cars, but she was glad he had chains and a good heater.

A flash of the badge at campus security got them into Perry's building. From there, the security guard led the way while Baines talked to someone on his cell about search warrants and witness statements. It sounded like he was trying to pass off their adventure as business as usual.

So far he'd been as good as his word. Every indication was that he would keep his part of the bargain. Fine, then Talia would keep hers.

There was yellow crime scene tape crisscrossing the door to Perry Baker's office.

"Have you searched here already?" Talia asked, suddenly cold. Had the videos already been taken?

"We've done the place where he was hit, but there hasn't been time for anything else. Too little manpower over the holidays. Too much else going on."

She breathed a sigh of relief as the guard unlocked Perry's office. The door had a nameplate and a hazard sign that warned students that their professor really was a monster—in this case, the silhouette of a wolf inside a red warning circle. All the carnivorous nonhumans had such signs on their office doors.

If Talia had rated a room of her own, her sign would have shown a bat. Stupid, since even the oldest vampires couldn't fly more than a block or two—something she hadn't mastered yet—and none turned into winged rodents. Go figure.

Baines was looking at his watch. Talia wondered if

he'd had plans—maybe a New Year's Eve dinner dance with his wife. If he had a wife. He'd said almost nothing personal on the drive over.

The security guard retreated, saying he'd check back on his next round. Baines turned to Talia. "Why do you think the professor was targeted?"

"I'm not sure. He's not stupid, so I doubt he told many people what he was doing."

She followed Baines into the office. He flipped the overhead light on. The fluorescents flickered to life, bathing everything in a harsh glare.

A laptop sat on the desk, hooked up to a large flatscreen monitor. Other equipment was everywhere—hard drives, a printer, routers, and boxes with blinking lights that Talia wasn't sure about. It all looked untouched.

A thick sweater hung over the back of the chair, a tennis racket hung in its case from a hook on the back of the door, a basketball perched on a stack of books. Deli containers filled the trash can. Framed degrees and awards marched in rows across the wall. Young as he was, Baker had doctorates in math and computer science. He must have been a real boy genius, because he couldn't have been much more than thirty years old. Talia felt a faint sting of nostalgia, thinking of her own years spent in study. Being back on campus made her yearn for the classroom, both as teacher and student. *If only I could get out of this mess with my job.*

If only was a dangerous game. She turned her attention back to the desk.

There was the usual clutter of papers, pens and a Dracula PEZ dispenser. Talia studied the drifts of paper, trying to guess what each heap was about. She picked up a box of flash drives and stirred them with her finger, wondering which one might hold the surveillance video she wanted. This could take longer than she'd thought.

"Hello, little duck."

Talia started at the voice, freezing where she stood.

Belenos! Her heart plunged, cold terror folding around her until she was drowning in it.

Baines took my knife and my gun.

He chuckled. "You've got to learn to pay attention. Leaving the door open like that? I thought a Hunter like you would know better. But then, you never were particularly wise."

Talia forced herself around, bit by bit, as slow as if she were in a nightmare turning to face the monster. Oh, wait. She was.

"Where's Baines?" she demanded, surprised that she'd managed to keep her voice steady. But she could hear the faint rattling of the data sticks in the box as her hand shook with fear. She set the box down. Wouldn't do to advertise the fact that she was about to faint.

"Where's Baines?" Belenos mimicked. "Where's my money?"

Talia forced herself to look him in the face. It had been well over a year since she'd seen him, and time had smoothed over some of his injuries. His fox-red hair had grown back to shoulder length, hiding the places where his scalp had been torn away. His face was still scarred, but the lumpy flesh had paled from red to pink. He was healing, but slowly. Whatever Omara had done to him had been from the extra-special column of the torture menu. *Too bad she didn't finish the job.*

"I spent your money," she said without expression. "All of it. On pretty clothes."

He looked her up and down with an angry sneer. "You would."

She swallowed hard, both angry and relieved that he believed such a stupid answer. She wanted to keep that money out of pure spite. He owed it to her.

"Where's the police detective?" she repeated.

"What do you care about a human?"

"He's just doing his job." She gripped the back of Perry's chair, holding herself steady. Part of her was waiting for him to zap her to smithereens, or whip out a sword and take her head. This civilized conversation was just painful anticipation.

Belenos looked heavenward, as if bored. "For now, your detective is in the hallway. He made a nice little snack. Oh, don't make that face. He'll be up and around in a few hours, but he won't remember a thing." Her sire narrowed his one topaz eye. "Here you are defending him. He'll blame you for sure. You're the only vampire he'll recall."

"Whatever." As long as Baines hadn't died because of her. "Why are you here?"

"A little bird told me that you were visiting to look at the poor professor's things. Such a shame, what happened to him. But then, he shouldn't have gone snooping in things that aren't his business."

Talia gulped. How had Belenos known any of that? Who was betraying them?

"Yes, little duck. It's been like watching you step off a cliff. Part of me wants to cry out a warning, and the rest wants to see blood and bones strewn all over the rocks below. Guess which part of me won."

He made a gesture, as if grabbing something from the air. A crushing force slammed into her rib cage and squeezed her skull in an invisible vise. Talia dropped to her knees, suddenly too weak to hold herself up. *Help!* she cried out in her mind, but the impulse never made it to her lips.

"You forget that I made you." Belenos closed his fist, bringing the pain to an exquisite pitch. "I can take back that life just as easily. Good. You're finally looking at me with the proper respect."

She wasn't looking at anything. Colors floated toward Talia like the bad special effects from a 3-D film. Black spots exploded before her eyes. A human would be dead.

Just as suddenly, the pressure released. Talia collapsed in a heap. She drew in a small breath, testing her lungs. Everything still worked. *I'm going to kill him. I don't care how ridiculous that sounds, or how afraid I am right now.*

Belenos hauled her up with his good hand.

When she could pull it into focus, the hallway beckoned like the stairway to heaven. Surely that security guard would be back soon. He'd see Baines, call more cops, who would shoot her sire. Maybe there was a way out of this yet.

She took a shaky step forward, as if she were going to bolt for the door.

"Talia," he said, his tongue relishing her name. "I wouldn't try anything, if I were you."

She froze, her arms held out to her sides a little, letting him think he'd stopped her.

Now!

Talia wheeled and lunged for the door, her wordless cry echoing in the hallway. Belenos grabbed her hood, hauling her back. The force of it popped a button. She heard cloth tear, the sound nearly as sharp as a whimper of pain. She fell against him, the weight and smell of him bringing back waves of terror. He kicked the door shut.

"Let me go!" she shrieked, landing an elbow in his ribs.

He flinched, then chuckled, long and low. "Sh. I'm going to help you."

"Help me what?" she asked in a low, hoarse voice. She knew him all too well.

"I'm going to help you remember what it is to be the servant of a master and not a rebellious whore. Oh, yes, I know what you've been up to with your dog. That little bird simply talks too much."

Oh, God, no, she didn't want Lore mixed up with this lunatic!

"Such long, delicious shudders. One would think I was going to punish you as Omara punished me."

He crushed her against him in a nauseating embrace. He brought his lips close to her ear, his breath tickling her nose and cheek. "We can't have that, now, can we? Why copy a job when one can improve upon it?"

Chapter 27

"All I want is a quiet beer," Darak said to Nia, raising his voice over the din. "Where's the mystery?"

The New Year's crowd at the Empire was rocking, the bar three and four people deep. Darak had both elbows out, guarding his territory. Daisy was asleep at his feet.

Nia seemed to hold her spot by being female, exotic, and wearing nothing to speak of. There was more of that cosmetic glittery powder against her ebony skin than actual clothing. The werebear beside her looked ready to offer marriage.

"The mystery, my friend, is in how you think you can prevent me from helping you to pluck the guts from this King of the East." Nia gave him her squinty-eyed look, which said he was likely to end up with an arrow in his ass if he tried to sneak away. "I am the perfect choice for your hostage. I am beautiful. Men never expect a beautiful woman to cut their throats."

"No."

"Who else would you choose?"

"No one. No hostages."

"You think you can get close to him without playing his game?"

"How close do I need to be? I'm just stepping on a bug."

"Bugs bite."

Darak sighed. There were only a handful of people he let backtalk him, and they'd all known him since before the Dark Ages. It was hard to fool someone who'd been at your side since togas went out of fashion.

There was the whole problem: You couldn't replace people like that. They were his chosen kin. "I want to go after this fool alone because he's a crazy sorcerer. They're always bad news. How can I hand you over to him?"

"Bad news is my meat and drink." Nia took a sip of her cocktail. It was mauve with a flower floating in it. "And I'm bored. Stop trying to keep me—all of us—safe. After this long, it's getting very old. You should have told us what the ghost girl said right away. You should have let us help you look for the necromancer. Enough of that. In three hours you will take me to the pier, and I will play my role as a poor, helpless slave girl. You're not doing this alone."

Darak grunted something that was neither a yes or no. He was watching the bartender, Joe, who was holding a cell phone to one ear and his finger in the other. By his face, he was getting bad news. It seemed to be going around.

Joe's gaze flicked up, meeting Darak's face. He began walking toward him, closing the phone. He leaned on the bar, bringing his face close to Darak's so that he could be heard. "You met Lore, the Alpha hellhound, a few nights ago?"

"Yeah."

"He has a message for you."

"What?"

"He needs your help."

Darak sat back on his stool. *Great. Now what?* "What makes him think I care?"

Joe shrugged. "He does this prophecy thing. He said you made a promise to a ghost."

Darak's skin went cold. "What did you say?"

"He said to say the airports are open. If you plan on doing something, meet him at this address now." Joe grabbed a napkin and wrote something down. He slid it across the bar.

Nia picked it up. "What has this got to do with your ghost?"

Joe gave them a dark look. "Our friend Talia is missing."

Friday, December 31, 9:15 p.m.
Perry's condo

Perry Baker lived in an apartment on the ground floor of a Victorian-era warehouse in Spookytown, the entrance off of a parking lot at the rear. Iron stairs zigzagged up its brick face, a few of the railings sporting Christmas decorations. Security lights winked on as Lore made his way around the building, casting harsh shadows in the snow. Someone had cleared a path through the drifts. Bit by bit, Fairview was getting a handle on its Winter Wonderland status.

His mood was far from festive.

Lore had dreamed last night, or perhaps it was a prophecy. As usual, he wasn't sure which and he had no idea what to make of what he saw: Talia throwing a knife at him, a look of deep anger in her eyes. He could still see the whirling blade, the *thwop-thwop* of it as it spun through the air. In the dream, he was leaping, trying to get out of the way. Fear rippled through him, but he wasn't sure what was the real threat. In the murky dream-state, he'd known there was something worse than the knife coming his way.

He'd jerked awake next to Talia's still form, his heart pounding. He was sick to death of nightmares. First Mavritte with a blade, and now Talia. How come the women in his dreams never had plates of food, or mugs of beer, or scented massage oils? Just for a change, it would be nice. But now he couldn't find Talia. Was that what the dream meant? Was the knife the sharp stab of worry in his heart?

Lore had called a meeting of his friends. They needed to regroup and make plans because the airports had opened and Omara was on her way. The timing sucked. He had a splitting headache, and he was deeply worried about Talia. He had to find her, but he had no idea where she was—not at the condo, not at the Empire, not in Spookytown, and not at the cop shop. He needed help.

The headache was one of the curses of being the Alpha. He'd been sitting in Bevan's living room and talking to the Elders when another prophecy had ridden in on a mother of a migraine headache. Through the blinding lights and nausea, he'd seen Darak making a promise to a filmy presence Lore couldn't fully make out, but he'd heard Talia's name. Whatever happened next, the rogue vampire would play a role—and it would involve her.

Two prophecies in twenty-four hours? Unusual to say the least. That in itself set his ruff standing on end.

The headache would fade, but worry dug in like the talons of a raptor. Talia had a talent for vanishing—from his condo, from the hospital, and now from Osan Mina's house. *The woman is pure chaos.* At least this time, he was almost certain that she was with Baines. But why? Had she gone on her own? Had Baines forced her? Why hadn't she told him where she was going?

They weren't at the police station. As the cop on the phone had pointed out, they'd not been gone two hours. Talia was an adult. Lore should chill out. *Sure.* After all he and Talia had been through, it was impossible not to fear the worst. He wanted to wrap her in his arms, as if he could protect the spark between them with his own bones and muscle. Last night had meant everything. Talia had been everything. Brave, vulnerable, generous—those qualities that drew him to her had been there in her lovemaking. Also, that chaotic, unpredictable element. After living by the rules of the pack for so long, the surprise of her was intoxicating.

When the storm of lovemaking had been spent, he'd slept beside Talia, his body desperate for rest. On top of crime, death, and Mavritte, the venom had taken its mind- and body-blowing toll, but more than an urge to sleep had kept him there.

Hellhounds guarded—and he wanted to guard her. Forever. No one else brought the kind of peace he felt when his fingers brushed her skin. No one—hound, human, or anything else—drew his eyes and filled him with her scent the way Talia did. In a matter of days, she had become the center of his thoughts.

But she wasn't a hellhound. *This isn't supposed to happen.* Too bad. His soul knew who it wanted, and that was that. *I don't care. I want her, and she obviously needs someone to cover her back for once.* What she had been through in her existence was appalling, even by Castle standards.

Anxiety sparking through his limbs, Lore crunched through the snow with extra force. He crossed the parking lot. Some of the cars were dusted off, others still lumps of snow. A trail of footprints led the way to his destination. He wasn't the first to arrive.

Sometime before Christmas, Perry had hung a stuffed toy on the door—a wolf's head with a Santa hat and flashing red nose. Santa Claws. Lore had to push it aside to find the knocker.

He'd barely rapped twice when Errata opened the

apartment door, looking like someone had stepped on her tail. Behind her, he could see Perry's black and white kitchen. It was a little messy, but well stocked with cookbooks and cans of food on the open shelving. Lore knew Perry had wooed more than one woman with his spaghetti Bolognese.

Errata met Lore's eyes with a desperate expression. "I can't stand the man. Would you *please* take him back to the hospital and chain him to a bed."

Lore decided not to touch that one. "Silver poisoning makes werebeasts crazy."

"I know that," she snapped. "I didn't realize it also made them stupid enough to try playing detective when they're full of bullet holes. He just got home an hour ago. He's barely unhooked from all those machines. Yesterday, he was supposed to be dying, for the love of—"

She turned and stalked back into the apartment.

Lore stepped inside, smelling chicken and onions from the soup pot on the stove. *I had no idea Errata could cook.* He shed his coat and walked through to the living room. It was mostly bare brick with black leather furniture. Perry had taken the place for much the same reason Lore had moved into his friend Mac's old condo—to gain a little distance from their respective packs. They were both considered rebels for adopting the human custom of finding a place of their own.

At the moment, though, it appeared Errata had taken charge. She was frowning down at Perry, who was stretched out on the couch, cushions propping him into a semi-sitting position. Perry's arm was in a sling, probably to immobilize his wounded shoulder. His color was bad, skin pale against the shadow of his beard, and his scent was tainted with the sweat of pain.

"What part of bed rest don't you understand?" Errata fumed.

Perry's eyes narrowed to slits. "The part where I take a nap while the bad guys finish me off. That's why they let me out of the hospital, remember? Too hard to run a medical center with assassins roaming the halls, so you send the target home so he can be murdered off-site. No, thanks. I'd rather cut to the chase and catch the bastards."

Lore didn't see Perry angry very often, but the wolf was on a slow burn. Lore didn't blame him one bit. No hospital would send away a human patient like this. "How many guards are there around this place?"

Just because Lore hadn't seen them outside, that didn't mean they weren't there. Most of the Silvertail pack knew Lore, at least by sight, and wouldn't stop him.

Perry started to shrug, but winced when he tried to move his shoulder. "Dad said he had it covered. Of course, he wanted me to go back to his place."

"Maybe you should have," said Lore.

"No way. I do that, and as far as they're concerned, I'm twelve again." Perry smiled, but he sounded like he was only half joking.

Errata gave a little hiss. "Stubborn idiot."

A knock sounded at the kitchen door, two quick raps. Errata went to answer it. Lore glanced over at Perry. His friend had his eyes closed, lines of pain around his mouth. Errata was right. Perry should be in bed, not hosting a meeting.

At that moment, Errata led Darak into the room. The werecougar, tall as she was, looked like a child next to him. "Lore, your, uh, friend's here."

Lore and Darak exchanged a wary look.

"Hellhound," Darak rumbled by way of greeting. Then he turned to Perry. "You look half-dead."

"Working on it," Perry replied, opening his eyes to slits. "Do I know you?"

"Perry Baker, Errata Jones," Lore said, pointing to his friends. "Everyone, this is Darak.

"Of Clan Thanatos," Darak added.

At that, Perry opened both eyes. "We're going with the heavy hitters."

"Damned straight." Darak made himself comfortable in an overstuffed chair. "What's this I hear about Talia being gone? How long?"

"Two hours," Lore said.

"That's not missing. That's out for coffee. What else is going on?"

Uneasy, Lore took the other chair. Errata sat on the arm of the couch next to Perry.

Lore got to the point. "First problem: The airports are clear and Omara will be landing shortly. It's New Year's Eve and the town is packed with strangers. It's the perfect time for this attack we're anticipating."

"Where is she going to be?" asked Errata.

"She's staying at her usual hotel downtown. The Hilliard Fairview."

"Shouldn't she go someplace different?" asked Errata. "She knows there's a problem, right? With the fire and the election and necromancy, etcetera?"

"Queens don't move," Darak replied. "It would be a sign of weakness."

"Great." Lore rubbed his eyes, wishing aspirin worked on half-demon headaches. "Problem two: Talia is missing. I think she's with Baines, but I don't know exactly why. Her cousin was beheaded by a necromancer we think was her sire. Her brother is a Hunter who may well be the sniper who shot Perry. Against everything we know about Hunters, they're using magic."

Darak made a noise that said he'd just figured something out. "So the Hunters are the interested parties."

They all looked at him, Lore getting the creeping sense that matters had just got worse. "What are you talking about?" he asked.

"Belenos wants to destroy Omara," Darak answered. "It's not a leap to believe the Hunters would consider the election an abomination, and they'd cheerfully punish the queen whose influence made it possible. They're working with Belenos. That's why the Hunters have access to magic. A truce in order to kill a common enemy."

"Wait a minute." Confused, Lore got to his feet and began pacing. "The Hunters and Belenos? Belenos killed Talia. He addicted her brother. The Hunters would never work with him. Belenos has a feud with her father. She told me."

"Am I missing something?" Perry asked.

"Talia was born a Hunter," Errata said.

"What the hell? No way."

"Her brother came to finish you off and she chased him through the hospital. You slept through the whole thing."

"Thank God for that." Perry winced. "Fido's balls, Lore, I know you like the wild girls, but wow."

"She is not a Hunter now," Lore retorted, feeling his defenses rise. *Where is Talia? Why hasn't she called?*

"I don't know this tribe of Hunters," said Darak. "But the ones I do know always put the killing of monsters ahead of their personal affections. Their children are the pawns and tools of their fathers. It's an honor to sacrifice them to the cause."

Lore stopped pacing and sat down again, feeling sick. "That fits with what Talia has said."

"Not to be self-centered," said Perry, trying to hitch himself higher onto the pillows. "But on the subject of my foiled assassination, I take it that Belenos sent the brother after me? Why?"

"Belenos must have found out that you have video images proving he's in town," Lore said. "I'm not sure how they knew."

"I was working as fast as I could. Maybe I left a trail." Perry winced and closed his eyes. "But still, how would they even know? More to the point, why do they care? What does it matter if we know Belenos was in town once the attack is over?"

"He needs time," Darak said. "And he will try to get away without being discovered. He will try to stick the Hunters with the blame. And my people."

"Why you?" Lore asked.

"Belenos hired me to kill the queen." Darak's words were matter-of-fact.

Lore's heart began to speed. "Then why are you here?"

Darak shrugged, an earthquake in that massive body. "I care nothing for the queen, but Belenos is a pig." And he told them how he'd found Belenos, and what he'd seen. "My guess is the attack will come through the sewers."

"It fits," said Lore. "Talia chased Max from the hospital into the underground tunnels."

"If all this is true, at least we know what game they're playing." Errata rose to stand by the Christmas tree, hugging herself. "The next move is ours. Where do we go from here?"

Lore answered, his hellhound instincts utterly certain. "We confront them in their headquarters. Then we chew their bones."

Perry cleared his throat. "Hell, Rover, this is Belenos we're talking about."

"The sorcery could be a problem," Lore conceded. "But they are still flesh and blood."

"From what I saw, Belenos has men stationed over a wide area. To catch them all, you'll have to sweep all the tunnels under the city," Darak put in. "That's a large area. If Belenos is smart, he's going to be on the move himself. His magic is one of their greatest weapons. He's not going to make himself a stationary target."

No one answered that one. A stray thought of Talia, the way she had looked at him from her pillow, reminded Lore of everything he could lose. He rose, anxious with what they were about to set in motion. He knew what had to be done, was willing to accept the responsibility, but that didn't stop dread from crawling like cold lead through his veins.

He had to mobilize the hounds and wolves and invade the tunnels.

Taking his cell phone, he stepped outside the back door, not bothering to put on his coat. The night felt muffled by clouds, the sky hovering just above the rooftops. The square of light from the doorway splashed into the darkness, an island of homey warmth framing his shadow. He sucked in a lungful of the icy air, exhaled a cloud of frosty breath.

He tried to let go of enough tension to think clearly. Part of him was proud of what had just happened. He'd pulled together a team and figured out Belenos's plan. Perry had paid a high price, but that only made Lore more determined to make their work count. He pulled out his phone and began making calls, first to Bevan and then to Perry's father, the Alpha of Pack Silvertail.

Lore rubbed his hand over his face, willing to trade anything to be back in bed with Talia, lost in lovemaking. His skin remembered hers, the curve of her collarbone beneath his lips, the faint spray of freckles in the cleft between her breasts. The idea of her brought such a weight of joy and sadness that he struggled for the next breath.

The last thought had barely formed, when a familiar dread leached the softness from the gray winter night. Something evil was watching, just as it had on the night Talia's cousin was killed. Lore's gaze snapped upward, scanning for any clue. *This has to be Belenos at work again.*

He'd felt this same dark miasma just before the fire—except this time he was sure it was watching him. Lore banged back into the apartment, the door crashing shut in his wake. "We have to get out of here. Now."

"Why?" Darak demanded.

Lore struggled for a moment, searching for the right

words. "There's dark sorcery watching us again. I felt it in the parking lot."

"What?"

Perry struggled to a sitting position. "Fido's balls, not again."

The last time he had described the evil, Perry had teased him. Now his friend sat white-faced with pain, a hard expression in his eyes that Lore hadn't seen before. Perry gave a bitter smile. "In case you hadn't noticed, I'm not really up to running."

"It's Belenos," Darak said, understanding sparking in his eyes. "Now I understand. He has a scrying ball. He's using it to spy on his enemies."

"That's why he's been a step ahead of us all along." Lore looked at Perry. "If you used a spell to locate his image on surveillance video, that's how he found you."

"Shortcuts," Perry said sourly. "I should know better than that."

Darak pulled a carved wooden amulet from his pocket. He turned it over in his hand and shook it. "Nia, my second, made me take this to hide from the evil eye. Maybe its battery's dead."

"How do we block Belenos out?" Lore asked.

"You don't. I do," said Perry.

"You can't," Errata shot back. "You're full of holes."

Perry flushed with temper. "Are there any other sorcerers in the room?"

Errata folded her arms, her expression hurt and angry at once. "Just don't complain to me when you bleed to death, okay?"

Perry shook his head, as if shaking off her words. "Cats, always with the big drama. Hand me that red stone on the bookcase."

With his good arm, Perry pointed to a sphere of red jasper about the size of a man's fist. Lore did as he asked, finding the sphere was heavier than he expected. He passed it over carefully, afraid that one of them would drop it. Perry braced his hand on his knee, cupping the stone.

"Drama my hind paw," Errata muttered. "You're just another macho idiot."

"Better that than an idiot in that evil entity's cross-hairs."

Errata clamped her mouth into a thin line.

Lore shot her a look he hoped was sympathetic. He didn't blame her for worrying. Perry was reciting something in a low voice. The wolf stared hard at the ball of jasper, a deep furrow creasing his brow. A faint glow was gathering around the ball, but it was obviously coming at a price. His face was falling into hard, tired lines, his skin draining of any remaining color.

Then, as suddenly as if a switch had turned on, the ball of red jasper began to radiate a thick, ruddy glow. Perry's shoulders sagged. At first the light spilled over his hands, heavy as syrup, but with a single word from him, it feathered into the air, fanning out like a drop of ink in a pan of water. It crept farther and farther in every direction, a splash in slow motion. As it thinned to cover every inch of space, the color grew so thin it was barely noticeable.

Lore and the others watched, looking up, down, and to every corner as the room filled with the faint light. "What's it doing?" Lore demanded.

"Call it magical anti-spyware," Perry said softly. "It'll scrub any unwanted spells within a city block."

He set the ball on the coffee table and sank back against the couch cushions, closing his eyes again. "We're safe enough for the moment, but we've got to fix this, quick. I can't shield the whole town."

"If you attack the tunnels, expect resistance," Darak said grimly. "Chances are, Belenos will see you coming."

Lore's phone chose that moment to ring. He flipped it open. "Hello?"

"It's Baines."

The phone line crackled as if the connection was breaking up.

"Detective." Lore's heart leaped. "Thanks for returning my messages. Is Talia with you?"

"She's gone. I need your help. I'm willing to bet she does, too."

"What happened?"

"The only clue I've got is a pair of fang marks in my neck."

There was static on the line.

"What did you say?" Lore demanded. There was another burst of static that made Lore growl at the phone.

Finally, a clear sentence came through. "I can't get through to the station. I'm underground. I don't have a clue where I am. It's freezing cold. Someone bit me and then dumped me down here."

The call went dead.

Chapter 28

They were going into the tunnels.

They'd gathered in the alley outside the Castle door. It was cold and it was snowing again, a steady drift of fat, white flakes that made the crowd around the open manhole cover look like a scene from a demented Christmas card.

For the last ten minutes, Lore had been giving everyone their instructions, the logical part of his brain still working even if the rest was MIA. At the moment, Lore didn't care about evil bubbling up through the storm drains—he wanted Talia in his bed, and the rest of the world could line dance its way to hell. But she was missing and probably underground with Belenos, so down the manhole Lore and his makeshift army would go.

There were wolves and hounds, both in beast and man form. Joe had spread the word to some of the local vampires, too. They stood at the back, lounging against the brick wall and smoking, flashing fang as they laughed at their own jokes.

Darak had left to meet the other members of Clan Thanatos. Besides the two that Lore had met, a handful of others had just arrived from down the coast by private boat. They would carry out their part of the plan separately. Clan Thanatos would cover the operations aboveground, Lore and his friends below. As they'd expected, Belenos had given his assassins the word to set Omara's doom in motion. Lore hoped Darak was as good as he claimed, because at a rough estimate Belenos's welcome party for the queen, not counting the Hunters, outnumbered Clan Thanatos ten to one.

Mavritte stood across from Lore, on the other side of the sewer entrance. She'd planted her feet as if she were braced for another attack, her hands fisted on her hips. The strappy leather outfit she wore showed the deep scars in her skin, reminding him of the sacrifices she had made fighting for her people. It was good to have her on his side. It meant something that, despite their differences, she'd brought the Redbones when he asked.

Time was their enemy. Hurrying through his instructions, Lore forced himself to look calm and in charge. "Any questions?" he concluded, scanning the crowd.

"Go over the bit again about how we're not going to be made into throw rugs by the Hunters," said Joe, who had left his bar to support Lore in the fight. "Just for me."

Joe was carrying a weapon called a bardiche, which looked like a thin, curved ax on a long pole. The blade was almost as long as his arm, but Joe handled it with the ease of long familiarity. No villain in his right mind was coming near that thing.

A camera flashed. Errata was there, documenting everything. Lore wanted to snap at her. Sure this was news and she was a journalist, but the constant retinal assault was getting old.

Perry wasn't there, and that left a hole. Since coming to Fairview, they'd been friends, always together in a fight—against the demon Geneva; against their foes

in the Castle; and in a dozen bars in Fairview and sur-
rounds. Perry's absence was the marker of just how serious this was. He was the first casualty. There could be
more.

Talia might be tied up and at the mercy of her sire. A
sick lurch jolted Lore's stomach.

And where the hell was Detective Baines?

With his heart in his throat, he gave the order to
move. He'd prepared his people as best he could but, ultimately, they didn't know what they'd find down below.
The nonnegotiable was that Lore never, ever left his
people behind. One way or another, he would get everyone home.

Once they were into the tunnels, the company split
up. Errata had insisted on being embedded with the
troops, whatever that meant. The company split into
four groups, each taking a quadrant of the tunnels. Lore
had deliberately kept the units small. There wasn't much
room to maneuver underground, and he didn't want his
people getting in each other's way. An efficient strike
force, experienced with close quarters, was the best
choice he could make with the information at hand.

Lore took his group of hounds to the southwest quadrant, close to the Castle entrance. A few of these tunnels were newer, lined with cement and lit with a string
of lightbulbs along the ceiling. His plan was to sweep
through this area first, because it included the basement
of the old hotel where Darak had met Belenos. With
luck, the king would still be there. Lore prayed that Talia
and Baines would be, too.

Talia sat on a straight-backed chair in the middle of the
old, dusty room, bound with silver chains and gagged
with a strip torn from her own blouse. Her skin felt
grimy with dust, every tickle of her hair a reminder of
the rats she was sure lurked just outside of visual range.

She was somewhere in the tunnels. Wine barrels were stacked against the walls, coated with decades of dust so thick it looked like cotton batting.

Now would be a good time for Lore to burst in and save her—heck, she'd welcome Mavritte—but she knew it was a selfish thought. It was better if she could escape on her own, because this was Belenos. The last thing Talia wanted to do was to bring his special brand of crazy down on the man she loved.

So far Belenos hadn't done anything more dramatic than tying her to a chair, but she wouldn't be surprised if he pulled an iron maiden out of a utility closet. Belenos was good at pain. Some said it was his only real hobby anymore. Talia knew better. His hobby was fear.

Which was why she kept her face as blank as possible when he unlocked the squeaky old door and stepped inside.

"Hello, my duck," he said, his voice silky. "How are you?" He shoved his hands into his pockets, drifting into the room.

She tracked him like a downed bird watching a slinking cat. A bird with attitude, though. She made a growling noise around the gag.

"Sorry. Didn't quite catch that." He bent and untied the strip of cloth.

He peeled it away from her face. Automatically, Talia hauled in a deep breath, winding up to scream. Instead, she started coughing, a reaction to the stale, dusty air.

"Poor Talia," said Belenos, walking in a circle around her chair. She could feel his presence like a cold, slippery finger along the back of her neck. "So sorry this isn't much of a room, but privacy is hard to get when you're on the move. Or, in your case, on the run."

He put his mouth close to her ear, his fox-red hair swishing against her cheek. "But you know all about that, don't you? You can run, but you can't hide. You know your daddy's here, don't you?"

Talia couldn't help a twitch, but said nothing.

"Oh, yes, he's my new best friend. We're working to-gether. Isn't that nice?"

What? Shock made her jerk, which seemed to amuse him. Then she understood. Big Red was a nickname for vampires, but a lot of people used it specifically for the red-haired king. Max had posted to the bulletin board that he was following Big Red. Following, not hunting. *I can't—I won't—believe this!*

"It's quite true," he said as if reading her thoughts.

She couldn't protest, the hot rage of betrayal too thick in her throat. How could her father agree to this?

"I asked for Max as our special go-between."

Oh, God, Max! She turned to meet the king's one topaz eye. Belenos licked his ruined lips. "I remember how good he tasted, don't you? Dessert."

Talia squeezed her eyes shut. "Stop it."

"Are you hungry yet? Give it a day or two and I'll bring Max in. I daresay it's been a while since you've had anything but a dog to eat."

Oh, no. She locked her knees, fighting the shud-der that quaked through her. She couldn't feed on her brother. It was bad enough that she'd betrayed him to Baines in the car as they drove to the university. But that's exactly why her sire would starve her and then send Max in. It was her worst nightmare.

Belenos bent, and pressed his twisted mouth to hers. She could feel the scar tissue of his skin against hers, cold and hard and vampire dead. As she fought the im-pulse to gag, he thrust his good hand up the hem of her sweater, working his fingers under the lace of her bra. Clenching her body, Talia stayed perfectly still, know-ing that if she recoiled there would only be more to come.

"You're so frigid, I'd almost say someone had killed you." He gave a soundless laugh that filled the room like a dirty secret.

"Let me go." She didn't open her eyes, but whispered the words like a prayer.

"It's not time yet."

His last reply made her flinch. What had she heard in his voice? Anticipation. "I've waited for this for months. Oh, I've known where you were, Talia. This is the computer age, after all, but I let you think you were safe. What's the fun of having the humans send you back to me when I was just waiting for the right opportunity to come after Omara? The bonus of paying you a visit made this trip well worth the air miles. You're my kill-one, get-one-free special."

He leaned closer. "There's something I want you to see."

Talia kept her eyes closed. She was shutting him out. Denying what he had to offer.

"Look at me," Belenos said, suddenly furious.

She squeezed her eyelids tighter, like a toddler having a tantrum.

He grabbed her chin, pulling her forward as far as the bonds allowed. "Look at me!" he roared. As he squeezed, she felt the slide of flesh against her jawbone.

Her eyes snapped open, glistening with the pain.

"That's better." With his free hand, he pulled a quartz sphere out of his pocket. "I'm in charge. Don't forget that."

He released her chin, letting her slump back against the chair. Her jaw throbbed, a pain for every place his fingers had crushed her.

He lifted the quartz. It sparked to life, a firefly of light glowing at its center and then blooming to fill the sphere. Talia watched with deep suspicion as the bright ball glowed in his hand, rimming the edges of his fingers with transparent red.

He shielded the quartz with one hand, hiding it from her view. "Let's see who is down here. Where is Detective Baines? He was last seen bumbling into the *wrong* part of the underground."

The image of Baines was blurry at first, but came slowly into focus. The detective was sitting on the ground, loading what looked like the last clip of ammunition into his sidearm. Baines looked dirty and in a desperate hurry, but there was no blood or broken bones that Talia could see.

Oh, wait. Baines was getting to his feet now, but struggling, using the wall for support. Something was wrong with his right leg. He couldn't seem to put weight on it.

Belenos zoomed the image out a little, getting more of the surrounding area. "There are plenty of places where the tide has chewed caves into the soft rocks beneath the harbor, and many more where the tunnel floors are just wooden planking over the pits beneath. After a hundred years, some of that wood has rotted away. I'm afraid our brave detective has fallen through."

Talia's chest seized with tension. When the tide came in—around midday—all those underground caves would fill up, but that was a future problem. Right now, Baines had other issues. He wasn't alone in the cave. Something had fallen in with him.

The cat looked like a creature made by magic, or it might have escaped from the Castle. It looked like a standard tabby alley cat—scraggly, thin, and mean—except it was bigger than nature intended. It must have weighed a couple hundred pounds.

It was looking at Baines as if he were a baby bird. Easy, tasty pickings. Baines was hurt, trapped, and running out of ammunition.

"Oh, this is too good, don't you think?" Belenos cooed. He rose from his chair and crouched down beside her, showing her a better view of what he'd conjured in the stone. "What you see is what's happening right now.

How do you like my kitty? I made him specially to keep the detective from getting bored."

"No!" she cried, forgetting herself and trying to rise from the chair.

It rocked forward, forcing Belenos to grab the back to steady it. The lapse of concentration made him lose the image.

"Bring it back! I have to see what happens!"

The desperation, the *begging* in her voice was a mistake. His mouth curled into a smile. "I bet you think your dog is going to ride to your rescue like a true-blue hero."

He waited for the doubt, the wounded look as she took in his words, but her gaze remained steady. *Lore doesn't leave his people behind.*

He gave a low huff of amusement and waved his hand again, and then she saw Lore, a fireball flying through the air over his head.

"*Tsk*, bad aim."

"What is that fire?" Talia asked.

"Why, that's how sorcerers fight, my duck. Basic wizardry. I've been teaching my troop leaders to use more than just guns. It's hard for the enemy to shoot back when they're burning to cinders. And werebeasts hate it. Teeth and claws are of no use, so all your hounds and wolves are just fish in a barrel, if you'll forgive the zoological contradiction. The tunnels will positively stink with burning dog hair."

Talia could see the hilt of a knife in his belt, but her hands and feet were bound. She wanted so desperately to grab it and slide the blade into his heart, she could feel the texture of the hilt against her fingers.

Belenos stood, checked his watch. "Tick-tock. Time to run. Next time I come back, maybe we'll check on your friends. Maybe not."

"For God's sake, what do you want from me?" Talia let her fury show.

"Still plenty of fight left in you. Good. Next time, I'll

bring some toys. I'm dying to try out some of Omara's techniques."

Belenos slid the quartz into his pocket.

"What. Do. You. Want?" she hissed.

He picked up the gag, wrenching it back into her mouth. "Entertainment, my duck. It's that simple. *Le roi s'amuse*. You owe it to me after stealing my money and running away. But that's the last time—I've learned how to keep track of my things."

He patted the pocket where he'd put the scrying ball. "Don't forget that I'm watching you. There's no escape from me. Ever."

He ran a hand down the curve of her cheek, and then planted a kiss on her forehead.

Belenos's men had one important strategic advantage, Lore decided. They knew the map of the underground warren, where the turnings were, where the dead ends could trap their enemy. What had begun as a rescue mission and sweep of the underground was turning into an all-out battle. Belenos wasn't the only magic user on deck. His minions had training, too.

Where Lore had four bands of fighters, the sorcerer had dozens of small groups armed with fireballs roaming the tunnels. Lore had expected resistance, but nothing so deadly.

He'd gone to hound form, along with the others in his fighting unit. They were better trackers and faster runners on four feet. Plus, they were harder to kill—and the fireballs were coming thick and fast. Some of the creatures in the Castle had used similar ammunition, and Lore knew from experience how deadly it could be. There was a score down his back where one had skimmed over him. If he'd been on two legs, he'd be toasted. As it was, every step pulled and twinged.

It made him twice as determined to secure the area so he could search for the captives. He'd sent out volunteers to begin looking for Baines and Talia, but the danger was extreme. *If only I could go myself.* But he was the general of the hounds, and he had to lead.

Lore crouched on his belly and crawled along the base of the tunnel wall. He could smell a mix of human and vampire. He wished he'd brought a troll or two. Or a dragon.

Lore stopped his advance. His hounds had been chasing a larger group of fighters, and they'd entrenched themselves in this passage. Lore was close enough to see what his team was up against now. There was a pile of rubble across the tunnel forming a barricade. The bad guys were behind it, using the rocky debris for cover.

Okay, not imaginative but effective, up to a point.

The king's lieutenants should have watched more Westerns. Lore backed up, reversing the crouched shuffle until it was safe to turn and trot back to his men. They were waiting in the darkness of a tunnel mouth, nine pairs of glowing red eyes. Lore gave his instructions. Four of the hounds trotted back the way Lore had come, prepared to draw fire. Lore led the rest down an adjoining hall.

Anyone with brains—or a passing knowledge of old action movies—knew enough to sneak up behind the barricade or fort or wagon and get the enemy that way. He just hoped there was a tunnel that looped back to the right spot to launch his attack. Surprise and timing were his best weapons.

The hounds flowed through the tunnels at a fast trot, turning left and then left again. It felt like they had been down there for hours, but he'd lost track of time. Like a pendulum, his mind returned to Talia. Was she hurt? The thought spun through him like a whirling blade. He wanted to break away and go find her, to flee instead of risking both their lives in an insane battle under the streets.

The fight with Mavritte in Joe's hotel had clarified

much in his mind. Vampire or not, Talia was his mate. He knew it by her scent, by her touch, and by the way his heart clung to hers. He'd known it that moment in the parking lot, when she'd taken his hand. His brain hadn't put it together then, but his soul had known.

It explained why he felt he had always known her, and yet they had only just met. It explained why he would stop at nothing to have her. He wasn't going to compromise. If he was the type to give up, the hounds would still be rotting in the Castle. Compromise wasn't who he was.

He was the one who faced a fully loaded sorcerer, because it was his job to stand guard.

Some days it sucked to be Alpha.

Lore stopped, listening to the noise ahead. The other hounds gathered close around him, flanks touching. *Voices. The hum of magic.*

This fight was about to get interesting. The route he'd chosen had been the right one, leading to an unde-fended junction about fifty yards behind the barricade. He'd found the launch point for their attack.

But Lore hesitated. Why had they left this point un-defended? He used all his senses, but there was nothing to detect. Nothing but the bombardment of fireballs and the frantic yips of the brave hounds he'd left at the other end of the tunnel. They were doing a good job, making enough noise for ten hounds under attack instead of four.

It was a nightmare moment, his instincts telling him to wait while his brain demanded that he move forward. Lore bargained with himself, weighing the risks. Was he underestimating the enemy? Was he giving them too much credit? What hadn't he anticipated?

Well, he couldn't stand there all day, while his follow-ers shifted from paw to paw with muffled impatience. In the end, he had to take the chance.

Silently, they glided into the main tunnel, taking position. The hounds spread out, fanning across the width of the passage. From there they would silently pad close to their fireball-throwing assailants, and then show them what hellhounds could do.

It wasn't until Lore was in formation, in the center of the pack, that he saw the problem.

These new tunnels were wide and high, and just as the walls began to curve into the arch overhead, there was a jog in the brickwork that formed a narrow shelf on both sides. There were snipers sitting up there, wearing drab green vests marked with the crossed-blade symbol of the Hunters. *Hunters!*

The muzzles of their rifles were pointed straight at the hounds. There wasn't much that could injure hounds, but ammunition laced with quicksilver would—the metal of Mercury, who ruled the hounds as they guided the souls of the dead to the beyond. Obscure stuff, but the Hunters would know that. They taught that kind of thing to their kids in nursery rhymes.

Lore gave a single, sharp bark to signal retreat.

They turned tail and ran, leaving the snipers to splatter the tunnel with bullets. As the bullets hit the brickwork, explosions of silver liquid blotched the walls.

The hounds raced, outrunning the rifle fire, but there were also fireballs, sailing low over their heads, singeing the fur from their backs. The heat cut like a razor. Lore flattened his ears against his head, making himself as long and low as he could. He heard a yelp of pain. One of the other hounds wasn't as quick or as lucky.

Wait. I've been here before!

The tunnel narrowed, the side tunnels coming less and less frequently. They ran so fast, the brickwork blurred into a red-brown wash. They were being stampeded. At the end of the tunnel would be a dead end, where they all would die.

He'd had this prophecy. He knew how it ended.

Slaughter.

This is how his father had died: the pack racing for their lives, herded into a killing zone by demons. When Lore's father had turned to defend his people, it had been too late.

Not this time. Lore wasn't playing their game. He wheeled on his hind paws and began racing back the other way.

Right into danger. With what breath he could spare, he began baying a distress call.

The others took it up.

He had forty-five seconds before he was in range of the Hunters' rifles.

Chapter 29

If one didn't like spiders, the underground tunnels were a lousy place to be. Darak's cooler body temperature made him unappealing to most biting insects, but they still creeped him out. Give him a Bengal tiger in a snit; spare him the crawly things. Not that he'd ever admit that.

Webs and broken egg sacks lined the stone walls. Something down here was good eating, if the spiders liked the place that much.

"Is this the only way we can go?" demanded the queen.

It was the first complaint she'd made, so he was okay with the question. "It's the least expected one. This passage should be unguarded. We'll have you at the Hilliard Fairview in fifteen minutes."

Rather than risking a long, exposed drive on the highway, Omara had taken a connecting flight from the airport to the inner harbor via float plane. Nia—who had avoided playing hostage because of the queen's early arrival—was in charge of guarding the motorcade that was supposed to be carrying the queen. The plan was to trick Belenos into thinking Omara was in her limo aboveground, even while she was hoofing it through the sewers. The ruse would hopefully buy enough time for Lore to put Belenos out of business.

Darak stole a glance down at Omara. She ruled a vast territory in the Pacific Northwest, but she was tiny, dressed in a long coat of fine white wool trimmed with a fluffy white fur collar. One long black braid hung over her shoulder, a sharp contrast to all that white. Her eyes were the shade of dark honey, her skin of pale cinnamon. Though she barely looked twenty, she was far older than Darak.

A relay of phone calls through Lore and some guy named Caravelli had prepared her. Otherwise, a hi-how's-your-flight from half a dozen rogue mercenaries would not have gone well.

She sighed with relief when they reached a main junction. Darak and Iskander held up their flashlights. They were in the front, the queen and two of her personal guards were next, another two of Darak's men bringing up the rear.

They swept the flashlight beams around, identifying a fork in the tunnels. One had a stream of water down the middle. The unmistakable stink of rotting kelp hung in the air.

"What is that?" Omara asked, putting a hand to her nose.

"We're close to the harbor, Your Majesty" said Iskander, who was far more polite than Darak. "Some of these places fill up when the tide comes in. The tunnels were used to haul goods from the ships."

"Smuggling, you mean," she said, sounding a bit amused. Like all women, she seemed to think Iskander was adorable. That had been his talent as a body slave.

When they came to the next fork, they went right. Now the tunnels looked dirty and dark, but blessedly dry. In the beam of the flashlight, Darak could see where the layers of sand and dirt formed smooth carpets, and where it looked like feet had churned it up.

"These tunnels are definitely in use," the queen murmured. "Are you sure this route is secure?"

Darak traced the path with the light. "Whoever was down here went this same way."

They went into what looked like a narrow service passage lined with bricks. He guessed it was part of an old coal delivery chute, rebuilt to serve another purpose. Farther along, there was still black dust clinging to the bricks.

Iskander consulted the map he'd printed off the Empire Hotel's computer. "I think we're under Fort Street. That utility door to the left must lead to the basement of another hotel."

"Is that good?" Darak asked irritably.

"This passage connects two tunnels. Shortcut. We're where we're supposed to be."

"That's all I care about."

Omara gave a quick shake of her head. "Something is watching us."

Darak looked around. They'd loaded up on charms and protections, but none of them packed the wallop of Perry Baker's magic. "Then the plan's gone wrong aboveground. Belenos knows we've double-crossed him."

Omara's eyes flashed. "Then get me up there so that I can deal with this face-to-face. Now."

He liked a woman who was willing to fight, even if she was a queen. Damning protocol, he grabbed her hand, pulling her down the narrow brick passageway to the tunnels. Iskander ran ahead, graceful as a deer, a long knife drawn in one hand. They'd just gained the main passageway when Iskander stopped dead in his tracks. Omara rammed into Darak. They stumbled together, his arms around her to keep her from falling. She felt pleasantly female, if a little too small for his taste.

"What the hell?" he demanded, and then caught sight of what had stopped his friend.

Something—no doubt Belenos and his magic ball—had been watching them. And found them.

Their flashlight beams vanished into a wall of blackness. It was black as ink, or jet, or the edge of the world. A shred of the darkness tore itself off and began inching toward them like an ambitious slug.

Darak's stomach rebelled, trying to crawl up his throat. Pushing past Iskander, he stomped the shadow-slug with his big boot, grinding it into the dust. When he lifted up his foot, it had vanished. "Illusion."

Omara clenched her jaw. "I don't like this kind of pretend. If he wants to play magic games, I say bring it on. I'll show that worm a few tricks."

A bright speck arrowed out of the darkness, whirring like a dragonfly. They ducked in unison, Darak feeling a sting as it zipped past his cheek. It splatted against the wooden door behind them, and it exploded. Darak pulled the queen to the ground, hoping none of the flying splinters were stake-sized. He rolled once, coming up on his elbows, and fired into the wall of darkness. The other guards followed suit. Muzzle flashes lit up the tunnel, blinding him for an instant.

Once the echoes of the gunshots faded, there was a moment of expectant silence.

Another bright, whirring blob came sailing straight at the queen. She tracked it for a microsecond, then shot it out of the air with a ball of energy she conjured out of thin air. The collision flared into a chrysanthemum of sparks, banging like a giant firecracker. Pain stabbed Darak's ears.

Two more fireballs came toward them, close enough that Darak had to fling himself out of the way. One caught his left arm, searing through coat and shirt to shred the flesh beneath. He swore, blood streaming from the wound.

He turned to see one of Omara's guards dead on the ground, a hole where his heart should have been. Not even a vampire could heal that.

Omara screamed something in a language Darak didn't know, thrusting a hand at the wall of darkness. The black barrier exploded into a shower of tiny black pellets. Darak flinched, but the scraps of shadow vanished in midair. Behind the wall a dozen figures scrambled to get away. Darak braced himself and fired, dropping one. Omara's other guard and two of the Clan Thanatos bolted after them, leaving Iskander and Darak in charge of the queen.

Darak was on his feet, forcing himself to ignore the pain in his arm. "We've got to get moving."

Omara was looking around, her bottom lip caught in her teeth. Her white coat was smeared with dirt from the floor, but she didn't seem to notice that. Fear was seeping into her eyes. "Can you feel it?"

As soon as she spoke, Darak could.

Iskander swore under his breath. A wave of menace so thick it was touchable seeped out of the walls. It was followed by a strange crackling noise, like something sticky rolling across the floor, or a million maggots all squirming at once.

Horror bubbled over Darak's skin, every primal instinct going on alert. *What is that?* His imagination couldn't come up with an image, just emotion.

"Move," he ordered.

They moved, hurrying for the tunnel ahead.

Omara covered her nose. He smelled it, too—rot beyond description, as if the entire cemetery had come out to play. He choked back his gag reflex, motioning the others to hurry faster.

The sound was growing louder, emanating from an intersection in the tunnels about thirty yards away. Darak held out his hand to stop and shone the flashlight toward the noise. His hunting senses were on full alert, probing the darkness.

"Any guess as to what it is?" he asked Iskander.

"Bugs."

"Bugs?" *Crap*.

The queen made a disgusted noise. "He is using the creatures of the tunnels against us."

The atmosphere of terror grew, freezing every joint in their bodies. *These are bugs on magic.*

Iskander dug the map out of his pocket and shone his flashlight on it. "Alternate route, right side tunnel, twenty yards ahead," he said in a tight voice.

"Do it. Fast." Omara didn't sound any happier. She had her fallen guard's gun, and was holding it like a pro. "There's a problem using magic on live creatures that are already enchanted."

Darak looked down on her. "What?"

"I could try to blow them away only to have them come back bigger and stronger than before."

"No, thanks."

They ran forward, Darak hating the fact that they were running toward the threat. The rustling sound grew louder as they approached the side tunnel, the sinister fluttering and scratching making his skin crawl.

A giant, hairy, claw-tipped appendage speared into the passageway, followed by a second that seemed to probe the air. Omara gave a revolted cry.

They turned right and bolted, grateful to give in to the need to survive. Darak pushed the queen and Iskander ahead, putting himself closest to the enemy. The snap, crackle, rustle sound was growing closer. It was only as they rounded a curve that he saw the *thing* out of the corner of his eye. A fat, globular body swung amidst eight scuttling legs, a cluster of eyes glistening wetly in the center of its head.

And he remembered the millions of webs they'd passed earlier. The snap-crackle-breakfast-cereal-maggoty sound was the patter of tiny feet. Spiders were swarming in rivulets down the tunnel walls and across the tunnel floors.

They had no option but to run across the tide. Darak tried not to feel the slippery crunch of it, and then the tickle of something crawling under his pant legs.

Vampires ran supernaturally fast, but the big spider was just as agile, squeezing through a narrow neck in the tunnel by flattening itself and folding sideways through what space there was.

Crap! They reached the passage they wanted, but it was webbed completely over. Iskander, who had been ready to launch himself down the passage, recoiled with a backward leap, nearly crashing into Darak.

Another exit up ahead was rimmed in webs, as if the spinners had just gotten started on that one. Darak thought he could see the white mesh growing in the few seconds he looked at it.

"This way!" They wheeled and bolted through it.

"I know where we are!" Iskander cried. "There's a street exit about a block away!"

Blessed Persephone. This passageway was wide and new, recently used for city maintenance because there were pieces of pipe and other construction materials stacked against one wall. Frost furred the odd piece of metal, giving the debris the look of an exotic beast.

Darak had not gone fifty feet when he realized that the rustling sound wasn't behind them anymore.

It was up ahead, between them and the way out. His stomach dropped like a rock.

Iskander gripped his gun as if it were a talisman. "We can't go back. They'll have our retreat webbed off."

Without answering, Darak stopped and picked up a length of thin pipe, testing its weight and balance. He handed his flashlight to Omara. "Then we go forward." He took the lead, shifting the pipe to his left hand, the .357 in his right.

I hate bugs. I really *hate bugs.* Spiders zigzagged across the ground, crawling over one another in their crazed haste to get—wherever. Darak couldn't see a pattern in the movement, as if the creatures were driven by a panic of their own.

They grew thicker with each foot of ground. Iskander raised his flashlight beam a fraction, catching the dull gleam of a ladder to the street. For an instant, Darak's hopes lifted.

Then the beam went up another notch. The huge spider was just in front of the ladder, splayed on the ceiling. Now Darak could see its full size—the body was as big as the wheel of a monster truck. The little spiders were weaving a thick web over the exit to the street.

His whole body itched and prickled.

Would a bullet kill it? Only one way to find out.

He shot the spider. It fell with a heavy plop, flipping itself upright with surreal speed. The bullet had gashed its chitinous body, a grayish green ooze dribbling out. Its pincers worked manically, venom gleaming at the tips.

A very different kind of venom from a vampire's. One bite would surely kill a man.

Omara shot, aiming for the cluster of eyes. It squealed like a saw shredding violin strings. The spider rose on its hind end, front legs thrust out. Darak rushed forward, ramming the pipe into its belly. The spider fell forward, pincers slashing. With a wild leap, Darak flung himself into a somersault, barely escaping the cage of its legs. The spider jerked, struggling against the metal lodged in its flesh.

Darak aimed his Magnum and began firing with grim determination. Iskander and the queen followed suit.

Making another bone-wrenching scream, the creature rushed them. Darak dropped the gun and fell into a crouch right in the spider's path.

"Darak!" Omara shrieked.

As the thing swarmed over him, legs churning to grab and hold, he flung his arms around the pipe and thrust with a rasping scrunch. Green matter fountained from the wound.

The screech pounded against the stone walls.

The small spiders fled in a stampede of rustling feet.

Darak heaved on the pipe, shoving the weight of the spider away as he leaped back. It collapsed to the ground, bouncing once before it lay in a stinking heap. Green continued to bubble from the fat belly.

They stood for a moment, saying nothing. Darak stared at it, pissed that it dared to exist.

"Where did that thing come from?" he growled.

Omara answered. "Sorcery. Belenos surely made it."

"Do you think there's more?"

The queen shrugged, looking pale beneath her cinnamon skin.

Iskander cleared his throat. "Just in case, let's get out of here. Now."

Pulling a knife from his boot, Darak circled around the body, and climbed the stairs. The spiders' web sealed the exit completely. He hacked through the web, peeling it back with a sound like masking tape coming off the roll. He pushed open the manhole cover with a clang and climbed out. He took a lungful of clean, chill air, glad to be free. A moment later, he saw Omara's upturned face peering out of the manhole. He reached down to pull her out.

Iskander followed, already on his phone. He flipped it shut. "Nia's coming with the boys. There was a scuffle when a group of Hunters figured out the queen wasn't in the car, but she took care of it."

"Good news."

The queen's face was tight. "Even so, I underestimated Belenos. His forces are better organized than I assumed."

Darak gave her a long look. That was the problem with royals. They always figured they were smarter than the next guy. But Omara had guts, so he gave her the benefit of his opinion. "Look, Your Majesty. If he just kills you, there's a good chance someone will step up and continue your work. He wants to obliterate your base in Fairview. He wants everything you stand for gone."

She turned angry eyes on him. "Then we need to finish this tonight."

"No shit."

Chapter 30

Lore had less than a minute to save his people.

He charged the enemy, ducking, weaving, leaping the fireballs in a deadly dance. Their ammunition wasn't infinite, and he was determined to make them waste as much as he could. Every fouled shot was one less chance a hound would die.

Twenty seconds spent.

The scene was coming at him in a blur of detail: the sharp-edged rubble of the barricade, the startled faces of Belenos's vampires as they wheeled around to see the red-eyed hound hurtling at them. Lore knew the ones he wanted. If he took out the leaders, the rest would scatter.

Thirty seconds.

He would have to brave the snipers. He was gambling they only had a few bullets filled with quicksilver. After all, just about every hellhound alive was somewhere in Fairview. Such bullets were a custom-made item.

Thirty-five seconds.

His pack had turned and were following him, but they were far behind. He was moving faster than the sorcerers could take aim. Faster than he could think. Lore let go and let his instincts run.

Forty-five. Rifles cracked, the sound blaring against the stone, but he was too fast for them, too.

Men swore.

That's right. Do it.

Switching the rifles to automatic sacrificed accuracy for speed. It wasted lots of ammo.

Lore leaped, spreading his paws wide to catch the leaders in the chest, to crush them to the dirt for putting his pack, his woman, and the city he called home in danger.

Fireballs launched, and they were too close to avoid.

Poisonous bullets pierced his flank, tearing through flesh and bone.

He'd expected it. Lore let himself fall to dust.

In the spark of consciousness that was his essential self, he counted. *One-one thousand. Two-one thousand. Three-one thousand.* Holding himself between states was a difficult trick, one only the strongest hounds could pull off.

And he re-formed, his jaws around the neck of the leader, the bullets and fireballs sailing through the air behind him. Bone and cartilage snapped beneath his teeth, blood rushing over his tongue.

This was what hellhounds had been bred for: to search out and destroy threats to the common good. It wasn't pretty, but it was what they did.

Mavritte and her Redbones answered the distress call, leaping the barricade like a black, rough-coated nightmare. It was exactly what was needed. Their numbers tipped the balance. The vampires scattered like the proverbial chickens, screaming as they bolted into the tunnels. Mavritte's hounds followed, baying in chop-licking excitement.

Meanwhile, Lore's hounds found the stairways up to the narrow ledge the snipers were using. Hellhounds died, but eventually the Hunters broke and ran.

Lore had secured his quadrant and saved his pack.

But the search had just begun. The tunnels were vast and there was still no sign of Talia.

Or Belenos.

Munching of bones.

Talia's legs cramped from being held immobile by the ankle chains. Because vampires didn't exactly have circulation, her hands weren't numb despite being cuffed behind her, but her shoulders ached from the awkward angle.

Fear hovered like another presence in the room, poking at her with the claws of memory and dread. Talia tried to push it away, but somehow it managed to squirm past her refusals. It clung and it whispered, reminding her that her friends were in trouble, and what could she do? Talia was useless, stuck to a chair while Belenos and company studied www.WhatWouldVoldemortDo.com for evil inspiration.

He hadn't been back. Presumably he was busy stalking Omara.

Talia looked around, using her dark-adapted eyes to search her surroundings one more time. She'd killed Lore's clock and got out of her handcuffs once. Surely she could come up with a means of escape this time—but she wasn't seeing the possibilities just yet. There was nothing in the room but dust, spiders, and wine barrels. If there was ever an AAA poll on places to be held captive, Lore's bedroom beat this one-star underground hole hands down. Lore's cuisine was abysmal, but he'd at least cleaned since 1905.

Lore! She sent a silent prayer outward, to wherever he was. *Be safe!*

Talia tensed as she heard the key in the lock. Someone came in, holding a lantern. She squeezed her eyes shut, momentarily blinded by the bright light. And then she smelled him. *Max!*

When she opened her eyes, the sight of him sent a jolt

through her. He was holding a gun. She made a noise around her gag, half hope, half fear. He set down the lantern and walked to where she was sitting. Then he hesitated, shifting his weight from one foot to the other. Talia looked up at him, pleading with her eyes. *You're my brother. Don't leave me here.*

It must have reached him. Wordlessly, he crouched behind her, working on her leg chains. She twisted her head around, making noises around the strip of cloth binding her mouth. *Thank you. Thank you!*

He got her feet free and started working on her wrists. "Don't talk," he said gruffly. "I don't want to talk to you. He's going to kill you. Get out of here, and don't look back. If he catches you, I was never here, get it?"

Awooowowooo! The sound echoed through the tunnels, lonely and chilling. *Hellhounds.* Max's hands shook, slipping on the ropes.

She heard the thunder of heavy paws and heavy panting from massive lungs. It was so loud Talia could nearly reach out and touch the sound—the sliding, scraping, bumping of fur and muscle and claw in the narrow passage. Running right past the door.

"Shit!" Max muttered, fumbling with the keys.

He came back for me. My brother came back. Talia flexed her feet experimentally, the freedom of movement delicious. *Part of him still loves me.*

Something else howled, the sound like the desolate thunder of the eternal gate shutting forever. Despite herself, Talia shivered. Then the silver chains fell from her wrists.

"Get up," Max said. She could smell his sweat, sour with nerves. He would hate that loss of self-control.

Talia tore the gag from her mouth. "Thank you."

"Don't talk to me."

She stood, the motion stiff and unsteady. She was shaking, but it wasn't fear. It was pure emotion. She held out her hand to him, her fingers almost grazing his arm.

He jerked back. "Don't touch me. I wasn't here, remember?"

"Max," she said, her voice pleading, but then she stopped. He had done what he could. He'd betrayed everything he believed in to save her. She couldn't ask anything else.

"You'd better be able to walk," Max said darkly, opening the door.

Omigod! Talia's eyes flew wide, and Max wheeled back to the doorway. Her mind went blank with shock.

Belenos stood there, watching a miniature image of them in his quartz ball. "*Tsk, tsk.* I told you I'd be watching. Both of you. You know what happens to children who don't listen."

What was *he* doing back? Wasn't he supposed to be out killing Queen Omara?

Max blocked the entry, but Belenos brushed him aside. "Playing the big brother, are we? What will Daddy say about his beloved heir breaking the rules?"

Talia watched Belenos move toward her, every past horror rearing up like a cobra dripping venom. Instead of making her afraid, it was making her angry. He'd hurt her. He'd hurt Max, and he was planning to do it all over again.

She caught Max's hand signal from the corner of her eye, one they'd used together time and again since they were children. An evil kind of satisfaction filled her, but she wiped it from her face.

"You have to take care of this, Max. Plans have changed. We have to be prepared to move in a hurry." Belenos reached out and gave a lock of Talia's hair a tug. "She's betrayed us both, and now she's nothing but a nuisance."

"Leave her alone." Max took a step to the left, getting into position.

"Why should I?"

"She's my sister."

"Then the honor of taking her head is all yours, my boy."

Talia looked from one to the other, letting rage, terror, and incredulity flow over her features. Let him think she was frightened and helpless. Belenos undid the buttons on his jacket, exposing a shoulder holster that held both a gun and a long knife.

Maybe the same blade he'd used to hack Michelle's head from her body?

Max's face went hard and cold. "No way."

"Then you'll be the first to die." Belenos drew a Browning Hi-Power. "Loose ends need to be tied up."

It happened before Talia could form a thought. Vampire-quick, she grabbed for the knife at the same moment that Belenos aimed the gun at Max.

Max kicked, knocking the Browning aside. Talia had the knife, the grip smooth and elegant in her hand. Silver hilt, silver blade.

She shoved it between the Belenos's ribs. On the left side, slanting upward. Instinctively, she aimed for the heart.

But it wasn't his only weapon. He had a boot knife.

Searing pain sliced into Talia's side, turning her whole body numb. The hilt of her knife slipped from her fingers. "Max! Make it stop! Make it stop!"

Max fired his own gun, taking the top off Belenos's head.

The king fell to the ground, collapsing onto his right side. Talia dropped to her knees, blood oozing from her side. She pulled out the boot knife, feeling the ooze turn to a steady flow. Belenos was stirring. She groped for the Browning he had dropped, working by touch.

Horribly, with brains and blood oozing down his face, the king was sitting up.

Talia's brain short-circuited. Vision was no more than blobs of color. There was a noise in her head like the steady screech of a car accident, waiting for the crash. "Stand back, Max."

She'd found the Browning. She raised it, knowing she was a good shot. At this range, an idiot couldn't miss.

She started firing. A spray of lukewarm blood caught her face and arms, blowback. It didn't stop her. She kept firing.

And firing until there was nothing left but the click of the gun.

Belenos had no head left.

Max was gone.

And then the world began to fade to black.

Chapter 31

When she came to, Talia couldn't figure out what she needed most: rest, water, blood, medication, or a therapist.

A bath. She pulled herself upright. Her side twinged where Belenos had stuck her with the knife, but she'd stopped bleeding.

Belenos.

The gruesome ruin of his body lay there, an arm's reach away. He was melting, dissolving into a dusty slime as vampires did when they died for the second time. She'd well and truly killed him, a vampire monarch. Her sire. Her persecutor. Her killer.

She'd been a Hunter. She'd killed before. By rights, she should have felt remorse, jubilation, satisfaction, something—but no. Maybe those were emotions for later. Maybe this was too personal, too deep for ordinary feelings.

Right now it was more like ticking a mental check box. Belenos needed killing. No question. *Tick*. Done that.

Suddenly, she turned and threw up a spatter of liquid, missing herself but not missing the decaying splodge that had been his feet. Her body was experiencing something, even if her mind had checked out.

I have to get out of here. Her senses were coming back, and the smell of him was staggering.

Talia got to her feet, memories returning in a jumble. Michelle, finally avenged. Max, who had come to save his sister but had been too afraid to stay. Afraid of Dad.

Belenos was a crazy, dangerous sonofabitch, but in some ways was a stand-in for the real villain of this piece. Her father—the great Mikhail Rostov—was the one who'd given his daughter her real wounds. Without him, Belenos would never have had a chance to touch her.

And he was out there with the rest of the Hunters, killing her friends.

Lore. She knew he could take care of himself, but he was facing magic and Hunters. *I have to help him.*

I have to stop my father.

At the thought of that confrontation, Talia's hands began to shake. How long had she been unconscious? She stole another glance at Belenos. Couldn't have been too long. Vampires decomposed quickly, and there were still bits of him left.

She picked up his weapons, pulling the long knife from the remains of his chest. Without looking back, she left her prison and her jailer behind.

To find the first man who'd hurt her.

Talia walked for a while, listening to the sounds of battle around her, but not seeing anyone until she had gone some distance south. What was going on? What was it Belenos had said? *Plans have changed. We have to be prepared to move in a hurry.*

If he was packing up and killing the captives, he and the Hunters were losing. The first feelings of satisfaction began to warm her.

It was then she saw a party of four moving a little

way ahead. Gun drawn and held in both hands, she ran forward as silently as she could. It was a woman and three men. When one of the men turned to speak to the female, she recognized Joe's profile. By the height and shaggy look of the other two men, she was sure they were hellhounds in human form.

"Joe! Errata!"

They turned, Errata's eyes flared with surprise. "Talia! Where were you? What happened to you?"

Talia looked down, realizing that she was splattered with Belenos's blood. "I got sick of people trying to lock me up."

Joe and Errata exchanged a wide-eyed look. "We're one of the teams looking for prisoners," Joe said. "Now we know where you are, but Baines is still missing."

"He's down here somewhere." Talia accepted a bottle of water from Errata. "Somewhere where the wooden flooring has collapsed."

While she finished the bottle of water—it wasn't blood, but she was badly dehydrated—Talia told them about what Belenos had shown her in his quartz ball. It crossed her mind that what she wanted to do most was hunt down her father, but she owed Baines for treating her fairly. Revenge could wait a few more minutes.

"We're near the ocean," said Joe. "I've been down here before, looking at the sewers as part of the district business council. The area you saw is right around here. Do you think you'd recognize the look of the exact place?"

"Maybe," she replied. "I'll give it a shot."

As they set out through the tunnels, one hound was left to relay the news that Belenos was dead and Talia found. Yaref, the hound that remained with them, was silent, dangerous-looking, and in star-struck awe of Errata. The latter was focused on filming everything with a small, expensive-looking camera.

"Here we are," said Joe, holding up one hand to

signal a stop. They shuffled to a halt. They'd come to an intersection of three tunnels. Two looked old, with slabs of shattered concrete making up the floor. One was more recently built. Bare lightbulbs followed a track down the ceiling, but the power was off. Errata swung around, making sure she got the location from every angle.

"Maybe it was near here, but this isn't the exact spot." Talia turned to the hellhound. "Do you know Baines's scent? Can you track him?"

By way of answer, Yaref did the dissolve-and-reform trick, changing into a massive black canine. He applied his nose to the ground, snorting like a Shop-Vac.

"Where are we?" asked Errata.

"Under the old hotel row on Johnson Street," said Joe. "Look." He walked over to the wall, wiping off a few bricks with his sleeve and revealing an enameled metal plate screwed into the brick. "There's a few of these sign plates around."

Talia drew closer to see. It read FIVE LILIES HOTEL.

"There were old wine cellars down here," he said. "The Five Lilies was around a bit before the Empire was in its heyday. There's an apartment building on the old Lilies site now."

The hound woofed, and then stood still as a statue, one paw lifted, nose pointing down an old, wet-looking passage.

"Seriously?" Errata asked.

Yaref gave her reproachful eyes.

"Lead on." She sighed.

The tunnel was narrow and slimy. About a hundred yards on, Talia noticed a salty smell clinging to the old brickwork. "I can hear water," Talia said.

"Parts of the waterfront are riddled with caves," Joe said. "Watch where you put your feet. The tide has washed out the floor in places."

"What were these tunnels used for?" Errata asked,

looking more catlike than usual as she picked her way over the slippery floor.

"In the old days, they could deliver from the ships straight to the storage rooms under the hotels."

Yaref was trotting ahead, making excited woofs. Joe was keeping up with him, but Talia and Errata lagged a little behind. The dog reached a junction in the tunnels, did some more loud sniffing, but then continued on ahead. The air got colder and danker, and Talia envisioned the tunnel ending and dropping them all in the Pacific.

Yaref started to bay, the deep *awoowoo* that seemed to be their warning cry.

Errata gripped Talia's arm. "Hold on. Something's gone wrong."

Talia pulled herself free and crept forward, her gun in both hands.

"Talia!" Errata hissed.

A huge, angry fireball whistled down the corridor. *The enemy!* It was bigger, brighter, and faster than anything Talia had seen. Growling and snarling erupted and she heard Joe's angry shout. Talia turned and ran back to where Errata waited. The reporter was unarmed.

"Run!" Talia ordered.

Errata obeyed. Neither of them looked back until they reached the last place where two pathways joined. They crouched for a moment just inside the mouth of the intersecting tunnel, both silent and still in the dark. There was an angry growl, and then stillness. The hypnotic *slosh-slosh* of the ocean sounded right beneath Talia's feet.

"Now what?" Errata whispered.

A fireball burst past the tunnel entrance, making them jump. Talia could hear Errata's heart pounding fast. Yaref flew past, legs churning. Pause. Then a huge shaggy wolf burst past.

"Was that Joe?" Talia whispered.

"I think so." Then Errata raised a finger to her lips.

Four figures ran past, two vampires and two Hunters. Talia recognized both Hunters as lieutenants of her father. Seeing them together with the Undead was just *weird*. Unexpected tears filled her eyes, as if trying to wash away the sight. Her old tribe was violent and filled with hate, but now they'd betrayed everything they stood for in a bid for yet more power.

One of the vampires stopped, called fire to his hand, and threw it with the efficiency of a sportsman. Talia itched to shoot, but she couldn't take him and the other three in time to prevent return fire.

The vampire ran on. Talia waited a long moment until the sound of their footsteps had fallen silent before she stirred.

"Do you remember the way back?" Errata whispered.

"Baines is still down that tunnel. We've got to try finding him."

"We don't have Joe or the hounds." Errata looked doubtful. She pulled out her cell phone. There were no bars in this part of the underground.

"We could at least go look for Baines," Talia argued. "Yaref thought he was down here. It can't be far. This tunnel has to end sometime."

Talia could see Errata thinking, the call to adventure warring with caution. "Okay. Let's look."

They slowly slipped back into the main tunnel, stopping to look and listen every few yards. They stayed at the edge of the passage, close to the brickwork. In places, the floor was spongy, no more than rotten planks.

As Talia suspected, there wasn't much tunnel left. Soon they could see the end of it, a round brick mouth looking out at the gray ocean. Flakes of snow made a diagonal curtain across the opening. The wind was freezing cold.

There was a power boat tied up at the tunnel mouth.

Errata pointed the camera at it. "Want to bet that's
where those guys came from? Think they were patrol-
ling this entrance?"

"Watch it!" Talia cried.

Errata froze, pulling the camera from her face. About
twenty feet from the tunnel mouth was a gaping hole in
the floor. Errata looked down. "Omigod! Baines!"

Talia rushed over. The detective had propped himself
against the wall, his gun in his hand. He looked white-
faced and pinched with cold.

"Are you hurt?" Talia asked.

"I blew my knee falling."

"Maybe I can pull you out."

"Watch out for the cat," he said.

"Huh?" said Errata.

"A different cat. I used up my pepper spray getting it
to back off. It's still around."

Errata pulled back from the hole, whipping her head
around and sniffing the air. "Is it very big?"

"Let's just say Fluffy's on steroids, and he's mean."

With quick motions, she shut down the camera and
stowed it safely inside her leather knapsack. "Take this,"
she said to Talia, passing her the bag. "I'm going to get
changed."

Talia set the knapsack to one side and lay down on
her stomach, peering into the hole. She remembered
you had to lie flat when rescuing someone from an
icy pond. She guessed falling through soft ice and rotten wood involved similar physics. Spreading out her
weight would be a wise idea. Many vampires could
levitate, but she'd never mastered the trick. "Can you
reach my hand?"

Baines holstered his gun and hopped over on one
foot, hissing through his teeth with pain. Their fingertips
brushed. "Not quite," he said.

She wriggled forward a couple of inches, listening for
ominous moans from the flooring, and reached down

again. This time, she got a firm grip on his hand. He was as cold as she was, all of the usual human warmth having fled his fingers.

It was at that moment she heard a low, feline murmur. She twisted to look behind her. "Oh, shit."

Baines hadn't been kidding. A long, wiry tabby was stalking around the hole, staring at Talia with brilliant green eyes. As cats went, it wasn't pretty. One ear was torn. She could see its ribs. Its tail was missing patches of fur. And it was the size of a St. Bernard.

Talia froze, mesmerized by the lime-green stare. She could reach for her gun, but by the time she could draw it, she'd be vampire pâté.

"It's there, isn't it?" asked Baines.

"Uh-huh."

"It's fast. I'm a good shot, but I've only managed to wing it."

"That's so not what I want to hear right now."

A second yowl rippled down the tunnel. *Errata.*

The cat sprang to attention, forgetting all about Talia.

Talia immediately took advantage of the reprieve. Bracing herself the best she could, she gripped Baines's hand and hauled with all her vampire strength. She heaved him up, up until his other hand could grab the edge of the hole. That gave her a bit more stability, so she used her free hand to clutch a fistful of his coat and drag him forward. It was an awkward maneuver. He landed with a flop, using his elbows to lever himself the rest of the way out of the hole.

Talia got to her feet, grabbing Errata's backpack. Baines got to his feet, but it was obvious he wasn't up to much walking, much less running away. Talia wrapped his arm over her shoulders, taking his weight. Step one was accomplished. She'd found their man. The next order of business was to get him aboveground, preferably without getting chewed on along the way.

The first obstacle was the Evil Kitty. It was hunched

into an unhappy ball, tail lashing, sending up a nonstop chorus of warbling yowls. Errata was answering in kind, her own tail whipping against the floor.

The werecougar was smaller than Talia would have expected, her body only about four feet long. Errata was packed with muscle, her fur a tawny golden brown except for her white chin and underbelly. Rather than hunkering down, she had one paw in the air, ready to swipe at her opponent.

The caterwauling blended into a continuous *meeeow-wwwwwowrr*. Talia would have given a lot for earplugs.

She struggled to think past the racket. She'd never get Baines back through the tunnels to the Castle entrance, but there was a boat a short hobble away. Under the circumstances, a bit of piracy didn't bother her, especially when the rightful owner was a villain.

A hop at a time, they started toward it. Baines was silent, his face gone ashen with pain.

"Do you know how to hotwire a boat?" Talia asked.

"Not. Done it. Long time," Baines replied through his teeth.

But you have. Interesting. Talia eyeballed the vessel as they got closer. It was a small Ranger, okay for traveling close to shore. "It's got an old Evinrude outboard. There's a red plug on the main wire harness. Disconnect it and jump the starter straight from the battery. Just choke it down to kill the engine later."

Baines frowned at her. "I thought you were a Latin teacher."

"English Lit, actually, but I can say all that in Latin if you want."

The cat picked that moment to pounce on Errata. Talia and Baines wheeled around to see the tabby grab Errata's head and flip her, clawing her belly with its hind legs. The cougar raked the tabby between the ears.

"Into the boat!" Talia ordered, grabbing Baines by the arm and half lifting him over the side. "Call the cavalry. Try the werebears. Tell them we need more help down here. Bring everything they've got."

Baines gave a single nod, discipline warring with worry in his face. "I'll do that."

In the tunnel, the cats separated, but only for seconds. Errata boxed her opponent, using strength where the other had speed. The tabby caught her in another grapple, but this time Errata threw her weight against the cat, bearing down and gripping with her long, curved teeth.

Talia glanced back at Baines. He was already working on the motor.

"If you call in your cop friends, keep them out of the tunnels. This fight isn't for humans. Your guys can make their arrests topside."

Errata howled in outrage as the tabby clawed at her eyes.

The outboard motor sparked to life. Talia suddenly felt light-headed with relief. He would make it out of danger.

"Are you going to be okay?" he asked.

"I've got to help Errata," she said, getting to work on the rope tethering the boat to the mouth of the tunnel.

"Watch yourself."

"Dead already, and I probably taste like it." She cast the rope into the boat and walked away back into the tunnel.

One life saved. Now for the catfight.

She pulled her gun. This was getting to be one hell of a night. *Just call me Dirty Harriet.*

She braced her feet apart, raising the Airlite in both hands. "Here, kitty, kitty."

Chapter 32

"It looks worse than it is," Errata insisted. She'd wadded up some paper napkins she'd found in her knapsack and was pressing them against her head. "Scalp wounds bleed like crazy."

They'd come to another tunnel junction. Talia looked both ways, her gun cupped in two hands. In the end, she'd frightened off the cat, but Baines had been right—it was too fast to get a clean shot. Not without risking Errata, who'd already been giving her all. Now the werecougar's hazel eyes peered out of a mask of blood. The cat had ripped open her scalp badly enough that she hadn't completely healed changing back to human form.

Good thing werebeasts didn't smell like dinner, because she was starting to get hungry. "You look like you're trying out for a role in a slasher flick."

Errata rewadded the paper napkins, looking for a dry spot. "Harsh. Remind me not to take you shopping for bathing suits. My self-esteem wouldn't survive it."

"Actually, you've impressed me. Not everyone can fight."

Errata gave a low laugh. "I have four older brothers."

"That'd do it. Are you sure you don't need to rest for a minute?"

"And risk a repeat visit from Whiskers? I don't think so."

When Errata fished her camera out again, Talia decided she had to be feeling okay, and kept moving. By now, they had to be near the spot with the hotel signs. She'd been hoping to meet up with Joe or Yaref, but no such luck.

"Sh!" Errata cocked her head, listening.

Talia strained her ears. Footsteps in the passageway. Silently, Talia got to her feet and slipped around the corner to see who was nearby.

She saw a man up ahead wearing a vest with the crossed-sword design. Max. *What's he doing by himself?*

Errata was behind her. "Isn't that your brother? *The one who shot Perry?*"

"Yeah. I need to talk to him." *He risked himself to save me.*

"Are you sure he wants to talk to you?"

Her words sliced through Talia. "This might be the only chance I'll ever get."

"And after that?" Her words were cool.

Talia didn't answer. Half of them might not make it home alive. She wasn't going to make promises.

With vampire speed, she closed the distance between herself and her brother. When she was a few steps behind, she paced him, step for step, letting the emotion that jammed in her throat crest, and then drain away. She blinked hard, clearing her vision before she spoke.

"Max."

Her brother wheeled, bringing his rifle to his shoulder with the speed of long practice. Then he fell back a step, his mouth falling open.

"Talia." Her name came out in a croak. "Get out of here."

"We have to talk. I'm still your sister. We played on

the snow hill together. We sat at the same table every
breakfast and dinner." *Until Dad effing stole my chair.*

Max's face twisted with fear. "Talia, for the love of
God get out of here. If Dad finds you . . ."

Talia heard a scream, half-human, half-enraged feline. *Errata!* She whipped around, her gaze searching
the tunnel. She couldn't see the werecougar, but there
were more figures wearing the Hunter symbol on their
clothes. The Hunters were converging on the spot Talia
had left Errata. *They have her!*

Perry's face flashed through her mind. They'd show
no mercy to a werebeast, and what they could do to a
female was even worse.

Max pushed past her, running toward the group and
leaving her alone. He wasn't brave or foolhardy enough
to be caught talking to the enemy, even if it was his sister. *Damn him!*

Talia took a deep breath, shifting her grip on the
Airlite. She wasn't leaving Errata at their mercy. She
started running toward the Hunters, her mind scrabbling for a plan.

Hard hands grabbed her from behind. "What are you
thinking?"

"What the hell!" Talia twisted around. An enormous
vampire loomed there, wearing a leather jacket and a
ferocious scowl. Where had he come from?

"If you don't stop and think, they'll have you, too," he
said grimly, his ice-blue eyes so pale they looked almost
white in the gloom. "Come on."

He dragged her down the tunnel, not stopping until
they reached a hollow in the stonework where they
could take cover.

"Who are you?"

"Darak."

So this was the mysterious rogue from the Empire.
"Aren't you supposed to be fighting topside?"

"I did my bit there. I had a promise to keep about

dragging your ass out of the fire. Now I know why. You're a bloody cowboy."

"Lore made you promise?"

"No. Michelle."

A sick feeling burned her. *He talks to ghosts*. "Was she all right?"

"Yeah. And she loved you." His voice had the finality of a slamming door.

Talia turned away, hiding the tears that choked her. "Thanks. I guess.."

He grunted.

They were close enough that Talia could count the men. There were four, including Max. She knew all of them by name. One had been her neighbor.

Another was her father. Tall and lean, his gray hair shaved close to his skull, Mikhail Rostov was definitely in command. He turned her way for an instant, and Talia caught sight of his face. Deep lines cut from his nose to the corners of his mouth, emphasizing his unbending expression. Waves of anger and longing sang through her. She wanted to smash that expression off his face, to make him bend. In an anguished part of her heart, she wanted him to hold her and tell her she'd been a good girl.

She'd killed Belenos, but just seeing her father was infinitely worse.

Cold sweat trickled down the small of her back. There would be no reconciliation. The only thing she could do was make sure that he didn't hurt her friends. She hoped that meant capturing him, but it might mean more.

"Are you okay?" Darak asked, studying her face.

"Yes," Talia said, hearing her voice shake. "I used to be one of them."

Talia realized what she'd just said, and felt her whole body turn to ice. *This is where he fights me, or we fight the Hunters together.*

But Darak seemed undisturbed as a block of granite. "They'll kill you. You know that, right?"

"Yeah. I'm a monster."

He gave her a piercing look. "Only if you want to be. Being a vampire gives you power. How you use it is up to you."

Talia couldn't take her eyes from her father. "I want to pull their plug."

The huge vampire made a satisfied noise. "Got a plan?"

"The Hunters will use Errata as a living shield. They'll make their way to the exit assuming we'll hang back, but they always kill their hostages at the last minute. The only chance we have of saving her is to get close enough to take out the Hunters before they know we're there."

Darak looked at her, a crease between his brows. "How do we do that?"

"Just get me one of their uniforms."

"You sure about this?"

Frustrated, Talia snatched her sleeve, pulling it up, exposing the Hunter tattoo. "I know what I'm doing."

"Okay, then." Darak gave her a mock salute. "The killer babe is in charge."

"Damned straight."

"Stay here." He slipped out of the hiding place, seeming to vanish once he reached the corridor. For such a huge man, that was impressive.

She leaned her head against the cold stone wall, simmering with impatience. Every memory of her long years of training flooded back to her. Planning what to do next took less than a minute. Most of the rescue would have to be improvisation, based on what she knew of the Hunters.

The hard part was turning on her family. It should have been easy, but right and wrong was for the brain. Going against the loyalties drummed into her from the cradle was going to break her heart.

But, sooner or later, she had to decide who Talia was. She wasn't the soldier her father had left on the battlefield, or the monster he'd banished from his table—and she sure as hell wasn't the scared girl who followed his orders even though her conscience screamed every time they went out on a hunt.

And none of that would mean a thing to him. Whatever she did next had to be done because it was right, not because it settled a score or proved a point. She would never change the way her father thought.

Darak returned with a Hunter's vest, utility belt, and two rifles. "There were dead nearby," he said tersely, thrusting the gear at her but keeping one rifle for himself. "I'll lurk in the shadows. They didn't have anything in my size."

"You don't need to come with me," Talia said. "I can do this alone."

"Sure you can," he said, watching her pull the vest over her blood-spattered clothes. "Shut up and tell me what you're going to do."

A surge of gratitude loosened the knot of apprehension in her chest. "I catch up to them. The uniform will fool them for about a second, but hopefully that's all I need."

"For what?"

"Follow my lead."

"I don't like that plan."

"Too bad." Talia took off at a run, praying they weren't too late.

The Hunters were only a few minutes away from the exit in the Castle alley. As Talia had predicted, her father had a gun to Errata's head. Max walked next to him. There were two other Hunters following in the rear. She could see the red glint of hellhound eyes in the shadows up ahead, watching the Hunters as they passed, but the hounds were helpless to attack. Talia prayed the hounds recognized her as a friend, despite the borrowed gear.

Talia caught up to the uniformed men. Her father

turned to acknowledge the troop joining his team, and in that split second Talia had to act. She gave a short, sharp whistle, the band's signal for danger ahead.

As she'd hoped, every Hunter jerked their attention forward, away from her. Talia smashed the butt of her rifle into her old neighbor's head, knocking him unconscious, then delivered a solid kick to the man on her other side.

Surprise was on her side. Talia wheeled and kicked the rifle out of her father's hand and yanked Errata out of his grasp. "Go!" she yelled.

Errata sprinted for freedom.

Talia's heart leaped with victory. She spun around, ready to follow, but her luck ran dry. She felt her gun hand wrenched behind her back, the sudden pain forcing her to drop her weapon. She swung her free arm, only to feel the slice of a blade so sharp it took a moment for the nerves to summon pain. A moment later, there was the cold kiss of a knife at her throat.

"How dare you show your face to me?"

The rough, hard edge of her father's voice sawed through her, bringing a rush of confused emotions. Panic. Disbelief. Disappointment. Hatred. Somewhere under all that, the memory of loving him.

"Don't kill me, Daddy." She could see the tip of the knife from the corner of her eye. It was the big Bowie knife her father had always carried. Big enough to— eventually—take off her head.

"Please, Daddy."

"I'm *not* your father."

"No, don't!" yelled Max.

She felt the knife bite into her skin. The sharp, hot pain wrenched a scream from her.

The news from aboveground was good. The queen was safe and under the watchful eyes of Clan Thanatos as well as her own armed guard.

While Lore's hounds secured the dense south end of the tunnels, his Beta's crew and the wolves of Pack Silvertail had tightened the other sides of the net. Many of Belenos's vampires had been caught or killed. When the news came that Talia was safe and had killed their sire, the fight had gone out of them.

More hounds and wolves had arrived with the werebears. Baines had called them, and they arrived just in time to have a share in the final roundup. There was also a heavy police contingent aboveground, covering every exit they could find.

Lore was satisfied with the progress so far, but there were too many questions left unanswered. To begin with, where was Talia? No one had seen her or Errata since they'd been separated from Joe.

Instead, he found Mavritte leaning against a wall, her leathers running with blood. She was staring at the floor.

Lore studied her face. "Thank you for fighting so bravely today."

"I am no coward." She gave him a hard look. "I have not forgotten my challenge to you."

"Even with everything that has happened tonight?"

"What has this to do with the pack? It is a war of vampires. Hellhound business has not been resolved." She turned her face away, speaking so softly he barely heard her. "Though I see what you love in your vampire."

That surprised him. "You do?"

"She killed her sire. She is a warrior without fear. But she is not one of us."

"Does that matter so much?"

She looked sad and tired. "The pack leaders must put the pack before all. How can a vampire put the hounds first? It goes against nature."

Lore was silent.

"Without a strong Alpha, there will be no future for us. No anything. The legends say there will be no young."

"You speak of legends. Traditions. We live in a different world now."

Mavritte poked him in the chest. She smelled of sweat and blood and gunpowder. "Do you not dream in prophecy? Do you not smell evil on the air? Are we not demon kin? You cannot believe what you want and ignore the rest."

"I will not let tradition trample what I know in my soul to be right. And I will not fight you."

"Then you can wage all the wars you like and remain a coward. It is the battle on the hearth that counts." Mavritte turned away, contempt in her eyes. "If the home is not strong, the kingdom has no foundation to rest on. The Alpha must have the strongest house of all. You have no true mate. You have nothing."

Lore was momentarily speechless.

Then they heard Talia's shriek of pain.

Lore scrambled into the tunnel, morphing into hound form as he ran.

He looked first for Talia. She was down and bleeding from the neck and arm.

Errata stood to one side. She had a gun, but didn't seem to know what to do with it.

One Hunter was down on the ground, but another, who was bleeding from the head, flew through the air. Darak lifted a third over his head like a sack of flour.

Lore had to get to Talia, but there was an obstacle. Two more Hunters—Talia's brother and an older man—were wrestling on the floor and in his way. It looked like Max was trying to grapple for a knife. They both looked up to see Lore at the same time. In their surprise, the knife went skittering across the floor.

Lore gave a warning growl. The older one grabbed for a rifle that was lying on the ground. *Mercury bullets*. Bad news, because Lore's strength was close to tapped out. The odds of pulling off that disappearing trick again tonight were low to none.

Rage slammed into him. He had to try. That was his mate wounded on the ground.

Kill. Protect. Lowering his massive bulk into a crouch, Lore bared huge, white teeth, his growl echoing like an earthquake down the tunnel. Someone screamed. Lore bounded forward, massive paws raised to trap and crush.

The older Hunter raised the rifle.

But Talia had lunged for the knife and thrown it a fraction of a second before, a look of deep anger in her eyes. He could still see the whirling blade, the *thwop-thwop* of it as it spun through the air. It was the same moment as had been in his prophecy.

Lore twisted in the air, giving extra clearance for the knife's path. The rifle fired. Lore had a moment of free-fall as he waited for the tearing of the mercury bullets through his belly.

But they never did. He felt them skim by, a hot flick against his skin.

When he hit the ground, the knife had drawn a long, bloody slash down the older man's arm. Lore landed with a clumsy thump and roll, coming to his feet in time to see the two men disappearing down the tunnel. Darak chased after them.

Talia was weeping, the harsh, racking sobs of heart-break. Lore padded over to her. Her neck was bloody, but it wasn't bleeding. There was a wound in her arm that was far worse.

He didn't think it was the cut she was crying about.

Lore curled up on the ground, pushing his body against her thigh, and put his chin on her knee, peering up at her. Hellhounds weren't known for their appeal, but he gave it his best doggy-soulful try.

She hiccupped. "Oh, stop it."

He whined and licked her face, but just once.

She squeezed her eyes shut, burying her hands in his

fur, kneading the ruff of his neck. It felt like heaven. "That was my father."

A fresh bout of tears seized her. He melted back into his human form, and held her close against his chest.

"But I didn't let him kill Errata," she said. "I stopped him. I stopped my father."

Chapter 33

"Happy New Year and best wishes from your friends at CSUP Radio, coming to you from the University of Fairview campus. This is Signy White filling in for Errata Jones.

"Here's a piece of British folklore for you. Remember, ladies, that if the first person to enter your home on New Year's Day is a tall, dark-haired male, it's good luck. They call this man the first-footer. They don't say what they'd call it if he had four feet.

"What the heck. Tall, dark, and lucky? I'm open to that kind of visitor any day of the year."

New Year's Eve, midnight
Downtown Fairview

Once she was in the clear air aboveground, Talia remembered that the sewer exit was a stone's throw from the Castle doorway. Guards were there, two in hound form, two in human. The old, stained brick of the alley glittered with frost, waves of snow clinging to the bottom of the walls. The middle of the alley gleamed with ice. Just then, the carillon at the museum began ringing in the New Year. Above, the fireworks from the harbor started. A thunderclap filled the air as a Roman candle flared to life overhead.

A dozen yards away, a bare patch had grown around the back door of a Chinese food restaurant that someone had propped open with a huge white plastic bucket. The doorway exhaled gusts of chow mein–scented steam as if the whole of Fairview had ordered in for their late-night celebration.

As Talia got her bearings, one of the hellhound guards from the Castle doorway ran over, calling something to Lore in their own language. Lore replied tersely, and the guard reversed course.

"What's going on?" she asked.

"I asked him to get help."

She suddenly felt faint. "Help? Aren't we done for tonight?"

Lore turned her to look at her arm, his touch kind but no-nonsense. "For you. Your arm is bleeding. A vampire should have healed by now."

Talia realized what he said was true. She hadn't had a big injury since she'd been Turned, but she'd seen other vampires bounce back from the most horrific trauma. Life with Belenos was nothing if not educational. "Silver blade."

He looked up, a touch of fear in his eyes. "We'll get you looked after."

"I'm tough," she said. *I'm dead. Could I actually bleed to death?*

He slid his arm around her waist. "Good."

There was another explosion overhead. It sounded like a cannon shot, but incongruous sparkles of gold dusted the sky. Talia let herself lean against Lore's chest, his coat rough against her cheek. If she admitted it, the pain and hunger and slow blood loss were wearing her down—but she didn't admit it. That was the first thing a Hunter learned: If you don't believe in pain, it can't hurt you. *Yeah, right. So much for that theory. It bloody well hurts, Dad, so stick it in your ear.*

It felt good to lean on somebody for once.

The hellhound was running back toward them. "Mac says to come inside the Castle. He's got first aid."

It took a moment for what he said to register, but when he did, Talia pulled away from Lore. "Are you kidding?" she protested. "I'm not going in there."

"It's safe. Mostly." Lore looked like he was struggling, probably with his obligation to tell the truth. "As long as you stay near the door. You don't want to go exploring."

"But . . ." *But it's a prison for monsters. Only monsters go there. Wait. That's me.*

"I'll be with you the whole time." He took her hand. "We need to bandage your arm."

"Okay, but don't you dare leave me for a second." She pulled out her gun and checked it. She still had plenty of ammo left.

Lore watched her, a slightly bemused look on his face. "Check with me before you shoot anyone, okay?"

"Whatever."

He put his arm back over her shoulder and, flanked by hellhounds, they approached the Castle door. Talia noticed someone had strung a HAPPY NEW YEAR banner in front of the entrance. The gold foil flickered as fireworks bloomed overhead. She imagined a pack of ghouls with party hats and noisemakers, and it wasn't pretty.

Lore stiffened as the Castle door swung open with a mighty groan. He might be used to the place, but she guessed he wasn't a fan. Talia followed him, her skin crawling with the anticipation of something awful.

At first glance, Talia felt like she was on a horror

movie set. Dark corridors hewn of gray stone crossed
at regular intervals, each looking exactly like the other.
Every few yards, a torch was set into a bracket on the
wall. The fire was odorless and gave no warmth, just a
dim, flickering light. *Magic.*

The door shut behind them with a deep, hollow
boom. She heard the slide of a thick metal bolt. The motion sent a cloud of dust swirling around her knees. Her
first instinct was to whirl around and pound on the door
to get out.

"You grew up here?" she asked in a whisper.

"Generations of hounds lived and died in this place
without seeing the outside. I was lucky enough to find an
open portal and lead my pack through it. That was in the
bad days before Mac took over."

Talia scanned the endless maze of dark, spooky hall-
ways. It looked like *Escher meets Frankenstein.* She tried
to imagine Osan Mina, with her bright kitchen, or—
worse yet—the hellhound children trapped in the shadowy desert of stone. *You grew up in here. How is that
possible?*

All at once she grasped the long, long road Lore had
traveled with his pack. They'd come from this and still
made a functional community in Fairview in a few short
years. *That's a huge, massive act of will.*

"This way," he said, steering her down one of the
many identical, featureless routes.

He slowed his steps to match hers, and Talia realized
she was all but walking backward. She felt weak and
shivery, but how much was due to her wound and how
much was the Castle's atmosphere? She forced herself
to pick up the pace.

"Once, the Castle was a living world," Lore said in a
tone that said he was trying to calm her down. "That was
a long, long time ago, before it turned into a dungeon."

"What happened?"

"One of the sorcerers who built the place went mad.

To make a long story short, he robbed it of life. Mac gave up his humanity to give it the chance to recover."

"What do you mean?"

"The world is rebuilding itself now, but it's kind of happening in fast-forward. Just like on the Discovery Channel."

Talia stopped. "Excuse me?"

Lore looked at her arm. "There will be time to show you later."

"You dragged me in here. Satisfy my curiosity."

He considered for a moment. "Look at this."

He drew her down a short side corridor. A few yards along, the stone blocks stopped and grew irregular, piles of rubble clogging the path. The walls broke away, ragged as if something had nibbled at them. Instead of geometrical corridors, there was a clearing with a pool. Starlight glittered on the shadowed water.

Fascinated, Talia looked up. "There's sky in here!"

In the clear, clean air, with no other source of light, the stars looked huge and sharp against the absolute blackness.

Lore gave a smile that held the memory of sadness. "A year ago, the sky wasn't there. There's still no sun or moon, just stars."

"No wonder it's so dark in here."

"I didn't see the sky at all until I escaped this place."

Talia tried to imagine that, but couldn't. She squeezed his hand harder, feeling his big knuckles under her fingers. Her childhood had been dominated by her father and his Hunter ideals, but there had also been plenty of normal stuff. Playtime. School. A warm bed in a regular house. Lore didn't need her pity and wouldn't want it, but she still had a lump in her throat.

"There's something growing over there," he said.

She understood what he meant by the Discovery Channel comment. Prehistoric-looking ferns, green despite the lack of light, drooped into the water. Between them were small pink and white flowers—a carpet of the sweet-scented blooms stretching far into the starlit darkness.

"Beautiful," she murmured. "I've never seen these flowers before."

"Not too long ago, there was nothing here but moss," Lore said.

Talia's teaching reflexes kicked in. "That makes sense. The Castle needed to put down fibrous organic material before something larger could take root."

She felt another shiver, but this time it was the thrill of seeing something incredible and rare. *This is an entire ecosystem building itself in fast-forward.* Someone should document the phenomenon, share it, make others understand why it was so remarkable. *I wonder if they would let the university students in here?*

More to the point—would the students get out alive and still human?

"Come," Lore said. "We can look around later."

Reluctantly, Talia turned back, her mind spinning. "Would it be okay if I brought a camera in here sometime?"

"Ask Mac."

They walked for another minute, meeting more and more people as they went. Lore waved to some, but kept moving until they met up with a young man wearing a leather kilt.

"Hey, Lore. Mac's coming," he said, stopping to give them a hello.

Lore made the introductions. "Stewart is one of Mac's new guards."

Talia noticed that he was heavily armed, wearing a short sword, several knives, an automatic rifle, and at least two handguns. He also wore a thick leather collar around his throat, probably against vampires. It made sense. Stewart was human—she was too hungry to miss the scent of fresh blood—and the odds of survival weighed against him in a place filled with predators.

Most remarkable, though, was the creature perched on his shoulder. It looked like a tiny, feathery lizard, plumes of orange and scarlet mixed with pale gray bat wings. It gave Talia a glare and raised a colorful ruff, chittering. Adorably, it grabbed one of Stewart's many earrings and held on with tiny, birdlike claws.

"What's that?" she asked, wishing she could pet it.

"Dunno," Stewart replied affably. "I found him in one of the cliff areas. He looked like he'd been dumped out of the nest. A few of the avian species seem to be laying eggs these days. It used to be everything in here was infertile, but not anymore."

"Isn't there a legend about feathered serpents in Mexico?" Talia asked.

Stewart grinned. "I'll have to take him to Taco Bell and see if he gets excited."

"Don't you have a job to do, Stewart?" said a cheerful voice.

Talia turned toward it. *So this is the infamous Conall Macmillan, the cop turned fire demon.*

Mac was huge, dressed in a Harley-Davidson T-shirt and blue jeans. Blue tattoos covered his forearms. The most obvious sign of demonhood was the faint red glow in his eyes and the fact that the corridor warmed up the moment he was in it. Otherwise, he seemed fairly undemony to Talia.

Stewart excused himself.

"So what's all this I hear about tunnels and giant arachnids?" Mac asked. "Caravelli leaves town for two minutes and you young hounds are running riot."

He clapped Lore on the back with enough force that Lore had to catch himself. "And you gave me the boring job of first aid? Why didn't you call us for the fight?"

"Your guards are spread too thin as it is," Lore replied. "If you pulled them off duty here, we'd have bigger problems than Belenos running around Fairview."

"I wish you weren't right." Mac guided them down the corridor. "I'll forgive you, but I'm not sure Caravelli will when he lands tomorrow."

"I'm sure Queen Omara will keep him busy."

Lore and Talia told him everything that happened. By the time they finished, Mac had led them into a room with a low cot. He'd invited Talia to sit down as he laid out an array of first aid supplies.

Within a minute, Lore had maneuvered him aside and begun working on Talia's arm. She caught the demon hiding a grin, and she flushed.

"You both look done in," said Mac. "I'll let Connie know you're here. She'll find you a place to clean up."

"Thank you," said Lore as he finished wrapping a bandage around Talia's arm.

Connie turned out to be Mac's wife, and a tiny Irish vampire with long black hair and deep blue eyes. Lore greeted her with a huge hug. She turned out not only to know Joe like a brother, but also to be the stepmother of Lore's childhood friend. It was then Talia made the connection: This was the person who had taught Lore to read. She looked at the little woman with interest.

Connie was the opposite of the stereotypical vampire. She was perky.

"The bad thing about this place," she said, her words lilting along in a breathless flow, "is that no one's ever taken a paintbrush to it. Stone everywhere. It's depressing. No point in hanging curtains where there's no windows. Now, I've been looking into this interior design course, thinking maybe that's what we need around here. It's hard to be morbid in Swedish modern."

"I'm not sure how the trolls would feel about it," Lore said. "I think they like the stone."

"Well, what would you be expecting from them, anyway?" Connie said with disgust, stopping at a door set into yet another dark stone hallway. "If they had their way, this would be one big sports bar. Well, here we are. I did up some guest rooms."

She had indeed.

As Talia stepped from the stone hallway into the thickly carpeted bedroom, she saw that Connie had an eye for design. The room was done in shades of green, the odd white accent giving it a clean, crisp effect. It was neither too fussy nor too stark, a series of abstract collages the main visual interest in the room. The bed looked sinfully soft.

Connie watched Talia's response with pleasure. "Not a palace but nothing too bad either, is it? The room has a full bath. There's another shower in the next room over, if you need it. Watch the water, though, hot means hot. We pump it through the dragons' fire cave. I'll bring some extra towels and clean clothes." With that, she turned to go.

Talia sat down on the bed, looking up at Lore. He lingered in the doorway, chatting with Connie in the easy way old friends do.

Talia blinked, feeling the ache of exhaustion in every bone. She was hurt, weary, and in an alternate dimension run by a demon cop and a vampire who thought she was on Home and Garden TV.

Weirdly, she was content.

Images ran through her head: Stewart and his lizard, Mac, their chattering hostess. The primeval ferns and the stars in the water. For a moment, she was too overwhelmed to know what she thought about any of it. There was fear in the Castle, but there was beauty, too.

A good, quiet feeling settled over her. She'd been through hell that night, but she'd reclaimed huge pieces of herself. She never need fear Belenos again.

Even better, they'd caught the Hunters. Darak had personally delivered Maxim and Mikhail Rostov to Detective Baines. It had been Talia's choice. He'd offered to tear off their heads. Just part of the service, he'd said.

Let the police have them. As bad as her emotional wounds were, the Hunters owed justice to many, many families. She would testify. But her moment of truth had come when she'd finally faced her father in the tunnels and helped put an end to his reign of terror. Maybe her brother would have a chance to heal now.

There was more adding to her contentment. She had friends who didn't care what species she was. No one was forcing her to do anything against her will. She had something to fight for—she'd realized she cared for Fairview and the people in it. She had a job here. It was home.

Plus, she had Lore.

Talia's mood dimmed. The question was how long she got to keep him. The pack was going to want him back.

Chapter 34

Lore kept talking with Connie and then again with Mac, who wanted to set up security arrangements in Fairview for the rest of the night. The hellhounds and werewolves were battle-weary. Omara was sending some of her personal guard to keep New Year's Eve civilized in Spookytown.

It was important, but Talia couldn't think straight anymore. She was happy to leave this one to the others.

With no signs of Lore's conversation winding down, Talia retreated to run a bath and get the blood and everything else off her skin. The water was blessedly hot, the soap and shampoo standard brands that she could buy at any drugstore. She lay back in the tub, trying to keep her bandage dry, and let her eyelids drift shut.

Lore. Daydreams aside, did she have a future with him? Would he be forced to choose between her and the rest of his people? She couldn't replace all the bonds that tied him to his pack, nor should she. A person was supposed to grow by falling in love, not lose by it.

Take her parents. Her father was a Hunter. Her mother wasn't. They'd been miserable, her mom cut off from everything she'd ever loved. Taking Lore from his people wouldn't be much different—even if she adored him.

She remembered Osan Mina's words about the Alphas and their reincarnated mates: *Strong hounds find them. The weak die alone. Alphas must be strong. Finding mate is test.*

Talia hadn't had a moment's breathing space to dwell on what the old woman had said, but now the words bit hard. Did Lore have a soul mate? Shouldn't he be looking for her?

Mina was insistent that Lore mate one of their own. Apparently their collective reproductive cycle depended on it. The Alpha had to get it on or the pack got another Alpha in a bloody, violent fight.

She refused to be the cause of that.

Talia got out of the bath, her heart heavy with unease. Giving him up might be ethical, but it would be awful.

She'd lost so many things in her life, most recently Michelle. Her death had taken away the only family who had welcomed her as a vampire. Talia had lost the last good connection to her old life.

But then Lore had made her feel like a person instead of a void. His simple kindness, the fact that he'd accepted her help, the fact that he'd introduced her to his friends—that had made her feel like herself again. She'd been crushed down to nothing, but Lore had shown her that she was worth finding and forgiving.

How could she not want to keep him?

She could be selfish for a little while longer, couldn't she? After all, they had defeated evil that night. That had to buy some karmic credits.

She looked at herself in the mirror, pale and thin, her hair clinging in damp tendrils around her face, a big bandage on one arm. Not exactly centerfold material. She picked at the bandage, loosening the tape Lore had so carefully applied. Slowly, she peeled back the gauze pad.

Since she'd arrived at the Castle, her wound had tingled. Something in the place had neutralized the magic that had allowed the silver knife to wound her. Now her Undead healing abilities were at work. The wound had already scabbed over, days of healing done in a matter of hours. She patted the bandage back down, happy that at least her body was in one piece.

Her need for blood had also eased, apparently another benefit of the Castle.

If only her heart could be as easily cured.

She left the bathroom, drying her hair in a thick, thirsty towel as she went. The bedroom was empty. Lore's absence gave her a twinge inside, part emptiness, part relief. If he wasn't there, she wouldn't feel guilty for loving him.

But then he came through the door wearing no more than a towel around his hips and a hungry look in his eyes. Obviously, he had gone next door to shower. She could only stare at him, stunned by a rush of desire.

"I want you," she said. *Even—especially—if there's not going to be a lot of time for us.*

Her body ached for him. It wasn't that he was familiar—they hadn't been together enough for that. It was the loss of never having the chance to know him, to learn all the things he liked. That took the luxury of hours for exploration. Hours they'd never have after he took a hellhound mate.

Lore was still damp from the shower, drops of water sliding down his biceps where the towel had missed. *One little towel has to work hard to cover that much male.* Talia delicately licked his skin, catching the drops with the tip of her tongue. She could taste the soap, a plain, simple brand.

I want you to come home every day, dirty from a hard day's work, and shower with that soap. I want the taste of you in my mouth every night.

She took his mouth, teasing his lip with her teeth, being careful not to draw blood. There would be time enough for that later. She touched her tongue to his, fencing a little as he drew her into his mouth. He had used the same minty toothpaste as she had, his taste echoing hers.

The mundane detail made her throat ache with the anticipation of bereavement. *Stop it! Stop it. You're not there yet.* She pushed it out of her mind, determined to not let sadness destroy the moment.

He used his size to crowd her against the wall, pressing her close. The roughness of the terry towel she wore rubbed against her nipples, her arousal amplifying the sensation to maddening heights.

"How do you want me?" he said, his voice little more than a growl.

"Sunny side up?"

He gave her a scathing look. "Are you never serious?"

"I'm very serious about this." She slid her hand between their towels, teasing his hard length with the rough cloth.

He caught her wrist. "Don't end this before it begins."

With his other hand, he tugged at the knot she'd made to hold her towel closed. It came apart easily and he backed away just enough to pull the cloth away. It dragged across her thighs and backside, its roughness giving her a pleasant shiver.

"That's better," he said, running a possessive hand down her bare flank. "You're so beautiful. Like the starlight."

How can you say that?

A moment later, he dropped his own towel with an impatient flick. It pooled around their feet, warm from the heat of his body. He pressed close again, his enthusiasm fully evident. Cupping her face with his hands, he kissed her eyes, her cheeks, her ears, taking possession of her an inch at a time, marking all of her with his lips. Making her feel as beautiful as he claimed she was. Finally, he dropped his mouth to her breast, rolling the nipple with his tongue.

Talia made an inarticulate noise, burying her fingers in his thick, dark hair. He finally released her, his breath cool on the wet, swollen tip. Her teeth ached, yearning to bite, but she held back, fighting for control. He took her other breast, giving it the same treatment. Talia gasped, praying for strength. She wanted to pleasure him as a woman before she took him as a vampire, but he sure wasn't making it easy.

"Bed," she groaned.

Instead, he pressed between her thighs, rubbing against her. She squirmed, feeling her readiness in the sweet ache teasing her core.

"I burn for you," he whispered, his lips intimate against her ear. "Let me lose myself inside you."

Talia was beyond putting words into sentences. "Okay."

He picked her up by the waist, holding her close to his body with no more than the strength of his arms, and delicately kissed her mouth. "I will take you."

The phrase sounded oddly formal, but it got lost in the chaos of sensations storming through her. He carried her to the bed, setting her down as carefully as if she were glass. Talia rolled over, crawling across its wide expanse, making room for him to join her.

Without warning, he caught her by the back of the neck, one hand big enough to immobilize her. She was caught on her hands and knees, vulnerable and exposed. A moment later, she felt the rough stubble of his cheek along her backbone, stroking against the sensitive curve of her back. She trembled, a little spooked to be held so still, unable to see his face or what he would do next. It gave new meaning to feeling naked.

His hand began to work her, stroking the soft, vulnerable places, questing inside to test her slickness. A shudder passed through her, and then again, and again. Automatically, she adjusted her knees, finding a better position to take more of him, to offer more of herself.

And then she felt the tip of his sex at her opening, sliding inside, spreading her farther and farther. *Oh, God!* The position, the sheer size of him offered a whole new range of sensations. She thought she'd split apart at the same time she wanted more and more right *there*.

"Lore," she begged, feeling a trembling in her arms. She dug her fingers into the sheets, doing her best to steady herself. "I need you *now*."

The grip on the back of her neck tightened, and he thrust again, driving deeper. A cry tore from her, tears filling her eyes.

He thrust again. Tension spiraled through her, pushing her toward orgasm. She tried to speak, to offer words, but they came out as strangled sounds. Tears slid out from beneath her eyelids. He was still moving inside her, sending her insides into explosions of bliss—again, and again. Sweat trickled down her ribs, slicked the places he was touching her. The moisture felt cool, another set of fingers tickling her in secret places.

It was too much. Talia felt like she was going to melt, or smoke, or start sending out sparks of frantic energy. She twisted, trying to bite, but her teeth snapped on air. He held her harder, forcing her head still while he had his way.

A mix of frustration and sheer animal pleasure rolled through her. He was picking up speed, pushing faster and faster. Each collision of their bodies drove Talia further from reason. Her mind blanked, losing contact with sight, sound, every sense but touch. Rapid shocks of pleasure pulsed through her. "Oh, God, Lore!"

He thrust one last time, filling her with heat and wetness. Her body started to let go, but her teeth ached so hard, she thought they would crack. Suddenly she smelled him close, right in front of her. She opened her eyes, tears blurring her vision. He was offering his wrist. She grabbed it with one hand, pulling it to her mouth, and bit down.

Hot tangy blood filled her mouth. Lore shuddered as her venom released, slowly, slowly collapsing to the mattress as if slain. She let him go, panting, her body still pinging with aftershocks of pleasure. After a long shudder, he stretched his massive body, bones cracking. Talia lay down beside him, running a hand over his chest, feeling a moment of intense possessiveness.

He pulled her close, bringing her face so close to his, their noses touched. His eyes were hazed by the venom, his smile a little dreamy. "That was my way, now we do it yours."

"Wait," she said, making herself face up to at least a little piece of the inevitable. "What are we doing?"

"Do you want me to draw you a picture?"

She shook her head. "I said that wrong."

He kissed her forehead, gently this time. "Don't worry about the future. Hellhounds are loyal unto death, and they always return to their mates once they are reborn. I will always come back to you. Is that what you wanted to know?"

Talia's chest ached with his simple, certain words. "You've got this all figured out." *But what about the fact that I'm not one of you? What about the children?*

"I've thought about it." Lore raised an eyebrow, nothing left of the venom stupor in his expression. "Would you wait for me? Hellhounds are long-lived, but the good part is you get a fresh new lover every century."

Talia spluttered with shocked laughter. "But you wouldn't remember me!"

"We do. We remember the scent of our loved ones." He pulled her close, covering her with his warmth. "Now stop talking. Everything's fine."

"Only every century?" she said petulantly.

He chuckled. "I adore you."

And he proved it to her, one gentle touch at a time. Talia willfully ignored everything else.

Chapter 35

Lore left the Castle, heading toward Osan Mina's. He'd talked to Caravelli on the phone, officially ending his term as acting sheriff. The nonhuman community was shaken, but still in one piece. He'd done his duty. Now he needed to debrief the hounds. With luck he'd be back in bed with Talia before she woke, but just in case he'd left word with Mac that he would be in Spookytown.

His mood was half jubilant, half belligerent. He had been Alpha for seven years, and in that time, he'd freed his people, built a place for them in Fairview, raised their status among the nonhumans, and given them economic independence. He was ready to take a mate, and he had found her. He would have Talia, and no myth would stop him.

He was going to prepare his pack to accept his bride. *Or else.*

Maybe not the best attitude for the occasion, but it had been a hard few days. Lore felt pared down to essentials, with no spare energy to give an inch.

The row housing along Spookytown's streets looked almost pretty in the snow and sunlight. The houses where the hellhounds lived were well loved, the walks shoveled, pups playing in the yards. True, none had been born since his mother had passed, but could that not be coincidence? Could not all the wars and struggle they had suffered be the reason why the females had not come into season?

Even if that were true, would the pack ever believe it? The Elders liked to have their way. Tradition to Lore was comfort and continuity. To them it was an end in itself.

But he needed this one thing. He needed to break with custom this one time.

He needed a miracle.

"*Madhyor!*"

Lore wheeled to see Helver sprinting down the street toward him, arms and legs pumping. A dozen yards behind him, Grash thundered in hot pursuit, clods of snow kicking up with every stride. Lore got the fleeting impression that something was wrong with Helver's face.

The young hound threw himself at Lore's feet, prostrating himself on the ground. "Help me, *Madhyor!*"

Grash skidded to a halt. Neither he nor Helver were wearing coats. Grash's coveralls were coated in sawdust from his carpentry shop, as if they'd started the fight there and run into the street. "He drops my tools. He blunts them. He is careless and lazy!"

Grash bent, grabbing Helver by the scruff of his collar and hauling him upright. It was then that Lore saw why Helver was begging for help. The youth's face was pulp, one eye swollen, nose streaming with blood.

Lore's vision hazed white with anger, rage leaching color from the world. "What is this? I gave him to you to raise up in the pack. You are his *trainer*!"

"He cannot be trained!" Grash growled. "And now

he fawns on his Alpha like a pup begging for his mother's teat. He will never earn the name of warrior."

Lore ripped Helver out of Grash's hand, pushing the youth to one side. "If you cannot manage him, you have only to send him back to me."

Grash spit in the snow. "Good luck to you. He has never been of use. He never will be."

Studying the big hound, Lore considered Grash's speed, his weight, how fast he thought. This wasn't the best time for it, but an opportunity had dropped into Lore's hands to bring him under control. "What do you mean by *never*? How would you know? You've been training Helver only a few days."

Grash's expression suddenly closed, a window slamming shut. Mavritte had asked Lore to give Helver to Grash, but had Grash already forced the young hound to obey in other ways?

"What did you have Helver do for you before you were his trainer?" Lore growled.

Grash was silent. Lore turned furious eyes on Helver. "What was it?"

The youth was breathing through his mouth, blood still bubbling from his nose when he tried to speak. "The campaign office. Grash sent me there."

Damn his hide.

Crack! Lore's fist connected with Grash's face, and then he was on top of him, blinded with frustration over the Redbones, with Helver, and simply with being Alpha. His fist smacked into Grash three more times, re-creating the damage he'd seen on Helver.

Lore caught his breath long enough to snarl. "What the fuck do you think you're doing running our young into danger?"

Grash bared his teeth. "There are drugs in the clinic we can sell. There was money there for the taking. I say why not? The hounds work to death while the bloodsuckers wear jewels."

"Because I say not!" Lore roared. "It's not what hell-hounds do!"

He dragged Grash to his feet, and then sent him crashing back to the pavement with another blow. Lore's hands hurt, his lungs sore from sucking in the ice-cold air, but the sheer physical brutality of the moment was necessary. Grash would respect it.

He wasn't the only one. Lore caught sight of Helver. The youth's eyes were bugging out of his head, mesmerized by the show of dominance. Common sense had failed to turn him around. Maybe this would.

On one level it disgusted Lore, but it was also part of being a hound. It would take decades in the human world to change the fundamental dynamics of the pack. Biology was involved. *Just like when the Alpha has to choose a mate.*

Talia. He wouldn't even consider not having her. She was part of him. Something had happened between them last night, as urgent and primal as this fight. *She is my mate.*

Lore stepped back, watching Grash redden the snow with his blood. His fingers twitched, as if considering another pounding.

Grash rolled onto his back, his eyes blazing with anger. "Damn you."

The words were muffled, barely token defiance. Lore felt a brief tingle of satisfaction. *Time to drive the point home.*

He put his boot on Grash's cheek, crushing the hound's face into the snow.

"Respect our young. Got it? Maybe you should repeat after me."

* * *

Saturday, January 1, 4:00 p.m.
101.5 FM

"Hello and a Happy New Year from your hostess Errata Jones, covering the afternoon and all night tonight on this special holiday show from CSUP.

"It was a busy night last night in Spookytown, and we'll have special coverage of all those events. But first, a special get-well wish to my dear friend Perry. If you're listening, dude, why aren't you in bed and asleep?

"Second, a farewell to Darak and all your crazy clan, who are on a plane and going places. Thanks for dropping by and lending a hand. You guys know how to work hard, but you are scary when it comes to after-game playtime."

Saturday, January 1, 4:00 p.m.
The Castle

Talia woke to find the bed covered with flowers. They were the delicate six-petaled blooms she'd seen by the starlit pond, white and pink and scented like warm honey. They were a symbol of the rejuvenating Castle, a gift of life where there had been only darkness before.

Though Lore was gone, he'd left this token of his affection behind. She lay beneath the floral carpet for a long minute, picking one of the blossoms off the comforter and twirling it in her fingers. *If these can grow in constant night, in a place where nothing is supposed to live, maybe there's hope for me yet.*

She felt so close to Lore, as if every beat of his heart somehow pushed blood to hers. It was pure romantic fancy, but she floated on it, enjoying the feeling of adoring and being adored. All her misgivings about the pack and their future were for that moment suspended.

Lore had left word with Mac that Talia should find him at Osan Mina's. After borrowing fresh clothes from

Connie, Talia made her thanks and left. She slipped quickly through the streets, conscious that last time she'd walked into the hellhounds' domain, Lore had been at her side. She took extra care, watching who was around her as she passed through Spookytown.

When she reached Osan Mina's door, the old woman responded before Talia had time to rap twice.

Mina was bundled into a heavy dark coat. "You're here. Good. We go now."

"Where?" Talia asked, stepping back so Mina could close the door of her town house behind her.

"Mavritte has challenged Lore for rule of the pack."

Talia's jaw dropped. "What? Now? They were in a huge battle last night."

Mina shrugged her coat closer around her bony shoulders. "It is past time he settled things with her. Pack business had been pushed aside too long."

"But—"

"Lore punished Grash. Grash is Redbone. Mavritte will not accept him beating one of her people." Osan Mina gave Talia a shrewd look. "Grash needed beating for Helver's sake."

The names flew by Talia in a meaningless rush. "Can't Lore refuse?"

"Pack law says Alpha must fight if she demands. She demands."

That Talia could believe. She remembered Mavritte threatening to challenge Lore when they were at the Empire Hotel. Lore had seemed confident that he could refuse, but maybe whatever happened with this Grash guy had changed that.

Mina led her down the street to a small playground. Talia trailed after, having a flashback to her high school days when the tough kids would scrap behind the school—a spectator event for every teen from a mile around. Here, hounds crowded around the site, but were oddly quiet. No one seemed happy about what was going on.

The fight seemed so bizarre after the huge battle to protect Fairview and Omara from Belenos. In numbers it was insignificant, and yet in many ways it was more crucial to her happiness. A vampire monarch had fallen last night—she'd killed him—but the fate of this tiny hellhound pack mattered more, because she loved Lore.

The playground was lit by streetlights that threw the onlookers' shadows across the frozen grass. The area had been cleared of snow, the picnic tables pulled to one side. They'd prepared for the fight, an added sign that it was important to the pack. A low, worried murmur buzzed around the crowd, which had split into two halves. One was more numerous. The other was smaller, but looked meaner. Those had to be Mavritte's Redbones.

Osan Mina led her to the larger half of the crowd. It parted, letting them through so they had a good view of the playground. Many of the bystanders bowed to Mina. Even more gave Talia curious looks—not hostile, but not really friendly, either.

"Lore asked me to explain." Mina folded her arms and snorted. "Explain pack business to a vampire. Ha!"

Talia rubbed her hands together, wishing Lore were next to her. He was always warm. "So, what's going to happen?"

Osan Mina shrugged, but the strain on her face was obvious. Hellhounds usually hid their emotions from outsiders, which meant Mina was truly worried. "They fight. One dies. The other is Alpha."

"Dies!" Talia knew that much already, but the words still jolted her. Before, a challenge to the death had been talk. Now it was staring her in the face. "Does anyone ever *not* die?"

"Only if they swear forfeit."

"What does that mean?" Talia looked at the empty space in the middle of the playground. The volume of the crowd's murmurs had gone up a notch, but she couldn't see anything yet.

"Their life belongs to the victor," Mina said. "The winner can ask for it whenever they choose. To swear forfeit is the act of a coward."

"Neither of these two is going to do that."

"No. If you have sworn forfeit, you cannot mate. Your life is not yours to give anymore."

Talia had a sudden, horrible feeling. Was that how Lore was going to get out of taking a mate in the pack? But that would mean losing, and Mavritte being Alpha. Lore would be honor bound to die for her whenever she chose.

Well, that won't work. "Have you tried voting for an Alpha?"

"We like someone. That is one thing. We trust someone to protect the pack. That is another." Mina's eyes turned hard. "In Lore, we have both. He needs a mate. It must be one of his own people."

Talia felt anger rise in a hot prickle. It just wasn't fair. It was surreal and stupid. "There's something I don't understand. If hellhound souls are born again and again, how come there are fewer hounds now? You said a lot died in the Castle, but shouldn't they be reborn?"

The surrounding babble got louder. "Magic can kill a soul," Mina answered, and then turned her attention to the empty ground ahead.

Talia stared at Mavritte as the she-hound strutted into the middle of the playground. It might as well have been a boxing ring. Lore's side stayed silent, but hers gave a ragged cheer, pumping their arms in the air. The sound brought gooseflesh to Talia's arms.

For once, Mavritte wasn't bristling with weapons. All she wore was a loose T-shirt and yoga pants.

"How do they fight?" Talia asked.

"No weapons. The beast form cannot be hurt, but the two-legged can."

Talia thought of her bullets passing through Mavritte in the Empire. As canines, they did seem to be invincible—except for quicksilver bullets and demon fire. "Why not just stay in hound form?"

"They can stay hound only as long as five counts. Otherwise, where is the battle?"

Talia rubbed her face, wishing that when she looked up, she would be back in bed with Lore. *What did you do today, Talia? Oh, I watched my lover in a bloody death match.*

She wanted to throw up, tension corkscrewing through her gut. *I'll stop this myself if I have to. That she-bitch is going to have to come through me.*

Then Lore walked into the makeshift ring. These cheers were loud and heartfelt. No mystery who the favorite was in this event. He peeled off his jacket, then his shirt, leaving only his jeans and sneakers. Talia's breath caught at the sight of his body, the rich tan of his skin flowing over powerful muscles. He tossed his clothes to one side and scanned the crowd. Talia stood on her toes, willing him to look her way. *Over here!*

He stopped, their eyes meeting. In that instant, she saw him not just as Lore, but as Alpha. He was every inch the hellhound king, strong, just entering his prime, the favorite of his people.

I love you! she thought desperately. *Don't forfeit your life to Mavritte. Be Alpha. Win. I'd rather lose you than watch you lose what you care about.*

He could never belong just to a mate. In many ways, he *was* the pack.

Sacrificing everything for love was a nice dream, but this wasn't like quitting a job and moving towns. This was life and death. And she loved him. She wanted whatever would be best for his sake.

Her mouth trembled, wanting with every cell in her body to be lying next to him, lost in the Castle's darkness.

He looked away, his expression that careful, neutral face he wore when he didn't want his feelings to show.

So what am I going to do? There wasn't a damned

thing she could do, unless she climbed into the ring and shot Mavritte. But as she thought it, she realized she couldn't. This moment wasn't about her; this was about the pack. She was on the outside. Lore had to settle it.

The fight was starting. It looked wildly unequal because Lore was simply bigger than Mavritte, but that didn't seem to faze either of the combatants. They circled, half-crouched, snarls so low that Talia might have imagined them if not for the chills that ran down her backbone.

Mavritte struck first, coming in low and fast under Lore's guard. He seemed to roll out of the way, letting her momentum carry her past him. He grabbed her by the waist as she passed, throwing her to the ground— but not before she lashed out with one heel, landing a bruising blow to Lore's thigh.

Talia realized she was gripping her hands together like she was praying. Maybe she was—for a quick end before the suspense killed her. Rekilled her. Whatever.

Mavritte was up again, landing another kick—this time to Lore's shoulder. Talia could hear it connect, and winced.

She analyzed the moves, remembering the lessons she'd learned from years of Hunter training. Mavritte didn't have a man's upper-body strength, but she was agile and knew how to use what power she had. Mavritte could have used that to advantage, but she repeated the same moves too often, allowing Lore to learn her patterns. Lore blocked the next shot, getting in one of his own and sending her staggering back.

"Good," murmured Osan Mina.

Talia bit her lip, and then remembered why vampires shouldn't do that. *Ouch.*

Lore flowed into hound form, but then so did Mavritte. The two wrestled, snarling and clawing in a ball of red-eyed shadows. The crowd began chanting in another language, but Talia got it: the five-second rule.

When they hit five, Lore turned back to human form, dancing away from Mavritte. Then she was human again too, but now had long, red scratches down her arms. She had turned a microsecond too soon, letting his claws touch her human flesh. Her eyes were glittering with wild excitement, her mouth stretched in a mocking smile. Lore was still stone-faced, but his cheeks were flushed.

"He could end this," Mina grumbled.

"I don't think he wants to kill her," Talia replied, once again remembering their confrontation at the Empire. "I think if there was another way, he'd take it."

Lore had done something to send Mavritte tumbling to the grass at the edge of the ring. Her fall hadn't looked entirely natural, and that set Talia's alarm bells off. In fact, the whole crowd gasped—and gasped again when Mavritte rose holding a stiletto. The long, thin blade gleamed in the streetlight.

"Knife!" Talia yelled, lunging forward.

Mina grabbed her arm. "No."

"You said no weapons!" But Talia had her gun.

But there was an underlying logic. If Lore died, they still needed an Alpha. Mavritte was the next strongest hound, whether or not she fought fair.

Mina's iron grip clenched harder. "Let them settle it!"

Mavritte grabbed Lore, clinging to him like a desperate lover, and drove the knife into his back.

Talia screamed.

Lore vanished.

Mavritte stumbled away, tripping over herself in confusion.

What did Lore do?

The seconds dragged on interminably, the hounds as one beginning to call out in agitated voices.

"He can't hold it this long!" Mina cried, gripping Talia's coat sleeve.

"Hold what?" Talia's eyes were blurred with tears of fright.

"The state between man and hound!"

Talia thought about it—there was a brief second between forms where the hounds looked like a cloud of black dust. What happened if he stayed that way too long? Did he ever come back?

Oh, God, Lore . . .

But the hound dropped from the air, crushing Mavritte beneath his weight. Lore gripped Mavritte's throat in his jaws, one massive paw covering the knife.

A cry of wonder sounded from the hounds. Apparently the vanishing act was a big show of power, but Talia was focused on what came next. The throat-ripping part. *Is he going to do it?* Talia wanted to turn away and needed to watch.

"He can't!" Mina hissed. "No, the fight was over! He should finish it."

There was no tearing of throats. A sob mixed of frustration and relief escaped Talia's throat.

Lore was back in human form, holding the stiletto. He stood under the streetlight, his figure dark and sharply defined against the backdrop of snow. "Mavritte of the Redbones, you broke the laws that rule the fight for dominance," he said in a deadly voice.

Mavritte scrambled to her feet, putting some distance between her and Lore, but the crowd tightened around the ring, blocking any escape she might have planned.

"Kill me," she snarled. "If you think you've won, end this!"

Lore's face was back to that neutral expression. Somehow it was worse than if he'd been screaming at her. "You lose the right to challenge me, Mavritte of the Redbones. Your people and your property belong to the Alpha of the Lurcher pack. To me."

She fell on her knees. "Will you protect my people?"

"They are my people now. I will protect them."

That's why she did this. She knew this would happen if she cheated. She sacrificed herself for the sake of her hounds.

Talia's skin prickled with shock. She hadn't expected selflessness from Mavritte. "Is her life forfeit?"

"Not unless Lore demands it."

So he doesn't have to kill her. Talia narrowed her eyes. There was something suspiciously convenient about the match. Lore lost nothing. Mavritte got something she wanted. She had secured the best king with the most resources to watch over her hounds, even though it cost her pride and rank among her own people.

Talia felt a wave of respect for the she-hound, but it was short-lived.

"Will you take a mate?" Mavritte asked Lore, in a loud, clear voice.

The crowd went utterly silent. Talia could hear the hum of the streetlights above. Lore hesitated, turning the knife over and over in his hand. Talia froze as his gaze veered her way, touching her face.

"I will take a mate of my own choosing."

Talia's spirits sank as every hound turned her way, disapproval and anxiety in their eyes. She stood between them and their future. If Lore stayed with her, there would be no young. Hellhound souls couldn't be reborn. Soul mates couldn't be found. The life of the pack wouldn't go on.

Their expressions all said one thing. She had no business with their king. She wasn't even properly alive.

Lore couldn't lie. His choice was clear—he wanted her.

But she wasn't what they needed or wanted in their Alpha's mate. But he *was* what they needed in their leader. Even Mavritte knew it, and was willing to pay a huge price to have him lead her pack.

Talia's body ached. She was dying all over again.

I can't be that selfish. I have to let him go. She exchanged a long look with Osan Mina.

"Okay," was all she said.

Mina gave a single nod, and turned her face toward

her king. The connection between them stopped dead, suddenly sliced away. It was as if Talia had instantly ceased to be.

Talia turned her back and walked away, her whole body burning with anguish. She heard commotion behind her, cries of disbelief and confusion.

Don't let him be coming. Don't let him. This is hard enough.

"Talia!" Lore ran past her, turning, blocking her path. "Why are you leaving?"

His bare chest was heaving, though he couldn't be out of breath from such a short run.

I love you.

Kind, brave, in love with her, practically declaring himself in front of the whole world—how much more perfect could Lore be? She began to feel tiny sobs bubbling up through her frame. "You know why. They need you—all of you. You have to be with someone from your pack. If you leave them and come with me, it will destroy you. Maybe not right away, but you'll come to hate me."

Shock widened his eyes. "What are you talking about?"

"The pack doesn't have a future if you take me. I can't be a pack mother."

"Those are all just myths!"

"That doesn't matter. It's what they believe that counts. That's the hound tradition. Even if it doesn't make sense to anyone else, that's who you are. Turn away from that and you lose as surely as if Mavritte cut out your heart."

He shook his head, beyond words.

"You know it's true."

"Talia, I love you!"

She clenched her teeth, trying to summon anger to get past the sadness robbing her strength. "Don't be ridiculous. We barely know each other." *But I love you.*

He reached for her, but then dropped his hand when she skirted around him. "If you doubt how much your people count on you, think about what Mavritte just did. She gave up everything so you could be the king."

"Talia, damn you." He grabbed her arm, pulling her close. "I'm not leaving my pack and I'm not letting you go. If the Prophets want me as Alpha, they're going to have to fix this."

"Lore, if I've learned one thing, we can't change what we are."

He kissed her face, starting with her eyes, her cheeks, her lips, wordlessly pleading with her. "I know you're the one I have to have. I know your scent."

"Lore," Talia said, his name more a sob than a word.

He cupped her face, forcing her to look into his eyes. "Don't tell me that you don't love me. Don't lie to me."

"Pick someone else."

"Don't I have a say in any of this?"

The pain in his words ripped through her. She pulled away. "Not unless hellhound soul mates are reborn as vampires."

He fell back a step. The movement was awkward, unsteady. Not like Lore at all. "You can walk away from here, Talia."

"Don't," she said desperately, knowing exactly what was coming.

"You can walk away, but I'm not letting you go. I'm fighting for you."

Talia pulled herself together, scrabbling for enough strength to go on. "You're smarter than that."

"I didn't get my hounds out of the Castle by giving up." A stubborn look she'd not seen before settled over his features. "This isn't over."

Talia swallowed, shoving her hands into her pockets so she wouldn't reach out to him. He looked angry, but he also looked hurt. "Think about what you're doing," she said.

Then she walked away from him, the most gorgeous, half-naked man she was ever likely to meet, however immortal she was. And his beauty was the least of her loss. There would never be another Lore.

Cold tears streamed down her face.

But she'd done her bit to help the pack.

Chapter 36

Wednesday, January 19, 7:30 p.m., Election Day
101.5 FM

"This is the CSUP special news coverage of the municipal elections. Polls opened at eight o'clock this morning and will remain open until midnight to accommodate all voters. Exit polls favor vampire candidate Michael de Winter. If he wins, he will be the first nonhuman elected to public office—a landmark on the road to securing full civil and legal rights for supernatural citizens.

"Many attribute the rapid progress in this area to the hard work and political acumen of the vampire queen, Omara. If one considers that the existence of nonhumans was a mystery until the year 2000, this is indeed a remarkable achievement that opens a new chapter in the history of relations between human and nonhuman species."

Wednesday, January 19, 8:00 p.m., full moon
Talia's condo

Talia walked through Saint Andrew's cemetery, her steps crunching on the last patches of snow. The cold snap had finally broken, and she could hear water rushing through the nearby storm drains. A heavy mist—something between rain and fog—dripped from the trees. It was night, but the moon gave an eerie glow to the veils of moisture cloaking the graveyard.

She stopped at Michelle's grave. It was one of the ones nearest the water—small, with a modest granite plaque. Talia laid the bouquet of lilies she held on the grave. She'd been there nearly every night.

Hi, Michelle, I started packing up your things today. It's not easy, and I don't want to do it. Your mom's letting me stay until I can find a place. I know you're not there anymore, but leaving is going to feel like parting from you all over again.

Talia stopped, swallowing hard. A group was gathered around a spot a few yards away. A small figure broke from them and walked over.

"Talia Rostova?"

"Yes?" Talia took a moment to look up. The speaker was a female vampire, very beautiful and very regal.

"I am Queen Omara."

Oh!

Talia sank into a curtsy. "Your Majesty."

"Rise, child," she said. "I've been meaning to speak with you for some time now. It will be a while before I need to join my candidate to hear the outcome of the election. Perhaps we can talk?" It wasn't really a question.

Talia drew in a shaky breath. "As you wish, Your Majesty."

Omara began walking along one of the paths that wandered the cemetery. Talia fell into step beside her, nerves on high alert. Wind hushed through the cedar trees.

"There are three subjects I wanted to speak to you about," said the queen. "First, you killed a vampire monarch. That is punishable by death."

Stunned, Talia stopped dead in her tracks.

Omara gave a slight smile, as if she rather enjoyed Talia's moment of fright. "However, it was Belenos, and he was after my life. The vampire council voted to consider the killing justifiable self-defense."

Talia thought she would faint. The queen started walking again. Talia hurried to catch up.

"You were granted leniency by a margin of one vote," Omara added. "In other words, count yourself lucky and don't do it again."

"He killed me, Your Majesty," Talia said. *They tried me without my knowledge. What would have happened if the vote had gone the other way?*

"I know," Omara replied. "That was taken into account. The council is sorry that you were Turned unwillingly. This is not an easy existence, especially if you did not choose it."

Talia took a breath. "May I speak, ma'am?"

"Of course."

"I was raised to hate monsters. Becoming one should have driven me mad, or made me destroy myself, or made me turn evil."

"But?" the queen prompted.

"Instead, it made me look at things and at myself in a different way. I'm not going to say I'd be a vampire if I had a choice, but I am stronger now, and not just physically. It made me start over and think about what I really believed. It made me break old patterns. I'm more Talia than I was when I was a living woman."

"I congratulate you. Not everyone could manage to transform themselves that way."

Talia hesitated. She could hear the ocean rushing against the shore. "Most people would be starting from a better place."

"Do you still hate monsters?" The queen started walking again.

"Some of my best friends are monsters."

"What about your father and brother? Where do they fit in this new worldview of yours?"

"There's a chance my brother may come around some-day. He's written to me. He's agreed to be a witness for the prosecution. He'll still do time, but a lot less."

She slid her hand into her coat pocket. She'd carried Max's letter with her since she'd received it. It was a connection to her brother that was real and honest—not spying on him from an Internet bulletin board.

It was an awkward note, but it was a start. The best news was that Max was getting some counseling. Ironi-cally, prison might be the salvation he needed.

Omara made a considering noise. "I understand the biggest problem with the trial of the Hunters is the com-plexity of it. Where does one crime end and the next begin? Perhaps it is good some of us involved are im-mortal. The case could go on for a while."

Talia was silent. The mere mention of the trial wrapped her in a blanket of confusion. It was impos-sible to see how it would end, though no one believed Mikhail Rostov would walk a free man ever again. That made her feel both sad and safer.

Omara was watching her expression. "I know it was not your direct intention, but you have done me and the community as a whole great service in these matters."

"Thank you, Your Majesty." She'd just been trying to survive.

"In light of that service, consider yourself my subject. There is no reason to carry on as a rogue." Omara gave her a smile that said no was not an option.

Talia felt a bittersweet relief. "I'm greatly honored. There is something I'd like to offer in exchange."

The queen showed a moment of surprise, then smoothed it over. "What's that?"

Talia held in the words for a moment, but then let them go in a rush. "I stole a great deal of money from King Belenos. I spent some of it, but I'd like to offer the rest to replace the medical clinic. I really don't want any reminders of him, even in my bank account."

For a moment, the night was heavy with surprise. Then Omara laughed, and it was an unexpectedly rich sound. "I like you, Talia Rostova."

"I'm not a good thief." She'd felt entitled to taking the money, but not spending it. It was useless to her, except as insulation under the floor.

Omara gave her a knowing look. "Lore of the hellhounds returned money one of his whelps stole from the campaign office. He offered free labor for replacing the clinic and campaign office as an apology for the theft. Between the two of you, we can have a very fine new building."

At the mention of Lore's name, Talia looked away. Her longing for him hadn't dulled one bit, but she hadn't wavered from her decision. He would get over her. Someday, he would thank her.

Again, Omara watched her carefully. "That brings me to my last topic. I am a sorceress, Talia, and I have been alive since Babylon was a great power. No one would accuse me of being a warm and fuzzy romantic, but—I dislike unnecessary grief."

Talia inwardly cringed. A lot of people had tried to give her advice about Lore—Perry, Errata, and Joe included—and now the queen was throwing in her two cents. None of them had seen the fight between Mavritte and Lore. None had seen the faces of the pack, hoping she would release their Alpha to choose a proper mate.

Omara tucked her hands into her coat sleeves. The wind from the ocean was cold, biting deep into uncovered flesh. "I walked the earth before the hounds were sent to the Castle. They were made from men and demons and the great temple dogs of the Egyptian sands. I know their magic. I would be patient with it, if I were you, and see what happens with the pack."

Despite herself, Talia was curious. "What do you mean?"

"Don't underestimate your young hound's willpower. One way or the other, magic is all about manipulating the energy of desire. He has plenty of that, I can tell. And don't underestimate the time you spent in the Castle. It has been known to have a transformative effect."

Talia flushed, wondering exactly how much the queen knew about the night she and Lore had spent there.

They had come in a full circle back to Michelle's grave. The queen stopped, signaling in some invisible way that the conversation was done. "Good night, Talia Rostova. I wish you well."

Without waiting for a reply, Omara turned and walked away, pausing only to call over her shoulder, "Don't forget to vote! You're not a rogue anymore!"

An hour later, Talia unlocked her condo door. She had voted, and she'd cast her ballot for de Winter. She was curious to see how a nonhuman would do. Plus, she'd never voted before. Exercising her opinion felt good. She was finally, ultimately her own woman.

She crossed to the balcony door, passing between the stacks of packing boxes she'd started to fill with her belongings and Michelle's. She hadn't started looking for a place yet. She'd made only one decision about what she would have in her very own solo living space. She'd keep the bobblehead poodle. It reminded her of the silly moments she'd shared with her cousin, and that was a memory she wanted to keep.

She stepped out onto the balcony, the cold an antidote to a wave of hot grief. The night was gauzy with moonlight, mist, and twinkling lights. She looked down at the cars passing below, the old neon signs of Spookytown flickering on and off.

Her reverie was interrupted by the sight of a tall, dark-haired hellhound standing on the sidewalk, gazing up at the balcony and waving at her. Fifteen floors up, the figure was tiny, but her vampire sight could pick him out. Talia inwardly groaned.

Lore. Everything about him—the way he moved, the set of his shoulders, his shaggy, thick hair—salted her wounds. She'd expected time to lessen what she felt. Part of her hoped maybe what they'd had was just a fling. An intro to the nonhuman dating pool. A walk on the furry side.

No. Not a bit of it, and it stung like sin every time they spoke, every time she saw him. She was never getting over him.

And here he was flagging her down for one more minute of torture. She started to back away, but Lore began making bizarre, urgent gestures. He looked like he was trying to direct traffic through the running of the bulls.

Irritated, she pulled out her phone. She somehow hadn't been able to resist putting him on speed dial. It had helped feeling that he was just a button push away.

"What?" she said when he picked up.

"Go around to the parking lot."

"Why?"

He held his arms out in mock exasperation. "Just do it."

"Okay." She shut the phone, feeling a lump in her throat. *Dammit.* She didn't want to get close to him. Smelling his scent, standing next to him would undo her for sure. She'd cried buckets already. She was going to end up a mummy from the moisture loss.

She pulled on a coat again and went down the fire escape—the same one he'd dragged her through at gunpoint—and out the back door—the same one she'd used the night he'd finally let her go—and into the parking lot—where he'd offered her his hand and promised to build a fire and keep her warm. *Oh, God, does everything have to be Lore-specific?*

Standing in the parking lot, she caught a blast of mud-scented air. For a moment the wet earth made her think of spring.

Except that Lore was standing next to a seven-foot, fully decorated Christmas tree. It sat in a bucket of sand, smack in middle of the fire lane.

"You look beautiful," he said.

That always threw her off guard. "What's with the tree?"

He looked pleased with himself. "Do you like it?"

Talia blinked. "I'm missing the punch line. Did you check the calendar? It's January."

His self-congratulation became a full-on smirk. "The hounds celebrate their winter holiday on the first full moon after solstice. That's today."

"Um, okay. Happy hound day."

He shifted from foot to foot, nerves creeping into his body language. "I thought we should have trees. A blending of cultures, humans and hounds."

"Nice."

He shifted again. "You said you didn't celebrate Christmas as a child. I decorated this tree for you."

"Oh." Talia felt tears prickling under her lashes. "Thanks. That's really sweet."

"I'll carry it upstairs."

She sniffed, pretending it was the cold air making her nose run. "Safety tip—next time, get the tree where it's going, then decorate it."

"Oh." He looked it up and down. "I guess that would be easier."

He sounded like he really didn't care, or that logic wasn't what he was going for. *What a weird conversation this is.*

The parking lot was where they'd had their first real talk. She could barely think for wishing she was back at that moment where their brief happiness still lay ahead.

Maybe he remembered that, too. *Let me go, Lore. Just leave me alone and let me go!*

She looked up at him. His dark eyes were sparkling—very different from the sadness that had been clinging to both of them the last few weeks.

He shouldn't be happy. Talia was suddenly suspicious. "What's up?"

"There are a few things to celebrate."

"Like what?" As she'd predicted, his nearness was an aching, empty throb. If she'd had the willpower, she would have stopped talking, left him there, and gone back to her packing—but she simply didn't have the strength to walk away from him twice.

"You saw that Errata published her article."

Talia tried to focus on his words. "Yeah, she sent me a copy."

The article on the fight in the tunnels had got the werecougar a foothold in the human press, and the paper wanted another story. "But her byline said Amanda Jones. Is that a pen name?"

"That's her real name. She says it's time to stop hiding behind her radio persona."

"She doesn't look like an Amanda."

"Who knows what we hide inside?" For a dog, Lore still looked like the cat who got the canary.

Suddenly, Talia was tired. "Lore, you've got news. What is it?"

"Did you notice the decorations?" He pointed to the tree again.

"Are those little bones?"

"This is a hellhound tree. Candy canes are for humans. We wish for other things." He tapped a gold foil star hung with thread. There were hundrcds of them on the tree. "These are for the mates who have gone missing. We wish for them to be reborn and come back to us."

"Weren't they destroyed by magic?"

A funny look came over his face. "But maybe they weren't destroyed."

"Then why can't they come back?" she asked, remembering their conversation in the Castle. *And afterward, he covered the bed in flowers so I'd wake up knowing he was thinking of me.*

"The pack likes you, you know. You put the common good before your own. You fought beside them. You're a teacher, and you offered to help set up a school. Osan Mina likes the fact that you know how to darn socks."

Talia didn't know what to say. *Why does any of that matter?*

"You may not believe this, but they've changed their minds. They wish you were their queen." He touched the star again, making it spin and sparkle. "I think that wishing is powerful."

Talia wanted to scream with sadness and frustration. "I'm not a hellhound. I love you. I want you. You can't doubt that. But I'm not the right species. I can't make the right biological magic happen."

His face fell, suddenly serious. "The female hounds went into heat."

"They can't do that." She stopped cold. "Unless you took a mate."

"You—I mean—you and I did. Then they did." He shoved his hands into his pockets, suddenly looking very, very young. "I don't know how. I mean I do, but—"

Talia's mouth dropped open, and then she burst out laughing. "You want me to draw you a picture?"

He grinned at her, her laugh straightening his spine, opening his expression.

Her heart caught in her throat. "You're serious?"

"Absolutely. It's, um, active in the neighborhood right now. There will be a next generation. It just goes to show you the old traditions aren't everything. Or else there's a new kind of magic. Whatever the case, you're my mate."

Oh, my ... He'd said if the Prophets wanted him as Alpha, they'd have to solve the Talia-as-mate problem. The double-dog dare had worked.

She flung her arms around his neck, smelling the delicious, musky scent of him. "I don't understand. Why did this happen?"

He wrapped his arms around Talia, cradling her against his chest. "Perhaps our lost souls went to other species. Perhaps there are too few hellhounds left, so we have changed in order to survive."

Perhaps a vampire queen who understood ancient hellhound magic had played a role? Or the Castle?

"The Prophets only know, Talia. I'm just a dog."

"But something's going on." Yes, something was going on. She was happy. Deliriously. Emphatically.

"It means we share something deep. It means I'll always find you, no matter where you go. I'll walk at your side. I'll sleep beside you and watch over you. I'll walk the passages between life and death to come back to you."

He took her mouth, kissing her long and hard until her toes curled and all she could think about was the feel of his hard, young body under her hands. The night wind was soft against their faces, smelling of the damp cedars, of restaurants and cars and of the deep, rich life of the city around them.

A city where anything at all could happen.

Did you miss the book that launched
Sharon Ashwood's Dark Forgotten series?
Read on for a preview of

RAVENOUS

Available from Signet Eclipse.

Prologue

Being the evil Undead wasn't fun anymore. For one thing, it was increasingly hard to get a library card.

Even borrowing a book required identification. The same applied to finding an apartment, renting a movie, or leasing a car. Sure, in the old days there was the whole vampire mind-control thing, but now the world was one big bar code. Just try hypnotizing a computer.

In the end, it was easier to give in than to hide an entire subpopulation from the electronic age. The vampires—along with werewolves, gargoyles, and the ever-unpopular ghouls—emerged into the public eye at the turn of the century. While Y2K alarmists had predicted millennial upheaval, they sure hadn't seen this one coming.

In fact, they hadn't seen anything yet.

Chapter 1

"Why didn't you say you were calling about the old Flanders place?" Holly's words were hushed in the street's empty darkness.

Steve Raglan, her client, pulled off his cap and scratched the back of his head, the gesture sheepish yet defiant. "Would it have made a difference?"

"I'd have changed my quote."

"Thought so."

"Uh-huh. I'm not giving a final cost estimate until I see inside." She let a smidgen of rising anxiety color her voice. "Why exactly did you buy this place?"

He didn't answer.

From where they stood at the curb, the streetlights showed enough of the property to work up a good case of dread. Three stories of Victorian elegance had crumbled to Gothic cliché. The house should have fit into the commercial bustle at the edge of the Fairview campus, where century-old homes served as offices, cafés, or studios, but it sat vacant. During business hours, the area had a Bohemian charm. This place . . . not so much. Not in broad daylight, and especially not at night.

Gables and dormers sprouted at odd angles from

the roof, black against the moon-hazed clouds. Pillars framed the shadowed maw of the entryway, and plywood covered an upstairs window like an eye patch. A real character place, all right.

"So," said Raglan, sounding a bit nervous himself, "can you kick its haunted butt?"

Holly choked down a wash of irritation. She was a witch, not a SWAT team. "I'll have to go in and take a look around." She loved most of her job, but she hated house work, and that didn't mean dusting. Some old places were smart, and neutralizing them was a dangerous, tricky business. They wanted to make you dinner in all the wrong ways. Lucky for Raglan, she needed tuition money. Badly. Tomorrow was the deadline to pay.

The chill September air was heavy with the tang of the ocean. Wind rustled the chestnut trees that lined the cramped street, sending an early fall of leaves scuttling along the gutters. The sound made Holly twitch, her nerves playing games. If she'd had more time, she would have come back to do the job when it was bright and sunny.

"Just pull its plug. I can't close the sale with it going all Amityville on the buyers," Raglan said. Fortyish, he wore a fretful expression, a plaid flannel shirt, and sweatpants with a rip in one thigh. Crossing his arms, he leaned like limp celery against his white SUV.

She had to ask again. "So why on earth *did* you buy this house?"

Raglan peeled himself off the door of the vehicle, taking a hesitant step toward the property. "It was on the market real cheap. One of those Phi Beta Feta Cheese frats was looking for a place. Thought I could fix it up for next to nothing and flip it to them. They don't care about looks, as long as there's plenty of room for a kegger."

He dug in his pocket and handed her a fold of bills. "Here's your deposit."

Prompt payment—heck, *advance* payment—was unprecedented, un-Raglanish behavior. She usually had to beg. Holly stared at the money, not sure what to say, but she took it. *He's worried. He's never worried.* Then again, this was his first rogue house. Before this he'd only ever called her to bust plain old ghosts.

He looked her up and down. "So, don't you have any, like, gear? Equipment?"

"Don't need much for this kind of job." She saw herself through his eyes—a short woman, mid-twenties, in jeans and sneakers, who drove a rusty old Hyundai. No magic wand, no ray guns, no *Men in Black* couture. Well, house busting—house taming . . . whatever—wasn't like in the movies. Tech toys weren't going to help.

She did have one prop. Holly pulled an elastic from the pocket of her Windbreaker and scraped her long brown hair into a ponytail. The elastic was her uniform. When the hair was back, she was working.

"Surely you knew the Flanders house has a history of incidents," she said. "The real estate companies have to disclose when a property has . . . um . . . issues." Holly eyeballed the place, eerily certain it was eyeballing her back. As far as she knew, Raglan was the first to hire someone to de-spook this house. No one else had stuck around long enough to pony up the cash.

Not a good sign.

Maybe next summer I should try dishwashing for tuition money.

Raglan blew out his cheeks in a sigh, fiddling with a thread on his cuff. "I thought the whole haunted thing wouldn't matter. The kids from the fraternity thought it was cool. Silly bastards. The sale was all but a done deal up until yesterday."

Holly walked up to the fence and put one hand on the carved gatepost. The flaking paint felt rough on her fingers, the wood beneath crumbly with age. The house had a bad attitude, but still the neglect made her sad. The old place had been built from magic by a clan of witches, just like Holly's ancestors had built her home.

Houses like these were part of the family, halfway to sentience. They lived on the free-floating vitality that surrounded any busy witch household—the life, the activity, and especially the magic. It was that energy that kept them conscious. Take it away, and the result was a slow decline until they were nothing more than wood and brick.

Reports of abandoned, half-sentient houses came up every few years. Centuries of persecution, combined with a low birth rate, had taken their toll on the witches. There were only a dozen clans left in all of North America, most with a scant handful of survivors. As their population dwindled, their houses perished, too. Most of these old, dying places were just restless, but a few turned bad, fighting to survive.

Like this one. Only its designation as a historical landmark had saved it from demolition.

Holly's pity mixed with a lick of fear. A gentle tugging was trying to urge her through the gate. Gusts of chittering whispers draped over her body like an invisible shawl. A caress, of sorts. The mad old place was inviting her in, embracing her.

Come in, little girl. So lively, so sweet.

A starved house would drain power from any living person, leaving them tired and achy. A magic user, especially a witch, was much more vulnerable. They had so much more to take.

A flush prickled Holly's skin as her heart sped up, filling her mouth with the coppery taste of fright. The strain of keeping still, resisting the whispers, made her teeth hurt.

Come in, little girl. The path to the front door was just flagstones buried in moss and weeds, but to Holly's sight it glowed. It was the one path, the only important route she would ever take. *Follow it and everything will be better. You'll be coming home at last. Holly, my dear, come to me.*

Holly pulled her hand off the post, putting a few paces between her feet and the property line. Sweat plastered her shirt to her back.

She felt the touch of a hand on her sleeve, but she didn't jump. That particular pressure, the curve of those fingers, was familiar, expected. Instead her heart skittered with a roller-coaster swoop of bad-for-you pleasure.

"I didn't hear you arrive," she said, turning and looking up.

Alessandro Caravelli was about six foot two, most of that long, lean legs. Curling wheat-blond hair fell past his shoulders, framing a long, strong-boned face that made Holly dream of fallen angels. The leather coat he wore had the scuffed, squashed look of an old favorite.

"I think the house had you." His voice still held faint traces of his native Italian, a slight warmth in the vowels. "I called your name, but you didn't hear me. I was crushed."

"Your ego's hardier than that."

"You make me sound conceited."

"You're a vampire. You're in a league of your own."

"True, and so is my ego." Alessandro gave a close-lipped smile that both invested meaning and denied it.

Holly pressed his hand where it rested on her sleeve, keeping the gesture light. Her pulse skipped at the coolness of his skin. Touching him was like petting a tiger or a wolf, fascinating but fearsome. Full of deadly secrets.

Some thrills were bad news. Working with a vampire was chancy enough; anything more would be insane. Besides, she already had a boyfriend—one who didn't bite. Still, that didn't stop the occasional soft-focus fantasy about Alessandro, involving satin sheets and whipped cream.

"So, this is the big, bad house on the menu," she said. *There goes the food imagery again.*

Dark as it was, Alessandro still wore shades. Now he slid them off, folding them with a flick of his wrist. The gesture was smooth as the swipe of a cat's paw, revealing eyes the same gold-shot brown as Baltic amber. He studied the Flanders property for a long moment, his face somber. Even after a year's acquaintance, he wasn't easy to read.

"Is this going to be difficult?" he said at last.

"No cakewalk. Raglan actually paid me the deposit already. He's afraid."

The sound of a car door opening made them both turn around. Raglan was standing by Alessandro's vehicle, peering in through the driver's side. The car was a sixties American dream machine, a red two-door T-Bird with custom chrome and smoked windows. Holly felt Alessandro coil like a startled cat. Where the car was concerned, he didn't share well.

The round headlights blinked on and off in an impertinent wink as Raglan fiddled with the dash. Alessandro always left the thing unlocked and half the time never removed the keys. To the vampire way of thinking, the car was his. No one would dare touch it. Until now he had been correct.

Raglan backed out of the car and slammed the door. "Sweet ride." Tension rolled off him as he skipped away from the car and gave a sheepish grin. He was acting out like a nervous little kid.

Alessandro made a sound just this side of a snarl.

Holly gripped his arm. "Not now. I need this job."

"Only for you," he said in a voice that whispered of cold, dead places. "But if he touches her again, he's dead."

Raglan cleared his throat. "Is this your partner? Pleased to meet you." He drew near but warily kept Holly between him and the vampire.

Alessandro gave an evil smile, but Holly poked him before he could speak.

Oblivious, Raglan cast a glance at the house, and his expression went from strained to about-to-implode. "So, what now? Can you get started?"

"I'd like to check one thing first. You mentioned that something happened yesterday, something that made you call me," she said. "Can you tell us what, exactly? We need the specifics."

"Yeah, well, like I was saying, yesterday things went wrong." Raglan's voice shook.

Foreboding fondled the nape of Holly's neck.

Raglan hesitated a beat before going on, shutting his eyes. "From what I hear, four frat boys went in late yesterday afternoon for an end-of-vacation party. Not supposed to, because the final papers aren't signed yet, but they forced a window. Wanted to start christening the place, I guess. They never came out."

"Maybe they're still in there, sleeping it off?" Holly said hopefully. She knew denial was pointless, but it was traditional. Someone had to do it.

Raglan shook his head. "There's more to it than that. The police have already been around asking questions."

"The police?" Holly said, startled.

"They went through the house this afternoon, but didn't find a thing. The cops were spooked as hell, but there was no sign of the boys. That's when I called you."

"I can't help you if this is an open police investigation! Not without their permission."

"Please, Ms. Carver." Raglan wiped his mouth with the back of his sleeve, as if he were fighting nausea. "I'll never sell this place. I don't even dare go in it!"

A spike of anger took her breath away. Her voice turned to granite. "You didn't tell me any of this on the phone."

Raglan went on. "Two more went in this morning,

some of the professors who were supposed to be, uh, academic sponsors for the fraternity. They never came out either. The department heads called the dean to complain."

"Six people have disappeared inside that house? Since yesterday? *You couldn't have mentioned this on the phone?*" She felt Alessandro's hand on her back, steadying her.

Raglan sucked in air, as though he'd forgotten to breathe for a while. "Ms. Carver, you've got to get those people out of there."

"You're right," said Holly, her voice thick. *The house is hungry.*

"Two questions, Raglan," asked Alessandro, his voice quiet and chill. "How did the department heads know what happened? Who called the police?"

"Witnesses," Raglan replied. "Neighbors saw the kids climbing in through the window. And then there was the screaming."